Jake & Emma

The Carrero Influence

Redefining Rules

L.T. Marshall

Published by Pict Publishing

ISBN: 978 1 9803194 3 6

The Carrero Series

Jake & Emma

The Carrero Effect ~ The Promotion

The Carrero Influence ~ Redefining Rules

The Carrero Solution ~ Starting Over

Arrick & Sophie

The Carrero Heart ~ Beginning

The Carrero Heart ~ The Journey

The Carrero Heart ~ Happy Ever Afters

Bonus Books

Jake's View

Arrick's View

Other books by L.T. Marshall

Just Rose

Acknowledgements

I want to take a moment to thank everyone who helped on this journey to getting my Carrero book 2 completed. To Grace, my editor, for sitting and painstakingly correcting my mistakes and to Emma for polishing this book to perfection. To my fans who have kept me going with laughter, encouragement and Facebook support while I battled to finish all three books.

To my long-suffering partner who endured a messy house, microwave food and a laundry pile the size of Everest while I was engrossed in completing book two. My children who became so used to a mother glued to her computer screen that they learned to make toast for themselves.

I am not one to ramble on with lots of thanks, so instead I want to say. You know who you all are, I have told you many times and this one is for you.

Thank you! xx

For Jackie, Grace and Shirin.
You kept me going when I wanted to give up. xx

Chapter 1

The subway to work is crowded as usual, even at this early hour. The smell and noise are overwhelming. I'm feeling fragile, nausea plaguing me all the time these days; the stress of moving offices and away from Jake making me ill. I check my watch for the fiftieth time this morning.

I'm late again … What the hell is wrong with me lately?

I groan inwardly.

I can't seem to get my head together or get back on track with anything. Giovanni Carrero has yelled at me so many times these last three weeks, I feel like resigning. He's demoted me to coffee bearer for now and I'm slowly losing everything I've worked for. My reputation as an efficient PA is shot and I've heard the rumors circulating the building.

Jake Carrero dismissed me for my incompetence and moved me to his father's building because he felt sorry for me.

The lies upset me, but I push them down into the depths of my mind along with everything else about Jake Carrero. It's better than people knowing the truth, that the stupid, naive PA fell in love with her boss and he didn't feel the same way.

That truth hurts more than rumors and lies ever could.

His father has more assistants than he needs but he likes to be surrounded by a swarm of servants. I am surplus to requirements it seems. So, instead, I've become a glorified receptionist; without a desk or any actual tasks or responsibility. I am *that* person who is asked to do the menial things, like hauling files to the library, making trips to Starbucks, and serving hot drinks to stuffed shirts when a meeting is in full swing.

My life is over.

I've thought about leaving so many times, scanning the classifieds in the paper almost every chance I get, but something always holds me back.

More like someone!

Somehow, still working for the Carrero Corporation is my link to Jake and I'm not ready to let him go just yet, if I ever will be. The pain is still too real even though I haven't seen him or heard from him. This is the true definition of being frozen out, even the office gossips don't seem to know about anything going on in Jake's life since he dismissed me.

That's the whole point of him keeping his staff small and in his trust, I guess. Unlike his father, who has an army of minions and everyone seems to know Senior Carrero's business. He's so public about a lot of things, and loud, and commanding. He yells at staff frequently and isn't shy about his movements or dragging an entourage of staff with him wherever he goes. He has a mix of security, assistants, and god knows what else, always crowded around him pandering to his every whim. I miss Jake's less inflated, uncomplicated character. He's only ever needed me … as ironic as that is.

I walk the last block to my new office building, it stands tall and blindingly bright, another column of pointy glass and harsh edges—just like Executive House, a sharp knife looking building amid the Manhattan corporates, standing as tall as most. I shudder. I hate working here. I hate everything about this place. I miss what I had at Executive House, in so many ways, beyond Jake.

The sterile interior and staff at Carrero Tower are always so afraid to step out of line under the command of Senior Carrero. The relaxed aura of Executive House is completely absent in this building and I never thought I'd see the day where I missed Jake's laxness and personal touch. The whole atmosphere between the two is so different.

The receptionist gives me a disapproving look as I walk past in a hurry, knowing for a fact I look disheveled. I slept in, rushed about and practically got dressed while running out the door. This shorter wavy style in my hair is always doing its own thing nowadays but I simply don't care anymore. I glare back at her.

Yes, I'm late … I don't fucking care.

She looks away. She's met my anger before; during the first three days I was here. She spilled coffee down my cream pencil skirt when passing, so I unleashed teen Emma in a rather grand fashion. I'd been a touchy, aggressive, nightmare those first few days, one wrong word got her a tongue lashing from hell. My face twists into a snarl, thinking of the calm and controlled Emma of the past. Where is she now?

She's jumped off a goddamn bridge! I can't seem to muster her of late. I miss her. Jake Carrero pretty much killed her; weeks of tears can do that to a person.

I drop my bag and cell on the desk in the office among the sea of temp desks. It's pretty much a free for all, sit when you need a seat. I miss having my own office and my own space, but it's not like I deserve it anymore. The inclination to run and organize my new boss's life has deserted me. I have zero interest in his calendar or responsibilities. I'm a train wreck nowadays and probably couldn't organize an alcoholic's party in a brewery.

My cell vibrates across the table, Sarah's name lights up the screen along with her face brightening it with a grinning selfie. She never calls me at work so concern rises in my stomach as I reach for it. She's my best friend and roommate, but even she knows not to bother me here.

"Sarah, what is it?" I ask, with nervous apprehension, inner dread that something is wrong.

At least I still have anxiety by my side.

Nothing changed there then.

"Emma, I'm really sorry to bother you at work … I know you don't like it … But, your mother is here," she replies sheepishly then silences at my angry gasp of air.

"What the f—?" I cut myself off, looking around the room for listening ears. There are a couple of assistants milling about so I lower my voice, bringing my mouth to the receiver to quietly hiss.

"What the hell is she doing there?" I know I shouldn't take this out on Sarah, she's only the messenger but my anger is seething from every pore at the mere mention of Jocelyn Anderson's appearance. Weak pathetic woman who chose another abusive boyfriend over sense or logic.

She has no right to show up like this! Invading my life after what she's done.

"She says she came to see you … To talk … What shall I do with her, Ems? I need to leave for work soon, I'm on an early shift today." She sounds genuinely upset, knowing she's stuck between a rock and a hard place. But, my girl knows which side she should be rooting for—if she has any sense at all. I take a steadying breath, pushing down my internal rage in a bid to remain calm.

"Show her the door," I say bluntly. "I need to get back to work, Sarah. Goodbye."

"Emma, but—"

I hang up quickly. I know Sarah will try to talk me around, but I can't deal with this right now. I can't deal with anything lately. I just need everything in my messed up, pitiful life, to take ten steps back, give my brain time to stop reeling and find its feet again. The last few weeks have been one constant headache and I feel like I'm drowning, I can barely breathe with it all.

My cell rings again but I reject the call. Sarah is persistent, more so of late since the changes in me have hit her hard; I feel like she's been smothering me with over-protectiveness. She doesn't know this version of me, this unraveling mess of tears and bad moods, the scatter brain behavior or the chaos I'm leaving in my wake. I think even she longs for a hint of the old Emma to come back and I'm really trying, for both our sakes. Her insecurity over my new persona is obvious and upsetting.

Somehow the mention of my mother has flipped a little switch inside me though and I feel a wave of the numb seeping in as the icy controlled part of PA Emma takes a hold. I'll have to deal with my mother at some point, just not right now, and it only angers me further that she thinks she can just waltz in unannounced as though I owe her my time. I lift my chin defiantly.

That's right, use the anger to fuel your return, cling on to that tiny piece of defiance and get your goddamn life back on track!

I feel relief at the tiny inkling of fire burning deep down inside my belly once more.

You're still in there, Emma. You can do this.

Walking into the board room I see the mess left behind from the breakfast meeting I obviously missed. Not that I really care. I sigh, heavily, since it's me who is going to have to clear this up, despite this floor paying cleaners to keep the place tidy—but they usually only appear after hours. I pout at the monotonous tasks that have become mine. It's so deflating considering I used to travel the world as the right hand of an accomplished CEO.

What the hell happened to me? This time last month I was PA to Jake Carrero! I was organizing his entire life, sitting in five-star hotels, pouring over contracts with him. We were friends and the whole time I was trying to ignore the fact I was head over heels in love with him.

I shake my head, discarding the thoughts that came uninvited into my mind, and start picking up the scattered documents and brochures from the table and returning them to the cart to be filed away. I stack the empty mugs and plates on the trolley, meant for serving food and drink, by the door. At least I can lose myself in cleaning up this room and bringing some calm back to the chaos in my head. I set myself to task, submerging my brain into deep cleaning the room and wiping away the mess made by its previous occupants; hopefully some of that deep clean will wipe off on my thoughts and help me get back to myself.

***

"Emma? Mr. Carrero wants to see you." A small childish voice comes up behind me causing me to drop my duster. My heart takes a sudden stop and my hair is stuck to my face from the exertion of my enthusiastic cleaning.

What? Jake?

My head reels a moment.

No. Giovanni!

I feel like an idiot. I throw a tight smile on my face before turning smoothly to acknowledge the girl. It's one of the small receptionists, all blonde hair and big boobs—like most of Senior's staff. He's sickeningly singular about the women in his employ, finding those whose looks are less like the woman he's married to and more like the "bunnies" of the Hugh Heffner world.

"Okay, where is he?" My voice is even, despite my irritation and I feel a familiar wave of control move across me unexpectedly.

"In his office, you'd better go right away, he's in a bad mood." The tone in her voice betrays her fear of Senior Carrero, but I ignore it. He doesn't scare me in the slightest. His attitude toward his employees grates on my nerves at the best of times, I'm used to that familial Carrero glare and its wily ways. Jake hadn't been against using that glare when bad moods struck, impossible scenarios or general mess ups. I think, somehow, coming here, I've lost all unease around Giovanni Carrero. My heart being ripped out by a man who shares his name has made me immune to the effects any Carrero could've tried to pull on me.

I push memories of him aside, I can't think about him right now.

Ever!

If I do, I'll just dwell on how much I miss him and how much I think about the night we had sex … repeatedly. I'll torture myself into insanity, and I can't afford to do that. Mentally, I was only just starting to see glimpses of the old me and didn't want to scare her back into submission already.

I follow the girl silently from the room and head toward the long hall leading to King Carrero's domain with my chin in the air once more, showing pride and defiance. I was not going to be intimidated by this man. No matter how badly he thought I was doing at my job.

Senior visibly bristles as I enter his office, for once he's alone, and sat in his leather throne behind his huge, polished walnut desk. The sun is blazing in from the wall of glass behind him and the breath-taking New York scenery. He looks like a formidable billionaire, small and tanned with highlighted brown hair and dark evil eyes. He watches my every movement as I walk nearer his desk, knowing that he would never ask me to sit, so I don't even try.

"You asked me to come see you?" I say tonelessly, my body rigid under his scrutiny. There is no love between us, I am merely another irritation to his life and another faceless employee.

"Yes, Miss. Anderson, I did … My son sent you to me as a PA, yet I've no need for more assistance. Your performance has left me with a sour taste in my mouth and I think we need to have a little chat." He doesn't even have the grace to look up at me while saying it, his eyes on his laptop as he types.

He's not one to mince his words, I stare at him blankly, unsurprised. I've expected this moment for a while, amazed it's taken three weeks for us to have this conversation.

"My son obviously saw something in you, so I'm not ready to dismiss you just yet … In fact, he insisted you stay in this company, indefinitely." His unexpected confession causes a sharp pain in my chest and brings a slight confused expression to my face. When he looks up, his uninterested gaze sweeps toward my face with a very deadpan look, betraying nothing.

Jake asked his father to keep me employed? No matter what? Despite sending me away … But why?

Emotion tugs in my throat but I push it down harshly. I'm not ready to dissect Jake's reasons yet, if ever.

Senior never says anything lightly, always direct and

to the point, not wasting his breath on small talk. I know he's not embellishing. If he thought I was a drain on company finances, excess to requirements, then I'd be gone already.

"So, what's to be done with me?" I ask drily, feeling less confident at the turn of this conversation. Grasping my hands together, I lay them across my waist to regain my posture, trying to look business-like, despite the pounding in my chest.

Right now, I wouldn't care if he sent me to Timbuktu if it meant I didn't get fired.

"You're going back to Executive House, floor thirty-two … Public relations, organizing events and the like …" he waves his hand around, uninterested "… Jacob told me you excel at planning and juggling a high workload, so I hope you finally prove it to me." His harsh gaze rests on me coldly, assessing me, but I steel myself against his stare.

The thought of going back to that building surges through me like fire, igniting my fear, manically, but I remain impassive under his scrutiny.

"I don't know what happened with my son, Miss. Anderson, but I am pleased with your discretion on this transference. There has been no real gossip as such, but I do want to point this out … You're still employed under duress of my son, he was very clear on this, and as you know, my relationship with Jacob is somewhat strained so this …" his hand points to me then back to himself, "… is the compromise I made to keep him happy. If I hadn't made such promises to Jacob, I would've fired you in under a week." His eyes release me as an end to our discussion and he goes back to tapping away on his laptop.

I lower my lashes and swallow, involuntarily, I suppose I should be grateful for this, despite my inner organs trying to shrivel up and hide. I still have a job.

What the hell has happened to me?

My job was my universe. The one thing I excelled at and pushed through. My life, consumed with work, got me to where I was because of it. Yet here I am, saved from unemployment because Jake felt guilty enough to ensure I kept my job.

The thought is sobering, and Giovanni's revelation is a surprise. Jake and he were always so formal, distant, and cold, it made me wonder at his willingness to please his son.

There may be more to their relationship than either Jake or I realize. Maybe Senior loves his son more than he shows.

"Jake didn't need me anymore … That's all there is to say." I point out blandly, avoiding the eyes that have once again come to rest on my face. In a way, it was the truth. He didn't need me … not in the way I needed him, so, there was no reason to keep me any longer.

"Right …" His voice is drenched in sarcasm. I glance up and for a moment I catch a hint of challenge in his eye, maybe even a slight thawing of his normally cruel tight mouth. He's almost as unreadable as his son. "Pack up whatever you brought here, you're going there today. Wilma Munro is expecting you." He moves his focus back to his laptop; a clear move to signal my dismissal. He's issued his demands and now wants me to remove myself from his presence.

"Yes, sir." I nod briefly and turn on my heel, needing no more direction. I walk out, confidently, despite my insides turning to mush.

I'm not sure how to feel right now. How can I feel about this?

I'm going back! Back to Jake's building, back to being only floors below him and I don't know how to feel about this, or how to process it.

Chance sightings … chance meetings. I don't know if I can handle it. I don't think my heart can handle it.

Waves of nausea return heavily, my hands tremble at the thought of possibly seeing him again. I feel sickening dread, this has to be the worst decision ever made in the history of mankind.

Chapter 2

Wilma Munro is a shock to the system. She's Scottish and her accent is thick, but not completely alien, with hints of a long New York residency. I can understand her for the most part, she's a resolute force to be reckoned with.

Wilma is small with dark coppery curly hair and huge brown eyes set in a love heart face, standing at only four and a half feet tall. She catches me, immediately, in her whirlwind of enthusiastic energy. Loud, yet not in a commanding way, she is direct, yet friendly and slightly terrifying. She whisks me into my new domain, assigns me a desk near her office, and outlines my responsibilities as part of her team, thrusting a box of files at me. She believes throwing someone in at the deep end brings out their inner worth.

"I've heard enough about you, Miss. Anderson, to know you were being wasted at Carrero Tower. I've great expectations of you." She smiles warmly, soft eyes twinkling merrily.

"Mr. Carrero seemed to imply I was only seconds away from dismissal," I respond drily, instantly regretting letting my mouth jump in before my head. I look away, nervously, my fingers finding my jacket to twist the hem, anxiously.

Nice move, just tell your new boss how useless you are.

"I'm very good friends with Margo Drake, my dear. I spoke to her only this morning, when I was informed you were coming to me. She only had good things to say about you ... and maybe some insight on recent behaviors."

I spin to look at her, sudden shock on my face, blood draining away and leaving me cold.

What did Margo say to Wilma? What did Margo know? Surely Jake didn't tell her about sleeping with me? Everything that happened?

My head is reeling. Of course, he would. He tells Margo everything, she's like a surrogate mother to him, and my old mentor. She would've pushed him to give her the real reason he let me go, unsatisfied with excuses and seeing through any untruths. He would've told Margo about that night for sure.

But would Margo have told this woman?

Even when I was with Jake, I kept Margo up to date with how he was doing; she always wanted to know, she always seemed discreet to me, so I hope right now she has been. Wilma winks at me knowingly and I pale, my body turns colder as the blood leaves my veins.

Oh, my god.

She must know!

I feel sick and betrayed by my old mentor, the pain is almost overwhelming. I swallow hard, unable to think of a response, but Wilma doesn't dwell. She sweeps away from me with a wave of her hand, leaving me reeling in panic and nothing more to say on the matter.

"The schedule is on top of that file, Emma ... We're arranging a dinner and dance for the Carrero anniversary. Read the files, we have press releases and a guest list to sort out, that's going to be your job. Look over what's been arranged, then we'll talk. The suggested guest list is in there too."

I watch her walk away, completely overwhelmed, my head somewhere in outer space and gob smacked. I feel like I've been hit by a tornado, but I push it all down deep inside.

Forget Margo, forget Jake. This is my life now and they owe me nothing.

Wilma doesn't seem to care about the past, so neither should I.

I look down at the box in my shaking hands, the schedule looks full and exhausting, but I see potential. I can work my ass off on this and regain some of my reputation. This job should be easy, easier than facing Senior Carrero and handing out coffee like a mindless minion every day. This is exactly what I need, a new challenge and a new distraction. Time to get my complicated head back together and file everything into that little black lock box in my mind.

I set to work, finding myself engrossed in tasks I'm more than capable of. The hours fly by for the first time in weeks, I look up seeing people leave, realizing it's the end of the work day already.

This is exactly what I needed to forget him.

* * *

The apartment seems quiet when I put my key in the door and my heart pounds through my chest wondering if Sarah made my mother leave. But, something deep down tells me Sarah hasn't. I open the door slowly and take a deep breath. The small hall which opens into the sitting room, smells of cooking food and I sigh.

Sarah won't be home from her shift at work, Marcus is unlikely to cook so that means someone else is here. I stiffen as I walk in, seeing my mother leaning over the stove, her arm still in a cast. There's a young brunette hovering by her side helping with whatever food she is currently massacring.

Figures. My mother's cooking expertise stops at heating a can of soup.

I take a moment to work out that the brunette is the nurse Jake's still paying to take care of her. He's honoring his promise to Sophie, a runaway we met when she was living with my mother in Chicago and who is now being adopted by family friends of the Carreros', to take care of her until her injuries are fully healed, despite cutting ties with me. It causes a dull aching lump to form in my throat.

Throwing my briefcase on the nearby couch I tense up, ready for this little altercation. They haven't heard me come in, too busy making noise in the kitchen with bubbling pots and pointless chatter. My rage simmers at the sight of her. I'm still reeling with the fact that she let Ray Vanquis back in her life, after everything.

"Mother," I snap, loudly and firmly. Both heads spin round, minor surprise replaced with quick smiles.

"Emma." My mother gushes as she comes out of the little kitchen toward me, her face still bearing some of the yellowing bruises from being beaten to a pulp by the so-called man in her life. She attempts to hug me but meets my icy stance and unmoving posture. I flinch at her touch, so she quickly recoils to stand a foot away from me awkwardly.

I notice her nurse hovering in the background, her face a picture of confusion and embarrassment, at least she has the good grace to turn back to the stove and continue cooking, acting like she hasn't seen anything.

"Are you still mad at me?" My mother whimpers like a child, causing my anger to flare again. That childish, wide-eyed expression of hers, the one I've seen a million times on her frail little innocent face, reserved for an audience. I turn away from her before I say something I can't take back.

"I'm going to get changed," I snap and walk off, leaving her to stand in the center of the room like a lost puppy. I take satisfaction in the hurt evident on her face, maybe it's about time she knew what it felt like to have someone who's a part of you treat you like you don't matter to them.

* * *

In my room, I sit on my bed and take a moment to inhale slowly, despite my outward frosty reception, I'm shaking on the inside from her visit. She affects me in ways I'll never understand, no matter how I try to deny it. The woman knows how to make me feel worthless.

She always pulls the rug out from under me, is that the curse of her being my mother? On some level, that child inside of me still wants her to wipe away my pain, unaware that she's the one who causes most of it.

I smart at the thought and my eyes wander to my closed door.

I know that I dislike who she is. I don't hate her … I don't know if I love her anymore … But I don't know what I feel.

I get up and change into casual clothes, tight jeans and loose top, glad to be out of the confines of a suit. I used to love dressing that way, but nowadays it feels stifling and claustrophobic. My hair, already loose, has grown an inch since I had it cut, it brushes my shoulders constantly with its wild waves. I look in the mirror at my head of tawny hair, brushing it back to reveal tired eyes and a sad face.

Do I look like this all the time? Or is this the effect Jocelyn Anderson has had on me just by walking through the door?

I push back the sad expression and lift my chin defiantly, pasting on the face of self-preservation that I've perfected over the years.

Returning to the sitting room I see she's trying to help dish out beef stew into bowls with a smile on her face. Bad moods forgotten, pushed to one side, like always. This is just the way she is, acting like nothing has happened. The sad story of my life with her.

I feel myself bristle and grind my teeth. I'm on edge just watching her, while she acts like this is the most normal scene in the world. I glance at her young nurse, she seems capable and has a maturity about her.

I wonder how much she knows? I wonder how much Jocelyn Anderson has let her see?

"Food's ready." The young woman chirps brightly, lying the bowls on the small dinette table. I watch my mother hesitantly, stay back. She's waiting on my reaction before she makes a move.

I slide into a chair at the table and concentrate on picking up the cutlery, starting to eat. I know I'm being cold and rude, and right now I just don't care. The last time I saw her she was in a hospital bed, battered and broken and I'd just learned that the man responsible was the same one who tried to rape me when I was eighteen. She'd gone back to him, the abusive prick, without a second thought to what it might do to me, or to our relationship.

They both sit and begin to eat; the silence is awkward and tense, but no one attempts to initiate conversation. The nurse looks around timidly before deciding staring at her plate is the best option and lowers her head. Finally, feeling my irritation rise beyond control, I break the glass-like atmosphere with a sledge hammer.

"Why are you here?" I blurt out, with not so subtle venom.

"I … We needed to talk about things, Emma." She lowers her lashes, attempting to be coy, maybe even feebleness, but it only angers me. Putting her fork down and crossing her hands on the table she leans toward me.

"About what exactly? The fact that you're screwing the man who loves to beat both of us up and tried to rape your only child?" I spit, harshly, taking delight in the nurse's gasp of shock and the color rising up her cheeks.

I guess she didn't know after all.

"Yes … Emma, he's gone … I know what I did, I see what I did." She tries to reach for my hand, but I yank it out of reach.

How many times have I heard this bullshit? How many times has she pushed men away after they hit one of us, only to have him crawl back into her bed days later.

"Too little, far too late, Mother! You think you can just show up here and smooth it all over? Do you even know what he did while you were lying in a hospital bed?" My voice is raised and agitated, I need to regain a little control in this if we are to have it out. I hate that she always makes me break this way.

"No …" Her weak tiny voice betrays her nervousness, she's afraid I'm going to tell her he succeeded this time. I see that moment of doubt, casting my mind back to the look on her face when she caught him trying to hurt me once before … The fear he would want me instead of her. It makes me sick to my stomach, which only helps fuel my rage.

"He attacked me!" I snarl. "He's just the same evil man he was eight years ago, nothing has changed!"

"What?" her eyes widen in alarm "Did he?" She can't formulate the words, but I can read her like a book. All she wants to know is if he *had sex* with me. This isn't about me or my getting hurt, it's about her boyfriend *cheating* on her.

"No. He didn't. He just wanted to prove his dominance over me, to scare me, and he did," I yell at her, feeling the twist in my gut as her expression confirms my thoughts. She's relieved. Her boyfriend didn't betray her. She's happy. She never gave a shit about me, it was always about her and her men. I just got in the way, I was collateral damage.

"Jake beat the shit out of him and I'm glad … I wish he'd killed him." I scream, jumping to my feet, sending the table into chaos. The bowls spill and glasses tip over, knocking drinks everywhere. Her face pales in sudden realization of how Ray incurred his injuries and I see the look she gets as it clicks in her brain. The nurse tries to grab the cups to set them straight, without success, all the while her face flaming.

Yes, Momma! Jake did that to him … Jake beat him to a pulp for laying his hands on me … Someone who didn't have any obligation to love or protect me, my boss! Not my mother … My mother never would've stood up for me in that way, never chosen me over her man.

The thought makes me want to lash out and beat her stupid face.

"Why can't you see what you do to me?" I scream again, tears flowing down my face, emotions getting the better of me.

"Emma … How is any of that my fault? Jake had no right to hurt Ray … He's the reason Ray left!" She yells at me, accusation and tears streaming down her face. She's on her feet trying to bring her small wiry frame to my height. The nurse stays seated, staring at her hands in her lap as though she wants to be anywhere but here. I feel a tremor of pity for her, she wasn't paid to get involved in the Anderson women drama.

"What?" My inner body lurches at her words as I click on what she said. "What do you mean he left? You said he was gone … You implied it was your choosing?"

I was so stupid to ever believe she'd make the decision on her own to send him away.

"He left. He came by looking like he'd been in a car wreck, told me it was over and left. I haven't seen him since.

You chased him out of my life … again. I hope you're goddamn happy this time, Emma," she yells at me, accusingly, unaware that she's just incriminated herself with every word from that harsh mouth.

Is she so self-absorbed that she is so deaf to what she is saying?

The anger inside me, teen Emma, is unable to hold herself back any longer. All the recent weeks of agony without Jake build up, breaking my ability to reign myself in. I lash out uncontrollably, throwing the plate of food at her, missing her head by an inch and smashing into the wall behind her with dramatic effect. Both woman squeal and jump in fright and I push the table hard onto its side, so it rolls over onto the floor, spilling everything else down with a crash. The rage and aggression that have been tethered too long are flowing out of me uncontrollably, unbridled.

"Get out of my fucking apartment," I scream at her, kicking away my chair, grabbing at my hair, almost ripping it out in frustration. I'm pacing, trying so hard to hold in the last ounces of control I thought I had.

I haven't been this way since the week before I left Chicago, so many years ago, when I got to this stage of erupting and going insane, I ran away. I ran, to protect myself, and protect her, from this anger inside me that wants so badly to hurt her; to retaliate at her failings as a mother. I can't run away now, nor do I want to. This is my home … my space and my life.

"Just fucking get out!" I screech again, this time the nurse hurriedly picks up their bags, and pulls at my mother's sleeve in a desperate attempt to remove her.

"Emma …?" Her lip wobbles.

"No! Enough! Just go!" I throw my arms up, wild and seething, she needs to leave before I lash out directly at her. I know I'm more than capable of it. I've hit back before, at men in the past but I've never hit her even though right now I want to. I feel it like a pulsing need inside of me. The need to hit her stupid head against something hard and knock sense into her.

I hate her so much!

They both turn and rush out, leaving me behind in my own chaos and rage. As soon as the door closes I crumple to the floor, letting it all go in a devastating wail, tumbling out until my body has no energy left to make a sound.

* * *

I finally sit up and look around, taking stock of the mess, I've made but I don't care. I look at the food running down the light gray painted wall like a wound. It feels good to sit here, surrounded by broken things and ugliness, I feel like I belong here. I know soon I'll get up and clean it all away, hiding the evidence of my break down. I'll pull myself up, straighten my face and my clothes and go back to poised Emma before the morning.

This is what I do, this is what she taught me! That no matter what, I must contain all that is wrong with me and hide it away, show the world that I'm capable and strong.

No one gets to see vulnerable Emma, and no one, no one … gets to inflict more pain on me. By morning I'll have filed it neatly into my internal black box and will have pasted on my professional smile, ready to face another day.

That's who Emma is, who I am. She's a fake smile and cold demeanor. She's outwardly unshakable and cool. Jake saw that Emma and truly believed that's all there was of her. He'd chosen to send her on her way, rather than see the broken mess inside, literally falling to pieces at just knowing him.

Chapter 3

I get into the elevator, smoothing down my skirt, and glance at the narrow mirror by the door, sighing. I look better, feel better, and more in control. I've only been back at Executive House for a few days, but somehow the familiarity of this building, and the people who knew me as Jake's assistant so treat me with more respect than I received at Carrero Tower, have helped me get back on track.

I've barely slept the last few nights. My mother's appearance has left my mind in a constant cyclone of thoughts. I've replayed my mother's words a million times in my head, none of it makes sense to me, the obvious aside, I can't wrap my brain around her admission.

I should've known really. Ray isn't the kind of person to up and run off because another guy gave him a taste of his own medicine. He only left years ago because I threatened to involve the police. I'm sure something more must've happened after Jake left him lying in the street. What did Jake do to make sure Ray left for good? I need to ask him, but I know I can't. Seeing him would be agony and I can't bring myself to ask him via email. As much as I want to know if he did, I'm too scared to inflict that kind of pain on myself. Seeing him, speaking to him, would kill me all over again. I need distance if I'm going to get over Jake Carrero.

I cast the idea of confronting Jake aside, head to my desk, and get to work, something I'm getting better at doing lately. I flick through the guest list on my iPad, it's a sea of influential guests: business tycoons, minor royalty, A-listers, and a whole host of visiting dignitary. The anniversary dinner is going to be a star studded and spangle bannered event, the talk of New York and I'm a very huge part of it. I sigh, feeling pride as I think about how amazing this is going to be.

The lift chimes as we stop, I move to step out realizing it's not my floor. We're only on ninth, I go back to my iPad, scrolling down the list of names, making note of who I need to contact and when. A few men in suits walk in so I shuffle over to one side, eyes down. Checking the credentials of some suggestions from Wilma; a Hollywood playboy and his wife, a businessman from Europe, both seem possibilities for our invitation only event.

My skin prickles, unexpectedly, aware of a wave of heat soaring down my body, alerting me to something. I look up at the men who have crowded in and only see the backs of navy and black suits, nothing sinister, no one's even looking at me. Two of the men move back beside me as more people shuffle in and I freeze as my eyes connect with the "something".

Jake walks in last, his perfect green eyes catch mine for a millisecond, that handsome face, designer stubble and boyishness. A frown crosses his face and he looks away quickly. The effect is crushing, my heart instantly accelerates into overdrive and starts pounding in my chest like a war drum. I bite down on my lip to try to even out my heartbeat.

This is another reason why I could never ask him about Ray. That look said it all, he doesn't want to know me anymore.

He's wearing a tailored dark blue suit with a white shirt and tie. Looking impressively handsome, like the CEO I first met almost a year ago, my breathing shallows and my hands tremble but I'm fixated on his back, unable to move my gaze from his perfect physique. His wide, sculpted shoulders emanate strength, his perfect neck outlined by his short, dark hair.

The agony of his proximity is tearing at me. I ache to reach out and brush my fingers against him, the man whose touch was once as normal as breathing. The wave of emotion throws me a curve ball and I have to fight to keep the tears at bay. I never knew seeing him would hurt this much.

I'm still in love with him. Four weeks of separation have done nothing to quell the intensity of these feelings.

This is all too much. I knew there was a chance our paths would cross at some point. But I hadn't expected it to be so soon or for it to feel this awful. I stay stock still, finding it hard to breathe. Trying my hardest to keep my eyes on my iPad, looking like I'm in full control of my faculties.

The elevator stops a few times and one or two men get on, pushing Jake to move closer toward me, where I am trying to pretend he's not here. His gaze stays on the front of the small space, deliberately ignoring my presence, and never straying my way.

Oh, my god. Please, just acknowledge me … Please.

I stare at my iPad on the verge of tears. The doors open again, and a crowd of people move in filling the lift. Jake has no choice but to move closer, so he's almost beside me. The motion causes me to look up nervously. I catch his eye and he gazes at me for more than a second. But his eyes are clear and steady, expression blank, before turning to face the door again. Another jolt in my chest, another slice of pain in my frazzled heart. He has no idea of the damage he could inflict with his impassiveness. My heart is pounding, the weight in my chest is suffocating me. I can smell his aftershave, smell him, so close, yet so far, the tension is almost radiating from every part of me.

God, I can't do this.

I look up with relief as the lift chimes at the thirty-second floor and push forward to get out. I cross in front of Jake to leave and almost brush against him, my skin surging with electricity and face flushing.

"Miss. Anderson," he says quietly and politely as I go. His deep husky voice causing me physical pain. I look back quickly, seeing his tight emotionless smile, confusion running through me then overwhelming sadness. He doesn't seem surprised or phased to see me. In fact, he doesn't seem bothered in the slightest, just bored.

"Mr. Carrero." I breathe, holding in every ounce of heartbreak. I can't manage a smile. I can barely manage a normal voice. As soon as I get to the open door I flee, pushing my way free, ignoring the puzzled looks from the men in suits as I dash into the hall to solitude.

I'm hyperventilating by the time I hit my desk, overwhelmed and ravaged, struggling not to cry with the after effects of finally seeing him.

How can he still have this affect over me? How can I be so weak?

My emotions, already taut from the last couple of days are not helping. I'm overreacting and overtired. The chaos of events lately is destroying any hold I have on old Emma's composure, breaking me down into this sniveling mess I'm trying so hard to overcome.

Wilma throws me an odd look from her desk, through the glass partition. I slump down in my chair, trying to feign a smile, and turn away to conceal my devastation. My head is aching. I feel cold and dizzy and my throat is constricting so much I can't speak. I'm holding back tears with so much effort it makes my throat ache.

"Emma, dear … Are you okay?" Wilma appears beside me as I rush to claw myself back together, not wanting her to see the mess I'm in.

"Yes, I … Ummm. I'm fine." I try but my voice betrays me; wobbling and breaking, raw with emotion.

"Emma, what's happened? You left for lunch fine. Now you're as white as a sheet. You look so distraught?" She lays a gentle hand on my shoulder and I almost flinch at the alien contact. It's so unexpected from someone I barely know.

"Nothing." I stammer. "I just didn't feel well for a minute." I lie, expertly, pushing it all back down inside.

At least my mother taught me one thing growing up, how to lie like a pro.

"Do you need to go home?" She takes my arm gently, forcing me to look at her, her expression grim as though I may break into a million pieces. This woman is so motherly and nice, it's hard to keep my cold composure, it isn't helping my mental state at all.

Why couldn't I have had a mother like her instead? A mother who genuinely cared for my wellbeing.

"No … no. Honestly … I just need a moment." My breathing is shallow with the effort of struggling to calm the erratic beating of my heart,

"Emma, maybe lie down and relax. It's not like you to get overwhelmed." She pats my arm and gives me a knowing look. One that says, "do as I say. Now!" I nod, relieved when her expression lightens, and she moves away to leave me to get going. I look around at the other staff sat at their desks typing away or on their phones. No one looks my way and

Wilma is hovering over a new girl, showing her some files.

I don't hesitate. I take my bag and purse and head out as soon as I see her entering her office. I need some head space to fall apart and reel myself in privately. It's better than trying to hold this all in to self-combust later in the day.

* * *

I sit in the ladies' restroom on a soft plush chaise lounge in the washing area. It's the only place I could get to quickly that was private enough to bring myself back to inner calm. My head is all over the place. This is about more than just Jake. It's everything. I've been holding it all in since the morning after my mother left. Her, my lack of ability to stay in control, the aching loneliness of Jake's absence, and now seeing him. It's all too much.

Maybe it's time I faced reality and looked for another job. I was stupid to think I could work here, only floors away from him. Acting like we don't know each other anymore. I just can't do it anymore.

I can't handle the thought that any time I leave this floor I might see him. There's a chance we could run into one another anywhere in this building, and I've just proven I can't handle it.

Looking around at the contemporary furnishings I sigh. My heart rate calmer, for now, but I know I can't keep living like this, in the hope of feeling better.

How long before I'm an emotional train wreck again because I've spotted him across a hall? Or in a lift? Or even in meeting? I need to get a grip of myself.

I need to think about this rationally, think about what's best for me and moving on with my life.

* * *

I take the elevator down to the lower floors where there's a huge canteen for staff to eat in with a pleasant seated area that is surprisingly private. I need time to think in a calm and quiet place, take a moment to browse the classifieds again and really think this through. Think my future through and where I go from here.

I grab a chair and sit by the large glass windows, with my English tea and bagel, to spend some time pondering over my next steps. I have no intention of walking away from this table until I have a plan in my head about where I go next or what I do. I know one thing for sure, I can't work here anymore. I was an idiot to come back at all. I skim the classifieds in the paper someone had left on the table and I circle a couple of jobs, but neither have the lure of the one I'm in now, or even compare to being the PA to New York's richest playboy. They don't meet the salary I'm used to having either.

God, I need to try harder.

I pull out my cell and scroll through some online job sites. There's a position for a PA to some European business man so I jot it down on my note pad.

Am I really doing this? Have I really decided to leave Carrero House?

"Emma?" The chirpy voice draws my attention and I look up to see Rosalie beaming at me. My old assistant. She looks pretty today, long auburn hair loose around her shoulders and her fitted cream suit accentuates her olive skin and hazel eyes. She always was a friendly looking girl.

"Hello, Rosalie! It's nice to see you." I smile back, easily, folding my paper over and moving it aside, gesturing to her to sit. She smiles brightly and flops down in front of me.

"I really have missed you on the sixty-fifth, you were my ideal boss." She grins again, her smile overtaking her face beautifully and for the first time I realize just how much I've missed her. I never really gave the idea much thought when we worked together, she used to ease my stresses and organize finer details, leaving me free to be brilliant. My secret weapon. But above all, she always had a smile for me and I knew she was my back up, someone I could always count on. With her, I never felt like I was doing it alone.

"I miss you too. I really miss your hot chocolates, a lot." I laugh, being genuine with her, probably for the first time.

"You seem different now … I'm sorry if that's rude." She lowers her lashes. "It's just, I've seen you at a distance a couple of times and I don't know, it's like there's something different," a hint of blush creeps up her cheek.

"I feel different, Rosalie, it's not rude … I guess I'm the talk of the office, right?" I sip my tea and raise an eyebrow. It's inevitable they're all talking about the PA who was sent away, only to be sent back again a month later.

"A bit … There's so much gossip about why you left." She blushes fully this time, averting her eyes to the paper on the table.

"Ignore the gossip, it'll blow over soon enough," I say so calmly I surprise myself. I know the gossip's been running thick but not one ounce of truth has made it out there. Rosalie's never been one to push for information when it comes to Jake and I wonder how much she picked up on, and how much she guessed.

"He misses you, you know?" She watches me a little intently, I freeze with my cup mid-air and shake my head. Carefully placing the cup down.

"He was the one who chose to send me elsewhere, Rosalie. Jake and I …" I sigh. "We reached a place in our relationship that wasn't working anymore." I avoid her eye for a moment.

"I get that, I could see it happening. It's just ... Since you've been gone, he's not much fun to work for anymore." Her cheeks glow still, revealing her discomfort and she looks away quickly.

"He'll get over it, I'm sure. That's what Jake does best." I tap my nails on the table top, trying to end this line of conversation.

"Are you leaving?" she squeaks, alerting me to where she's looking, sitting up straight in a flash, she's noticed my notes on the pad beside me ... The European PA job. I mustn't have folded it away as discreetly as I thought I had.

Crap. Smooth move, Emma!

"Thinking about it." I cut in smoothly, flipping the pad over. I don't know why I care about her knowing. Everyone will find out soon enough if I hand my resignation in. I'm sure even that would make it to the sixty-fifth floor in a hurry.

"I know things went south upstairs, but I always believed you'd come back ... That whatever happened with you and Jake, it'd blow over. He misses you, regardless of what you say. You were both such a perfect fit, it's just so awful to see you drifting apart." Her face is so earnest it quells my urge to snort, instead I shake my head sadly, as a familiar lump in my throat resurfaces.

"It's complicated. I really doubt he misses me at all ... We wanted different things. This is for the best. I know that's not really an explanation but trust me." It's the only one I can come up with.

"Men are really complicated but I know one thing ... Men in bad moods? Angry, shouty men, like Jake has been for the last few weeks? Are usually angry and shouty because they're hurting in some way ... It started the day you left, and he's only got worse. Take from that what you will." Her pointed expression and raised eyebrow make my insides droop.

I look at the table knowing full well his recent mood has nothing to do with me. He came home with Marissa in tow, and the knowledge that he is going to be a father. His ex-girlfriend turned drunken one-night stand in a moment of weakness, made sure of that. No wonder he's gone off the scale with his moods. His life has always been so perfectly uncomplicated with no real ties or relationship commitments. Marissa dropping that bombshell on him upends everything that makes him happy. Jake isn't missing me, Jake is missing the life he had before he got a girl pregnant.

I cast a picture in my mind to one of his petty glares and it makes me smile for a moment, even mad or pissed in some way, he was too beautiful for words.

"Jake has a lot going on, Rosalie … I'm not even a factor in his moods … Trust me." I smile, tightly, as she stands. She lightly squeezes my hand on the table and straightens her jacket, picking up her paper cup of coffee.

"I need to head back, if I'm late he'll probably yell at me again … It's been nice to see you, Emma …I mean really, really, nice." She gives me a killer smile and it melts me. My reaction is almost spontaneous, without thinking, I jump up and give her a hug. Something inside tells me this is a goodbye hug. She hesitantly hugs me back after a moment of shock and pulls away.

"You really are so different … I like it." She turns on her heel, grinning, leaving me with a wave. I watch her walk off among the milling people until she's out of sight, a strange feeling of longing as she goes. She represents everything I had … The office, the job with Jake, her, my friendship with him, and a whole other world. Saying goodbye to her represents how I'm feeling now.

It's time to move on with my life.

* * *

I walk up the hall toward my desk glancing at the clock. I've been gone almost two hours, but something tells me Wilma won't mind. I've worked like crazy since coming here and she seems to trust my skills. I've returned a lot calmer and happier. I'll happily put in the hours at the end of the day to make sure she knows I'm not abusing my second chance at being here. She'll be happy with that. Plus, now I have some sort of plan about what I'm going to do, I feel better. I've always liked plans and control, knowing where I'm going and what I'm doing. Despite it not being exactly what I want in life, it's a step forward with a new focus. Determined to move on I have a notebook full of jobs to look at later tonight, resolving to apply for at least one of them.

I beam at her as I pass her glass walled office and she grins back, phone to her ear and animated hand gestures. I'll miss her, even though my time in her department has been brief. I'm comfortable working with her, there's something about her that makes me like her, she instantly puts you at ease with a feeling that you can trust her.

The files on my desk are full of guest list suggestions from this morning. She wants me to research some new additions, some big names, and big money to satisfy the media attention. People who sum up what the Carrero name stands for; elegance, opulence, and grandeur.

My cell rings as I'm reading through the list, picking up the receiver I put it to my ear, lost in the words before my eyes.

"Emma Anderson, speaking," I answer distractedly, holding it between my chin and shoulder as I flick over a page.

"You're going nowhere, Emma." Jake's voice halts me, my breath catches in my lungs. My stomach receives a sudden punch reaction to his deep familiar tone. He sounds pissed, his voice is deep and growling, terrifyingly close to my ear. I pull my cell away, scowling, as though it's offended me in some way before returning it, angrily.

"I'll go where I damn well please … It has nothing to do with you!" I spit, his domineering behavior has never been a hit with me, nor do I fancy his chances now. His reaction bringing out the fight in me.

"It's got everything to do with me … You're still under contract. I'll make it impossible for you to leave until your contract ends … To the fucking second it ends." He's yelling at me now.

What the actual hell? Why is he being like this? How is me leaving anything to do with him? Absolutely fucking nothing!

My rage seers dramatically.

"Why do you care?! You don't want me around, but you don't want me to leave either? That makes no sense … You can't dictate my life to me anymore, Jacob!" I snap, taking the wind out of his sails slightly.

"You can't just up and leave, New York is your home." His tone switches a little, pleading slightly. But, the moment I realize it, his voice changes back again, "Don't call me fucking Jacob!" His temper matches mine. Fire meeting fire. If there was ever hope in my mind of an emotional reunion with Jake, this proved I was so completely wrong. This here, sums up everything he sent me away for. This anger between us, always simmering, for no goddamn reason. It replaced how we used to get along.

Jake is pig-headed, domineering, stubborn, and an asshole!

"Last I checked it was the name your mother graced you with. Suits you when you're being an idiot. I'll leave New York if I want to. Hell, if I want to leave the goddamn country then you don't have a say. Back off, Carrero. I'm not your PA anymore." I let it all out in a gust of emotion, anger, and bravado. Steeling the internal tremors of having him finally contacting me, finally talking to me, he made first contact.

"Be rational, Emma. You've worked so hard and come so far in this company, don't throw it all away to spite me." His anger is wavering, he sounds more like he's pleading. I am so confused with this, and so angry. But I'm not backing down, not after the way he hurt me.

I'm so mad at Rosalie right now, I know she wouldn't have meant this reaction. She must have mentioned it to Margo and Margo, of course, has told Jake. I groan, inwardly, there's only one way to deal with commanding Carrero when he's like this.

"Butt out, Jake. I'm nothing to do with you anymore. That's what you wanted, remember?" I say coolly, hanging up. I turn my cell off, my hands shaking violently. I know what he's like, he'll call back and I won't have the willpower to be quite so brave.

I breathe deeply, steading myself against my chair and smooth a hair from my face in a bid to regain control. Taking a moment to still the absolute chaos of a train wreck inside me, looking around I see no one has raised eyes toward me. No one heard anything.

Good … No scene … No damage.

Wilma is still on her call, writing notes as she talks. The other few girls at nearby desks are engrossed in laptops and papers, there's a man wandering across the far wall toward the water cooler. No one has looked my way at all.

My desk phone rings and I automatically pick it up.

"Don't fucking hang up on me again." Jake snaps down the line, my body sagging into my chair in deflation. I clutch my temple, a headache coming on at his grumpy asshole mood. I know this side of him only too well and I've no energy for it. All I've done is make him angrier and antagonized the part of him that wants to lash out at me.

This is all I need. Well done, Emma, well done!

"I can't do this, Jake … Please." My voice has lost all its conviction. I sound weak and tearful. I'm exhausted, he exhausts me, this whole thing is exhausting. Last thing I need is this, him on the line giving me the Mr. Dominant Ice routine.

"Do what?" He sounds genuinely confused and I roll my eyes.

"I'm looking for jobs elsewhere, nothing you say can change it. It's better for both of us that way. Please stop calling me, I have work to do … Goodbye." I don't give him a chance to talk but hang up again. I've barely cradled it before it starts ringing again, a light on my phone indicates it's an inside line. I know it's him.

Screw you, Jake … Stop doing this. Leave me alone!

I get up and walk away from my phone. It's loud ringing drumming in my ears. Some of the others in the office have looked up to see the cause of their interruption at work, but they quickly look back down when met with my angry glare. I'm glad in such a brief time they've learned not to mess with me; at least I still have that part of PA Emma somewhere inside of me. I walk to the water cooler and get a cup of water as it finally stops ringing, relief at last … only it starts again seconds later.

Shit. I can't keep ignoring calls. What if they're from clients? Actual work?

I walk back and flick on my answering machine, killing it mid-ring. At least this way I can catch genuine calls, take messages and filter out Jake.

I grab my iPad and a file then head to the hall. If I go to the copy room to get duplicates of some work Wilma gave me then I can focus on doing something menial until he gets bored and gives up. Unfortunately, I think that may take a while seeing as Jake can be as persistent as toothache. He'll get the hint soon enough, I hope, knowing only too well that "dog trying to sniff out a bone" attitude he possesses.

I see Wilma catch my eye as I walk past her glass wall, waving and pointing to the copy room with a smile I wander off as she nods me away.

I may have wanted to talk to you again, Jake, but not like this. All you've done is show me how right you were to send me away.

***

I copy several sheets needed to make booklets about the status of the dance for the meeting tomorrow. Leaning against the side table I put the copies into piles for stapling. My head's spinning with Jake at the forefront of my mind. His reaction to my wanting to leave and his attitude. I don't get why he's being like this. It's got nothing to do with him.

Is he worried he'll look bad if I up and leave?

No. Jake never cares what people think, it's his most admirable quality; no matter how annoying.

Maybe he's just really annoyed that my contract isn't out. After all, I did sign for another year not long before I left, maybe he just wants to make sure he gets every second he can out of me. At least that's what he said on the phone anyway. He always saw my potential. I'm sure he'll want to keep face with his father after making such a huge deal about keeping me employed in the Carrero empire. This isn't about me, I don't matter to him, this is about him in some vague narcissistic way.

The door creaks open and I turn expecting to greet one of the girls but freeze, my face dropping and coldness sweeping up from my stomach to my neck. Jake is towering in the doorway. His eyes are glacial, his body emanating extreme power and rage as he stares at me like a rabid dog. He's dressed in navy suit pants, white shirt with rolled up sleeves and open collar. His tie is loose and hanging down his chest, jacket: AWOL. He's impeccably dressed but with the glare of a psychopath. He looks ready to take on a rabid beast.

Oh hell.

I swallow hard, feeling a wave of fear creep up from my toes and envelope my body.

"You and I need to talk … *Now!*" He slams the door, latching it so no one else can enter. I'm sure the entire floor heard the bang. I feel my body stiffen, this is the last thing I need. Being in here and feeling the way I do, I have no defensive play for him this way.

How can he just sweep in like a tornado and ruin me? All the control I mustered, all that inner calm, gone, with just his voice and a look.

I turn away, sure he'll see the emotion filling my eyes as I pull the file from the copier, throwing it among the piles I've laid out. It's a good excuse to keep my head turned away, using the task to stop tears from spilling over while I scramble to hold on to any control I have left.

The only thing I manage to say is, "Go away," my voice, small and fragile. His strong hand grabs my arm, yanking me round to face him, setting me off balance so I flail my arms out and plant my palms on his chest to steady myself. I recoil my hands at the heated touch as searing tingles race through me from the contact.

"You're not going to Europe!" His eyes bore into mine,

his jaw tense. He looks dangerous and wired, I think he's lost his mind. This is the first time I've ever truly been afraid of him physically hurting me, he looks ready to hurt someone and as I'm the only one locked in here with him, I feel nervous. The blood drains from my face, my body sending another surge of coldness through me in response.

"It's not even a possibility yet … I've only just seen the job … I haven't applied." I sound timid and afraid; his face softens realizing my fear, so he releases some of the grip he has on my arm.

This has nothing to do with him … He can't control your life. Stand up to him, Emma, don't let him stamp all over you.

"You belong here … In New York … In the Carrero Corporation." He looks away and I see the rage sizzling into something else, something unreadable. He lets go of me and I move away, fast, putting distance between us, standing against a table at the far corner. He sees me move and frowns, as though he doesn't understand why I would be nervous of him.

Really, Jake?

"Please, Jake … This isn't your concern anymore." I turn away, confusion and heartbreak fighting one another. He's standing straight and tense, every pore sending me mixed signals in the small, windowless room.

Why couldn't this have been different? Him coming to see me and treating me like this only serves to drive a wedge even further between us.

"You're always going to be my concern, Emma … Whether you know it or not." His voice is lower and softer now. I turnback to face him and find him looking at the wall to the right. His eyes are transfixed on nothing, as he sighs heavily, it seems his fiery burst of anger has fast burned out.

"You make it sound like a burden, like you have no choice?" I almost laugh as I say it, feeling anything but joyous, just broken. He looks at me, eyes slowly move over my face, his expression guarded. He says nothing, just frowns, infuriatingly, giving nothing away.

Someone bangs on the door, causing him to jump. From my corner, I can see he's lost his angry glare, his temper fully dissipating making his body slump a little. Burned out from being the giant fire ball of fury that barged in here, he seems to have lost all his fight and I realize he's not acting like the Jake Carrero I thought I knew.

"Open the door, Jake, before the office temps start a rumor that we're making out in the copy room." I sigh, feeling heavy and tired. I think I'm probably on the verge of fainting. Internally rattled but mostly just fed up of being an emotional wreck. I need a drink. All of this, today, with Jake, has been too much for me; from no contact at all to seeping into my entire day. Jake is like an all-consuming black hole.

"Maybe we should give them something to gossip about?" he smirks at me and I see a hint of my Jake … My cheeky Mr. Carrero, he hasn't changed one bit underneath the "bear with a sore head" demeanor and it makes me feel sad. Despite myself, I feel a smile tug my lips and I shake my head at him.

"I could still sue you for sexual harassment you know … since I still work in the same company." I look away, shyly, as he unlocks the door, letting in an irate receptionist. She looks from him to me and back again before turning cherry red and making excuses to disappear. Jake watches her go but leaves the door standing ajar. It seems neither of us have the energy for this anymore and he puts his hands in his pockets, his shoulders hunching like he's been deflated. Instead of making him look more vulnerable all it does is make him look so much more manly and strong, I feel a pang in my chest, hitting hard, almost winding me.

"I'd probably deserve it." He shrugs, looking me up and down. I can't read anything in his face, only that he's no longer angry. "Don't go, Emma … Please." He sounds so sincere. It's so unexpected, it causes a lump to catch in my throat.

"I haven't decided on anything, Jake … I need space to think … Not you, charging in here yelling at me and ordering me around. I need time to figure things out." I respond, firmly, watching him.

He sighs, heavily, looking me over slowly, more deliberately.

"I don't want you to go … I need you to understand that." I see a hint of that boyish Jake I love so much, and it rips through my chest. He pulls out his hands and walks toward me, closing the gap between us, forcing the air around me to thin so I can barely inhale.

"You wanted me out of your life a month ago. Nothing's changed between us. New York is my home, Jake, but maybe it's not where I'll find my happy ever after. If you're still my friend, then let me make my own choices." I step toward him slowly, impulsively, itching to reach out and touch him but stop a foot from his tall, powerful frame as I realize what I'm doing, we're standing face-t- face.

"I want you to be happy, I do. I just don't want it to be in a place that I'll never see you again." He frowns down at me, his green eyes darkening to almost hazel and the intensity of his frown furrows his perfect brow.

"The last thing you ever said to me was that we would never see each other again. Now it seems like you didn't mean it." The ache to fall against his body, and feel his arms close around me, pushes me to move a step away. I'm not stupid enough to believe we could ever go back.

"Maybe I just don't know what's good for me when it

comes to you. I don't know when to leave it alone." His hand coming to push a stray hair from my face, something he's done a thousand times before, but which never felt as unbearable as it is now. I turn my face so his hand falls away.

"You need to leave it alone. Leave me alone to get on with my life." I swallow down the tears, so close to breaking.

"I know." It's barely audible, more a breathy agreement. His eyes lose a little of their Carrero sparkle. We both inhale, slowly, acknowledging what we know is for the best. As heartbreaking as it is, for me at least.

"Walk with me, Emma … at least to the elevator?" It's such an odd request, one that leaves him looking so young and unsure. There's a vibration in the air between us, a heaviness full of tension. I hesitate, then nod and move forward. He takes my movement as acceptance and opens the door for me, following out at a distance.

"Does this mean you're sorry for acting like a stalker?" I throw him a shy smile, unsure how to navigate this situation, hoping humor, like always, would break the tension.

"No." He smiles back but it doesn't reach his eyes. At least we're no longer yelling. Now we're just quiet and reflective.

"Nice to see you haven't lost your touch, still overbearing and arrogant." I smile softly at him again, walking side by side, trying to act normal. The change between how we used to act around one another is highlighted even more. We're just pretending now, the awkwardness of this walk, cracking the air.

"You haven't even begun to see the depth of my overbearing stalker skills." He grins, the usual humor in his voice is missing. We're just going through the motions of how we used to joke and laugh. It's all very polite, hiding a sea of emotions under the surface.

"Talking of which …" I hesitate and look around. Ray flashes into my head but I pause.

Not here … People will hear.

He frowns at me, sensing I have something serious to ask him.

"What is it?"

"I need to talk to you about something … Well, actually, ask you something … Just not here, okay?" I look around again as we get to the elevator. Too many curious eyes are glancing our way, wondering why Jake Carrero is walking me to the lift. Too many ogling women appreciating the sight that is Jake Carrero. I hear the lift ping as the doors open and turn to him to say goodbye.

Suddenly, Jake hauls me into the lift with him and I stumble into his arms, hopelessly, as I gasp in shock, aware that most of the hall has just seen what he did. I push him away hard and angrily.

Why the hell does he do things like this? Always manhandling me any time he chooses, like a freaking child. Even after everything, he still thinks he has a right!

"What are you doing?" I snap, annoyed that my frustrations are met with a smile and a shrug. The urge to throat punch him is overwhelming. I try to straighten up, my clothes now riding up to my armpits.

"You wanted to talk, what's more private than in here?" The doors slide shut, locking us in.

"You're so … Aargh! Always with the grabbing!" I bark, turning away from him in agitation, ignoring the self-satisfied look on his smug, arsey face.

He's right though, although there are cameras in here watching everything, they have no sound. My temper simmers down to minor annoyance as I realize he's done me a favor.

How many times has he acted like this in the past? Too many to count.

The eternal child in him is frustrating.

"What do you want to ask me, Emma?" He leans against the wall of the lift and casually sprawls back, crossing a foot at the ankle over his other and perching his butt on the hand rail. His hands are in his pockets and he's looking at the floor. This is the Prince Carrero pose I've seen so many times before, relaxed, in his domain. I eye him up warily and sigh down my rejections to his manhandling.

"Ray Vanquis," I say, quietly. He looks up, but I'm unable to meet his eyes. When I don't say anything else he stands upright and steps toward me.

"Has he contacted you?" his anger evident with each word. "What has he done? Has he hurt you?" His hand grabs my wrist, pulling me to him, harshly. There is fire in his eyes, an instant anger almost boiling over. His body is hunched into me, as a sort of protective shield and his face is terrifying.

"No, Jake, no … I promise." I resist the urge to recoil, he'd never hurt me. He relaxes a little, letting me loose so I can move back, agitation over his face.

"I would kill him this time, I swear." He grits his teeth then runs his hand through his cropped hair, trying to bring some calm to his demeanor, yet only messing up his neatness. I missed protective Jake, seeing him like this makes me ache and tugs at my heart as I watch him. The urge to fix that ruffled hair almost overwhelming me.

"Jake …" I sigh, "I need to know what happened after Chicago?" I look at him, imploringly, his eyes come to meet mine, frowning.

"Why?"

"Something happened then?" His question confirms

more than he'd have ever told me if I hadn't brought it up.

"What makes you think that?" He's trying his smooth, *I can talk myself out of anything,* routine, moving back to the wall, leaning against it, stiffly this time. I know this side of him. I know when he's covering.

"Because men like Ray don't up and run the way he did … He broke it off with my mother and disappeared." I keep my tone gentle, I don't want a fight. I just want the truth and going up against Jake with anger never works.

"Did you really think I would just forget it, Emma? Come home and not do anything?" His eyes flame with aggression; I feel the heat rise in my cheeks.

"What did you do?" My voice is quiet and unsure. I've never known this side of Jake, and although I'm glad, I'm also scared by what he's potentially done.

"You want details, Emma, or confirmation?" He moves forward and closer to me, expelling the air from my lungs. I can't think when he's so close and moving to almost touch me.

"I don't know." My voice is cracking, and he sighs, tracing a knuckle down my cheek slowly. His touch is igniting a million sensations through my body, making my knees weaken. The urge to close my eyes and savor this is overwhelming, but I resist.

Fight it. Don't let him affect you. Be strong.

"All you need to know is that it was made clear to him, that you and your mother are out of bounds, that should he ever reappear, there will be consequences, Emma … Worse than what I did to him in Chicago … That's all." His voice is low, our faces so close I can breathe him in. The ache to kiss him overwhelming me badly, he pauses so close to my mouth, his eyes stopping on my lips briefly. An odd paused moment between us, then he steps back and moves away.

"Are we done here?" He sighs, the elevator pings almost at his request and opens, two men get in and I nod at him, working my way out to the hall. He follows me for a second holding the door open.

"If you ever hear from him again, you come to me … No matter what." His dark gaze sends a shiver down my spine. I nod, obediently, watching him, knowing that he means it. He looks at me with a satisfied smile and returns to the elevator, eyes glued to me as the door closes between us, blocking him from view. I stand, transfixed, staring at the elevator doors, feeling like I've been ravaged. I hate that he does this to me anytime he's close to me.

Pushing down the crazy turmoil inside I move to another elevator and wait until a door opens to return to my floor. I need to get back to my desk where I can recover from all that is Jake and process what he's just told me.

***

Back at my desk, I switch my answer machine off and turn my mobile on. There's already a notification waiting for me; an email from Jake. I sigh in frustration as I open it, torn between happiness and anger.

Jake Carrero has sent you an iTunes gift

"I Will Find You" by Clannad.

I guess it's a joke about his stalker tendencies, apparently, no matter where I go he'll find me. He won't let me leave New York, at this rate I'm sure I'm not going to be allowed to leave this company. I sigh and throw my cell down in agitation.

We'll see about that, Carrero.

I've no idea which way is up or down anymore … Jake sends me away and acts like he doesn't know me. Next thing

I know, he's all over my life, trying to tell me what to do and sending me songs. I'm more confused than I thought possible. He's like a roller-coaster ride with his emotions, and it seems my feelings are taking a cue from him.

It's all got to go. These stupid feelings and emotions, at least he confirmed my doubts about Ray Vanquis.

Do I never have to worry about him again? Will Ray stay out of my mother's life for good?

If he doesn't then I can only imagine what Jake will do. He isn't someone you mess with. For all his outward charm and laid-back manner, Jake has a dangerous side. I've seen it before, briefly, having his money and power means the sky has no limits. He could make someone disappear if he wanted to. He certainly has the mind set to do it. His family have ties with the mafia, they keep it out of the media attention, deny the links but they are old-world Italian. His grandfather founded this company amid mafia blood money rumors; stories which Jake has never denied nor confirmed. I shudder at the thought, but somehow take comfort from it. Whether he is in my life or not, he's protecting me … Still. His power, reaching out, and sheltering me from afar. I could never hate him for that, he is the only person I've ever met who cared enough to do that for me. That's why it hurt so much knowing I had to give him up when he pushed me away.

***

The afternoon goes by uneventfully. Jake left me be, and despite my shock at hearing from him and then seeing him; I'm once again wavering over my decision to leave this place. In one day, he's taken me down; then up and down again; from almost crying in rage, to smiles; then back to complete desolation as I realize we have no reason to see one another again. All his visit has done is remind me of how much I miss him; his anger, humor, and charisma. His beauty and ability to change mood like the wind. I miss every part of him and it makes me ache inside, seeing him only highlights how far I am from getting over him.

Wilma doesn't mention his appearance at all. I'm so bogged down with work the afternoon goes by quickly. I make up the lost two hours after most of the office staff leaves. I like having this quiet time to work through everything Wilma has asked of me. Focusing on work helps me ignore him and forget all about today and seeing him again.

Chapter 4

It's dark out by the time I look up. I stretch out my back and get out of my seat. I've placed more than twenty calls, emailed back and forth with several PAs dealing with invites for various important people, and I've liaised with the event planner. I'm sure there's nothing else I can do tonight since it's nearly 7.00 p.m.

The weather's moving toward winter so the sun's setting earlier. I didn't expect it to be this dark. I regret staying so late, since the walk from the station in Queens will be dark and slightly frightening.

I clear up my desk and power down my laptop then pick up my coat and bag; walking to the elevator with a stifling yawn. It pings, the doors open, and I enter, not surprised to find it empty. The elevator slows down and pings again, I look up to notice it's stopped at the fourteenth floor. Odd, since very few staff stay beyond five thirty. I don't think Jake and I ever left before seven when I worked with him, but he always was a workaholic.

The door opens and I'm expecting another empty floor; my eyes focused on my cell, checking messages. Someone comes in, a male. I can see his shoes and trousers from this angle and he stands close to me, a little too close. His aftershave takes over the space, sticking in my throat, pushing me to glance up. There's something vaguely familiar about him and I'm sure we've met before, when I was Jake's PA. He's in his late forties with silver gray hair and heavy-set features. He smiles at me before I return to my cell. There's something about him that makes me uneasy, so I move further away, subtly. I wrap my arm around myself, guarding my body.

"You're Emma Anderson, right?" his gruff voice interrupts my obvious disinterest in him and I glance over and frown.

"I am, yes ... Why do you ask?" Looking him up and down, I note the well-tailored gray suit, and expensive shoes, he must be one of the executives; rather than just office staff. He has an air of wealth and confidence about him, and the arrogance of a man who always gets what he wants.

You know? Like Jake.

"I'm Dan Gabrielle." He extends a hand and the name rings a bell, yet for the life of me I can't place it. I'm normally good with faces and names.

"Pleasure," I say coolly, shaking his hot, rough hand and retract to stand as gracefully as I can to the side. My brain connects the dots and I recognize him. Dan Gabrielle is one of the Carrero's top tier executives. He deals with merchandising the beauty and grooming products. I've heard so many rumors about this man, and his lifestyle, from the office staff. He's known as someone to steer well clear of among the women. It's only my stupid luck that I would get trapped in an elevator alone with him after hours.

"I heard you used to be Jake's PA? ... I've been looking for a new girl myself ... My last one left suddenly." He smirks, and an odd glint in his eye causes my stomach to lurch in apprehension. I wonder how many advances she rebuffed before leaving, knowing all too well the kind of behavior the executives sometimes like to use on their PAs, especially since I have first-hand experience of it with Dawson.

"I'm not looking for another PA position within this company … I'm working with Wilma Munro on events and such." I look away, pushing my cell into my bag to give me something else to focus on. He moves closer, gaze stilling on the neckline of the blouse under my fitted jacket. With a disgusting grin widening on his face I realize he's found the slightest hint of cleavage peeking out at the top of my clothes. I feel my stomach drop and my nerves start to flutter. Alarm bells drowning out everything in a crazy manic fashion.

Sexual harassment was common in the offices, more common than people like to admit, and this guy was giving serious vibes. I've been here before, handled this kind of thing multiple times before working for Jake. I know most of those high-ups here would never believe me. Jake never made me feel this way in all the time he was with me, not once, regardless of his hands-on approach.

"I'm sure we can come to some sort of agreement." He moves closer, so close his arm is against my shoulder. I'm against the elevator wall, there's nowhere else for me to go. "I need a pretty girl with good skills … I hear Jake couldn't keep up with you, so he had to let you go." The slimy snake-like tone in his smarmy voice causes my chin to snap up and glare at him. I know what he's hinting at, he's heard rumors, or assumed, that Jake and I were having sex.

Oh, my god.

"I don't know what your implying, but I'm not interested." I spit angrily, trying to move back but feel the wall come up behind me, it's closer than I thought it was.

It doesn't stop him shifting even closer.

"I'm a believer in never saying never, Miss. Anderson. I normally get what I want. I've seen you around the building … I particularly like the attire." He leans into me and talks into my ear, "Tight, fuckable skirts and sexy stilettos." He runs a hand up the side of my tight pencil skirt, from thigh to hip, then travels across the front heading toward the apex of my thighs. His touch causes revulsion and bile to creep up my throat and I shove him away hard.

No … No … No! Why does this shit always happen to me?

Just like Dawson when I worked for him and his wandering hands! What the hell is it about me that screams—Touch me?

"Get the hell away from me!" I yell at him, hearing the door ping. I run out at full speed, not caring if anyone sees my manic departure and run smack into a brick wall.

"Fuck," grunts the wall. There's an "ooomph" and a groan, then a thud as we both hit the floor. I'm lying fully on top of someone's warm, hard body. Their arms around my waist as I scramble to take a breath, the fall must've knocked the wind out of me.

"Jesus, Emma … A hello would have sufficed."

I groan at Jake's voice and raise my head, coming nose to nose with him. His perfect green eyes locking onto mine from a far too intimate angle, memories flood into my brain.

Really? It had to be him! Of all people. Why him?

I push myself up, quickly, from sheer embarrassment, and haul myself to my feet ungracefully. There's two men standing close by watching us with amusement, one of them leans down and helps Jake to his feet, picking up his cell in the process, handing it to him.

"I'm sorry." I breathe, panting. I look back at the lift, but it's shut … that creep has gone but my body is still vibrating with adrenaline and fear.

"What was that all about?" He smooths down his clothes before reaching out to drape back a strand of my hair, realizing what he's doing, he moves back quickly, dropping his hand to his side. I glance at the other men awkwardly, both seem to be staring anywhere but where we are, they mutter something incoherently and move off to give us space.

"Your employees are all assholes." I bite, shaken by the encounter and speaking without thinking. The past me wouldn't have said anything about this. But this isn't the past me anymore, and new me is sick of men thinking I'm a free for all.

"Why? What's happened? Is this the reason you came thundering out of the lift like a pro footballer, getting me in a take-down?" He smiles at me gently and adjusts his jacket again, looking down to button it back up and smooth his tie behind it. I can't help but begin to smile too.

"Maybe." I look away, embarrassed about this whole thing.

"Who was in there?" He thumbs toward the lift door, curiosity on his face. "Wasn't my father by any chance?" He smirks, knowing too well his father is someone I would call an asshole. Jake and I share that kind of love for him.

"No. Your father, unlike you, knows to keep his hands to himself." I regret it as soon as it's out of my mouth and I see the darkness move into his eyes instantly, the grim look on his face.

Crap. Good one, Emma!

"Someone laid their hands on you?! In there … right now? Tell me who! Tell me, Emma!" He steps close enough to make me feel intimidated, his voice laced with anger.

I sway over whether to tell him or not and know it's not wise to evade this. The two men have moved far off now, trying not to eavesdrop as Jake gets considerably louder.

Me and my big mouth!

"He said he was called Gabrielle … Dan, I think …" It comes out in a feeble mumble and I can't look him in the eye. I watch as his jaw tenses, he looks over my head at the lift door, his eyes narrow and jaw taught.

"I know exactly who he is," snarling, he grabs my hand and pulls me with him so I almost stumble. I'm jerked behind him, throwing a wave to his escorts, indicating he's leaving. They seem to hover for a second then walk off assured he is dismissing them.

"Where are you hauling me?" I try to pull my hand free, but he continues, holding tight, dragging me to the internal offices of this floor. My heart is racing, and my head is protesting every second.

Fuck, fuck, fuck.

"To use an office … You need a seat and I need to have that mother fucker fired." He sounds terrifying. His voice is laced with venom and his muscles are rigid, a jolt of adrenaline shoots through me.

Is this what I want?

Oh, my god, the drama that will come because of this. It's not the first time I've been groped in this building, but it's the first time I've told anyone … Told Jake.

"Wait, no. Jake, wait!" I panic, but he hauls me inside a small office and shuts the door behind us. Ignoring me, he swivels a chair round and sits me in it briskly, grabbing me by the arms, pushing me around like a rag doll. He perches on the desk beside me, pulling out his cell, his eyes gleaming with rage and I know better than to try to stand back up.

"Tell me exactly what happened … What he did … Every detail." He's spitting razor blades; his expression is serious and yet, I hesitate.

Maybe I over reacted or misjudged the scenario …

My face pales, unsure if I should tell him everything but I know he won't let this go.

"Now, Emma!" He growls my way and I realize this is futile, he won't let me leave until I do. I take a deep breath and look at him, telling him in detail, as much as I can remember. He sits the whole time in silence, jaw clenched and brows down in an angry glare, watching me intensely. I hate him looking at me that way. I'm doubting myself, wondering if he's thinking I'm being a drama queen. If he even believes me or is wondering why I would assume Dan had done anything wrong.

When I'm done, he pulls out his cell and barks orders at some poor soul, issuing marching orders on grounds of sexual harassment. He stills while they explain something to him on the other end of the line.

"Then set it up … Him, you and whatever legal team representatives are available, first thing … Offer him severance. I don't give a shit! … I want him gone! No one lays a hand on any woman in this company without consequence … There's footage from the elevator CCTV, I'll deal with security myself." He snaps the commands, eyes fixated on my face, showing contained rage.

I feel a rise of pride within me as I watch him on the cell, that surge of love I always felt around him.

Mr. Commanding "don't mess with me" Carrero … Scary as shit boss.

One thing that surprised me when I first encountered him, was how passionately he seemed to stand up for women, their rights and giving them respect in the workplace. I guess his relationship with his mother has a lot to do with how he is. It's one of the reasons I trust him so fully. I know he's probably one of the few men in this building I am safe around; despite his playboy, womanizing, status.

"No. The woman in question will not be there … I will … on her behalf." He's still angry, shouting down his cell to whoever was unlucky enough to have a direct line to Jake.

"Call me back when it's set up … No matter what time … I'll clear my schedule … Yes … Goodbye." He hangs up his cell, his mouth held in a tight line.

"I'm taking you home." It's a command, not a question and I know there's little point arguing with him when he's in battle mode. After the lift scene, I don't fancy walking to the station alone anyway. I'm shaken but all I can do is nod and look away unsurely. I sense him move close to me so he's almost touching my knees with his legs.

"Are you okay?" His voice is so soft and gentle I'm forced to glance up. He's holding out a hand to me and I accept as he pulls me to my feet. Slowly, he wraps one arm around my shoulders, pulling me against him and giving me a soothing hug. His chin rests against my temple, letting all the tension seep out of me.

This is the Jake I miss the most, the friend that he always was. This is the Jake who rips out my heart whenever he shows face.

I miss you so much!

"I'm fine." I sigh, trying not to sag against him, or react to his body against mine. The two of us stand embraced, but it's awkward and tense; nothing like our hugs of the past. He releases me, searching my face for a hint of untruth, but sees nothing. I'm so beyond used to men behaving that way toward me that I'm no longer affected by it as I should be; a sad fact.

"Come on, my car's in the garage." He takes my arm and guides me out of the small room, keeping me close beside his warmth and heads for the elevators once again.

Once inside the atmosphere becomes strained, neither of us knowing what to say or how to behave. He lets me go and moves away, giving me some space and I wonder if it's because of Gabrielle. If maybe he doesn't want to make me feel uncomfortable, enclosed in a lift with him, not the he ever would. Thankfully the trip to the ground floor garage is short.

He leads me to his car, something he rarely uses when coming to work. It's a low, sleek, and powerful sports McLaren P1. His baby. Yet, I've never seen it, or seen him in it, let alone drive it around New York. He's mentioned it many times before and I know it cost him over a million dollars and I'm stunned by just how seductive it is. It's jet black and looks almost sinister, sat in his personal parking space, like a shadowy bat-mobile in the corner, shiny and purring at him from afar. The car is the epitome of sexiness and I can't help but feel a little stir inside at how it looks.

Figures that his car would scream with as much sex appeal as he does …

This garage is only used by the higher paid execs and has a full-time security post wandering around, gated entrance, and a hoard of CCTV cameras, making it feel like Fort Knox. I follow him as the car beeps in response to our approach, signaling it's unlocking. I walk to the passenger side as he touches the handle and lifts the car door up toward the sky to let me into the molded seats and high-tech interior. He then pushes the door down, concealing me behind the tinted windows before gliding round to the driver's side, getting in smoothly.

This car just screams Jake, from every pore, something about its relaxed coolness, sleek sportiness, and intimidating shape. He presses a button by the steering wheel and it roars into life, sounding like an expensive jet plane, purring with vibrations as he hits the gas. The interior lights up from a display in front of us, whirring and electrical noises from the rear as a tail fin comes up from the smooth sleek flat back. It's hard not to feel a rush of excitement with this car.

"I like your car." I smile his way, seriously impressed. It feels like I'm sitting in a Formula One dream machine and even though I've never been interested in vehicles of any sort, I can't help but feel like this one is special.

"I like my car too." He grins over to me like a boy with his favorite toy, all bad moods lifted at being re-united with it. He reverses out of the space, expertly in control of his beast and head outs of the underground park, waving to the men who lift the barrier to let us out. The tunnel exit is lit by ground lights guiding us to the outside traffic, giving it a sense of driving out of some concealed spaceship into the light above. The loudest, most roaring machine I've ever heard. I can feel the way we're sticking to the road as it moves effortlessly out into traffic. It just adds to the excitement of feeling like I'm sitting next to Bruce Wayne.

"Why do you never drive it? I've heard about it, but this is the first time I've actually seen it?" I blink around in the dark interior, feeling like the co-pilot in a private airplane.

"I only got it back a couple of weeks ago, it's been away for months, having adjustments to my specs. I also had the color changed … it used to be bright orange." He's keeping both eyes on the road, driving carefully as we hit traffic. The engine's louder than I expected in the open air and I can hear a whizzing wheeze of a turbo. This car is sex on wheels and I can't help but feel my adrenaline rise at its vibrancy around me.

"Black is more your color." I smile at him, awed by how good he looks sitting in the control seat of this monster, effortlessly taking control of something so powerful. He belongs in a car like this.

"So, is this the reason you learned to drive with Formula One favorites?" I tease. "So, you can drive your own ridiculously expensive car?"

"No. I bought the car after many years of lessons, and a lot of research ... This baby is a car made for people who can actually drive." He flashes me his *because I can* grin and I shake my head. His ego untainted by his latest admission.

"Seems like a waste for the streets of New York."

"I have it transported every so often to my family's home in Italy ... They have amazing tracks over there to give this girl a run for her money." He swells with pride, patting the dash, and smiles at the dark interior, stopping at a red light. The car drops into purring mode, reducing the noise greatly.

"Girl? Please tell me you haven't named her?" I laugh at him, but he looks my way with a shocked expression.

"That's sacrilege! Of course, you must name your baby. She's my girl!" He rubs the dash again and croons a little as though soothing an offended woman. "She's called Miss. Anderson!" He winks at me with a grin, receiving a sigh and a shake of my head in return.

"Of course, she is!" I look out the window, away from his smile and cheeky expression. Ordinarily I would give anything to have the casual humor between us back, but this, *normalcy*, hurts.

"You doubt it? She's stubborn, fast paced, and fiery. Miss. Anderson made perfect sense." He shoves my shoulder lightly with his fingertips as if to prove the point. I frown and shove him back with a haughty pout.

"Actually, now you mention it, seems like it should be called Jacob. It suits you." I smile and look away triumphantly.

"Thin ice, Anderson!" He throws me a warning look steeped in humor. He despises his birth name with a passion, so, of course, I use it to tease him.

"Like I care. I spend my entire life walking on it when it comes to you." I stick my tongue out at him and he just pushes my face childishly, his palm squishing my nose for a second. I muffle a, "Hey" and pull his hand from my face.

"Jerk."

"Diva."

We smile at each other but drop our hands, looking out the windscreen as though suddenly realizing this wasn't right anymore. Funny how we'd forgotten for a moment, only to come crashing back to reality and then silence. Jake seems to mull over something for a moment before breaking the tension.

"How've you been, Emma?" He glances at me, then concentrates on the road, watching for the lights to change. I shrug.

How can I be honest and tell him I've been dying inside since he made me walk away? That this situation just highlights how much I miss him, and us.

"Okay, I guess." I can't look at him. I can feel his eyes on me, then the car bursts into a roar again and we're moving. I don't think Jake has ever driven me home himself before, this feels too intimate somehow, just the two of us.

"I've missed you," he says, so honestly I can't help but look at him. His eyes on the road. His perfect profile showing no hints of emotion. Just honesty.

"I've missed you too." I sigh. Our eyes meet for a second then we both look away, tension rises fast, cracking in the air. He tenses his jaw, looking as though he wants to say something but bites it back turning his eyes to the road. I can't say a word, I don't know what to say, conversation is harder than I imagined it ever would be. Especially when all I want to do is crawl into his lap and be enveloped by every part of him.

"Do you like working with Wilma?" he finally asks, keeping his eyes steady, nothing in his voice betraying what he might be thinking.

"I guess … It's not as challenging as working for you though … Feels more like a holiday." I giggle as he tries to grab my leg, squeezing it in punishment. I bat his hand away, we're forgetting ourselves again. He straightens back up and shakes his head at me with a mock glare, his features relaxing as he sighs and smiles instead.

I miss that smile.

"I missed that sound." His revelation silences me, the ache inside grows bigger, and I try not to look directly at him.

"I missed your grumpy bad moods and overbearing demands." I reply wittily, trying to shift the deep ache before it consumes me.

"I miss drunk Emma." He retorts with a cheeky glint in his eye. I hate that he likes that version of me, a little jealousy seeps in.

"You would … You're a terrible influence on her." Every word he says is making my heart heavier with longing.

He has no idea how much he affects me or how hard this is sitting here with him.

We're swerving through traffic and I can't help but be impressed with his ability to drive this car in the chaotic New York traffic. I feel relaxed, despite the lurches in my stomach every time he hits the gas. This car is immense, getting up to speed so quickly. He's quiet for a few moments, seemingly thinking, then turns to me with a serious look.

"Gabrielle will be gone before the end of the week, Emma … I promise. He had no right to lay a hand on you or say anything to you that made you uncomfortable." The serious tone and dead pan expression remove the traces of lightness from the atmosphere.

"I seem to attract it somehow," I reply, quietly, catching his frown from the corner of my eye and he sighs heavily.

"Men want what they can never hope to have … You have no idea just how beautiful you are. It's part of the allure … You're vulnerable and young, yet there's something so unbelievably sexy about you. You turn heads with zero effort. Men like that should be strung up … You deserve far more in life." His words startle me, and I look at him, catching my breath.

"You think that about me?" I squeak. He's never said anything like this before or told me anything about how I look to him. I always assumed men looked at me like an easy target, someone who longed to be abused. Just like I assumed Jake only ever saw me as his mildly attractive assistant and friend.

"You mean, do I think you're beautiful and sexy, yet vulnerable and innocent? Yes, I do" His eyes lock onto mine, my insides sizzling.

Oh my god. His words seduce me as much as he does. Is this a Carrero line? Is he being genuine? No one has ever told me anything like this before, all I see when I look in a mirror is the shadow of an awkward girl in the body of a cold, plain woman.

He pulls up to another set of lights, the car powering down to a gentle purr.

"I don't know what to say." I squirm in my seat, my face burning. I let my hair fall forward, concealing my blush. I have absolutely no clue how to react to his confessions.

"You don't need to say anything … I'm being honest. Looking like you do doesn't give men permission to behave the way they do … I can't exactly take the moral high ground, can I?" He sighs.

Our eyes meet quickly. I flush, the memory of him making love to me floods into my mind. I look away as emotion hits me hard in the stomach, that night will haunt me forever and continuously break my heart.

Crap … Yes, he could. That night was consensual, and I wanted him just as much as he wanted me. I still want him!

"You're nothing like the rest of them," I say morosely.

"I wish I felt like I wasn't," he mumbles, barely audible, eyes forward.

I have no words.

Does he really believe he forced me? Does he think he's done to me what other men have done and forced himself upon me? How can he think that?

We kissed more than once, long before that night in the hotel, I kissed him back. I clung to him with a fever so hot it almost consumed me.

"I wanted it … Please don't ever say that again." I breathe, softly, laying a hand on his leg without thinking about what's appropriate. Our eyes lock, heat building in the small confines of the car. Tension sparks almost instantly. I want him to kiss me so badly, I can almost taste it. His lips part and his pupils dilate. I want to throw myself across the car into him, my body responding insanely fast.

How the hell did this start?

He snaps his head away, looking around, and throws the car into a right turn which shunts me in my seat. Luckily, I'm restrained by my seat belt. He steers us down an alleyway into unlit darkness. With a roar and a lurch forward, we slam to a halt. He jumps out, leaving me bewildered and shocked as he comes around and yanks open my door.

Confused and shocked, I stare at him as he unclips my belt and hauls me from my seat, pushing me against the rear body of the car. He crushes his mouth into mine, knocking the wind out of me with the sheer unexpectedness of it. My hands come up to wrap around his neck, his fingers tangle in my hair, and his other hand swings around my back. My ass grinds against the cold metal as his body pushes hard into mine; kissing me with fevered abandon. We groan in unison. Our tongues meet and our mouths mold perfectly, in rhythm. Effortlessly matched movements, that ignite my fire. I love kissing him, he makes it feel like the easiest thing in the world, all thoughts of what we're doing fly off in abandonment.

His hands release me, coming down under my butt to my upper thighs. He hoists me up as my legs open to come around his waist, my skirt seam rips up the back to allow for extra movement. My body slides up the sleek hood of the car to rest on top of it, our heads at the same height for once. My inner body is spiraling out of control, heated and sizzling inside, my heart pounding erratically, almost jumping through my chest.

His kiss deepens, our tongues caress erotically and there it is, kissing like we've always been made to do it. Hot and fire fueled, consumed only with how it feels. I want to fall into this kiss and never wake up. I want to be devoured by him endlessly. This is everything I've needed to heal my heart. The pain melting away, replaced with hunger and a sense of completion.

I feel his growing desire against me, and it makes me burn inside. My body is clenching with heat as his hands still cup my butt. He pulls me tighter against him.

I need him. I want this more than anything I've ever wanted in my life.

My hand trails down his front, skirting his abdomen to pull his shirt up so I can feel his naked, taut skin. My fingers crawl under the thin material, greedily along the tickle of hair, down toward his waist band and hard as iron muscle. He groans, pushing against me firmly, one hand slides up my inner thigh until his thumb comes to the lace edge of my panties. I thrust my pelvis forward, aching for him to keep going as his thumb traces over the outside of the material, over my femininity, sending tingles and waves of pleasure through me.

God …

I groan in ecstasy.

Pulling me off the car he walks with my body wrapped around him fiercely, mouths still connected. I feel the air around my underwear and my naked legs, one of my shoes falls off, hitting the ground with a clatter but I don't care. His mouth pleasures mine as he maneuvers me. I feel him sit me on hard sloping metal, tipping me back to lay down as he scoops forward on top of me, his mouth moving to my neck. Warm breath causes a million sensations to flow through me as I grapple my arms out to stop myself sliding down, realizing I'm on the hood of his car, sheaved in darkness under the edge of a fire escape. His groin comes to meet mine, stopping me from falling, and pushes against me for a moment, a hard thrust as we collide. Dizzying lust soars through me before his hand finds me again.

I push my fingers into his hair, arching my body up to him, with one swift tug he rips my lace underwear off. I squeak in surprise as his hand moves back to tease me into submission, exploring my warm depths deliciously. I writhe around under his expert touch, savoring the weight of his body over me. His hands explore me and I'm more than ready to lose all control, surrendering to him. I'm soaring, my heart is lifting at his attention, my emotions reeling with mounting happiness.

Suddenly, his attention snaps up, unexpectedly, leaving us both breathing heavily. His eyes focus on mine and his expression changes; from heavy and fiery lust to sudden ice-cold blankness. He pulls my hands from what they're doing to him, grabs my wrists and harshly pins them to the car by my head. His expression is so angry suddenly, and his glare is so frosty, it makes me catch my breath.

"This is why I made you leave, Emma … This shit that I do to you! This shit we do to each other!" He rasps then lets me go, pulling away so I slip down unexpectedly. He catches me and slides me to my feet, almost aggressively. Missing one stiletto, I stumble against him and grab his arms for support. He picks me up like a child and walks me around the car, wordlessly, depositing me into my seat. He retrieves my shoe and hands it to me before slamming the door shut, almost in my face.

I don't know what to say. I'm completely dumbstruck into silence. I want to rewind to seconds ago when his mouth was on me and his fingers inside of me, I didn't want him to stop. I'm reeling with confusion, stung by his instant rage and close to tears. My heartache returning with a passion. He walks off from the car into darkness for a few minutes. I can barely make out his powerful figure as he paces back and forth. He seems to be really pissed off, trying to regain some control, arguing with himself. If it wasn't so traumatic it would be kind of funny to watch.

I try to reel in my thoughts, pulling my skirt around me a little, trying to conceal as much nakedness as I can before he returns. I see him spin toward the car, and he walks back with a look of sheer fury as he slams into his seat with a closed off expression on his face. He doesn't look at me, just throws us into reverse at speed, causing me to shoot forward. His hand grabs me and stops my collision with the dash.

"Put your fucking belt on," he barks, angrily. I feel like he's slapped me in the face. I remove his hand from my waist and scramble to pull my belt over, harnessing myself in obediently. I can't speak … On the verge of breaking down because I have no idea what I've done wrong.

What the hell happened?

He flicks on the stereo with a push of a button and music blares around us. Nickelback's "Rockstar" is mid-chorus, loud and invading, drowning out the ability to talk. He's making it very clear he has no intention of talking anymore. His focus is on the road as he reverses out into a clearing, a little more gently this time, but his face is a picture of rage. He gets us back on route, jaw tight and frowning. I can see the darkness in his eyes, even from this angle, and know he's in another shitty mood.

He's driving a little more aggressively, just like he did on the way back to the boat when we went away on holiday. Even that nightmare ended with me not seeing him for over a week. I don't feel quite so relaxed anymore as he makes full use of the car's responsive acceleration. I know a severely pissed Jake when I see it, but I don't understand why. I slide down in my seat, trying to look out the window away from him. My heart is pounding through my chest, manically, so afraid to even look his way. I have so much I want to say to him, but this reaction, and the way he's acting has killed the words on my lips. I want to cry and get as far away from him as possible, so I can sob this night away.

I maneuver my skirt around my waist, so the split is up the outer side on my thigh, at least I'll be able to hold it together when I make my exit and only expose my leg instead of ass. I catch him glancing at me, his expression harsh. He clenches his teeth, making his jaw move in agitation and looks away again quickly.

The rest of the journey is tense and conversation free as loud music blares around us, adding to the heightened fragile atmosphere.

* * *

When we finally pull up to my building, he gets out, and comes around to let me out of the car. Yanking the door upwards, he stands back, keeping his distance as I clamber out, ungracefully holding my skirt with one hand and gripping the doorframe with the other. We avoid looking at one another, the icy air between us sending out chills. I long for him to say something ... anything. But he doesn't. He just closes the door behind me and walks off, getting back into his beast, pulling away, and leaving me standing on the curb. The sound of his tires screeching on the road adds another slice to my already slashed heart. One more Jake scar for the collection.

Chapter 5

Sarah looks me up and down in confusion and worried alarm; questions held on her lips, yet she says nothing. She's waiting for me to explain, watching my expression earnestly. I'm holding my skirt together with one hand at my thigh but it's not doing much to conceal my naked leg, she can probably see my lack of panties too. I shake my head, sighing, my face pleading with her, as though to saying, "Please don't say a word" and walk past her. She moves aside, her mouth agog but thankfully, she leaves me alone, letting me walk to my room and shut her out.

I strip, quickly pulling on sweats and a loose T-shirt before sinking down onto my bed, letting loose the scrambled thoughts in my brain. I groan inwardly. My aching heart is solidly back in place. I run a hand over my eyes and rubbing harshly, smudging my make-up.

What the hell did we do? Again?

I'm more confused now than ever before. I thought Jake sending me away had been so final. It told me he wanted me out of his life, that he wasn't into me at all. Yet look what just happened. I didn't initiate any of it this time, he did. But he also ended it just as abruptly. He even said doing those things to me were why he sent me away in the first place.

Jake will never want what I want. He's not looking for a girlfriend, especially not one like me. Yet, somehow, I seem to have had as much of an effect on him as he did on me. I want to cry but there's a tiny glint of hope inside of me, not just from the last few minutes together but about the entire day. The events leading up to his kiss, his touch.

He was going to have Dan Gabrielle fired. He'd already warned Ray off, then he forbade me to leave New York; almost pleading with me not to go. If I think logically, he's acting like a man with some deep feelings for me. But, if I listen to my heart, it's telling me I know Jake's ways better than that. He's always been protective of me. He cares because I'm his friend, he's a good man who defends any woman's right to be respected, more than any man I've ever known. It only makes him even more appealing.

But kissing me? Almost having me on his car?

And then, there's Marissa. Something neither of us broached. Marissa and his unborn child. There's no way I could ever forget her presence in his life.

A gentle knock on my door interrupts my train of thought and Sarah comes inside, shyly bearing two mugs of cocoa. She slides them down on the bedside table and climbs on the bed beside me, lying down, mirroring my pose across the quilt.

"What happened to your skirt?" she asks, reaching down to the floor to try to grab it. She untangles it and holds it high, smirking in admiration.

"Jake happened." I shrug. We've come so far in our relationship lately, we no longer have secrets. I've learned how to communicate with her a little better and enjoy having someone to confide in nowadays, about Jake anyway.

"Wow! … As in … You had sex?" She turns to look at me.

"Ripped skirt says sex to you?" I blink back.

"The lack of panties under ripped skirt says sex to me." She grins but her smile falters when she sees my dark expression and shaking head.

"Well, if you call getting me to the point of almost screwing me on his car bonnet, then walking away, and dumping me out front without a goodbye, sex then …" I feel the tears bite at my eyes.

No wonder I'm confused.

"…Wait … He did what?" She turns to stare at me, her eyes boring into my profile.

"I don't even know. It's been a long day, so much has happened, and it sort of led to being dragged out of his car for a heated make out session that he ended … And now he's pissed at me for something he started." I raise my hands in agitation, voice pitched. "He drives me crazy."

"Holy hell … I thought you didn't even see him anymore … You left for work in a funk and come home half dressed … How the hell did you get from there to … Well, here? In a day!" She grins at me, but I shake my head again, more confused than even her.

"I don't even know, Sarah … I don't know what to think anymore … I ran into him in the elevator, then things just seemed to escalate from there. I saw him twice after that and he brought me home … The kiss happened on the way here." My eyes drop to the satin bed spread and I fumble with the surface threads.

"Did he say anything?" She narrows her eyes, studying my face. She's been trying to analyze everything "Jake" since he sent me away a month ago. "You know about making out with you, then stopping it?"

I shake my head and take deep heavy breaths, trying to

stop the thundering of my heart. Calm the trembling of my body.

"Maybe you should call him then … He owes you an explanation, Emma … You can't just keep second guessing him all the time." She picks up my phone and lays it on my chest, but I don't move. The last thing I want to do is call him. He'll be driving back to Manhattan anyway, back to his apartment, miles away from me. He wouldn't pick up.

"Can we drop this?" I sit up, the phone slides down my body and lands on the bed. She sighs and flops back beside me, flat so her head is nestled in my cushions. Thinking for a moment, she sits up and takes my hand.

"You know what the biggest problem with you two is?" Sarah blinks at me but I just glare at her and offer no response.

"You don't communicate with one another when it comes to feelings. You're as bad as each other. Neither of you seem capable of just coming out with it and putting your heart on the line. I don't think he's as immune to you as you believe. I think he's scared, and so are you, and if this continues then neither of you will get anywhere." Sarah crosses her arms triumphantly and sits back.

"You finished?" I slide my legs out from under me to make myself a little more comfortable. "I know you think you have this figured out, but remember, I know him. I know what he is. Jake likes uncomplicated and he knows we're exactly the opposite of that." I raise my hand as Sarah goes to say more. I don't want to listen to it. Every time I talk or hear a single word about Jake it just makes me feel more depressed and anxious. I don't want to analyze it anymore. I just want to drop it. She narrows her brows at me then changes tact, her face turning coy. I can almost see her drop the subject mentally. She wavers for a moment, then something else sparks in her face.

"Your mom called me." Her tone is gentle, but I still stiffen as though she's slapped me hard.

She really chooses the most epic of topics!

"Did she now?" I bite back emotion through gritted teeth. I certainly don't need this line of conversation either.

"She asked if you'd calmed down yet … Told me you'd launched a bowl of food at her head … I did wonder where half the crockery had gone." She pushes some of my loose hair behind my ear, watching me closely. My face betrays the fact that I don't want to talk about it. "Anything you want to let out?" She smiles at me, encouragingly, but I shake my head and pull myself free to retrieve the mugs. I hand her one and avoid eye contact.

"When it comes to her, I think it's safe to say, our story has ended … There's nothing more for us to say to one another." As much as it hurts me to say it, I know it's true. My mother and I have reached an impasse, a road in our lives where too much has gone on to ever be set right. She chose her bed many times and now she must lie in it. I'm done being dragged back, time and time again, to a place that causes me pain. If Jake taught me anything it was that I deserve more from her. I didn't deserve the men she dragged into my life. He showed me that what those men repeatedly did wasn't my fault. It was hers for not protecting me. The thought causes a tear to run down my cheek.

"Are you okay, Ems?" Sarah's hand comes to my shoulder in gentle comforting affection. I close my eyes swallowing the tears down, empty and defeated with all of it.

"I'm just really tired, Sarah … It's been one hell of a couple of days. I think I just need some sleep." I turn and give her a weak smile. Relieved when she takes the hint and gets up to leave me be, she knows there's still a huge part of old Emma in me, the one who sometimes needs space to be alone.

"I'll let you get some shut eye … Marcus is working late so I won't be going to bed until he's home … If you want me, I'll be in the lounge with my old friend Netflix." She grins back at me, blowing a kiss, shutting my door behind her. Leaving me alone with my thoughts.

I should eat, but I have no appetite. Instead I pull out my oversized Joey bear. I never found the heart to throw this gift away from Jake. I curl up on my bed into its huge furry belly, sliding the mug of cocoa, untouched, back to the side table. I just want to sleep today away and forget it ever happened.

* * *

I'm half asleep when I get to work the next day. I tossed and turned most of the night, seeing every hour on the clock despite my exhaustion. Anytime I dozed off, Jake plagued my dreams, the memory of his mouth on mine, the feel of his arms around me. Torturing me over and over. My mother crept in there too, haunting the depths of my mind with a ghost like face, her arms outstretched trying to pull me back into the darkness. Jake's arms solidly folded around me, pulling me back with him into the sunshine. The irony of the dream isn't lost on me.

Wilma hands me an envelope as soon as she arrives, sliding it onto my desk with a smile that makes me stop what I'm typing and look up questioningly

"Margo asked me to pass this on." She grins, walking off toward her desk, looking almost smug. I rip open the envelope and pull out the letter, opening the folded cream paper, a ticket slides out and I read the note

Dearest Emma, this was bought quite a while back and as it's a named guest list, only you can use this. Jake insisted I send it to you. I hope you do go and have some fun! See you there. Xx Margo

The ticket has my name, plus guest, printed neatly on it, in gold foil. It's the Marie Curie charity ball in Manhattan tomorrow night. I was the one to get Jake these tickets for his entire staff on the sixty-fifth, a goodwill gesture from Jake, as each ticket raised funds for the event. I groan inwardly, if I don't go then Jake's wasted hundreds of dollars on my ticket. But, if I do go then he'll be there and so will half the people I worked with.

Do I go? Can I see him again so soon? If I do, then who do I take with me? How can I face him after last night?

As his PA, we decided to go together. No dates required, but that was then, at a time when he seemed to be going off his endless casual dates and was happy to have me escort him everywhere.

Who am I kidding?

I only have Sarah to ask and I already know she has shifts tomorrow night. Apart from her, there is no one else I felt comfortable asking and I'd never ask a date. I sigh, heavily, sliding the envelope and its contents into my bag. Thankfully, the days of working for Jake have left me with a wardrobe full of expensive clothes, I'll have no problem finding a suitable dress if I do go alone.

I check the time, it's only mid-morning. I submerge myself in the details of the Carrero Corporation anniversary event. The one-hundred-year celebration of the Carrero empire. Today's job is dealing with an array of mind numbing details; liaising with the event designer over napkins and such. Wilma has a week of press releases to get through. Somehow, in the brief time I've been here, she's designated me as her own PA rather than just another member of staff. It's given me a little pride. I haven't lost my skills after all and my confidence is slowly ebbing its way back to me.

My phone rings just before lunch and I pick it up, in my usual cheery tone.

"Hi, Emma, it's Rosalie … From Mr. Carrero's office." She sounds sheepish. I guess she's wary after Jake's little angry appearance down here yesterday. I feel a tad sorry for her. I know only too well what he can be like and she was never one to deal well with him directly, always seemingly intimidated by him, if I'm honest.

"Yes, Rosalie, how can I help you?" I keep my tone friendly, I won't mention yesterday. I have no intention of making her feel uncomfortable or lay blame.

"Mr. Carrero has asked that you come up to see him, immediately to discuss a matter, he was dealing with this morning … He says on your behalf." She hesitates, trying not to say too much on the phone. We all know that most of the calls inhouse are monitored and she probably has ears listening in, nearby.

"Right now?" I ask. It's so like him to expect me to drop everything and come running when he clicks his fingers.

Has he forgotten that he dumped me on the pavement last night, without a backward glance?

"Umm yes … He did say … Immediately." She gulps. I get the impression he's either close by in the office or has his door open and can possibly hear her. If he knows I'm arguing against him then he'll no doubt take his mood out on her. I sigh.

"Okay … I'm on my way … Goodbye, Rosalie." I place the receiver on the cradle then send Wilma an internal message that I've been summoned to the sixty-fifth for a minute and walk out. She's engrossed in a call, but I see her reach over to her laptop as I pass her window. Upon reading what I presume is my message she turns and waves at me with a smile, in confirmed approval of me leaving the office.

* * *

"Rosalie." I smile, graciously, as I arrive. I don't wait for her to announce my presence to Jake, his door is sitting half open, so I walk straight in. He's typing on his laptop, eyes narrowed in concentration. The sight of him jars me, pale blue shirt, open, as usual at the collar, sleeves rolled up. He looks too divine for words and I can almost forget how pissed at him I am. His dark hair is freshly trimmed and styled. He looks like a model for businessman of the year. I still my beating heart and clear my throat to catch his attention.

"Sit. Emma." He thrusts a thumb to the chair which always sits at the side of his desk, without looking up.

Hmmm.

"You'd better shut the door too." He adds as I go to move forward. I sigh loudly, then turn and shut the door. I should be acting grateful instead of irritated. I know he's calling me here to talk about Dan Gabrielle but what happened between me and him last night, has left me feeling raw and really irritated.

The look on his face doesn't bode well, maybe he wasn't able to fire him after all. I walk around his desk and slide into the seat closest to him. It reminds me of the many times I've sat here before, wasting time, chatting to my ex-boss and laughing until my sides ache, and now here we are, like strangers. I miss "Funny Jake".

As I sit, I catch his eyes running over my exposed legs under my skirt, then he shifts in his chair as though he's suddenly extremely uncomfortable. He shuts his laptop and swivels his seat to face me. His expression grim.

"So, this morning I sat in a board room with half of legal, three from HR and Margo, negotiating Gabriel's early retirement … He accepted the severance … He's gone." His tone is almost nasty, his fire filled green eyes are narrowed and he doesn't sound happy at all.

"You're mad about that?" I feel guilty, wary of his unusual mood and feeling like this is my fault.

Has he changed his mind about sacking Gabriel after all? Maybe he thinks I overreacted last night?

"No, Emma. I'm mad that the son of a bitch got paid off to leave. That I couldn't just outright fire him... Legal was all over my ass and brokered a deal, they didn't want a messy sexual harassment case... Bad for business." He snarls through gritted teeth, turning back to his desk and clenching fists on either side of his laptop.

"I see." I sound small and childlike. I should've known this could happen. Sexual harassment was still taboo in this crazy world of high profile business and men in suits.

"I did some digging, his last four assistants left quickly. I managed to contact three of them and they've agreed to come forward about his advances on them too ... He's a snake ... You weren't the only one." Jake growls at his fists.

"If he's going then why are you pursuing it?" I feel agitation lift to my shoulders, making me tense. He has no idea how hard it is for me to sit here with him, clearly avoiding all talk of last night and acting like nothing happened.

"Because making him take an early retirement and a huge sum of money is not *dealing* with it ... I'm pissed ... I want his ass raked over coals and I'll make sure he gets what he deserves And what he deserves isn't my money!" He slams his palms on the table.

"Why are you taking this so personally? You just saved a lot of future assistants from being groped, regardless." I snap, nervy with his aggression and not in the mood for his Carrero temper today.

"Because it *is* fucking personal!" He snaps back, rising to stand and stalking past me to his drinks cabinet. "He laid his hands on *you*!" He clatters decanters, indicating just how angry he is, and I take a steadying breath. My heart aching but this time not in pain.

Why does he always have to say things like this? Making me hope that there's more to us than this weird toing and froing thing we do.

He comes over and thrusts a glass in my hand, returning to his seat with his own. I look down at the amber liquid, I can smell it from here, the strong stench of brandy. I hesitate but take a sip of the burning liquid, coughing and placing it on his desk. His temper seems to dissipate slightly as he slugs it back and slides his glass next to mine.

"What happens now?" I eye him warily, he's turned to gaze out on the skyline, every muscle in his body taut.

"I told you … He's gone … As far as you're concerned, it's done. No one knows anything about you … I made sure of that."

"So, I guess … Thank you, Jake." I smile as he turns to look at me.

I really do mean, thank you … He's no idea what he's done for me.

He sighs heavily, his body relaxing slightly. He turns to me and watches me closely. His brows furrow, and his gaze intensifies on mine.

"Look, Emma … About last night? I'm sorry I acted like such an asshole." At least he sounds sorry.

I'm taken aback by this revelation. I never thought he'd ever mention last night again. Especially with the way he was acting a moment ago. I look away, embarrassment enveloping my face, it wasn't all one-sided, yet I still feel shameful.

"You confuse me," I say quietly, keeping my gaze on the art on the far wall, unable to make eye contact while this subject lingers in the air. I can see him from the corner of my eye, he leans forward in his chair, resting his elbows on his legs. He rubs his palms together slowly and then rubs his face.

"I know … Which is why I need to say this." He slides up as I turn to look at him, his gaze is boring into mine. "You and I … We don't work … Not as friends, not as boss and PA … Not as anything …" He sets his gaze on the New York skyline outside, breaking the spell, he has over this situation, "I think it's best if we both try to keep our distance and keep things civil … I'll back off over this Europe job, Emma. Maybe it's a great idea. If you want I can make some calls? Ensure that you get the position?" His voice is low and husky with no hint of emotion.

My throat constricts painfully, it feels like he's thrust a knife into my heart. I can't swallow, or move, my hands are frozen on my lap, my breathing has stilled. He has no idea of the impact his sentence has had on me. In one fell swoop he's broken my heart and killed me. I can't stay here and wait for anymore.

"Don't bother," I snap, rising from my chair, scolded by what he's said. "I don't need you to do anything else for me." My pain fuels my need to leave. I go to storm away but he's on his feet fast and catches my arm.

"What? So now I've pissed you off? I thought running to Europe was what you wanted?" he yells at me, pulling me toward him angrily. I stumble and try to wrestle myself free of his hold.

"You've no fucking idea what I want," I yell, yanking my arm free. Enraged by the pain he's causing me, infuriated by his never-ending need to manhandle me.

"You know what? You're right! I've never fucking known! You're like a goddamn enigma to me. Anytime I think I get even remotely close to figuring you out, you turn on me like this. Screw you … I'm done with this shit between us. Go find a job elsewhere. I'll dissolve your contract so you're free to fuck off anywhere you please." He barks, letting my arm go and raising his palms in agitation.

"Fine! Maybe you should! Maybe I will! It's obvious you feel like you have some weird obligation toward me … I'd be better long gone, out of your life and your company!" I spit, and this time successfully storm off, slamming his door in grand fashion, behind me. Then jump as I hear a loud smashing sound coming from inside his office. He's obviously hurled his glass at the wall, or the door.

I'm seething, spitting nails as I storm back to my own floor, giving glacial looks to anyone foolish enough to glance at me. Caught up with an argument inside my own head in which I hurl every goddamn thing at him which pisses me off. My blood is pumping at an alarming rate, but I know the second the rage calms down I'm going to crumble.

When I get to my desk I thrust my drawers open and begin slamming things on top.

I'll leave right bloody now. I'll show him. I won't even wait for another job. I'll just go and be done with this crap.

I lose my resolve and slump into my seat dejectedly. Energy wavering and temper fast dissolving away. Fighting to hold back the tears that are now overwhelming me as my heartache clambers out on top.

Why does he do this to me? He knows how to wind me, and the worst thing is, I don't even think he knows he does it. I hate him so much but … I love him. More than anything in the world. I'm so done feeling like this. I'm so done with hurting.

"Emma? Darling, are you okay?" Wilma's concerned tone breaks into my train of thought and I realize she's standing almost in front of me. The scattered contents of my drawers strewn across the desk and some on the floor. I look up at her tiredly. Jake saps all the life from me.

"Men!" I mumble and feel mortified as a fresh bout of tears pour down my face, shocking both of us.

* * *

"Feeling any better?" Wilma's arm is around my shoulder. Her soft voice is in my ear as she rubs my back in her office. I had a full-blown emotional break down and did something I never ever imagined PA Emma would ever do. I told her everything about Jake, and how I really feel about him. Things I haven't even told Sarah. I blame the maternal pull Wilma has over me and the darn gentle look she manages to throw my way at every opportunity. I'm using an almost empty packet of scrunched up Kleenex to mop up my mess of a face, sniffing down the last dregs of my self-esteem.

She's sat and listened, and nodded, and some of the time, I saw a knowing look in her eye and assumed Margo had told her the odd tidbit of my sorrowful tale. She listened quietly, her gentle touch on me the whole time, letting me get it all out. She seems unsurprised to know I had sex with Jake. But then I guess most of New York's single women had. His headboard's probably run out of space to keep tally years ago. It's not exactly a small or hard list to get on.

"A little." I sniff, using the new tissues she's given me to blow my nose again. I feel like a complete mess.

"Sounds to me like you two have got it really bad, yet neither of you has the ability to admit it to each other." She smiles knowingly, but I shake my head. She doesn't know Jake the way I do. She has this so wrong in so many ways.

Yes, I've got it bad … Jake just … I don't even know anymore, he's just Jake. It's all sex with him.

"You sound like my flat mate, she said the same. Jake's complicated. He doesn't feel the same way … He pretty much told me to leave and go to Europe." I smile tightly, she's no idea how much of a roller-coaster ride Casanova Carrero is.

I like her stroking my back, it's motherly. My mother never did this for me, ever. Not even as a small child. I've never had a motherly figure in my life, not really. No one soothed my tears or hugged me back then. My mother was all about *her* pain, *her* drama. I was the one who smoothed back her hair and wiped her tears.

"I want you to go home, Emma, for the rest of the week … You need some time to really digest everything. What you've told me is so much in such a small amount of time. Take some R and R. Don't come in until Monday. You're due some holidays anyway, so you won't lose any pay." She pats my back and smiles softly.

"I can't …" I begin to protest but she catches my hand and squeezes it tightly.

"This isn't a suggestion, Emma … I need you sharp and focused. This is for my benefit as much as yours, sweetie. You also need time to figure out if your future is in this company or in Europe." She gives me a full body squeeze before standing up and walking to her desk from the couch where we were perched. She pours me a glass of water and brings it back to me, sitting down once more. "Go to the dance tomorrow night. I'll see you there. And, if you still feel like you don't need time off, then we'll talk."

"I don't know." I move uneasily.

Jake will be there, probably with a date. How can I even contemplate going after what's happened? I'm so done with this roller-coaster.

"You need a good night off, a pretty dress, and a lot of

alcohol. Take a friend, have a blast, kick back, and set these gorgeous waves free." She picks up a strand of my hair and pushes it behind my ear. It seems everyone has the urge to tame my wild hair nowadays. Maybe I should grow it back out and return it to "sleek poised Emma mode" since my life seemed to start unraveling not long after I cut it all off.

Chapter 6

I walk into the empty apartment two hours later, dump my bag on the table and survey the room. I don't even want to be here, I should be at work, organizing. Instead of coming home to sob into my pillow. I need to get a grip of my life. Wilma is right, all of this has been non-stop. Yet, all I've done is bury my head in the sand and pushed myself to go to work, never taking the time to absorb it all. I need time to think. Real time to myself, to figure out what I'm going to do.

Do I want to work in Europe?

No … I don't want to leave New York.

Do I want to leave Carrero House?

No. I love working there, it's familiar and stable. Plus, I adore Wilma, Margo, and even Rosalie. I would miss the people I see every day even though we don't interact much. I couldn't leave Sarah. I mean, I know she has Marcus and lately, I'm starting to warm to him a little. I even laughed at a joke he made a few days ago, but still … She's my best friend.

But, on the other hand, things aren't going anywhere. I feel like every time I see any light at the end of the tunnel,

Jake appears and blacks it out. He's all I can see, all I can focus on and it's driving me slowly insane.

How did we get here? He used to be my everything, my friend, my protector, my lifeline … and now he's the cause of everything that's wrong with me.

It feels like we've been apart for months, but the reality is, it's only been weeks, just a month. Dragging days and sleepless nights have caused time to stand still. I need to get over him.

Pulling on jogging clothes I decide to go for a run. It's mid-afternoon in Queens and the sun is out, kids playing in the street. It's getting late in the season so it's unexpectedly warm for the time of year. Christmas will be here soon and that's going to be an ordeal and a half. My mother wanted to come here this year for some reason, I don't want her to. I've invited Sophie on Christmas Eve to spend some time with her, and the last thing I need is my mother anywhere near her or me.

God, I miss that girl.

She's been emailing me religiously. She seems to be doing well in her new home. In such a short time she's settled so well. She can't believe how blessed she is, getting used to a wealthy family and all the perks that go with her new lifestyle.

I pound my feet into the pavement, working up a sweat and it feels good. I've missed running. I only seemed to do it when I was staying in hotels with Jake. It had become part of the ritual of our life. Since I've come home my running shoes have glared at me angrily from the corner asking why I'm neglecting them. Not anymore.

I'm going to start doing this every day again, it helped before, helped me get my emotions in check, helped me work through my internal dialogue. I'm sweating like crazy, working over everything, emotionally, mentally, and physically, but I push on.

I'll go to that dance tomorrow night. Show everyone who I am, who I used to be. I don't need a date at all. I'm PA Emma and I was always happy to stand alone with my chin held high.

There will be plenty of people I know there. All the staff from sixty-fifth, Margo, Wilma, Rosalie, Leila.

I miss Leila. Jake's childhood friend and my ally when he took me on his family boat for a week.

Her emails are less frequent than Sophie's, but we've stayed in contact and I know her family are all going to attend this event. Sophie sadly won't be, it's adults only.

I need this, I need a social outing where people I know and like will be present. Wilma's right, lots of alcohol and dancing with Leila is just what I need.

Jake can stay the hell away from me. Since it's what he said, right? We should avoid one another … Well, Carrero, you're the one who sent me the goddamn tickets.

I wonder if Marissa will be there and my stomach lurches, up until now I've done well to ignore that little issue. It pains me in so many ways to know that she and Jake hooked up and could potentially be together again. It kills me to know she's carrying his child, whether he wants it or not. I wish I could see inside his head and really know how he feels about her, and the baby, gain some insight. She's the one person in the world I hate as much as Ray Vanquis. I can't see what her appeal is. Jake and Marissa are so unmatched. I've never understood how he could fall in love with her, even as a teen. She's so vain and self-centered, cold and domineering in so many ways. Her poor child will have one loving parent, at least, one rock to rely on. And, as much as it hurts me, so much more than I'm capable of enduring, I know Jake will be a good father.

***

I hit the shower on my return and eat with Sarah and Marcus. It's late and they have no clue that I've been home for hours. Conversation is light. I watch them and for the first time I see it, the compatibility, the companionship between them. Despite still thinking he's a smarmy creep, I can see the genuine affection he has for Sarah. It humbles yet pains me. I want this with Jake, so badly. We had something close once. But we let this mess and sex get in the way and we destroyed everything. I destroyed everything. I only have myself to blame.

I don't tell Sarah anything. She's too happy and comfy in Marcus' arms watching a movie. I endure the romantic comedy for a bit then excuse myself and head to bed. Faithful old sleeping pills working wonders and getting me through my current tragic life.

Chapter 7

I get up with renewed vigor. I've slept better than I have for days. Somehow, I feel more able to cope. I eat, wave Sarah off to work and tell her I have a day off to get ready for the dance. It's not a complete lie as I intend to get ready in grand fashion, going to lengths I've never bothered with before. Wilma is right, a good dress and a girly night with Leila will help. I intend to follow Leila's example. Something she taught me on the yacht, pampering is an enjoyable girly pursuit and can almost fool you into believing you don't have a broken heart. She also told me that a good night with a girlfriend can change your whole outlook on life.

I manage to book an appointment at a beauty salon for just after noon and I'm having the works. Nails, hair, waxing, make-up. I have a room full of people to impress, who have seen nothing but gaunt and lifeless Emma for weeks. Senior Carrero will be there, and I want to regain some of my pride in front of him. This dance means so much more than a night of fun for me, it's a chance to save face and present my old self again.

I spend the morning trying on dresses and finally settle on a floor length, red, slinky dress. It has a low cut back, corseted front and no straps. It clings to every curve and falls in a pool of fabric on the floor. It's one Donna chose for an elegant banquet we never attended weeks ago, at his request, she's his personal shopper and shops for anything he needs on demand. Jake's Armani tux was sent back but this was mine. Jake never expected me to return anything that was bought for me, generous to a fault. I find the shoes to match in the pile of unopened boxes in my bathroom. She's gone for Hollywood glam, vintage red heels in matching satin to the dress. Jake always said red suited me and I hope he's right. It's a color I've only worn once … at his pushing on that damn boat.

I make my appointment with time to spare, feeling nervier than I should. This is something I've rarely done in my life. Leila was my first proper experience with salons and beauty treatments. So, I'm glad when they don't keep me waiting for the full glam treatment, starting with a hair trim and highlight retouch. I want my hair back to how it was the first day I cut it. It's grown so much and tickles my shoulders a lot. Somewhere, in the back of my mind, I know I'm thinking about Jake's reaction, the first time he saw my hair and deep down I want him to see me that way again.

Don't go there. Tonight, is neither about him or for him. It's about moving forward.

* * *

Standing at the mirror in my bedroom, I feel sick with anticipation. I look every bit red-carpet ready, it even wows me. I wish Sarah was home to see. I look, for the first time in my life, elegant and dare I say, a little bit beautiful. They've given me subtle nineteen-fifties make-up with a nude lipstick and winged eyeliner. My skin looks flawless; my cheeks blushed and high; my nails a natural French manicure; so clean and polished. My hair is left down in its natural waves. It's shorter again and brushed to one side. I look seductive. I can't believe the girl in front of me is my own reflection. The dress sculpted to a body I'm rather proud of and I stand elegantly in my heels.

I feel a tremble of nerves course through me, anticipation and dread in equal amounts. I know tonight is either going to be wonderful, or disastrous. I just hope that it won't be the latter. I know Leila can get me through this and I need to see her so badly.

I grasp my silver clutch and pull on the silver fur stole that Donna chose for another outfit, but it looks good. I've booked a cab and it'll be here any minute. I feel sick to my stomach; my hands are shaking badly when I slide the ticket into my bag. I steel down my nerves and head out to wait for my ride in the cool evening air.

This is a new me. Be brave. Take a deep breath, and smile. You can do this.

* * *

The huge venue is every bit as glamorous as any I've been too with Jake before, complete with a red-carpet entrance, flashing cameras, and tuxedo wearing security. I pass easily with my ticket, getting slight interest from photographers as they try to decide if I'm a celebrity or not, a few flashes just in case. I feel a little proud. I keep my chin down and walk inside. Leila knows I'm coming, her text said she'd find me, so my only task is to get inside and amuse myself until then. Find something to do until she rescues me.

The inner floor is full of people mulling around in various degrees of expensive formal wear. The music from the full orchestra is loud and invading. The noisy bustle of chatter and scraping chairs, chinking glasses is almost overpowering. It's been going on for an hour already and seems almost full; no huge wave of late comers to this merry event.

I weave my way through the crowd, looking for my table, names are placed on cards at the plates for the main meal. I refer to the huge easels in the corner, holding large printed seating plans, and feel myself pale as I locate my name among the guests. I'm still seated at the Carrero table next to Jake, seated as his date.

Shit! What was I thinking? I should've known this would happen. No one would've informed them of a seating change … Margo would've known this.

I lose all my bravado, turning, I panic, and rush off toward the entrance feeling flustered and emotional.

I'm not staying and doing this; the meal takes up more than an hour of the night. I can't sit beside him sipping wine and acting like all of this is okay.

What the hell was Margo thinking?

I can't breathe, I need to go. Go home and forget all of this. All my confidence is gone, and a sickening feeling is rising inside of me, urging on the breathlessness of an anxiety attack. I feel my face heat as color creeps up my skin and I desperately push my way across the overcrowded floor, rushing to find my escape through the crowds haphazardly. I feel like an idiot.

I'll just text Leila and tell her I felt unwell.

I move forward into the room and realize the only way out is across the dance floor. It's less crowded and easier to navigate than the bustling walkways. I push on, rage and emotion spiraling inside of me. I'm not looking where I'm going, blinded by watery eyes and complete disappointment in myself.

I look up as I push through a tight group of people in black formal wear and come face-t- face with Jake, mid-dance floor.

Shit!

Literally two feet away.

My breath halts in my chest painfully, the sight of him spins my world and drowns out everyone around me. His eyes meet mine with equal trepidation and I'm captivated, a prisoner to him, under that steady green gaze pushing away everything else that surrounds us.

We stand motionless, feet apart. I can feel the tension around us, making me want to crumble. He looks like my dreams, flawless perfection in a black tuxedo and white shirt, a doorway to my soul. He looks every bit James Bond and bad boy rolled into one and it's painful to see. His gaze is steady on me, never leaving my eyes. Neither of us move or say anything. His expression is calm. I want to know what he's thinking. Long for him to say something instead of just staring at me that way.

"Oh, my god, Emma!" Leila's excitable voice grabs my attention as she dives on me from the left. Jake was obviously with her. She begins hauling me into an overeager embrace around the neck, turning me to her. I grimace in surprise but let my arms find a path around the energetic creature and tear my focus away from the one man holding all my attention.

"Whoa, Leila." I choke, laughter breaking over me at her exuberant welcome. Glad of her sudden distraction. She releases me and grabs my hands, bouncing up and down excitedly. I catch a glimpse of Jake watching us. His expression unchanged, his body language stiff.

"I've missed you, millions! Emails are not the same, Miss. Ems. You look freaking sensational!" She spins me around, surprisingly strong for someone so small. I gasp at the movement, lose my footing on the high heels and fall sideways. Strong arms catch me, pulling me upright, instant searing heat at the contact flows through me. I know without looking that Jake has me. He expertly stands me and holds my upper arms, releasing me once I'm steady. Trying for composed and cool seems to be my only focus. I just hope he doesn't see the way I trembled at his touch or closed my eyes until he had put me upright.

I take a slow breath to regain my composure, but Leila seems oblivious.

"Careful, Leila." Jake scorns in a maternal tone. I try to avoid looking at him, my body fluttering at his touch even though he's let me go. I catch his eyes skimming my dress and flush inside, he looks away and watches other people in the crowd. That unreadable face and taut body hiding everything going on in his complex mind.

"I can't help being so happy to see her, Jake, you keep her hidden from me." She smarts with a smile. I glance at him quickly, seeing the frown flicker across his face when he looks back at Leila.

He hasn't told Leila that I don't work for him anymore? I guess neither have I, it never crossed my mind to tell her or anyone that Jake removed me from his life.

"I've been working." I cut in smoothly, avoiding his eyes again. Music overtakes our conversation as the instruments heat up, a slow ballad comes across the air, making conversation near impossible.

"Oh, I promised someone a first slow dance." Leila turns me, shoving me into Jake, hard. His arms automatically catch me, again, keeping me upright as I collide with his chest. He lets me go as though I've burned him, shifting apart and upping the awkward tension between us. "Keep her warm for me until I come back, Jacob!" She grins cheekily and takes off.

"That girl …" he says tightly, avoiding my face.

"You've got to love her though." I shrug, biting my lip. The nervousness is overwhelming me, unable to look at his face. The music is moving into full swing as couples move around us, joining together to sway. I fidget with my hair awkwardly and shuffle my feet, looking around for a quick exit. This is beyond unbearable and incredibly awkward. I catch him glaring at my fingers mid-twirl and release the strand nervously. He can still close me down with a look.

"Want to dance with me, Anderson?" His low tone halts me. I feel my stomach flip and hesitation jump in. I don't know if I can bare this. "I don't bite …" He smiles, and I see the flicker of amusement in his eye, remembering the last time he'd said it to me, so long ago.

No, he didn't bite, he just devastated hearts.

He doesn't give me a moment to answer or think, just reaches out for my wrist and pulls me into him so my body softly collides with his, and I reach up with flat palm to his chest. He maneuvers me perfectly in his arms and sways me in time to the music, his face above me and turned away, so there's no confusion as to what this is. I tense, his touch is all I've craved for days, all I've thought about, but not like this. He's forced into this, standing in the middle of a ballroom floor surrounded by important people. He doesn't want to cause a scene. He doesn't want to be here with me. I feel a swell of emotion overtaking me and my eyes well up.

I can't do this. I can't pretend like everything is okay and we can just put the past behind us. I can't put the past behind me, I can't pretend that I don't still feel the same way about him. It's agony.

"I can't do this …" I whisper, emotion breaking in my voice and I pull myself free. I try to turn away, but he catches my chin with his hand, lifting it up to him quickly. I know he sees my pain and my eyes are almost overflowing with the effort of not crying. I've become so useless at finding my mask nowadays, it's long since deserted me. This close to him I'm defenseless. His lips part and he frowns but he lets me go. I see some sort of recognition run over his face. He's seen something he doesn't like, maybe he's finally realizing why we can never go back to before. Because his stupid ex PA has become so utterly devoted to every part of him that she can no longer function in his presence.

That's one thing for sure that could send him running for the hills … Love.

"I need to go." I turn my face downwards trying to hide the tears as they spill down my cheek. I go on my heels, walking away as fast as I can, taking deep breaths, trying to calm the inner chaos begging to erupt all over this ballroom floor. Trying to get the feel and smell of him away from me so I can breathe. So I can function. He stands motionless on the floor, but I can feel his eyes watching me leave. It hurts me more than I can bear.

I walk through the crowds on the dance floor until I find open space, maneuvering among people and faces trying to find a way out of this infernal room. My heart is beating erratically, I'm afraid to turn around and see him again. I need to stay strong and leave. Pushing until I get to the edge of the dance floor, I stop to take a deep breath, my legs weak as I try to steady my pulsing heart rate.

My cell vibrates in my clutch bag and I curse, whoever it is has really picked the worst moment to summon me. I grate my teeth as I yank my cell out, anger growing inside me at this damn job and the way it always imposes on every part of my life.

Jake Carrero has sent you an iTunes gift.

I freeze, almost dropping my phone in shock. My breathing ups a gear, making me afraid to move.

What? Why would he? Why now, after everything? Our long-forgotten mode of communication.

Jake sending me songs as way of giving messages is lost and forgotten since he severed our tie and sent me away, along with our friendship. I don't understand why he would try and get to me this way now, how much this hurts me.

I screw my eyes closed.

I'm dreaming, this is all a hallucination and when I open my eyes, it'll be gone. I can't do this, I can't have him acting like we used to. I just saw him, and it was obvious it'll never go back to how it was.

Is that what he wants? PA Emma back, friend and platonic assistant? I can never go back there.

I swipe the screen slowly, scared and hesitant. My breath catches as I read the email, a small gasp leaving my lips and eyes filling with moisture.

Jake Carrero has sent you:

"Say You Love Me" by Jessie Wares.

I feel the tears fall before my brain has time to connect.

What does this mean? He knows I love him?

I don't know what to think or feel. I spin around scanning the dance floor, looking for him, for some hint of an idea at what this means or what he wants from me. All I see is an ocean of people. I've come too far, my sight of him hindered by the crowd and I stay facing the floor, my head whirling. I made the mistake once before of not being honest with him. No matter what this means, I won't make the same mistake again. Sarah was right. We didn't ever just say what we felt, we never talked about feelings. I don't want to be that girl anymore. Even if I humiliate myself, then at least I'll leave him in no doubt as to how I feel this time. If anything, maybe he'll finally leave me alone and stay out of my life.

I open iTunes and scroll; every title lacks what I want to say. I try some keywords and there it is—it's perfect. I know the song, it's what I should have told him a long time ago. I purchase and send.

Emma Anderson, you've sent Jake Carrero

"Only Love Can Hurt Like This" by Paloma Faith.

I look up again, scanning the crowds, searching the floor. I don't see him. It pains me more, every face a disappointment. I shove my phone back in my bag and push it aside. My body is in chaos, my mind floundering and my breathing is labored. I've never been so terrified. If only I could see him, figure out what all this means. I want to see his reaction, I want to know how to feel. I feel like I'm hanging from a cliff by my fingernails torn that maybe I should go back and see if I can find him.

And then, there he is.

Pushing through the wave of bodies toward me, looking around, his eyes search every girl with tawny hair in a red dress and finally fall on me. He falters, his body straightens, his eyes lock on mine with a force that make me stand stone still, caught in his spell. I'm in no doubt that he was searching for me.

He strides toward me. His eye on his target, he's homed in and his look is stern with intent. He marches toward me, without breaking eye contact, not stopping to look at the people beside him who try to get his attention. Just me and he's moving fast, he doesn't hesitate. Two more strides and he's at me, his hands on my face, cupping my jaw, pulling me forward hard and his mouth molds to mine.

The power of his kiss makes me melt, grabbing onto his arms for support. The emotion behind it opens me up to him and I surrender. Letting him capture me, drag me into him and lose myself. His lips mold to mine and our tongues caress in perfect unison. I'm free falling and time ceases to exist, everyone disappears and it's only him. Pulling me under into a wave of euphoria that's untouchable. It doesn't matter that we're surrounded by people, doesn't matter how many see this, all there is in time and space is him and I. Locked this way. My heart soars, my stomach flutters with a million butterflies.

After what seems like forever he pulls away from me, breathing hard, matching my own breathlessness. His hands are on my jaw, gently holding me still. Holding me close, his forehead against mine, my hands on his upper arms are holding on tightly. We don't speak, just breathe each other in, our eyes locked, pupils large and focused, passing a million messages in just a look.

The doubts I had about Jake in the past are dispersed with the strength of the look he's giving me. I see his pain and heartbreak mirrored in mine, that same longing to have me as I have wanted him.

I think Jake loves me!

My world spins, the realization that everything I've felt, everything I've been so afraid of is right here in his green depths, staring back at me without hesitation.

"Come with me?" he whispers, even though the room is noisy, I hear him loud and clear and nod. His eyes are focused so intently on me, flicking from my eyes to my mouth. His face flickering as he concentrates on my lips as though he's experiencing internal pain. He kisses me again, lightly, sending flutters through me, tingles to every cell. A sweet kiss, not one of passion and misunderstanding but a "You're mine" kiss.

He lets go of my face and grabs my hand, interlocking our fingers possessively as he pulls me in the direction of the grand exit. I can't stop myself devouring him with my eyes, my heart's in a frenzy and my blood rushes through my entire body.

I love him so much it hurts.

A pain so severe I think I may fall right here, my heart giving out under the pressure. His tall, strong body guides me, pulling me out of the room. Spiraling crazy thoughts.

Is this really happening?

My heart's soaring, my chest heavy with uncertainty yet beating fast with anticipation. Someone stops us, I vaguely remember them, business acquaintances, someone important. That irritated wave of disappointment and impatience hits me hard.

No, no, no. We have things to work out, things to say. Go away!

He pauses, throwing me an unreadable look, then shakes hands with the suit before him. He tightens his grip on me as though he's afraid I'll run away or leave him. He pulls me into his side, his muscles tense and he tucks my arm under his possessively. He's making it clear that he's aware of me, wanting me to know I'm not far from his mind. Another man intervenes, and Jake gets impatient, he tugs me forward and slides an arm around my waist. Pulling me against his body so my head leans into his shoulder and chest, turning to plant a kiss on my temple. The excitement rises inside, threatening to unravel me as I wait, so hard to stay still and not scream in frustration. Finally, he makes an excuse and moves fast, jerking me with him, then glances down at me as I stumble, pausing to right me on my feet.

"I'm sorry … I just need to get you out of here quickly … I need us to be alone. To talk." He rushes his words in a very un-Jake-like manner, his voice is so husky. I almost feel my inner body explode. He looks around the main hall and seems annoyed, hauling me with him. He heads for a door concealed behind the sweeping staircase. I can barely match his steps with my flowing dress and high shoes. I lift the hem of my skirt to stop myself tripping and catch his eyes on me, a look of sheer lust and longing. My stomach tightens.

This is happening!

Checking around he opens the door into a dim abandoned hall and pulls me inside, closing it behind us. He turns me, so I'm pushed against the wall in front of him, sweeping back to me, capturing my mouth, without hesitation. His hands bracing the wall at each side of my head. This kiss out does the first. Every single longing and insatiable ache being poured into this meeting of our lips. I feel myself crumble under the force. His hands come around me, pinning me to him with my back against the wall, breathing heavily. He's just as lost as I am, my hands slide around his neck, holding on for dear life, crushing one another with a vehemence so powerful it's terrifying. After a moment he pulls away, leaning against me, our bodies heaving with desire, forehead to forehead. Breathing each other in with eyes locked together. I see apprehension followed by a frown and it causes my voice to stifle in my throat.

Is he regretting this already? Maybe I was wrong about how he feels. About what I saw in his eyes.

"I'm waiting on it, Emma." His voice is low and pained, he seems upset. Suddenly so different and my stomach drops.

"On what?" I sound meek, scared and confused by his expression and this quick change in him.

Not again, Jake. Don't leave me again. Please.

"The door to hit me in the face again … Another reason you think we shouldn't be together," he says sardonically and it's only now I see the flicker of fear in his eye.

How many times have I done that to him? How long was he waiting for me to let him in?

I shake my head, lifting my fingers to trace his lips softly, the chiseled curve of the perfect mouth. He makes me ache for his kiss again. He catches my hand with his, pressing my palm to his mouth and kisses it lightly, closing his eyes at the touch. I feel the smile tug my mouth.

"I'm not going to do that … Jake. I won't push you away again." I breathe softly. The agony of time apart has chased my fears into the darkest recesses of my mind, nothing can hurt as much as not having Jake in my life. I lost all the things that mattered to me. In the end, I realized he was the only thing I had that was worth losing in the first place. His pupils dilate at my words, sending a surge of power through me.

Jake's here with me … For once we're on the same page and I know by looking at him that we want the same thing.

"I love you … I think I've been in love with you for a very long time …" He smiles shyly, unaware of the devastating effect those little words have on my soul. My heart constricts in joy, my tears falling with happiness and I become a mess of emotions melting in his arms.

"I … I …" I can't get the words out and fall to pieces in a flood of tears and sobs. I've been waiting so long to have him feel this way about me. It's all too much and I fall to pieces. He wraps himself around me, burying his face in my hair. His strength and power, holding me where I need to be. I could lose myself completely to him and know I'd always be safe, held like this.

"Don't cry, *bambino* … Please, Emma … I didn't think telling you I loved you would cause this." He sounds ravaged, his voice torn with emotion too. I cling to him as though I'm adrift in the sea and he's my lifeline. "Say something …"

"I … love … you." I sniff and sob incoherently, feeling

his body relax. He pulls my face from his chest, lifting my chin, kissing me softly on the mouth. Savoring the touch, so gentle and perfect that it sets me off again. Like an erratic overemotional women on her period, I literally burst into tears, just shy of wailing like a cat.

"Jesus, Emma … If I'd known this was how it would be, I would've brought some tissues and a lot of chocolate." He grins at me, fingers tangling themselves in my hair and I giggle through my tears, falling against him again. He can always make me laugh, despite everything, despite the sheer deep emotion of what we're doing, what we're saying. Here we are, smiling.

"They're happy tears." I sniff back the waves of emotion, trying to regain some composure. Digging in my purse for tissues and finding nothing to stop the wave of mascara pouring down my cheeks.

"Should I be crying too then?" He smiles, wiping my cheek with his thumb, doing his best to dry my face by using his jacket sleeve to dab the worst away. He's caging me against the wall with one of his arms, lowering his face to stay close to me.

"I don't think I want to see you cry." I smile up at him through watery eyes, feeling a rush of warmth as he delivers another soft kiss to my mouth. I could let him do this for an eternity.

"Good. I'm not much of a crier and you're doing a grand enough job for the both of us … I'm happy, though, you have no idea. I never thought we'd get here. I didn't think this was how you felt about me." He rests his brow against mine, tracing my face with his fingers. Breathing so closely. This time I lean up and kiss him, feeling brave enough to do it, in the knowledge that he loves me. It ignites into a more passionate kiss with his hand sliding behind my neck and his tongue finding the warmth of my mouth. We both groan and sag against each other. Sexual tension igniting with rage and he pulls away, sucking my lower lip slowly and gently. Both of us look at one another through heavy lids, seeped in lust.

"If we keep doing this then I can promise you I won't be a gentleman for much longer." He warns with the softest voice, his eyes glued to my mouth. I'm fascinated by the way his perfect mouth looks so right nestled among designer stubble and chiseled jaw line.

"Oh, I always knew you weren't a gentleman." I jest, biting my lip unable to tear my gaze from his mouth.

You're perfection.

"Hey! I've been very well behaved. You have no idea the kind of thoughts that went through my head concerning you." He catches my wrists and pins them over my head with one hand, his other sliding up from my waist and along my ribs suggestively.

"None of that surprises me, you and your ex-rated mind. I always knew you had Casanova tendencies." I tremble with shivers as his touch ignites feelings inside me that are equally ex-rated.

"Cheeky!" He plants a swift kiss on my lips then leans back to continue watching me. He lets my hands go, "You're beautiful, and you're all mine!" We smile at one another, then he quickly delivers another lip grazing kiss. Trying it out, enjoying the fact that he can. I can see kissing becoming his number one hobby quite soon.

"I'm still mad at you." I push my palms up his abdomen and slide them over his chest, exploring, being able to freely roam.

"I don't blame you, *bella.*" He frowns. "I'm mad at me too," there's a tint of regret in his eyes. He brings a hand down and smooths my hair behind one ear, stopping to play with the delicate diamond cluster earring, his eyes focused on it as he moves it around gently.

"Makes a change from being mad at me, I guess." I smirk. I've finally gained control of my emotions again, as much as I can after a love confession from the man of my dreams. He stares at me for long agonizing moments, his eyes locked on mine, taking in every detail of my face, his expression unreadable.

"I only got mad with you because of how I feel about you, Emma … It was ripping me apart. I didn't know how to behave around you or how to deal with all this crap inside of me … Overemotional men are just narky shits." He softly smiles.

So, all those times he seemed so crazy pissed off at me … All came down to this? Surely not?

"I get mad at you because you're an asshole sometimes; nothing to do with emotions or love." I smirk and look up at him shyly. He breaks into another heartthrob smile and I can't resist running my fingers across his mouth again. I feel him move into my touch; being able to freely touch him like this is beyond any of my dreams and desires. It feels like I've died and woken in a heavenly place.

"We need to make this work." He breathes. "I can't walk away again … I don't want to. This past month has been unbearable, like I had my insides wrenched out."

His confession is sobering, his voice strained. Rosalie was right. Jake had been missing me as much as I was missing him.

Jake loved me. All that denial and second guessing him was for nothing.

"Are you asking me to be your PA again?" I ask quietly, bravely, soothed by knowing he'd had the same suffering I had when we were apart, a pang of hope rises in my chest.

I've no idea how that'll work now, things are so different.

"I'm asking for way more than that, *miele.*" His voice softly caresses me, his fingers still in my hair, sensually moving over my scalp, sending shivers of desire through me.

"Tell me what you want from me, be specific." My inner strength takes a step forward.

Be brave, Emma … stop hiding and put all the cards on the table. Sarah said we didn't ever lay it all out, well, here we are.

I need him to be straight with me. I need to hear him say it. No more second guessing.

"I want you … All of you … I want us. Just you and me and no one else. No games, no hiding, no more misunderstandings … I want you to be the one woman I share my bed and my life with. I want a real relationship with you, *bambino.*" I've never seen Jake so open and honest and … raw in my life. The fear in his eyes and the trepidation, because for him, this is just as huge as it is for me. His brokenhearted past, his need to keep women at arm's length for fear of being hurt and here he is, offering all of himself to me. I throw myself around him, holding tight, my heart gushes with love as his arms tighten around me too.

This is everything, this is what's meant for me. I love him so much I can barely breathe.

"I want that too," I whisper, as his hand comes up into the back of my hair, fingers entangling to hold me tight.

"You better not be crying again." His voice is laced with humor and I lean back shaking my head, face wide with a happy smile.

"No tears … Brownies whatsits." I attempt a girl guide salute and watch Jake shake his head at me pitifully. He pushes my hand down with a frown and kisses my forehead with a "nice try" kind of look on his face.

"This … Us … It's really happening?" Jake suddenly

looks so young and vulnerable, tipping his head back and letting his eyes run over my face.

"It looks that way." I manage, tangling his fingers with mine, tugging his hand against my chest to feel his skin on mine, becoming greedy.

"You may need to pinch me a couple of times to actually believe it, shorty." He moves in again, brushing his mouth against mine tenderly. His hand skims my throat and across my shoulder seductively, reigniting his obsession with touching me again.

I pull away, my mind racing ahead and look at him seriously. There's one thing plaguing me, and I need to know. One thing that causes a pain in my heart, even amid the elation now bashing me in the face.

"What about Marissa?" I curse inwardly at how feeble I sound saying it. His jaw tenses but he smiles at me gently, bringing our noses to touch.

"I don't want her. I didn't want her. It was a stupid drunken mistake. I'll be there for the baby but as far as she's concerned, she means nothing. It's you, it will always be you." His fingers trace my eyebrow gently, then smooth back a strand of my hair that's fallen forward. I see only truth in his eyes.

"How do you feel about the baby?" I ask. I want to know everything that's ravaged my mind for weeks. He frowns, wondering where I'm going with this, but he's my Jake now and I get to ask him this because he loves me. That thought gives me confidence and power, opening parts of me that I never knew I had.

"I'd be lying if I said I was happy … I'm not … But I did this, and I need to take responsibility. I hadn't ever thought about having kids, so this is all pretty overwhelming right now." He screws his face up cutely, looking far too appealing.

"Don't walk away from your child," I say. I know better than anyone what a father who didn't want to know could do to a kid emotionally, for a lifetime. He kisses me softy on the lips. Each time he does a look passes across his beautiful face, disbelief that I'm letting him so freely do this.

The feeling's mutual. Did I really torture him that much?

"That's not me, Emma … I'm nothing like your father. I won't walk away." He gently pushes my forehead with his. "Can we drop this conversation for now, there's something I would much rather be doing." He grins, the glint of "Cheeky Carrero" in his eye. All signs of doubt and vulnerability moving out and sexually confident Carrero moving back in, even his body seems to suddenly get bigger.

"Such as?" I smile. Deep down a slight wave of insecurity moves into my mind.

Is he going to leave me here? Where else does he need to be? Surely, he isn't planning on leaving me here now? After this?

"Taking my girlfriend home and fucking her brains out. It's long overdue." He grins, capturing my mouth as I inhale sharply in surprise, a passionate kiss stilling my words. His hands come to pull me into him again. This time harder, making his intention clear. Taken aback by his declaration, my body tingles in anticipation.

Girlfriend? Me?

I squeal internally.

And what he wants to do … Most definitely!

My body is practically convulsing in excitement. Only Jake could make crass sound like the most romantic suggestion in the world.

* * *

The car journey to his apartment passes in a flurry of back seat grinding and fumbling, lying flat across the smooth leather seat. Jake heavy on top of me with his hands and mouth all over me, pushing me to a searing heat that has me panting, kissing me as though he's been deprived for years. Toe-curling kisses that have me begging for more. My fingers find his shirt and bow tie, undoing both so they hang freely open, his naked strong chest covered in my lipstick kisses and his jacket discarded on the floor.

If the internal, blacked out window of the limo hadn't been there, I would have been ashamed at what Jefferson was witnessing. Jake almost has me on the seat, his desire set free, my body no longer out of bounds for him and he's making the most of it. All my inner voices and fears chased away by his kiss, the doubts and panic gone.

He bites, nips, licks, and kisses every exposed part of me, rips my underwear off under my dress and explores me with his hands, making me climax on the seat in a way I could never have imagined with his fingers exploring my point of ecstasy. He devours my mouth with his. I had never done anything like this, never imagined I could allow myself or trust a man enough to let one. It feels like heaven under his practiced hand, for once his experience not something which upsets me.

I never had the urge to do anything like this until Jake, he's insatiable and irresistible, from the second he had me locked in this dark box of a car, I had been his. His growing desire kept firmly locked away, he stills my hands telling me, "No … My turn first." He has a year's worth of fantasy about me to catch up on and he wants to take his time.

* * *

I can't walk from the car to his building, my legs are shaking from what he's done moments before, so he scoops me up with a look of a sexy devil and carries me to the inner building. Trussed up in his arms like a fragile prize as the doorman opens the door at our arrival and Jake looks down, winking at me naughtily. He looks like the cat that got the cream

"That was just the starter, *bambino.* I have weeks of pent-up sexual frustration to take out on you yet." His voice is heavy and laden with sexual intent, my insides clench, held fast in his arms. Melting under his scrutiny.

Oh god!

There is no going back now, I am hopelessly his and I want this more than anything.

In his apartment, he carries me to the living room and places me on my feet in the middle of the floor, leaving me standing and takes my stole and bag, tossing them on a nearby chair. His fingers trail across my naked shoulder and down my arm as he walks away, tingles igniting across me and my heart lurching up. He walks to his side unit and pushes his phone into the station dock and turns on slow music that fills the air soothingly.

"Are you trying to seduce me, Carrero?" I smile coyly, biting my lip and watching him move around the semi-dark room. He seems nervous, much like I am now we're here.

"I've learned, that when it comes to you, nothing is a certainty. I'm definitely seducing you." His eyes come and meet mine as he slowly walks back to me, lifting my face by cupping my jaw with his palms, he lowers his head and kisses me slowly and deliberately. A slight touch of his tongue across my bottom lip. I open my mouth and kiss him back, letting my arms slide up between his and around his neck. We move against each other firmly so every curve and line meet, his kiss deepening and sending a spiraling pit of longing through me.

His hands skim my ribs, my waist and then come around behind me, cupping my butt and he lifts me closer to his height, my feet lifting me from the ground, so I tip my heels up. I give a little squeak in response and pull away to look at him.

"This isn't your first rodeo, is it, cowboy?" I giggle as his hold tightens on me. Holding me high against him.

"First one that matters." He grins and moves to my throat, kissing and sucking. I feel myself go weak and close my eyes, sagging slightly as I let him devour me, my grip around his neck loosening as he slides me back to the floor. Each touch sending a thousand sensations through me, my body erupting and my stomach fluttering so much I feel my insides shaking.

My hands come up to the back of the bodice of my dress, fumbling with the catches that are concealed in the corset fastening, eager to be naked with him, but he stays my fingers, cupping them and pulling them away from the clips.

"We have all night, there's no rush." His eyes are heavy and hooded and despite slowing me down, I can see the lust in his dark green eyes. "I've waited for what seems like an eternity for this. I don't want to hurry it." He kisses me again slowly and then lets me go, takes my hand and pulls me toward the door of the bedroom.

"Where are we going?" I look at the bed longingly, after what he had done in the car I had been sure we would get in here and go crazy with passion. Jake seems to want to savor every second and delay the actual moment but I'm too hot for his body to be with mine; I want to be naked and writhing right now and put all the months of anguish behind us. I want that night in the hotel again, only this time with no doubts and internal voice trying to stop me from enjoying it.

Who the hell are you and what have you done with Emma?

"Patience, *bambino* … All good things come to those who wait." He pulls me into the sitting room to the larger clearing between the couches. Lifting a remote from the nearby table, he switches on a concealed stereo which plays the bedroom music across the room. Soothing soft music made for lovers. He pulls me into his embrace and starts dancing with me, slowly and tenderly stroking my arms and neck, his mouth gently pressing to every exposed part of me. He's keeping the tempo slow and seductive.

Feeling a tad frustrated, I lift my hands and wave two palms in his face.

"Stop! What's this?" I flick my hand up and down his torso as though gesturing him.

"What?" He looks amused, if not a bit confused.

"This slow and smooth, easy, lovey dovey, seduction? Jake from the hotel was more of the slam me to a wall and take me kind of a seducer. This feels too much like Casanova putting the moves on." I pout, frustration brimming.

"That Jake was a little sexually frustrated, this Jake is crazy in love and knows you're all his for an eternity." He moves in again to start kissing my neck.

"Nope, no … Nope!" I grab his hand and turn on my heel, yanking him with me toward the bedroom. When he doesn't follow I yank his wrist with a tug and hear him laugh. He's like unmovable stone and is just regarding me as one would a child.

"I didn't agonize for the last month to be made to wait now!" I huff and pull him harder. Trying to back into his room and tugging with all my might. He doesn't budge.

"Are you telling me you want me to throw you on the bed caveman style and screw you?" He's still holding his ground, hardly moved by my feeble tugs. Watching me with a look that just screams "you're so fucking adorable right now."

Ughhh.

"Yes!" I yell it at him in frustration. I don't want soft and gentle Jake, I want "fuck this shit" slam me to the wall Jake. The heat of how he was when he just needed to have me. I want that to seal this deal.

"You have no sense of romance, baby, something we need to remedy." He shakes his arm, testing how tightly I have a grip and sighs. "Fine … This time! Next time is my way!" He steps forward, bends down and flips me over his shoulder, smacking my ass hard, which gets an excited squeal from me, before striding into the dark bedroom and tossing me on the bed.

Yesssss!

I giggle as I bounce and watch him slide off his loose bow tie and then shirt. The beauty of that body on show at last, it's enough to make me drool. Heart elevates, and palms get sweaty, the inner nerves pushing to the forefront.

"Turn over." He commands, and I do as I'm told, I feel him kneel over me and his hands start undoing my dress. I feel my body sag a little at the release from the tight corset. "This dress is coming out to play again, next time we'll keep it on." He almost growls, his voice has turned raspy and deep. He sounds more like passionate Jake now and it excites me beyond belief. He catches my hips, pulling me down the bed until my feet slide to the floor and stands me up. When I do, the dress falls around my ankles so I'm left standing in lace panties and I feel the warmth of his naked torso against my back, his hands trailing down my exposed waist. I close my eyes and let my hands drop to my sides, exposing my naked breasts.

"These can stay on." He helps me step out of my dress,

his hand cupping my foot in my high stiletto shoe and he runs a finger up the back of my naked leg, causing me to shiver in anticipation. I feel him move away and see his trousers being thrown to the side of the room from the corner of my eye before he's back against my back.

"Are you nervous?" his soft voice brushes against my ear gently, sending a wave of tingles and electricity rushing around my body. Goosebumps prickling every inch of me.

"A little," I admit. It was partially the reason I had wanted it to be fast and passion driven, no room for nerves or shyness. Now we're standing, almost naked, and my anxiety levels are dwindling to be replaced with desire, the way Jake always makes me feel, calm, and safe.

"It's a first for me … being nervous I mean," he says softly, and I feel his breath against my neck, a soft kiss placed on the apex of my shoulder blades, his hands slide softly over my hips and he takes my panties down slowly to my ankles. I lift a foot at a time and let him remove them fully. Watching as he carefully maneuvers them over the shoes he wanted me to keep on. I say nothing, just glance down and catch his smile from his lowered pose before he slides back to standing.

"I know I said caveman style screwing … How about we just go with the flow instead." He kisses my neck gently, tracing the curve below my ear lobe softly. I can only nod, my voice caught in a groan as I relax into him, his hands come around, slowly turning me toward him. Despite having sex with him so long ago, he'd never seen me fully naked and I'm more than aware of it now as his eyes roam over me appreciatively. The look takes away my shyness and apprehension and I can see he wants me badly. It's written all over his face as his eyes slowly take me in, he makes me feel desirable and sexy. He's naked too, all hard angles and lines and black ink tattoos, making me weak at the knees.

He's the perfect male specimen and I can barely contain the longing tearing through me.

He leans down, lips to mine, not so softly now, the evidence of how turned on he is pressing against me. His tongue smooths against mine and he deepens the kiss, heat notching up a gear, I let my hands skim his muscular biceps, up to his carved shoulders and to his strong neck. I trail across the hard, even plain of chest and tangle in the slight scattering of hair there, feeding on the way he's moving to me and kissing me hard.

With a swift move, he scoops me up, so my legs are drawn around his waist and I'm holding on around his neck. He walks us forward, still his mouth on mine and I feel him go to his knees on the bed and shimmy us fully onto it. He drops me down onto the padded surface and grabs my ankles, a little tug to pull me down the bed and I'm catapulted onto my back. He's not slow in getting on top of me and nestling himself between my legs, nudging them open so we're connected fully.

"I love you." He looks me straight in the face, eyes pure green and heavy with longing. His face so smooth and relaxed.

"I love you." I bite my lip to stop the wobble of emotion coming over me. That ache deep inside, love fueled and ravaging. He kisses me softly then sucks my bottom lip a little harder, I can't help but close my eyes and groan against his mouth, igniting so many ripples of desire.

"Doesn't mean I'm not going to fuck your brains out though." He grins up at me and all softness is replaced with hard core lust, his hand cups me between the legs and slowly circles me. I gasp and arch back, his mouth coming to my exposed breast and sucking down on my nipple. I convulse in pleasure.

He moves his thumb to rest on my clitoris, small circular movements sending me wild as he goes back to kissing and sucking on my mouth and lips. I start squirming and clawing at his back with my nails, unable to stop the moans and groans from deep down inside of me. He expertly slides a finger within me, circling and teasing while kissing me into submission as my body reacts to him. It doesn't take long before I feel the waves building up inside, that same feeling of climbing again and I brace my hands on his chest, pushing him up, he stops and looks at me, wariness on his face.

"Not like this … I want you, I'm ready," I say it so breathlessly, but he understands, pulling his hand from between us, he leans to the bedside unit and pulls open the top drawer.

Moments later he's slid on the condom and is back on top of me, easing himself between my legs. He runs a gentle finger over my breast, up my throat and to my face, where I surprise myself by catching his hand in mine and pushing his finger into my mouth to suck. He groans and tenses over me, the tip of his hardness pressing against the opening of my softness, I feel him twitch in response to what I'm doing, and it empowers me. I ease my hips down and up and feel him push inside of me, stretching me and hitting that ache inside as he pushes in, he exhales slowly.

"This is so much better than I remember," he groans, coming down to press his lips to mine.

I arch up so he's filling me completely and claw at him as he slides back and forth, painfully slowly. He stops to look at me, savoring the sensation and I see the expression on his face go to pieces as he pushes again with a little more intent. He catches my hand and props it above my head, pinning it down, then he does the same with my other arm and brings them together. Holding me down this way and looking straight into my eyes, he begins moving inside me slowly, his lips parting, and his eyes glued to me as pleasure sweeps through us. I resist the urge to arch my head back and close my eyes, I want to look at him as the pleasure takes hold of me, I want to stay focused on those perfect green eyes and that perfect face. Imprint this moment to memory.

It's as though we're made for one another, I'm already panting and groaning as the waves of heat start tingling at my toes. The slow steady wash as it begins to move up through my legs, my body so in tune with his and so responsive, he seems to sense the approaching orgasm, he thrusts harder, letting my hands go kissing me, his tongue probing my mouth. He quickens the pace; his movements have more force behind them and I grip at the sheets beneath me. Each thrust has me gasping out, my legs tightening around his waist, my nails clawing up his back and tangling in his hair. I can feel his hot breath against my neck as the pressure of his hands push into the mattress, making it dip by my head. Harder, faster, bodies moving in unison, moans and groans entwined.

"Fuck … Emma … I'm not going to last … This is too good." He grunts into my neck and thrusts again; one hand grasps my hip, so he can increase the pressure of each movement. I feel the wave move up over my body, my tingling senses igniting as it hits me right in the core and I completely unravel around him, my body spasms and I cry out in sheer ecstasy.

"Oh, my god … Jake …" I moan out, losing all control as he thrusts twice more and falls hard on top of me with a groan, muttering my name huskily.

Chapter 8

I wake in the early morning light entangled in Jake's limbs and bed sheets, my body aching and heavy from everything he's done to me through the night. I can't help but smile at the memories, a warm blush traveling over my skin.

If I had thought Jake had a high sex drive when dating his string of floozies, I had severely underestimated him. Last night, he'd been addicted to my body, barely giving me time to recover. He'd been true to his promise and brought me to dizzying heights of pleasure more than once, his expertise and confidence in pleasuring me. There was not a single inch of my skin he had not kissed or licked or massaged softly and I had finally passed out from exhaustion, rather than his wavering libido. My brain too confuddled to function anymore. My Casanova was truly a master in the bedroom, with the confidence of a man who has no sexual inhibitions. I was literally glowing.

Old Emma has been reborn.

I manage to free myself from his arms and slide out without waking him, standing by the bed in all my nakedness to look at him for a moment. His beautiful body sprawled, possessing the bed in the way he'd possessed me over and over. My heart swells to almost bursting and I know I'm smiling like an idiot.

I love him more than words can ever express.

His perfect, dark hair messily ruffled, his dark lashes closed on flawless tanned skin and that designer stubble, sexily hot against crisp white sheets. He looks like the cover of an erotica book, naked torso and tattooed shoulders, carved in perfection.

How did I ever manage to get him? To win his heart? I must be dreaming.

My head is still reeling over the fact that I'm here, that I'm with him. I'm in his apartment after sharing his bed all night and that he told me so many times already that he loves me.

Jake Carrero loves me … Emma Anderson, a nobody PA from a nothing existence. Jake Carrero … Infamous playboy heartbreaker, actually fell in love.

Ti amo.

Maybe I should learn Italian, just to understand the many pet names he bestowed on me now, I might understand just what he's calling me.

I go to the bathroom to shower, so that I'll look fresh when he wakes up. The downside to a specimen like him is it makes me feel a little like an ugly duckling in comparison, especially when last night's make-up was first cried off and then sweat all over me through vigorous pursuits. I'm sure my hair has seen better days and the fright awaiting me in the mirror is so not worthy of someone like Jake. I'm tired and I should be asleep, but my body is hyper actively awake. Still tingling from his touch, his mouth, and his love making.

I stand under the water, my head tilted up to the jets, so it blocks everything out. Noise, thought, bodily aches and just revel in the heat and pounding massage it gives me. For the first time in my life my thoughts are completely blank, there's nothing. No doubts, no niggles, and insecurities, no memories or anything of the sort. I just feel at peace. Peaceful and something else, a small lifted weightlessness deep inside of me I can only describe as contentment.

Who is this new person?

I feel the small draft behind me of the shower door opening, a grin spreading across my face immediately. I know his presence, I could feel him feet away without even trying. His hands come around me, his hard, chiseled body against my back as he joins me under the huge water jet, his mouth instantly on my neck and teasing me gently.

"Hey there, beautiful. Mind if I join you?" He sounds hoarse and tired.

"Bit late for asking, don't you think?" I wiggle my butt into his groan and feel him respond with vengeance, a hardening I cannot ignore. Despite the amount of times he's had me already, I feel myself respond, my insides clenching with desire. A heat rises within and I turn in his arms to capture his mouth, feeling brave, letting my hands run over him then push him back hard against the tiles and launch myself at him. He seems momentarily shocked then grins, his pupils dilating almost instantly. He picks me up under the thighs, so my body wraps around him, every naked inch to every naked inch, walks me forward so my back is against freezing tiles and water is pouring over both of us.

"Better hold on, *mio amore*." He sounds low and gruff. "This is going to be memorable." His eyes heavy with longing, I bite his lip and suck it in response and lose myself in his low groan.

* * *

We're laid out on his bed once more, loosely held in his arm as we both stare at the ceiling. For the first time in my life, I feel calm and truly happy. We're saying nothing, just laying side by side, his hand twirling a strand of my hair and gazing up, finally sated and it feels like perfection. It only took half a dozen times, in as many hours, to stop him wanting to have sex every moment we had stilled to catch our breath. My body is tingling in ways I never knew it could, embarrassment at being naked with him is gone, just sheer euphoria and exhaustion in its place. Months of pent-up frustration finally being realized and now here we are, comfortably silent and entwined.

We hear Nora in the kitchen making us lunch, it's late morning and the sounds of her clanging pots and the low mumble of the television she has on somehow sounds homely. The blinds are shut, the room still dim but everything feels right, like I'm finally home. Like I waited my whole life to find myself exactly here in this time and place with him.

"I can't imagine anywhere else I would rather be right now," he says softly, as though reading my mind, his eyes coming to rest on my profile.

"Not missing your big-busted, casual sex then?" I tease, grinning like a Cheshire cat. He watches me, a smile moving across his mouth as he shakes his head.

"Not one of them compares to you in any way, Emma …they never did, *amante*. Besides these are pretty big if you ask me." He cups my breast, leans forward so our noses touch with a wicked gleam in his eye and brushes them together softly. I giggle and slap his hand softly.

"You're my everything," he says with serious intensity.

"No, Jake, you're mine," I answer tenderly, my eyes filling with moisture at just how romantic my Casanova can be, he knows exactly what to say to me. That tugging ache going off inside of me again which I was starting to recognize as love.

"Do you want to come somewhere with me today?" he asks, his eyes still locked on mine, unmoving. Our bodies linked at the legs and torso. Arms casually intertwined.

"An adventure? With you? How could I resist?" I smile, the longing to wrap myself around him again already rising in me, he leans in and kisses me on the mouth. Gently yet seductively enough to fill me with heat again.

I'll never tire of this, never tire of his need to feel my lips on his, it's as though they were made to fit mine perfectly.

"I need to be with you. All of this seems like a dream … I'm scared I'll wake up … I just want to take you out, away from here, away from a bed." His eyes glint sexily. "I want to feel like we're actually real … Not just sex."

"You want to spend a day not having sex? Are you ill?" I laugh in disbelief, feeling his forehead for a temperature check. He slides a hand down under the sheets and cups me at the apex of my thighs to prove he's not sick. Then pulls away with a dirty look and a smirk.

How he could even have anything left after the last few hours performance was beyond me.

He looks shy and awkward suddenly, not a Jake trait at all. The humor dropping away.

"I know it sounds stupid … But this whole *serious* thing … It's a long-forgotten memory, I need some practice at having a girlfriend. I'm worried I may just keep you naked in my bed indefinitely, *bambino*." He grins again, coming to lay on top of me, his weight pressing me into the bed and he's gently kissing me again, his fingers playing in my hair. "I've never really had to evaluate what a real relationship was like, I have no idea what I'm doing." He leans his chin on my chest and looks up at me adoringly. A face that could melt the most frozen of hearts.

"I never imagined you could be so cute. This is all new for me too, I was eighteen when I last had a boyfriend and I never exactly had a steady or normal relationship." I smile up at him.

"Uh-uh." He covers my mouth with his palm. "You were an untouched virgin who's never had a single boyfriend in her life, lived like a nun." He moves over me so he's hovering above my head. "I was your first everything and will be your last everything, too." The wicked look in his eyes doesn't fully cover that tiny hint of seriousness. I pull his hand off my mouth.

"So, it's okay for you to have been a man-whore, but I'm a pure untouched maiden?" I laugh at him.

"I was a virgin too; all those girls were just all smoke and mirrors. I was keeping myself for you." He grins and nuzzles my neck.

"Of course, they were, I totally believe you." I shift under him so I can slide my legs open and move them around his waist a little more easily, he settles on his elbows, coming down to watch my face.

"Completely true story. Scouts honor." His face turns serious and he frowns at me a little. "It's just us, the past doesn't matter, it never existed before this moment." He sighs, eyes focused on mine. The hint of a little frown showing just how serious he is in this moment.

"Nope … You can erase the past if you like, but not from this point, reverse to last night on the dance floor and anything before then can get the giant push. I'm keeping that memory forever." I slide my arms around his neck, so I can pull him closer, the warmth of his breath fluttering across my naked cleavage.

"Actually, I think I may want to keep the hotel floor memory. It maybe wasn't our happy start, but it was something I never want to forget." He nudges my nose with his as though asking if I agree.

"Fine. If we're picking and choosing memories, then I'm keeping the boat kiss." I lower my brows to show I mean business.

"Yeah, I want to keep that too, just not everything in between that and the hotel fuck." He quirks an eyebrow and there's a cheeky glint in his eye.

"Please do not refer to what we do as that." I roll my eyes, sighing.

"As what? Fucking? Why not?" He laughs at me.

"Because it's a vulgar word and makes this sound so … So. Sordid!"

"I like fucking you." He sucks a small area of neck and I feel my toes curl in response.

"Ruining the moment." I mutter.

"Making love? Having sex … What about screwing?" he murmurs while distracting me.

"Hmmm, yes, yes and no. Equally crass." I close my eyes at the feel of his mouth running down my neck, igniting tingles and shivers through every part of me.

"Jesus, Emma, there has to be some sordidness to our … Making love." He sits up and looks me in the eye.

"See, there you go. Such a good boyfriend." I smile up at him, patting him on the head like a puppy and he shimmies his groin into me suggestively.

"Easy to train, great! I feel so proud. Can we now go back to my previous subject? You know, now that's all cleared up." He slides his hands around my wrists and pulls my arms over my head to pin them down gently.

"You want to take me on a date?" I reply with two raised eyebrows.

"No … Dates are all I've done for years, empty pointless things. I want to take you out. Something meaningful, I don't want to call it a date, that seems so far removed from how I feel, from what I think we have." He's behaving so unsurely, like a nervous teen again, it only makes him more appealing.

Who knew he had this side to him?

"So where to?" I ask coquettishly, fluttering my lashes. He makes me feel sexy and playful and I like this latest version of me. His eyes fix on my face, lust moving back in. He seems transfixed on my mouth once more, automatically parting my lips at his focus, my breathing becoming shallow at his expression of pure desire.

Oh boy, is sex all we think about?

"I was thinking." He clears his throat and pulls his gaze away from my mouth with a long pause "… The Caribbean … A yacht for some unfinished business." He looks away, he obviously wants to get to the point without another sexual interlude.

"In a day?" I laugh in disbelief.

"Okay, so maybe for a week, or three …" He grins back at me, his eyes so clear and alluring, sparkling green. "I need to undo the memory of the last time we were there." He kisses me tenderly again, my body heating under his expert mouth. His body shifts to fully pin me down and he brings his groin to mine snugly.

"I thought you just erased the past?" I smile up and wiggle my hips.

"Okay, so maybe I just want to take my very serious girlfriend on holiday. Romantic time out … I like saying that … Girlfriend." He sounds it out slowly and breaks into an adorable grin, I'm rewarded with a firm kiss planted on the mouth.

Jake seriously likes kissing.

"Don't you actually work anymore, Mr. Carrero?" I give him the innocent coy look that I'm getting good at. Amused by him, so in love with him.

"Not much since I stupidly sent my PA away, I've been worse than useless at my job … She's going to freak when I get her back in my office and she sees the chaos she's left in her wake."

"Is she now?" I grin at his admittance. "What about your stand in? Was she no good?" I ask innocently, knowing fine well my mentor Margo has been back at his side while he was searching for a replacement. Jake seems intent on twirling a strand of my hair now, softly tugging it across the pillow and flattening it out, fiddling. A tell-tale Carrero trait when he is uneasy in a topic of conversation, he fidgets like he needs a distraction.

"I think she probably hates me now, I've been a nightmare of a boss … She threatened to throw me from the sixty-fifth floor window more than once. Told me to get my head out of my ass and get you back." He grins again, only this time I see that hint in his eye that he's only half joking. Another gentle kiss on my mouth.

I like kissing too.

"You were always a nightmare of a boss, grumpy ass, and very trying on my nerves … …You really missed me that much?" I wiggle an arm free and prod him in the shoulder with a finger.

"You've no idea, *bambino,* I felt like I'd severed my own limbs…" He sighs. "When I saw you in the lift that first time back in my building, it was the worst agony I've ever felt … I wanted to say so much to you." He presses his forehead to mine, our eyes meeting. Our conversation taking another serious turn.

"All you said was my name, you barely looked my way." I remember sadly.

"I couldn't formulate the words, I definitely couldn't look at you. I felt like I was back in high school, nervous as hell, dying to just push you against that wall and kiss you until you surrendered to me. I could smell your perfume from the second I walked in, I could feel you in there without looking at you … I couldn't deny how much I was missing you, how good you looked, and it felt like shit."

Tears catch in my throat, I had felt the same way. I lean up and kiss him, letting my fingers trail across the perfect brows and down that sexy stubbled cheek.

"It felt that way for me too." I breathe.

"I still didn't know how you really felt, it was the only thing holding me back … Kept telling myself I never had a chance with you. When I heard Rosalie tell Margo you were going to Europe, I thought I might actually explode. I couldn't just let you go." He looks tortured, lost in the memory.

"Jake, it was always you," I whisper softly. "I was scared of how you felt, but I wanted you so much." Being open with him was proving so much easier than I had ever anticipated. The barriers between us finally gone, from the second he told me he loved me I had let go. I had let myself fall completely into his trust.

"I didn't see it, *miele.* So many times I got close and your wall slammed back up. I figured you didn't feel the way I did. That I was pushing you and you had no choice. The night we had sex I felt so confused after … I felt like you hadn't even consented. I tried to think it through a million times, trying to remember if I had just railroaded you into it." He frowns, his eyes darkening with emotion.

"I had wanted nothing else for so long." I choke back

tears. "I was so scared I would just be another conquest … A good time … That I'd lose you, my job, our friendship … I was terrified."

He leans up, brushing hair away from my face, tracing my mouth with his fingers.

"I wish I'd told you so many times how I really felt, I wish I had just come out and said *I love you, Emma*. I'm in love with you." His voice is raw with emotion, my heart swells painfully. "If I had, we could have avoided so much heartache. So much craziness between us." His eyes hold so much emotion.

Jake really loves me. As much as I love him.

Every time this realization hits me it takes my breath away, I want to pinch myself in case it's a dream.

"I was going to tell you the morning you sent me away." I smile, a tear pooling in my eye. He frowns and lifts his head so he can use his fingers to smooth it away as it trails down my cheek.

"Don't tell me that … It makes me feel like shit knowing that." He looks down at my throat and sighs heavily "Really?" His eyes flickering back up full of question.

"Yes, really. The whole time you were telling me that I had to go, I was fighting with myself to say it to you. But when you looked at me, you were so cold I knew I couldn't. You didn't want me." Tears fall freely down my cheeks, he groans and presses his mouth to mine, kissing me thoroughly, removing the pain of the memory in one fell swoop before moving back to look at me again, his face fierce with raw emotion

"Emma, *miele* … I was dying inside … I thought it was always going to be me on one side wanting you and you on the other trying to keep me away. I did what I thought was best, so I could function and move on. I wanted you more than air. I needed you. I need you!" He kisses me again, trying to push away the sadness on my face. My face his for the kissing, soft pecks to wipe away my tears.

"Why did you send me the song on the dance floor … After everything?" I break in, I feel inquisitive, we've never really talked openly about our feelings this way. We've always skirted the issues, never communicated and I want it all now, I want every detail. I want to devour all the knowledge I can, to understand. Bask in his confessions, hear him talk about things I always believed to be different, that had kept us apart. I want to know what changed.

"The way you looked at me … I know you … I saw the same broken heart I'd seen in the mirror for weeks, that agony of wanting someone and thinking they've rejected you. For a fleeting second, I saw it, I knew I had to ask you, but I had no words, I was scared to ask. When I watched you walk away I thought about our songs. Our last songs to each other and the song you had sent. I'd dismissed it as missing my friendship at the time."

"You listened to it right there?" I giggle, but he shakes his head.

"I realized I couldn't, because you were leaving, I panicked, I needed to stop you going. I'd heard that song a million times on the radio that week, every time thinking of you … Figured what better way to ask how you felt. Take a chance even if you rejected me." His mouth brushes mine again softly, achingly seductive.

"I'm glad you did," I whisper as his kiss deepens and I feel my body beginning to unfurl. He pulls away, brushing his mouth against mine once more, so delicately it tickles, making me smile. This, between us, it all feels so natural, so right. Like we were always meant to be this way.

"Not as glad as I am … I practically ran after you when

you replied. Okay, maybe I did kinda run. Felt like all my Christmases had come at once. I think I must have shoved at least five important clients out of the way," he mutters against my mouth, both of us breaking into bigger smiles, our breaths so close and erotic. "You're mine now … All of you … I get to touch and kiss you, any which way I want. No restrictions. No holding myself back. Anytime I want … It feels like heaven." He kisses me on the nose this time, cooling the heat between us a little. He's trying not to escalate things sexually and I feel a tad disappointed, but I know he wants more, more than sex, more than a casual fling. He wants forever.

"We don't need to go away to have some romantic time, Jake." I nestle in his arms, moving to get comfy.

"Not this argument again, what is it with you and refusing my offers of holidays in the Caribbean?" He pins me down, an evil look flitting across his face. "Don't make me torture you into a yes."

"It's only torture if I don't like it," I reply cheekily and push my mouth into his. If he isn't going to ignite this passion then I sure will, I slide my hands around his neck bringing his mouth hard against mine, deepening the kiss and bravely pushing my tongue against his. He groans and surrenders, his body instantly molding to mine fully and I know he's done for.

Chapter 9

He buckles me into the passenger seat of his car, leaning in to kiss me passionately once more, his green eyes alive and twinkling. Jake can't seem to stop kissing me and it's not like I can complain, after a year of being crazy for him, I don't want him to stop. I've not seen him this happy and carefree for a long time, since before the first time he ever kissed me.

Had I really been torturing him all that time?

My heart lurches at the thought. He closes my door and comes around to slide into his sleek powerful car in an effortlessly graceful maneuver.

"Your place for a change of clothing, I guess." He runs his fingers down the thigh of my satin dress, his pupils dilating. "I forgot to tell you how amazing you look in this by the way. I practically passed out when I saw you."

"You're so easy." I giggle watching his lips part, he raises his eyebrow and winks at me

"Can't help it, *bambino* ... You're sex on legs, and this dress only emphasized that fact." He throws me his killer smile and starts the car. "Maybe we'll get a replay of making out on the bonnet sometime soon." He tilts his head toward me with a raised eyebrow and I shake mine in response with an added eye roll, a smile breaking across my face.

Is this real? Is this really happening?

We've been together all morning, showered for a second time and managed to get clean that time, ate pancakes and bacon in bed and teased each other mercilessly. It's so easy and natural, it feels like we've always been this way, devoid of awkwardness. All heartache forgotten, all the tension, fights, and stupid behavior. All of it had faded away as though we were never just boss and PA, or even just friends.

It was well after noon and we were only now getting out of his building.

"We can't just hop on a jet to the Caribbean." I point out, he hasn't dropped this subject yet.

"I'm pretty sure we can. I own a plane and a boat and the company who employs you." He pulls into traffic, the hum of his powerful car sending excitement through me, something about this car gives me thrills. I guess because it's so *him* … Powerful, sexy, expensive … A thrill of a ride in that almost trademark black. I feel myself blush.

"I hope whatever's making you blush is something I've done in the past twelve hours, *miele*?" His hand comes to my thigh and he squeezes gently, his focus going quickly back to the road.

"It's the past twelve hours I'm blushing about." I smile back, our eyes lock longingly, I'm overwhelmed by the strength in the electricity between us.

Will it always be this way? Is it like this for everyone?

"It will only get better, *bella.* Once I get to know what really turns you on … Just you wait and see." I don't respond, just feel the heat ride up from my thighs into my face, and I'm biting my lip as the inner desires overtake me. I don't think it's possible for him to improve on anything he's done to me in the last few hours.

"I love you, Jake." It comes from somewhere inside of me, so impulsively it even surprises me. He turns to focus on me, his face happy, and his hand comes to stroke my cheek delicately.

"I'll never tire of hearing that from you … *Ti amo, bellezza.*"

I love you, beautiful.

I was beginning to understand some of the things he said to me but too many times I had asked the question—*What?*

I love that Jake litters his affectionate terms with Italian words and he sometimes slips into fluent Italian sporadically, it's sexy as hell, even if most of the time I can only guess at what the meaning is.

"We're still not going to the Caribbean." I smile stubbornly, "We both have jobs, and I'm sure my new boss won't be happy about my sudden sabbatical." I try for stern, PA Emma tone.

"I'm your new boss … Wilma will have no say." I see that flicker of dominance shining through but for once it doesn't annoy me, it excites me. We always did play the power game with one another, even when we got on well.

Does Jake really want me back as his PA? How in the hell will that work?

"Do you think that's wise? Me coming back?" I watch him maneuver the car confidently, my knees pressing together in anticipation of having those hands back on my skin.

"Do you think I would leave you down on Wilma's floor and hire some other woman to fly around the world with me to share cozy hotel rooms now?" He flashes a knowing smile at me and I feel jealousy twinge. He's right! I wouldn't like that at all and I know Margo is only his temp stand in. He could hire anyone and have them by his side the way I had been. Someone small and blonde and sexy who wore tight ass skirts and stilettos while bending over her desk.

No, I do not like that at all.

"You wouldn't find anyone as tolerant as me," I mutter darkly, contemplating some other woman sharing his room. He grins, knowing his hint has worked.

"I wouldn't want any other woman, Emma … Not anymore … Not ever again, my little green-eyed seductress." The seriousness in his tone sends a thousand butterflies through me and he pinches my cheek playfully. I never, ever, imagined I would hear words like those coming from Casanova Carrero's mouth, let alone his willingness to be with one woman in a real relationship.

I guess hell could freeze over after all.

"You don't think being together twenty-four seven will affect things?" I ask.

"I was with you practically twenty-four seven before, and I felt like it wasn't enough, Emma … I wanted you around all the time, I wanted you in my bed. Look, *miele,* we can try this and if it starts affecting our relationship we'll sort something else out." He looks at me again, I can see that he's deadly serious and it kills further questioning, he's right. I need to stop over thinking everything, all the time.

We don't know until we try and coming back to work with him is more than I could ever ask for. I loved working with him every day, organizing his life. I missed all of it so badly.

Somehow, knowing there would be no more leggy dates and separate bedrooms made it seem all the more exciting.

I inhale deeply and grin at him widely, the urge to dive on him and kiss his mouth to death over takes me but I steel it back inside. I guess this is what being in love is meant to feel like, a huge wave of euphoria and a severe lack of hormonal control.

"I'm still saying no to the Caribbean." I beam at him, I at least need to pretend I have some say over things nowadays.

"We'll see." He's still watching the road, quick glances at his mirrors. It's his "I know I've made up my mind tone and I just need to make you see sense or bully you into it". I sigh and wonder what I've let myself in for.

I mean, really! … I know him better than most, he can be stubborn and overbearing, dominant, and sometimes terrifying. But he can also be protective, attentive, gentle, and so very sweet.

"We shall." I challenge masterfully. He narrows his brows and looks at me in a way I've never seen before, a cross between determination and lust.

"I've new ways in which to bend your will to mine, *neonata* … New ways to torture you now that sexy body is no longer out of bounds … I wouldn't test my limits." He grins wickedly, and I see the veiled threat, catching my breath.

Well, this is new for us. I've never had the sexually competent Carrero make erotic promises of punishment and torture and actually mean it.

I feel my pulse quicken and I squirm in my seat, he's no idea how he can turn me on with a look. Or that his threat is more of a lure to behave badly.

"You don't intimidate me, Carrero … Bring it on," I whisper seductively. Turning with a satisfied lick of my lips followed with a bite of my lower one, I smooth my hands up my thighs in a bid to get a reaction, only it's more extreme than I anticipate. He literally swerves into the side of the road, slams the brakes on, unclips my belt, and hauls me into his lap in a quick, effortless move, crushing our mouths together. I'm forced into the smallest space ever, a window at my back and a steering wheel in the ribs, but his hands all over me are drowning out the discomfort, my mind reels at his assault.

I'm putty in his hands. He's showing me that with a kiss he owns me and it's working. I've melted to a gooey puddle in his lap, he could literally strip me naked right now on the sidewalk and I wouldn't argue. He's uncovered my weakness for him in one night and he fully intends to utilize it. Jake has always had skills in manipulation, so this doesn't surprise me in the slightest. He pulls his mouth from mine, keeping his hand around my jaw, holding us nose to nose

"We're going away for some time alone … We need it … I need this." His voice is thick and husky, he kisses me again before I can answer, pulling me back down into erotica, his tongue caressing mine until I feel like the longing will make me self-implode. His hand moves up under my dress finding what he's searching for, pulling my underwear aside and connects. I arch on his lap, gasping in pleasure, his mouth still on mine as I squirm.

"Say yes, *bambino.*" He breathes into my mouth, pushing his fingers inside me slowly, his thumb circling at the front. I wriggle and claw at his shoulders, the sensation overwhelming me. Every part of my already sensitive womanhood is throbbing with pleasure. His fingertips gently circling and teasing until I'm almost panting, almost begging. He withdraws, leaving me wanting and aching. "Say yes." He breathes again. The sensation is too extreme and too intense to fight, and I want more of it. I grasp his arm and try to force his hand back to its previous position, bite his lower lip in a bid to make him take me but he stays still, his eyes dark with lust.

"This isn't fair," I moan and grind into his lap trying to take control from him, but he only smiles. He's far better at this game than I'll ever be. I can feel his desire beneath me but he's still as a statue, amusement on his face. He likes this version of Emma.

"One little word, *miele,* and I'll do whatever you want, I'll screw you right here in the car." He smirks.

Only Jake could make that the most appealing sentence in the world.

I give in, saying, "Yes," loudly as I wrap my arms around his neck, falling into a passionate kiss, my inner self squealing out in ecstasy as his hand moves back inside me, and his other hand pulls down my bodice. I don't even care that he's just manipulated me without effort, most likely starting a pattern for things to come now that he knows he can.

* * *

I try to right my dress when I'm back in my own seat, pulling its skirt back down my body awkwardly, my face feels hot and I'm sure I must be several shades of pink and red, my skin is glowing.

Despite the tight confines of the car and invasive controls around us, Jake somehow managed to make good and made love to me in his car. Facing me forward to the front windscreen, sat in his lap with his arms around me, glad of the heavily tinted windows. It had been awkward but hot and I had ended up sprawled over his steering wheel gasping in the afterglow. I only then became self-conscious about our surroundings, feeling relief when I saw he'd put us in an empty alley, shaded by tall buildings on either side. He'd known he was going to have sex with me as soon as he turned the car. The appearance of the condom had been a huge hint, the cheeky wink and grin confirmed he'd pre-planned my surrender to his way of thinking. I had no chance with him as a lover … I would never have any say in this life ever again.

"So … Guess we'll be going to yours to pack a case then, right?" He grins at me, leaning over to clip my seat belt back on, always obsessed with taking care of me as though I am incapable. He looks completely unaffected by what we've just done, even his hair is still in place. I shake my head at him

"Is this what life is going to be like? You decide something then use your "sexpertize" to make me agree?" I watch him, trying to look unamused, but I can't stop smiling.

"Like you thought it would be any different?" He grins back, righting himself in his seat and pulling his belt on. "Now make sure there's a lot of bikinis … We'll be solo this time, I doubt you'll need any actual clothes." He winks and for some reason I know he means it … bikinis or naked, I can be sure that's how I'll end up if the last thirty minutes are anything to go by.

"Maybe I'll have a three-week headache, darling …" I say haughtily, trying to keep the humor from my face. He has us back in traffic, moving on, his face animated.

"*bambino*, best way to get rid of a headache is to have your hot Italian boyfriend sweat it out of you in various energetic positions." He throws me a serious look with a raised brow.

Arrogant sod! His ego is big enough for the both of us.

Who am I kidding? It's one of the things that make him who he is, his confidence and directness and he knows it. Damn you, Carrero!

* * *

Sarah is home when we get to the apartment, she looks frantic and I feel instantly guilty. My phone had died late last night, and I had been so absorbed in being with Jake I hadn't even thought. She looks us over in surprise then grins knowingly. I guess I still have that flushed, "just been screwed," look and with Jake's arm around my waist possessively, it pretty much tells her all she needs to know.

"Emma? Thank god! Well, I can call off the search party!" She grabs me in a hug and points a finger at Jake.

"You better be treating her right this time. Stopping all this nonsense and bullshit evasive behavior." She waggles it at him, bringing her tiny frame to his in a very aggressive manner. Jake raises his palms and tries not to smile.

"Like she's my queen … She was a little too busy to think about phoning home, Mom." He darts out of the way of her playful slap and she turns to me instead.

"I was worried about you. Next time a text to say … Oh I don't know … *My boss stopped being a schmuck and finally hooked up with me.*" I smooth back her stray hairs and try to fix her baggy shirt. She's obviously been in her nightshirt all day and pacing erratically. The old relationship we had would have never seen her worrying about my absence this way, it's a little cute.

"I'm sorry, I really didn't think you would even notice. I won't do that again … Promise." I hold up my brownie oath, despite never being one and try for a smile. She glares then shakes her head and resigns to a smile.

"Marcus said you would probably be away trying out some guy's bed springs—" She snorts.

"Hey! … Less of the *some guy*. Jake cuts in, a frown creasing his brow as he moves to lasso an arm around my neck and pulls me close, linking his hands in front of me. "There's only one guy Emma will ever test bed springs with and that's yours truly. She's a lady, a one guy kind of girl." He frowns, a little grumpily.

"Marcus is an idiot." I retort and look around for signs of him but find none. He's obviously at work.

"What about you, Carrero?" Sarah narrows her eyes and hunches forward to scrutinize Jake's face. "Are you a one girl kinda guy now?" she asks almost menacingly, I stifle the urge to laugh at her protective mother hen routine.

"Scouts honor." He holds up fingers in an attempt to

make a scout's oath and fails. He was obviously never a scout. We share something else, a severe inability to get an oath right. He leans out to tweak her in the face and gets his handed batted away.

"I swear you better treat her like a queen. She doesn't tolerate side chicks or any of that nonsense you hear? You hurt her, and I'll cut off your family jewels. I'm a chef! Trust me I have big sharp knives and a lot of skill." Sarah looks convincingly scary, so much that even I look at her in alarm.

Where the heck has this little psycho been hiding?

"Look, tiny scary person, I love her. I told her so many times and I'm telling you. No side chicks, I'll definitely be looking after her from here on in. You can stow the knives elsewhere, possibly in the back of the next guy who insinuates my girl has been sleeping around." Jake flashes her one of his Hollywood smiles and kisses me on the top of the head. Sarah seems satisfied, her manic expression drops and is replaced by a welcoming smile. I sigh with relief and pull myself out of Jake's arms.

"I'm going to get out of this dress and pack." I lift the skirt from the floor, so I don't trip and start heading to my room. Jake goes to follow me, but Sarah's raised eyebrow and come-hither look stops him. She obviously hasn't done talking to him yet. I throw him a supportive smile and gesture for him to stay, he looks like he might refuse, and I don't blame him. Sarah has the air of Gestapo and interrogation swarming from her in droves. I can also tell in a look he wants to come with me and continue what happened in the car.

I need to get my stamina up living with him, I'll never get through a week at this rate. He's insatiable; I may not be the most experienced woman on the planet but even I know his hunger for sex isn't normal, or the ability to go at it as much.

I wonder if this is his Italian blood or just Jake blood that makes him a sex addict with a stamina second to none. I can't really complain, since knowing he loves me I have become just as insatiable and it still shocks me. I never knew I had it in me or that it was even possible to even try to have it in me.

* * *

I finally finish packing up my case, my phone on charge in its dock by my bed. I take my time, breathing space from Jake so I can think. He's like a tornado that devours everything in its wake when he's with you and sometimes I just need some time to process things more slowly.

I'm wearing jeans and a T-shirt, which skim my figure, Converse on my feet and a denim jacket, this is probably the most casual he's ever have seen me other than my gym attire, but for some reason, I like being this way around him. So far removed from the Emma he met a year ago, she didn't even own jeans at all, he had to see how much he'd changed me. I wanted him to see how different I wanted to be with him.

My hair alone is a huge deal, changed from long, sleek, and always tied back immaculately, to short and wild waves hanging just under my jaw, with blonde highlights which make me look young and carefree. I catch sight of myself in the mirror, free of make-up. He'd seen me this way before, in hotels early morning, late at night, but I look different. My skin rosy, my eyes softer blue, my lips stained pink from being kissed endlessly. I look happy and almost beautiful. Even for me to see, it's amazing.

Love really changed you.

I pick up my phone, now it's charged, and call Wilma Munro.

"Emma, darling … I didn't expect to hear from you today." She sounds overjoyed to hear me, it makes my heart sink, I really do like this woman. I'll miss working beside her even though it's only been a couple of weeks.

"Wilma … Hey …" I sound as awkward as I feel. "I need to tell you something." I hesitate.

"I already know … I'm really happy for you, honestly. The sixty-fifth is getting a great asset back." She beams down the phone.

"How?" I'm confused.

"Oh, honey, you and Jake are the talk of the building. Apparently, his storming over and kissing you passionately in front of a few hundred people will do that … Besides, he called me about twenty minutes ago." I can almost hear her smiling.

"He did?" I'm beyond speechless. I don't even want to start contemplating the public display we put on and what gossip will be doing the rounds about it right now.

Why do these things always shock me? I know him … I should have known this. Eternal domineering boss mode.

"Yes, he told me that you're being rehired as his PA effective as of this morning and you'll come see me when you get back from a little trip." She sounds positively ecstatic, despite losing an employee.

"Right," I say floundering, heat in my face. I'm kind of lost for words.

I really need to get my man to stop doing this crap to me

"Okay, I guess I'll see you on my return … Right?" I say softly, there's so much more I want to say, she deserved more after listening to my woes and being my shoulder to cry on. I wanted to say more but I was dumbfounded.

"Just tell me, Emma … Did he tell you he loved you yet?" she asks cheekily. I feel myself blush and smile despite myself.

"Endlessly." I laugh, and she joins me.

"Good, thought he might. Was pretty obvious by the way he stormed into my office a couple days ago, demanding to know where you were. Just remember my invite to the wedding." She laughs again. "I better go, dear, I've some irate man in a suit glaring at me."

We say our goodbyes and she hangs up. I don't know whether to laugh, cry, or be angry at Jake, either way, I am relieved that Wilma isn't upset about my departure.

My door opens and Jake strolls in, as though it's the most natural things in the world. All anger dissipates when I see him, his jeans, white T-shirt sculpted to his body and leather jacket make me weak. Effortlessly Hollywood. I bite my lip as I try not to fall into a daydream about the things he does to me.

"Ready? You've been an age, baby." His perfect smile flashes my way, spying the case, he moves forward to pick it up, checks for my passport and iPad inside. I stand watching him, bemused. He walks over to my bedside table and lifts a couple of books I'm in the process of reading and slides them into my case along with my phone which is now on the bed.

"Need any help there?" I ask with a laugh.

Pretty sure he could have packed my clothes too at this rate.

"Toiletries?" He raises an eyebrow, ignoring my sarcasm, I steadily watch him feeling the overwhelming desire to sigh at him. Nothing he does should surprise me.

"In the case," I say blandly.

"Sexy lingerie? You know that corset thing I spied way back when I helped you clear out your clothes?" He looks me up and down. I guess it's been on his mind since then, that thought pleases me, the fact he still remembers, and I've never actually worn it.

"In the drawer." I point at the dresser and go to move

past him, but I halt as he yanks it open, empties the contents into my case.

"What are you doing?" I ask, laughing at him.

"I think, as your boyfriend, I should know every piece of your underwear intimately … For future gift buying." He smirks and closes the case, pushing it closed to conceal the bulge. "You can model it for me when we get to the boat … I think I should get a job as your un-dresser."

I sigh this time.

What the hell am I going to do with him? I don't think I'll be getting much of a tan on this yacht break. I'm starting to think keeping me in a bed as a sex slave has been his plan all along. And he said he wanted to take me away so our relationship would be more than sex! I'm starting to wonder if he's capable of that at all.

He stops by my oversized bear and frowns at him.

"You won me him in Las Vegas. He's called Joey." I remind him, following his death glare.

"You've been sharing your bed with this fella?" he asks seriously. I can't see any humor in his eye but he's obviously not being serious.

"I have." I smile demurely. He picks the bear up by the throat rather aggressively.

"By the time we come back, buddy, I want to find that you've moved back into the wardrobe or there'll be hell to pay … I share her bed now … I'm the only guy she'll be cuddling up with." He grins at me and throws the bear across the room at my door in grand fashion and I watch as it slumps ungracefully into an unloved heap.

"Poor teddy, he never did anything wrong … A perfect gentleman every night." I pout. "I never took you for the jealous type." I poke at him, he drops my bags, grabs my hand and pulls me into his embrace.

"I'm not the jealous type … I wasn't … But with you …

… Maybe." He kisses me, my body melting to his.

"Just don't turn cray-cray on my ass … I don't mind jealous as long as you don't take a lighter to my teddy bear." I smile. His face turns serious momentarily, leaning back to look at me.

"Don't put ideas in my head." He catches me with a swift kiss then turns me in a twirl and pats my butt to get me moving.

"You don't need any encouragement." I flutter my lashes back at him. Catching my face in his hands, he squeezes my cheeks slightly so my lips pucker up.

"You're just so freaking cute. I could eat this face." He leans in, nibbles my lip, then kisses me on the nose amid my giggles and protests.

Sarah meets me in the hall and gives me a huge cuddle, she adorns me with all her departing advice, obviously brought up to speed by Jake about our little holiday. Be safe, don't drink too much, don't sleep in the sun, send her updates. I smile and kiss her on the cheek. A little overwhelmed with the speed in which this is happening. Such is life with Jake and I should be used to the whirlwind that he is by now.

"Don't let Marcus sleep in my bed when you have a fight … Jake may take a blow torch to him, I think he just killed my teddy bear." I pass her with a pat on the head and move toward the front door.

"What can I say?" He shrugs at Sarah leaning down to plant an unexpected kiss on her cheek, she looks surprised and flushes. "Dirty fur-ball had been sleeping with my girl." She waves us off amid a flurry of giggles and I roll my eyes at him. Leading the way out of the front door and pulling it closed behind him when he gets out beside me.

"You can stop torturing girls wherever we go, Casanova

… I know you get your kicks out of the reaction, but your new "girl" might have reason to start feeling jealous." I mean it light-heartedly but somehow it comes out more serious than I intended, insecure Emma clawing free. He pushes my bag under his arm with one hand and grabs me with the other, catching my wrist and hauling me back to him.

"She gave me some good advice while you took about three hours to get ready…. I didn't want a reaction, *miele,* I was grateful. I'll never make you jealous either." He kisses me, breaking away to rub his nose against mine, a little show of affection I'm getting fond of. "I don't have any interest in getting reactions from other women … Only you." I smile up at him shyly, he always knows just what to say to me and I feel that inner anxiety fading away, replaced with a sudden desire to curl around him and squeeze tightly.

"What advice did she give you?" I question softly, my arms finding his waist even though we're still standing at the top of the stair in my apartment building. His mouth staying close to mine.

"To remember how easy it is for you to hide behind that wall when you're scared … To never let it stand between us again." He kisses my forehead softly. "She reminded me that despite seeming like you're always in control and capable, deep down you're that same kid from Chicago who learned to keep people out. No one protected you …… But I'm here now and I'll always look after you, *il mio amore.*" He kisses me again, slowly, more deliberately, sending my heart into a fluttering mess.

"I know you will," I answer honestly, my mind casting back to Ray Vanquis and his admission that Ray was gone from my mother's life for good. He smiles at me, locking eyes, before pulling me after him down to the car in the street below.

Some teenagers are gathered around admiring it and stand back in awe when he opens the door and throws my bags into the tiny rear seats. Jake gives the kids money and thanks them for watching his car, there are smiles and high fives all around. One of them whispers loudly that he knows who he is and they all seem to flush. I notice he's given them each a fifty and almost balk at it. Kids from around here aren't exactly well-off, he probably just made their month. Easiest way to spend a few hundred bucks. Something I'll never get used to with him.

They stand back in admiration to watch us drive off.

Chapter 10

Less than an hour later we're at the airport boarding Jake's private jet with all our bags , in tow. This has happened so fast, I've barely had time to think, let alone breathe. I feel like I'm running away from work, from life, from everything and taking a time out in some fantasy romance novel with a millionaire who can pull strings like no other. I should be used to this side of him, we used to take business trips at the drop of a hat and to him this is no different. To me, this is craziness.

Jake pulls me up the steps and leads me into the jet with him, I feel a sense of familiarity that feels so good. I missed this plane, I missed everything that was a part of him, of being with him.

He guides me to a window seat and slides in next to me, laying a hand on my lap with a smile and another kiss. Jake's constant kissing is starting to feel normal, but it still catches me by surprise how demonstrative he can be, I'll never tire of it. With hugging, hand holding, affectionate gestures, and constant verbal praise, I never imagined he would be this way. I never saw it with any of the women he hauled along or went out with, they were the ones who always clung to him, pushed him for a kiss or a hand to hold, always trying to get affection from him.

He shifts in his chair retrieving his phone from his pocket and looks down at the vibrating gadget, a look of frustration crossing his face. He glances at me, a fleeting moment of doubt but then answers.

"Marissa … How can I help you?" he sounds tense and glances my way warily.

I feel my stomach drop, turn away to look out the window and bite my lip in vain. I won't let him see me upset over this. She had to surface at some point, I couldn't go on pretending she didn't exist. His hand finds mine on my lap and pulls it back to him, entwining our fingers gently and giving me much needed attention.

My reassuring boyfriend.

Who knew that Casanova could be this attentive? So in tune with me he knows when I need his touch.

"I won't be here for the next couple of weeks, so that will be a no." He sounds irritated. I try not to listen and lean my face against the window instead, concentrating on watching the airfield while the crew load our luggage and get ready to take-off, the door is still open, and I have the urge to get up and go outside until he's off the phone.

"Look, I told you … No, I did … I'll be there at the end of the month … You're the one who doesn't want me at the other appointments … Because I'm not coming to see you. There's no reason to come more often." He snaps. "OK, Marissa, I need to go … I'm taking my girlfriend on a break … Emma! Fuck off, Marissa. Just hang up before you say something you'll regret." He hangs up angrily and throws his phone across the aisle at another seat, that fiery temper of his has seen many phones hurtling this way. He turns to me and tugs my hand, so I look at him, he looks worried when I face him.

"I'm sorry, *bambino*. I didn't expect her to call." He leans down, rubbing his nose against mine, catching my chin with his hand and tugging my mouth open a little so he can kiss me tenderly. I respond trying to forget my upset in the midst of his touch. I hear the click of the door being shut and pull back to look past him, we'll be taking off soon, so I move to fasten my seatbelt.

"You don't want to talk about this?" he asks warily, watching me, but I just shrug.

What is there to talk about? I don't want there to even be a situation with Marissa, but there's nothing I can do about it.

"What's there to say?" I finally answer because his eyes are boring into me.

"You haven't even asked for updates … What's expected of me before the baby comes." He's walking on eggshells trying to gauge my reaction, I look away, feeling the tears rise inside of me. I don't think I'll ever feel able to talk about this.

"What is happening?" I say softly, only because I feel he wants me to. He senses my distance and sits back, he knows Emma in closed down mode, knows when to step off a little. I may be improved Emma nowadays but it's early days and easy to revert to kind. Although Jake seems to be in new and improved mode too, and instead of old Jake pushing me for answers, he's being gentle.

"I need to fly to LA once a month … Go to antenatal classes with her, she wants me at the birth." He shifts, making the seat creak with his weight, and turns toward me so he can watch my profile a little better. I continue to stare out of the window, trying to detach myself from this conversation. Distancing myself from the pain that's clawing up inside me.

"She doesn't want me at any of the medical

appointments, scans et cetera, just the classes … Every four weeks for the next six months, then fortnightly until the baby comes."

"LA?" I ask in surprise, last I knew, Marissa lived in New York. Location seems like a safe topic, but also one that annoys me. He'll have to go there once a month to see her.

"Yeah, she headed out there after we came back. She's got a condo that she's living in … It means though, that when I fly there I'll need to stay over one night for the class and head home next day." He looks down at my hands, seeing it held loosely drops it, I hadn't realized I'd loosened my grip on his and instead he slides an arm around my shoulders pulling me toward him. "Talk to me." He pleads.

"I am …" I start but his look stops me, furrowing his brows.

"You're asking questions … Not really telling me what you're thinking, baby." He chides softly. "I want to know how all of this is making you feel. I want to know if my going to see her will upset you." He sighs. "You've never told me how you feel about there even being a baby."

I turn my face away and hold down everything, talking about this is too hard.

If I tell him how I really feel, what then? It's not exactly good … And then he'll know how much I hate this.

All I can manage is a shrug, the words too painful to spit out, he sighs and squeezes me a little tighter.

"You know the old me would have been pissed at this … You going silent and brushing it off. Acting like you're bored and don't care … I now realize that this version of you is when you're hurting the most, *miele.* You don't need to say it, Emma, it's pretty clear that you're distraught over this whole situation. It's okay to not be fine with this … I'm not fine with it either."

He pulls me tighter, his mouth coming to my temple and pressing softly.

I'm beyond *not fine*. I'm devastated. She's the thorn in my happily ever after.

"This is the last thing I ever wanted. I want you and I want to just have us and a clear future ... This shit with Marissa complicates things, all I can do is try to do the right thing at the same time as trying to make you feel better about it." His nose brushes the side of my face as he places a gentle kiss on my temple, over my hair. I feel myself relax slightly, as always, his touch soothing me.

"I hate it," I say softly, finally. "I hate her." The tears fill my eyes, he turns my face to him by holding my chin and comes close enough to inhale me.

"You'll never have anything to be worried about when it comes to her ...... I choose you, I'll always choose you ... She's my past, I'm only putting up with her for the sake of this kid. If I had a choice, she would be nothing to do with my life at all. Our life." He soothes me huskily.

"Why did you even go back to her?" I look at him imploringly, I've never understood it, he told me it was a drunken mistake, but I know how safety conscious he is when it came to sex, he always carried protection. I had ordered him bulk amounts to his apartment in the past. He'd also had his heart broken by this woman when he was a teenager, and had spent years after unable to commit to any girl because of her. It made no sense to me that he would be able to spend just one night with her.

"Honestly? I don't even remember it ... I'm not saying that to make you feel better, I'm serious. I went to a party with Daniel and some guys I know, I was already far too drunk. I don't even remember seeing her there, I woke up in a strange bed beside her. I left. She hounded me for days after and I told her to forget it." He shrugs, sighing, and holds me tighter. I should have known his rich, party-wild, idiot best friend would have been involved in him getting so drunk he couldn't see straight.

"You don't remember any of it at all?" I ask dubiously, I had seen Jake really drunk and he always seemed to remember most of his nights, regardless.

"Seriously, Emma. I swear ... You've never seen me as drunk as I can get. Last thing I can actually remember is downing shots with Daniel then waking up feeling like an elephant had stomped on my head and there she was, lying beside me. I felt like an idiot and got out of there as quickly as I could. I didn't even wake her to say *see ya*!" His frown deepens as he tries to keep my eyes on his.

I could imagine Casanova Carrero high tailing it without a backward glance, he hadn't been shy about telling women he wasn't interested.

"This was before the boat?" I ask, thinking back to her behavior and the way she kept trying to make eyes at him, some unspoken message.

"Yes ... And, no. I didn't know she would be Vincent's date on the boat. I never invited her. When she showed up I wanted to dump her ass over the side. I already knew I had feelings for you by then, she was the last thing I needed around, she manipulated being there because I wasn't returning her calls."

I look pensively at the front of the plane, we're already climbing in the air, I un-click my belt and stretch out taking a deep breath.

"I didn't like her from the second I met her." I shrug "There's something about her."

"Most of that is show on her part, she can be okay sometimes. Used to be anyway, we haven't exactly been friends for a long time." He pushes his arm further behind me, his other scooping my legs and lifts me onto his lap with a quick effortless movement. He sits me sideways across him, cradling me close so we're nose to nose.

"I love *you*. I'm not hung up on my ex … I didn't have sex with her because of any unfinished business, closure, or feelings that still linger. It's only you … It will always only be you. She's only in my life now because of circumstances, she would be gone in a second if there was no baby." He holds me close so we're forehead to forehead, I smile despite the pain in my chest and the doubts of insecurity within me.

"You always know what to say." My fingers trace his chiseled jaw, across the roughness of his stubble and perfect lips softly. Finding comfort and cooling the inner turmoil.

"It's easy with you … It's always been easy with you. I can tell you anything." He kisses me lightly, yet I feel pain constrict across my chest, I feel guilt rise inside of me and tears begin to fall involuntarily

"Hey, hey … *bambino*? What is it? … Don't cry." His hand comes up to smooth away the tears, his expression concerned.

"I know I'm really useless at talking, it just feels so one-sided. You're giving me so much and I clam up, the words won't come." I bury my face in his neck, wrapping my arms around him tightly, afraid he will disappear, clinging on like he's a life raft. His arms come around me tightly, hauling me close to him.

"When we were apart, I did a lot of thinking … How hard it was for you to tell me things, how much of a big deal it was that you told me the things you did. It still is. I know how much of an ass I was being, I talked to my mom a great deal after Sophie … Gained some insight into why you're both this way. I'm not expecting miracles *miele*. I know I need to be patient and not push you. You'll open up in time, it'll be worth the wait when you do." He soothes softly.

"What if I can never tell you everything? Some of it's too hard … Too shameful." I cry against his T-shirt, feeling it dampen slightly, his hands stroking up and down my back trying to comfort me.

"Then I'll live with it … Nothing that ever happened to you will change how I feel, it doesn't change who you are to me." He strokes my hair, his face pressed against it. "Knowing there are things which haunt you, *bella*, they make me so angry. I want to be the one to take them away, I'll always protect you." His voice is raspier, a hint of raw emotion which causes me to lift my chin back to face him.

I find his mouth fiercely, crushing mine against it, meeting no resistance, his hands come around my body and then head possessively. He deepens the kiss, pulling me hard against him, searing into instant heat. Panting, I pull away, desire flooding me, and I see his grin.

"As much as I want this right now, I'm pretty sure one of the flight crew will walk back here." He smiles, hovering close.

"I don't care," I say defiantly, catching the gleam in his eye, his lips parting.

"And I thought I was the wild and naughty one." He grins, needing no more encouragement. Lifting me up, he pulls my legs over, so I straddle him on the seat. He moves me back, so he can unzip his pants. "I love this side of you, *bambino* … My cute and sexy little wildcat. Who knew once I thawed out the icy exterior I would find such a fiery little number?"

"You bring it out in me, with all this crazy Italian hotness." I poke him in the cheek and give him a puckered air kiss. Watching the way he dips his brows, frowning with a smile, which I'm starting to realize is his, *You're too cute for words* look.

"Better make this quick then; can't disappoint my girlfriend." He grins and pulls me down for another skin scorching kiss.

* * *

"Wake up, *bambino* … We're almost there." Jake's mouth hovers over mine, his breath soft on my skin. I yawn and stretch out in the seat beside him, confused that I'm in a car and not the plane, I look up and around quickly.

"How the …?" I'm seriously confused, we're in a limo and the scenery outside is tropical.

"You fell asleep on my lap, I carried you to the car … We'll be at the port in a couple of minutes." He smiles at me, stroking back my hair from my face. "You look beautiful when you sleep, *bambino.* Completely at peace and cute as a button". I my face heats as the blush rises up, I don't know why I'm always taken by surprise when Jake is being so sweet, so non-Carrero. I knew he could be this way even when I was only his PA, but he's definitely upped the ante since telling me he loved me. Fewer sexual references and more cute ones, he makes me feel desirable and beautiful, like I'm floating on top of the world.

As for sleeping in peace, I had learned a long time ago that sleeping anywhere near him put an end to my night terrors. I don't wake with dark shadows looming over me when he's close by, protecting me, even in my dreams.

"Are we in the Caribbean already?" I rub my eyes and sit up in the seat to look out the window, despite the air conditioning blowing on full, I can tell we're in warmer climates, there's a stuffiness in the car.

"It's only a four-hour flight, the yacht's already docked here; my father likes to come out here a lot, so the boat has permanent moorings." He hauls me back to him, pulling me into an embrace. "I missed you while you were sleeping." He grins before sinking a kiss on me that fully wakens me up.

Will this burning desire he ignites ever calm down, I feel like I may self-implode every time his lips meet mine.

Moving against him fully, absorbing myself into the sensation of his kiss, his hands come up around my face and tangle in my hair. We always seem to ignite the passion quickly. He pulls away to lock eyes with me once more, simmering the heat.

"I never ever told you how much I love your hair … I could run my fingers through it like this for an eternity." He smiles again, melting the last ounces of me and I beam back. I feel the car come to a slow stop, I smile and flick my hands through the short waves with a wink. Cutting it had been the biggest change of all and now obviously one of my favorites.

"We're here." He grins with a raised brow, before turning to slide out of the car. He helps me out after him, the sun immediately blinds me, and I feel the familiar slide of his shades come down on my face. The movement, so familiar, so typical boss Carrero, makes me grin and hug him like a child.

He drapes his arm around my back and walks me out into the port, leading me along the concrete walkway past some expensive looking boats until we come to the familiar *Rosalina*. A beautiful, long, white yacht belonging to his family.

A boat that held only heartbreak for me the last time we were here, he'd left me alone and I shiver at the memory. He'd gone off with god knows how many women to put distance between us, to try to forget how he felt about me.

As though sensing my memories, he kisses me on top of the head and gives me a squeeze.

"Erasing the past … Remember?" He nudges me, and leads me on board by the hand, fingers intertwined like they belong together.

Chapter 11

The last few days have been like some sort of erotic fantasy, endless days of sex, sun bathing, and frolicking in the sea. We've been wrapped up like a couple on their honeymoon with only eyes for each other. He was right about coming away, we needed this time to just be together, to just get used to our new roles as a couple and no longer fighting our feelings. It's been more about bonding and getting comfortable, talking through the misunderstandings and just learning to co-exist in a new dynamic. Uninterrupted, eyes only for each other time, just to be.

We've been swimming, sun bathing, and reading, eating on the loungers on the upper deck and rarely leaving the close proximity of our bedroom. The staff have given us space and it feels like we're on the cruiser alone. I guess Jake has given orders that we're to be left in peace as some forewarning, he tends to have sex wherever he sees fit and I think we've christened every sun lounger, flat space on deck, and most of the rooms on the boat.

As I've come to learn, Jake's sex drive is never fading, it has kept us up late almost every night and in bed until late every morning. He's made love to me several times every day, until my body constantly tingles and glows with his attentions. I never knew it could feel this way, be this way. That someone could make me feel so desirable and beautiful or that I could trust a man enough to let him do any of this to me. I never knew that I'd have any reason to like that he had a past like his, littered with affairs and constant one-night stands, but now I see the benefits of it. Years of honing skills and now I'm reaping the rewards with a competent lover.

He's shown me so many ways in which I can be pleasured, his lack of inhibition at trying things out, his superior confidence at being able to pleasure the female body. He's taught me so much in such a short time, taking me forward into my own journey of sexual awakening, trusting him more than I ever thought capable, and finding confidence being in my own skin. He has a way of taking away my awkwardness, my shyness, and replacing it with a hot, wanton, version of myself who wants to be adventurous. I'm flowering beneath his capable hands, coming into my own, learning new things, and growing within myself. Finally putting part of my past to bed in ways I never thought I could , but it's because of him. The trust and love I have for him is making me capable of it, he's healing me just by loving me.

Our relationship has come on so much further than I imagined it could. Talking endlessly about things we like, things we hate, small talk, and general life. Even before, when I thought we were the closest friends, we never had the conversations or laughs that we've had the last few days. We talk about the vaguest things, laugh at each other's lame jokes, and have grown so much closer than I ever thought possible. I feel like I've finally got to know him in ways that had been denied me previously, that inner working of his mind and how he feels truly.

I've learned that Jake isn't all of the Mr. Confident he portrays, and his humor is sometimes used to cover what he's really feeling. All those endless jokes and sexual innuendos were his way of testing the waters, probing to see if I loved him back. The childish part of him, I sometimes see, which is so at odds with the alpha male everyone else sees there. He has insecurities about love, about himself, but he always seems able to shrug them down, ignores them for the most part and lets his stubborn nature tramp all over them. Letting me in, letting us happen has opened a whole new side to him, a vulnerable and scared side, the part of him who was too afraid to tell me he loved me, and it makes me want him all the more.

We're not so different after all.

Jake has opened up about things that I never knew, never shy at being honest with me and coaxing me to question him on anything I want to know. I've met the gentle, attentive lover, the guy who's forever touching me, cuddling, holding hands, and kissing. With me he's patient, never pushes me to talk about things anymore, giving me time to just let it happen and not saying anything when I can't. He tells me he knows it will take time, and for now I'm floating in the clouds.

* * *

It's late afternoon, I'm pacing on the upper deck in a mix of agitation, upset, and anger.

"I'm not talking to you!" I pout childishly, rage beginning to grow inside of me at his confession. Turning away from him on the main deck of the boat, I pull my sarong tightly around my waist and tie it off with an angry tug.

"*Bambino,* please." He tries to catch my arm, but I storm away. He stifles a laugh and comes at me again. "You're really mad at me?" He sounds like he's in disbelief.

I forgot how obtuse he can be.

He catches my face in his hands, trying to bring me to him and croons at me softly, his baby voice coming on strong. It only makes me so much angrier. I shove his hands off and glare fully at him.

"Baby? …… *bambino*? … Don't be like that." He tries to kiss me, sucks my bottom lip seductively, but I shrug him off. The doe eyed and faux boyish coy look completely lost on me.

Forget it, Carrero … That does nothing for me right now.

"Go away, leave me alone." I walk toward the metal railing of the boat, I feel like smacking him over the head and grip the railing with a vengeance. He has no idea how angry he can make me.

He'd no right to interfere without even asking me … He should have told me long before now.

"Emma? … You didn't want him in your life, I did what I thought you'd want …… He wanted money, I gave it to him on the understanding he stayed away." He catches my arm this time and hauls me to face him "*miele … bambino … Ti amo.*" He's trying to sweet talk me.

"Fuck off with your fancy foreign words." I spit childishly, pushing him away, my hands flat on his exposed torso. "I can't even talk Italian, so for all I know your calling me names!" I try to tug my arm out of his grasp, but he only pulls me closer. Smiling indulgently as though I'm a tantrumming child. In a way, I feel like one and could easily stamp my feet all over his right now.

"Do you want to see him?" He's trying a different

approach, trying to distract me from what he's done. His eyebrows raised in question.

Not a chance, Carrero … I'm seething with you!

"No! … It still gave you no right to pay off that asshole … He's my biological father, it should have been up to me to cut him off for good." I give up trying to pull my arm free and instead turn my body away, so I don't have to look at him.

"Okay, you're pissed because I didn't tell you … You're right … I did it without consulting you, but at the time, Emma, you were only my PA and we could barely talk about this stuff without you storming off and clamping shut." He tries to plead his case, stroking back my hair to turn my face to him, he sounds remorseful, but I'm not done being angry about this.

Doesn't he see how much this hurts me … Not what he did, but the fact that my biological donor happily took his money and agreed to never contact me again, for the rest of my life. It's Jake who's getting my rage but it's my father I'm really seething at.

"How much?" I snap, still facing away from him. "How much money did you give him? How much did you flush down the toilet?" I snap, heart crumbling.

I'm thinking he would have happily taken a couple of thousand dollars to walk away, he was that pathetic. What was I worth? Ten thousand at the most? Less? He would have agreed to a meager $500 when he'd approached me not so long ago.

"I gave him what I thought was a reasonable amount to stay away … I didn't give him a chance to ask for an amount, it would have pissed me off more." He smooths my hair back again, pausing as I shrug him away and only coming back to it when I still.

"What am I worth then?" I ask, emotion breaking my voice. Pain searing through my chest like a hot spear.

Do I even want to know? Could it be anymore humiliating than this?

"I would have given him millions, baby. To me there's no amount that you're not worth … My lawyers gave him $500,000 and made him sign a contract agreeing to stay away indefinitely," he says matter of factly.

I spin around in shock.

"You gave him how much?" I choke.

That's half a million dollars? Jake gave that slimy weasel half a million goddamn dollars?

I feel the blood drain from my face.

Why would he do that? Why would he give him so much money? For me?

"I would have given him twenty times that much, if he'd refused to go … To me you're priceless, there isn't enough money in the world that would make me walk away. I hoped he would put up a fight." He smooths my hair again, this time I don't pull away, too busy with my eyes glued to his face, my brow creased.

"Jake, that's so much money." I blanche, shaking my head at his shrug. I can't get over the shock and the disbelief.

"It's just money, baby." Jake turns me in his arms fully to face him, loosely draping them around my shoulders so his hands hang down behind me. Resting his arms on my shoulders out straight.

Only someone with too much money could make a statement like that!

"You didn't have to, you're crazy." I look down at his abdomen, a place to focus while I calm the rambling of my thoughts, his tanned, naked skin is definitely a good focus point.

"Get used to it, I haven't even shown you half the crazy things I get up to." I glance up at his humorous tone and shake my head at his smile. Adrenaline junkie and racing car addict, I'm sure I could guess what he means. I sigh it all away.

"He took the first offer, right?" I ask, swallowing down the pain my own question gives me. Trying to numb out the biting lump of heaviness in my stomach.

"Yes! He did … They low balled what I told them to give him, they figured he would negotiate an amount above that … He didn't." He looks angry. His eyes almost changing to the darkest of greens, betraying his rage. "He's lucky he never met me face-to-face."

I turn away this time, his arms sliding away. I can feel the emotion swell up from somewhere deep inside and a tear trickles down my face.

I can't believe Jake gave him half a million dollars, I wasn't even his girlfriend, I was only his PA. He did that for me anyway, regardless to everything else we had going on back then. My Carrero. So stupidly rich, sometimes he's on a different planet from me.

"I'm not really mad at you, Jake, well I am now I know how much money you threw away … I'm mad at him." I cry softly, his arms come around me from behind, his face nuzzling my neck. I cover his arms with my own and savor the feel of him around me. He has no idea how it feels to have someone who's supposed to love you from birth reject you repeatedly.

My own father used me as a way to get money. I always knew he would, I just didn't think Jake would be the one to give it to him.

"I wish you could see how little that guy deserves to even call you his daughter … He's scum, he's nothing. The money was nothing, *miele*. It was worth it to keep him out of your life and away from causing you more pain. I hated him upsetting you, he never once got to know anything about you. If he had, then there isn't anything in the world which could have torn him away, you're amazing. You deserve a real father. Someone who would do anything to be in your life … He's not that guy and it's no reflection on you, *bambino* … Trust me," he says it calmly, tenderly, breathing against my neck softly.

"Stop doing things like this without telling me." I chide, but there's no anger anymore, only deflation in my voice. Sadness always makes me tired.

"I'm sorry, *bella* … It was before you were mine. I did what I thought you needed me to do as your friend. I won't keep anything from you ever again … I promise." He kisses my neck and I close my eyes, relaxing into his touch, he always knows how to calm me, how to stop my mind from over analyzing myself into desperation.

I turn in his arms and hug him fully, savoring his naked skin on my bikini clad body, he feels hot and smooth and strong. Sending tingles and aches through me so easily, taking my mind far from the topic that's hurting me, my insides responding on some primal level.

"Make me laugh. Distract me," I whisper against him, indicating that I don't want to talk about this anymore, I don't want to think of that creep any longer. Burying my face against his chest.

For the last few days it's all he's done, even over stupid, tiny disagreements, he somehow manages to take it all away and get me to smile and laugh. I want that more than ever right now, to remove this heavy knot in my stomach at realizing my father was the scum I always believed him to be. The disappointment I always knew he was.

He moves me out of his arms so I'm standing in front of him, bends down and picks me up over his shoulder in one swift movement, making me squeal. Holding my thighs with a strong arm he takes a few strides to the side of the boat, to the open railing, and jumps in the ocean taking me with him. Sarong and all, even his sunglasses nestled on top of my head.

* * *

"I said laugh, not drown!" I cough, grinning and spitting out warm salty water when we resurface, he has his arms around me, treading water so we stay afloat, wiping droplets from his face. Devilish and grinning, his hair infuriatingly still in place; the boyfriend with the indestructible hair. I really should investigate Carrero grooming products.

"You're smiling so I got it halfway right." He grins, kissing me solidly. "Want to have sex in the sea?" He pulls my body to him, so my legs are around his waist, my arms around his neck, even in the cooler water he feels hot and smooth and inviting.

"Again? Oh, if we must," I say demurely as if it's the most boring request known to man, but my body is clenching in anticipation and I have a huge grin on my face. Best way to get over upset is to have your hot Italian Jake make love to you, works wonders every time. His eyes move to my lips as he focuses on them for a few seconds, I'm fascinated by the clearest green of their depths and the way his pupils contract and dilate as he thinks about something, his expression so serious. A smile breaks across his perfect face, throwing a kiss on the corner of my mouth, he lets me go, pulling my hand and makes me swim after him toward the edge of the boat.

"Where are we going? I thought you wanted to … Ummm … play in the sea?" I query, following him regardless.

"You're right, we've done it a few times now … Figured I would try something new with you, tiny." I feel disappointment tug at me, I liked when he made love to me in the sea, it felt wild and erotic, but a sense of exhilaration raises instead. New with Jake could be anything, he has no end to the sexual positions he puts me in, no end to his experimentation. I also have no qualms with letting him, trusting him always.

I follow him up the chrome ladder onto the boat, water pouring down my skin, and my sarong, molding to my legs. My sunglasses are surprisingly still stuck in my hair, he turns when he gets to the top and helps me the last few rungs before leading me to our bedroom on the lower deck, hand in hand.

Walking into the darkened room, he leaves me standing in the middle of the floor with a command to wait while he leaves. I pick up a towel and dry myself off quickly, peeling off the sarong and throwing it into the laundry basket, I pull the sunglasses off and lay them on the vanity for safe keeping. I'm rather partial to his sunglasses.

He returns carrying a black velvet bag and throws it on the bed and the contents empty over the sheets. I feel myself shiver with nerves as I watch him, we've never included anything in our sex sessions, just him and me and now here he has some sort of collection of Gothic looking cuffs and straps. I narrow my eyes and look at him questioningly.

"They're not mine before you start freaking out, thinking I'm some sort of Mr. Gray hiding some red room obsessions." He grins. "The staff found them after the last time we were here, I think they belonged to that porn chick."

"Miracle?" I laugh at the memory of the bimbo with the high-pitched squeal, Daniel Hunters entourage for that trip. He nods looking down at the things on the bed.

"Do you trust me?" He moves forward so we're nose to nose and lightly grazes my lips with his. "Trust me to tie you up?"

"I'm not so sure anymore." I giggle looking past him at the pile of restraining devices, there seems to be a blindfold too. I swallow and sigh, "Yes, Jake, I trust you." I sigh quietly, he kisses me hard, lifts me up to straddle his waist and carries me to the bed.

"Good, because I'm going to handcuff you to my bed and fuck you like there's no tomorrow … In a very loving way of course." He drops me down so I'm laid on my back with my legs still firmly propped up around his waist.

"You and that word …" I roll my eyes.

"Baby, come on … Would it sound quite so sexy if I said anything else? If I said I'm going to boink you like there's no tomorrow, it wouldn't have the same ring to it." He starts devouring my body with his mouth.

"When you put it like that …" My sentence trails off as I surrender to the sensation of his mouth tracing my stomach muscles, every touch sending soft, hot tingles of pleasure over my skin.

He makes light work of moving back on top of me, his damp body acting like a sensual distraction, cold and wet against my warm and dry, moving up the bed, he takes one of my wrists and pulls it toward him. He slowly straps on one of the wide, leather cuffs which is padded with a Velcro fastening. I wouldn't be able to get my hand out unaided. He takes my other hand and does the same, slowly and deliberately, watching my face for signs of disapproval. When he has them on he moves down my body with kisses, licks, and nibbles, making me groan, I close my eyes as I lay back on the bed, relaxing, letting him take control and enjoying every delectable sensation. Finally, he puts one on each ankle amid a flurry of gentle kisses and soft caresses, with the same slow deliberate movement and watching me for signs of refusal.

He comes to kneel over me, picks up the straps that look like wide nylon hiking cord and clips them to the metal rings on each cuff, long lengths that trail down the bed. They look more like horse leading ropes.

"You sure about this?" He stops and looks at me, kneeling over my body and caging me in. The excitement slowly building within me has knocked all sense of doubt away, tingles and nervous excitement shooting through me instead,

"Very sure." I breathe sexily and see his eyes darken, lust moving in. Things getting heavy and serious as our bodies awaken again.

He decides on using the light fixtures on each corner of the headboard as his point of connection and pulls my arms up above my head to anchor me close to them in mid-air. My breath catches in my chest, my body tingling with excitement as my hands dangle and the cuffs tighten with the weight. I've never been tied up, never had any urge to be, yet with him it doesn't feel wrong or weird or even scary. It feels achingly good. I'm powerless to stop him devouring me.

"Okay?" He scoops to brush lips with me.

"Perfect." I kiss him back and lick his bottom lip gently, a tiny teasing motion, satisfied in the reaction I see growing in his swim shorts.

The look on his face is almost boyish, he likes trying new things, he likes finding new ways to have sex with me. Jake and his love of games, spicing it up. I want this, I want anything he does to me over and over, never tiring of the endless ways he can make every time feel new and exciting.

He comes up to my face, pulling the blindfold over my hair so he covers my eyes and sinks a long, slow passionate kiss on my mouth. A gentle, perfect molding of two into one, his tongue exploring mine. A reassuring "I love you and I want you to trust me" sort of a kiss.

I can only wriggle my arms but can't move them from side to side, up or down, I'm completely his and the sensation is sending hot thrills through me.

He's tracing his mouth down my body again, slowly teasing and nibbling me, making me arch and move involuntarily. I'm moaning softly as he maneuvers me into submission, he tugs my legs apart with a swift movement that makes me gasp under my breath. His hands come down my inner thighs, his hot skin sending electric jolts through me. I feel him tie my ankle straps somewhere low down, the strain of the cuffs putting light pressure on me, so I'm spread open, completely unable to move at all and exposed. I feel his weight leave the bed.

I stay still and quiet, waiting, he's no longer touching any part of my body and the inability to see has heightened all my other senses drastically. I flinch and yelp when a warm hand touches my thigh, then giggle in reaction and hear him stifle a soft laugh.

A warm mouth follows, causing me to arch my back from the bed in response, it feels completely different and far too good. Held captive, completely at his mercy and unable to predict his movements. Every single touch is heightened to an intoxicating degree. I feel vulnerable and out of control, but I like it, it's exhilarating because I'm so completely trusting of him and know I am safe, even tied down and exposed.

He unties the straps of my bikini pants, slowly, he pulls them free and slides them away, my body lifting to aid the removal. His knees dipping the bed at each side of my hips, so I guess he's straddling me, but nothing else touches me.

Soft lips graze my cleavage, still held in my bikini top and his warm fingers trace the thin straps up to my neck, sliding behind to pull it free. The bow unravels, and I feel the soft slide of the fabric being pulled out from behind me, a hot hand slides under my back and I arch upwards, allowing the removal of the second tie, inhaling slowly and deeply when the bikini is slid away. I'm fully naked and completely his to do with as he pleases. This slow act he has going on is building up the energy inside of me, the anticipation, to feverish levels.

I feel his warm breath hover over my abdomen, the weight shifting down the bed as he moves, tilting my head to try and figure out what he's doing. I've never felt so alert, so in anticipation of a touch. His mouth comes to my skin and again I flinch, relaxing to the small gentle kisses, a lick, then his mouth moves to the apex of my thighs. He hovers, blowing gently, sending a thousand sparks through me before his hot sensual tongue probes me. I moan out loud, writhing within my confines and tug against them.

His mouth continues expertly licking and toying with me, I can't bring my legs or knees closer, I'm wide open to him, unable to stop anything he is doing and it makes it all the more erotic. This is a new level of sex for us, a level I didn't know we could reach, because what we had done so far already blew my mind.

I groan and arch my back again as the pleasure intensifies, his mouth doing things to me that makes my body tingle and writhe in ecstasy, wet, hot softness of his tongue entering me over and over, teasing. Gentle sucking jolts through me, bringing me to the brink, his breath on my most secret part is achingly sensual, and I bite my lip hard, groaning from deep down, feeling the build of internal heat and unable to stop my body from moving around. I feel warm wetness flowing, showing him just how much he's turning me on, making me open up and throb for him, begging to be devoured.

I strain on my confines, enjoying the feel of the pressure around my wrists and ankles, the harsh rasp as I tug again and the cuff jerks against me. It's so in contrast to what he's doing, it only adds to the effect. Harshness and a biting ache and then sensual softness and deep pleasure. There's something so highly sexual about surrendering myself to him this way, letting him have full possession of my body and being unable to stop him. As someone who always had to have control in life, never willing to drop her guard, I'm completely helpless to the lure of being his captive. It's a fantasy I never imagined I would like, but it seems to be exactly what I want.

I feel the heat building inside of me and the beginning of the waves which will climb to a higher euphoria, I'm climaxing quickly like this, whatever he's doing combined with being restrained this way is certainly talking to my inner goddess. His hands trace my curves as his mouth flicks and sucks at my core. I come seconds later, crying out in a thundering glory, unable to tense and pull my legs in makes it even more mind-blowing. He doesn't stop as I cry out, his tongue pushing in for a final assault, his hands on my hips, yanking me down to push me further into him and causing an almost instant second wave of cries as I convulse more harshly. This time the stars going off in my darkened vision, combined with the internal explosions cause a rush of moisture to run down my inner thighs as I pant and grind myself into him.

"Seems like I'm doing something right." His voice finally comes up to my ear, his body covering me as the waves begin to slowly subside, my body is reacting to his warm, smooth skin and desire already coursing through me again. His mouth grazes my neck, his hands on my body, stroking, teasing, exploring me. His fingers tug at my erect nipples and in turn it causes me to tug at my confines in reaction, but I'm held taught, his willing captive. I feel the hot rush course through me once more as my body cries out for more of this kind of love making.

He pushes against me, still wearing his shorts, the damp sea water is cold against my overheated body, it feels sensual and sends sparks in every direction. A jolt like a thunderbolt. I push against him savoring the feeling, the inner ache for his body to join with mine overpowering me so that I'm almost delirious with aching.

I'm still blinded by the mask over my eyes and can only anticipate his movements by sound and touch, it heightens everything inside of me to the point I'm panting helplessly.

"Who knew my cute little Emma was such a freak in the bedroom?" His husky voice is hoarse and low, sexily arousing against my neck once more, he slides up me, his lips meeting mine, his tongue slowly opening my mouth to him and sliding inside. I can taste myself in his mouth and it makes me groan, aroused by something so primal, so dirty yet so satisfying.

He moves off me, leaving me panting, longing for more as I listen to every sound he makes, moving across the bed. The noise of him opening a drawer, then the familiar rip of foil as he gets a condom. My hearing tuned in like it's never been capable, the anticipation has my body shivering, skin igniting with goose bumps.

Seconds later he's back over me, his weight making the bed dip, he's leaning on all fours caging in my body like a predator, his body heat surrounding me on all sides. I tingle in apprehension, alert and wanting as he leans down, capturing my nipple in his mouth, sucking and gently biting until I'm wriggling around, moaning softly. He tends to the other in the same fashion and I can already feel my body climbing back into the initial stages of orgasm. Already highly sensitized and responsive to him like I've never been.

I've never been like this, so effortlessly bringing me near to another body racking exploding orgasm and I thought

Jake had done a pretty outstanding job to date.

He moves back on the bed near my ankles, sinks down and I feel him rip open the ankle restraints, a surge of relief as I can pull my legs up again. Hot strong hands grasp me around the pelvis and he flips me over causing the upper restraints to cross my arms at the wrists and I gasp at the surprise. It's tighter and I'm even less mobile, held with them in mid-air, my head locked between my inner elbows and facing down like a submissive. I'm defenseless and held ready to be taken, something I would never have imagined I would ever be comfortable with, yet with him, nothing is out of bounds.

He lifts my body so my knees prop me up, pulling my thighs apart so he can move behind me. His hands come to my warmth and probe me softly before he enters me from behind in an easy, slow movement. I arch letting out a satisfied groan, pushing myself back against him so I can feel his full length filling me and hitting the ache deep inside that's been building and craving the feel of him. There is never a substitute for the feel of him inside of me, no matter how good he is with his hands or mouth, this here is what I crave.

His hands cup my ass and squeeze hard, moving his palms up my body he grabs my hips pushing me forward with his weight but follows me, the restraints biting in. It feels better than amazing. I feel nothing but fullness and pressure from him, completely filling me, starting a slow steady rhythm in and out which soon has my body climbing higher and higher. Groaning and whimpering out loud, I can hear his breathing becoming loud and labored. The rhythm of our joined bodies a sensual dance that is slowly unraveling me, blowing my mind.

He quickens the pace until he's slamming hard into me,

almost ruthlessly, both of us breathing hard. His hands gripping my waist so tightly I feel like it'll leave marks, passion overtaking gentleness and lust driving him further. I savor the roughness, I cry out with every thrust. I love what he's doing, I anticipate every movement, grind back to him, encourage it to be harder. Every jolt sending a deep wave of pleasure, my body losing all control as I begin to hit that dizzying height again. I moan loudly as the waves build, this time it's so fast and so close to the last stroke, it threatens to tear me apart. The build-up making me pant out loud; heat, and wetness which only seems to make him more excited and he thrusts harder and faster.

I'm unable to slow it down, held captive in my pose, his hard, hot, body is ruthless. I tug at my restraints harshly in fear of the precipice I'm almost on the verge of reaching, the intensity overwhelming me and I'm unable to move, the waves of my climax quickly enveloping me and making my body spasm wildly without warning. Splayed out in front of him, completely immobile, adds to the intensity of the orgasm, causing it to multiply and string out for endless mind-blowing minutes that are so much more intense than anything I've known. I cry out loudly again, racked with something so huge I can do nothing but surrender and scream out in the most earth shattering moment of my life. Body flushing with moisture at my release and I lose all conscious awareness of anything but the ripples of extreme deliciousness catapulting through me.

He falls over the top of me and we both collapse on the bed in a heap, my arms outstretched above me. Still inside me, throbbing at his own climax, spurring a sprinkle of tiny mini explosions within me. I'm still moaning in ecstasy and unable to feel anything but extreme release. Both of us lost inside our own internal pleasure.

It's like nothing I've ever experienced in my life, not even with Jake these past few days and I'm completely hopeless to do anything but languish here. He reaches up, tugs off the wrist cuffs, pulls me into his arms to lay and bask in what he's just done to me, our bodies sagging in satisfaction. I'm panting and tingling all over, my limbs have turned to jelly as he pulls the blindfold off me from behind, throwing it toward the wall and spooning me. I'm completely useless to move my own limbs and still trying to catch my breath.

I feel his smile against my shoulder where he's laid his head, and smile too, even after something like that, something so new and kinky, there's no awkwardness or shyness. He satisfies me in ways I could never have dreamed of and rocks my world with so very little effort. He kisses me gently on the back of my shoulder.

"Now that ... Is definitely in the top five. Might even be a number one spot." He pants breathlessly, I can hear by his tone that he's smiling still, I grin too. "I've never made you come like that before," he says nuzzling my neck softly. "I think we'll be taking this set up home with us, *bambino.* I'm definitely up for a repeat of this." His voice is deep and husky.

"Hmmm mmmmm." Is all I can say in response. I'm beyond exhausted, unable to formulate a reply. I never knew sex could be the way it is with Jake, every time different, mind-blowing, but this had to be a favorite now. He had literally just rocked my world.

"That good huh?" He kisses me on my cheek, a hand coming to stroke my jaw line and then he stretches out to yawn, a hand appearing in the air above me. I stretch out and nod, closing my eyes and snuggling against him, ready to just fall asleep. He wraps around me a little more comfortably, snuggling his face into my hair, his legs entangling with mine, this is his getting ready to take a nap pose, it seems we're both exhausted.

"Emma?" His voice thick and hoarse, so close to my ear it gives me goose bumps.

"Mmm hmmm?" I say lazily, letting my hands follow the curve of his arms and cover them possessively. Enjoying the strong, hard muscle under smooth skin and softest hair.

"It's never been like this ..." He breaks off as if he's not sure if he wants to say this. I open my eyes, listening intently.

Does he mean that he's never had sex like this? Or that it's never felt as good as this?

I turn slightly to gaze at his face in the now shadowy room, the sun must be going down.

"In what way?" I croak, finding some of my shaking voice, my body still tingling in the afterglow.

"Wanting to have sex with you every second of every hour, like I just can't get enough of you. No matter how much I get you naked, the urge never dies." He leans closer to me, stroking my face gently. "Long before I got to touch you, I wanted you, it drove me crazy." He pulls me so tightly it almost makes it impossible to breathe.

He has no clue that I've felt the same way about him from the first time I ever laid eyes on him, his effortless sexiness, his over the top hotness. I've been under his spell, aching at his every movement for so long. I turn to him within the loop of his arms, he loosens his hold enough so I can and our eyes to meet.

"You're the most adventurous girl I've ever met, there isn't anything yet that you haven't let me do to you ... You've no idea how much of a turn on that is. How much of a surprise it's been, considering everything I know about you, what that means to me." He looks so sincere.

"I trust you, I know you'd never hurt me or do anything I

didn't want." I smile up at him, watching his gentle expression with adoration. "I've been yours from day one, Jake, even before I could admit it to myself … Unable to function in your presence without fantasizing about your hands on me … The reality is so much more than the fantasy, everything you do only makes me love you more." I lean up and kiss him passionately, his mouth responding with equal fire. His hands sliding down my body to my naked butt, cupping it and pulling me up toward him.

"I'll never stop trying to fulfill your fantasies. Or making new ones together." He frowns lightly, a seriousness to that flawless face, he kisses me again, slowly and deeply, moving against me. My body responds instantly; he was right about one thing, no matter how often we make love, our bodies yearn for more. Even when I think I am beyond the capability, it surprises me. This ability to instantly recover and want it so soon. I feel his hardening against me and know he's reacting in the same way, with his subhuman skill.

"How about round two?" He grins, pulling away from my mouth, his hand reaches up to catch the cuff and pull it back down toward us with a glint of wickedness in his eye.

Chapter 12

I wake up and try to stretch out, but I'm restricted by Jake's heavy body, wrapped around me like always, if I have one complaint about my lover it's this unearthly way of sleeping. He literally manages to get as much skin on skin and limb twisting as possible and somehow maneuvers me into positions while unconscious that defy the human body's ability to bend.

I slide a leg out from between his, rotating my foot to get some feeling back and attempt at retrieving an arm which has gone to sleep pressed under his weight. He is impossible to get loose from in bed, the second I move free he reaches out and re-curls himself to me, pulling my limbs to how he wants them around him. He's sleeping heavily, I can tell by his deep, even breaths, so moving slowly I manage to get myself loose.

Sitting up beside him, I gently stroke his cheek with a smile on my face. His sleeping habits are more of an insecure child longing for cuddles than the confident awake Carrero, just another layer to my fascinating man.

I get up, finding a robe quickly and head out to the upper

deck for some air. It's dark but the horizon has hints of color as though sunrise is not far away, the air is cool and refreshing after his stifling body heat.

I had been dreaming about my mother again, lately she's been plaguing my thoughts. I don't know if it's because of Jake being in my life this way, I somehow feel obliged to tell her, or if it's just being with him which has started to make me feel differently about my decision to see her again. She is still my mother, being with Jake had shown me what she's always been searching for and never found, which, in a way, is sad. That one guy who can bring such happiness to her life, the way Jake has mine and I feel some remorse about it now.

Was it wrong to want to find love? To be that desperate for it that you push away all the bad and try not to see it.

There's no denying he's changed me in so many ways, he's brought that cold ice queen PA back in touch with emotions and feelings that I could never have imagined coming back to. Changed my way of thinking completely.

I've seen my mother in a different light and yet come back around to feeling some sort of forgiveness toward her in such a short space of time. Maybe it's because Jake told me about my father and somehow it's made my mother more appealing to me. Despite her flaws she kept me, raised me, and in her own way, I know she loves me. No amount of money in the world would have made her walk away, even when she chose her lovers over me, in the end it was I who had left and she never tired of asking me to come back to Chicago.

I breathe in deeply, finally cool enough to go back below deck, tiredness fogging out the thoughts which had woken me, the call of his body luring me back to lay beside him, as though it was starting to fade at his lack of presence. I am a butterfly who needs the sun to fly and he is that light for me.

I climb back in bed slowly, he's shifted in his sleep, so he's moved away to lie on his back and it's easier for me to lay beside him. Placing my head on his chest, his arm automatically comes around me, pulling me up tight against him, his chin comes to my head. He makes me smile, even asleep he somehow has this sixth sense that I'm here. I wrap my arm around his ribs and close my eyes, trying to push my mother out of my mind's eye.

"I'm awake, baby." His voice startles me. "I woke up and figured you needed some "you" time … I always wake up when you leave me." I feel his smile against my hair, the irony of his sentence. He told me that my going away had been a huge wake up call to how much he needs me. I shake my head at his cheesiness and throw a light kiss on his broad chest.

"I was thinking about my mother … I guess I'd been dreaming about her."

"You thinking you maybe want to see her?" he asks cautiously, he still has no idea how to tread over the subject of my mother. As far as I know, he thinks I should have a relationship with her because she gave birth to me. I've always known he had some mixed feelings about the woman who left me subjected to so much in my youth, but his own relationship with his mamma has made him ignore them.

"I don't know anymore." I sigh. "Part of me never wants to see her again …… Then part of me feels like I've so much more to say to her." His other arm comes across and envelopes me in a tighter hug.

"She's still your mamma. I think you'll always regret not trying to talk to her again. If you want to see her, I'll come with you … For moral support." His hand moves up to my hair and begins caressing my scalp gently.

"I think I'd like that," I say softly, closing my eyes and listening to the steady beat of his heart in his chest, lulling me back into calmness. I think about the fact that old Emma never wanted Jake near her past or her mother, yet here we are. I feel his chest rise and fall a little more quickly and his arm tenses a touch. I open my eyes, aware of how in tune I've become to him, he seems hesitant.

Does he maybe not want to come to Chicago?

"What is it?" I ask. He sighs heavily as though he's just been busted.

"I had a message on my phone when I woke up." He sighs again. "We might need to cut this trip short, *miele.*" He lets go of me and slides out of the bed, reaching for his jeans and pulls them on before coming to sit back down to take my hand. I can see his face in the moonlight coming in the uncovered window ports. I've learned that when he thinks an argument is likely he'll always get up and pull pants on. It amuses me as somewhere in my head I wonder if he's protecting his tackle in case things get frisky. Maybe he thinks I'll go in for the kill below the waist in anger. It only makes me anxious now that he thinks a fight is brewing.

"Why? … What is it?" I ask in confusion.

"Marissa … She's demanding that we sit down with lawyers, she wants our agreements in writing. A contract so to speak, and my father is pushing for it like crazy. She also wants to talk money and her requests. If I ignore her she'll only keep hounding me and ruin our time here." The tightness in his voice makes my skin prickle and irritation spark.

"She wants what? Does she think you're going to go back on your promises? She doesn't need your money; her family is as loaded as yours, and what goddamn requests? You owe her nothing, until that baby comes then she's nothing to you

… Your relationship will be with the kid, not her!" I snap, my anger getting the better of me and the rush of emotion fueling my outpouring. Sitting up quickly, my insecurity and jealousy showing face in unison. He leans forward grabbing me and pulls me over toward him, his hand stroking my cheek gently.

"She thinks I won't commit to the classes and being at the birth because I now have a vested interest elsewhere … You … It's also pushed her to demand that you'll not be included in the trips to LA or the relationship I have with her, and that after the birth you can't have anything to do with the baby unless I marry you," he says hurriedly, an edge to his tone.

I gasp in shock … Confusion crushing me.

What? She's threatened by me? She's trying to drive a wedge between us in the only way she can.

It's obvious she's still in love with Jake and this is her biggest weapon. She's going to use his child as a pawn to maneuver him to meet her demands and try to tear us apart in the process.

"You're going to agree?" I snap in anger, his hands tightening on me.

"No! Why would you think that?" He frowns. "She can't dictate who I take with me on my own goddamn plane to LA, or who stays in the hotel with me, she doesn't own me. She's not my goddamn wife. Once that kid arrives, if she wants me to have access then she'll need to get used to the fact you'll be there, whether we're married or not." He gets up, letting me go and paces back and forth in agitation. "She doesn't need money, but I'm giving her money anyway, for our child … Not for her. Marissa is manipulative, it's a fucking gift of hers, she thinks by throwing in the jibe about marriage that I'll run for the hills because she thinks I'm a commitment-phobe." He sneers. "She's no idea how different things are with you … If I need to marry you to let you see my kid, I'll marry you tomorrow, because I'll marry you anyway … Now or in the future, Emma, you're going to be my wife." He storms around.

My voice catches in my lungs and I can't formulate a reply, I just stare at him in open-mouthed surprise, inner tingles waving over me like hot sauce. Jake's never mentioned marriage before, I know he loves me, but part of me still finds it hard to believe he loves me as much as this.

"You want to marry me one day, right?" He suddenly sounds so young and unsure, my silence making him think I'm freaking out in a bad way. I guess a small part of me is, but mostly I'm shocked into silence. He moves closer and I see the panic in his face, the doubt that he's said something he shouldn't have. I reach out for him and he follows, wrapping himself within my arms.

"I just didn't think you would want that with me," I mumble, the tears stinging my eyes.

"Why wouldn't I? You know how I feel about you … I've told you enough times." His face comes to mine, his hand clasps my chin and tugs my eyes up to meet his.

"It's just … I'm broken … You can have any woman you want, why would you choose to marry someone as messed up as me?" It's the first time I've ever verbalized some of my inner insecurity and anxieties to Jake. Something I've always hidden because it's such an ugly way to think and I don't want him thinking me pathetic. He seems taken aback for a moment and stares at me with furrowed brows.

"Is this what goes on inside that head of yours? Is this how you think?" He seems genuinely surprised. I close my eyes and nod, painful to even admit this to him. This inner voice that's always with me, always doubting my worth, always hiding in the recess of my brain that I would never let anyone see. I feel his mouth against mine, his kiss forcing me to respond, his hands come up to cup my face and hold me close. I return the softness, parting my lips, sagging against him as our tongues meet, gently caressing. He kisses me until I'm panting then pulls away.

"You're not broken … You're scarred … You're the only woman I ever want! Even if you left me tomorrow, I wouldn't move on. Even when I thought I could never have you, I couldn't just get over you. I couldn't get you out of my head. Everything reminded me of you … … … Tell me what I need to do to make you feel secure, *bella.* To believe me … I'll do whatever it takes to remove those doubts from that beautiful little head." His gaze is so intent on mine that I feel like he's trying to see deep within my soul, trying to figure out why I would think this way. He's no clue to the depths of insecurity I have inside of me, the depths of self-doubt and lack of worth. I've always hidden them so deeply behind my mask that no one knows, not even Sarah.

"Everything you're doing already … Little by little, it helps." I finally say softly. I don't know what else he could do to make me believe that I mean as much to him as he does to me.

"*Non avete idea di quanto ti amo, bambino,*" he mutters, his eyes focused on mine, slipping into his second language. I giggle and raise an eyebrow.

"What?" I look at him indulgently, he breaks into a smile and looks down at his hands between us, holding mine.

"I really need to teach you the basics of Italian. I said: *you've no idea how much I love you, baby.*" He kisses me on the nose. "You tamed *il Casanova, mio amore*, that in itself should be proof of what you are to me." He smiles.

I close my eyes tightly and take a huge deep breath.

He's right, he's told me a million times, and now maybe it's time I told him why I'm so sure that I'm not worthy of anyone to love me the way he says he does.

I trust him, he shares so much with me, yet I hold back. There's a part of me that's always afraid that if I tell him about my past properly, he'll turn from me. Disgusted at what I am. But if I don't he'll never really understand me. I owe it to him to open up, to at least try. He opens himself to me in every way possible and yet, he no longer pushes me to do the same. I love him enough to let him in fully, it's time.

"Ray Vanquis wasn't the only man to ever hurt me in that way," I say it so quietly, with such fear that I can't even open my eyes and see how he's looking at me. I feel him stiffen, he isn't sure if he should say anything or move, still holding my hand in his. He can sense that my statement is something more than a random sentence. He knows I've decided to start talking about my past, he knows me well enough.

I reach over and cover his hand with mine, take another steadying breath. I gulp unsteadily.

"There were more than a dozen men in my mother's life who tried, some a little more successfully than others, to abuse me." My voice breaks but I swallow down the urge to cry. This is so much harder than I could ever imagine. Telling Jake of all people is the most devastating thing I've ever done. I don't want to open my eyes, I don't want to do this, but I know I must; If I'm ever to feel worthy of his love then he must know all of what he's trying to love. Give him the full picture, so he can run if he wants to. He needs to see that dark side of me, the part I keep hidden away and only then, if he still loves me, will I truly believe that he can love me as much as I love him.

He doesn't speak, or move, I think he's holding his breath

in case any sort of interruption stops me from going on, bringing that door closed in his face again, like so many times in the past. My hands begin to shake with the effort of doing this, but he stays unmoved; my breathing getting shallower and nausea swirling crazily.

"Some just managed to kiss me and touch me in places they shouldn't have … I was very young the first time, so young I didn't understand, I just knew it felt horrible and wrong." Tears begin falling down my face, more from the shame of having to tell Jake than the actual memories, I had long ago stopped crying over those men. Breathing so heavily, finding it painful to go on. I feel his forehead come to mine, grounding me a little, his own breaths shallow too. His thumb strokes my cheek, urging me to go on, to finally tell him and I swallow hard, my body trembling with the effort.

"Some hit me … Kicked me, it wasn't sexual with those ones … I saw them do things to my mother that I'll never forget though, things no one should see, especially not a child." I swallow down hard, a lump rising in my throat, threatening to choke my voice from me as images flicker through my brain. Memories I had long ago ground down into a tight little box away from the light of day.

"Some of them tried to have sex with me, but I learned quickly to fight back, they didn't like that and would leave me alone, but they tried. I still remember the feel of their hands on me." I shudder heavily and feel his grip tighten on mine, giving me the strength to continue. "By the time, I was seven I had been groped and mauled in so many ways, I felt sick to my stomach when boys would come near me in the street or at school … I became very introverted, very aggressive. I got kicked out of school so many times for my behavior, lashing out, hitting boys … Smashing things up. I had so much rage." I sob and feel him pull his hands away, wrapping them around me instead and pulling me against his chest.

If I stop now, I'll never have the courage again. If I let myself stop and think about what I'm telling him then I'll never find this voice again … ever. Those memories will only be driven down deeper inside of me to never see the light again.

"I started sleeping with a baseball bat that I bought with money from a paper round when I was too young to even know what sex was, I bought it because I knew the men wouldn't stop coming and I hated what they would do to me … I ended up in protective services by the time I was eleven; a neighbor reported my mother's boyfriend for beating her up, hearing the screams almost daily … You would think that losing me for a year, to a horrendous life in a children's home would change her, but no. I came back to exactly what I left behind." I feel his thumb move across my cheek, wiping fresh tears and I tilt my face into his touch. Still he stays quiet and just listens intently.

"Somehow it was better than what I had dealt with in that home, kids can be cruel and the carers were just as abusive, so I learned to lie and hide the things going on as much as she did. I didn't want to go back there, it was awful … But the older I got, the more sexual the advances became. She has a knack, you see, for finding men who were the same as the last. Perverted assholes with serious dominance issues and no qualms about using women as punchbags. I would fight back as hard as I could, the first time I got properly beaten up my mother wouldn't take me to the ER because she knew I would get taken away again. I had to strap up broken ribs myself for weeks on end and pretend I was fine." I gulp down more sobs; my face is soaked, and I can feel the sheet covering my breasts getting cold with dampness. Jake is still silent, breathing hard, gripping me so tightly it's beginning to hurt, but I don't care. I need him holding onto me, to find the strength to get it out and done with so we can move on from this. I can't bear to look at him, can't bear to see the rage in his eyes or the despair I can feel coming off him in droves. I just need to keep going, keep talking and get it all out there.

"By eighteen, I was good at defending not only myself but her, I would chase them out with my bat swinging. I'd learned to use my anger effectively, I had so much rage, so much hatred inside of me. I would just keep hitting until my arms ached with the effort … I smashed two of her boyfriend's cars up in a bid to chase them off." I shift position on the bed, pulling my legs out and stretching them out, sighing heavily.

"She would hate me after and make me go elsewhere to cool down; I slept rough for days on end because she wouldn't let me come home until I apologized to them for it, which meant returning to being abused in one way or another." I laugh sardonically, my wonderful mother and her screwed-up sense of parenting.

"Ray was the first one to put me back down on my ass and show me I was no match for a man … He wanted me to have sex with him and when I refused, he beat the crap out of me while trying to take me by force, he tried to rape me. She came home and stopped it, but she never forgave me." I feel Jake tense, his whole body emanating so much anger, sadness, pain. He's listening so intently, so silently and it's unnerving me. I know without looking that rage will be the dominant emotion on his face right now, I can feel it and just push on blindly.

"She always treated me like I caused it. I think Ray was the first man she'd seriously fallen deeply in love with and it blinded her in the craziest of ways, she couldn't see what he was. It was after Ray that I finally found the courage to run away with Sarah, to run away from her and what she kept doing to me … It's why I never go back, why I don't want to go back. To that house and the endless memories of things that went on. She wasn't a real mother, Jake … I was the one who cooked and cleaned and took care of things, took care of her. She was so wrapped up in her affairs and relationships it was like I was invisible. She didn't want to know what they were doing, she didn't want to face it. She sure as hell didn't try to save me." I sniff back my unshed tears.

"I still dream of things that terrify me, when I'm not laid beside you in bed, they haunt me … You keep them away, make me feel safe and stop the past from getting to me … You have no idea." I finally sag and more tears fall down my cheek, calming my breath and trying to push it all back down inside. I feel like I've just let a monumental weight from my shoulders but at the same time I'm being crushed with panic at how Jake will react. Afraid to look at him, afraid to breathe.

"That's pretty much a condensed version of everything you ever asked me about." I mumble, so quietly it's barely above a whisper, my head hanging in shame as I stare at the fingers I'm twisting together. It wasn't a detailed out pouring but it was as much as I could handle.

"Emma?" His soft voice makes me look up and I see the devastation on his face, his furrowed brows and tear-filled eyes, the tight clenched jaw, holding back raw emotion. I see nothing but agony in his eyes.

"My *angelico.*" He smooths his hand across my cheek, removing a fresh tear as it rolls slowly down my face.

"How can you love me knowing all that I am?" I ask with so much conviction in my voice, I sound hoarse. He lets me go and for a second, I feel fear grip my body, fear that he's walking away, that he's disgusted at me. As he moves back the panic grips me, my eyes widening but he shakes his head as though in answer, slides his arms under me and pulls me to his lap, wrapping me in a proper embrace torso to torso, pulling my legs around him so we're as close as humanly possible. With his hand cupping my jaw, the other around my back and pulling me in, our faces touching. I slide my arms around his neck, relaxing into his embrace. Eyes wide with apprehension, heart beating erratically.

"I want to find every one of those men, every single one and kill them with my bare hands … I would serve life in jail for what I would do to them for hurting you. For touching you." He growls, holding my face to his so we're only a breath apart. "How can I not love you, Emma? Everything you've told me just makes me love you more, want to fiercely protect you more. Your strength, your undying will to carry on despite it all … You're an amazing woman, and after all of that, everything men showed you about themselves, you still found it inside of you to trust me, *bambino* …To fall in love with me, to let me touch you. You've no idea how immense that is … I'm in awe of you … You didn't just survive, Emma; you built a life for yourself that completely transformed what you had come from, so that no one would have ever guessed." His mouth comes to mine, kissing me softly. "You've no idea just how amazing you really are. I think I've just fallen in love with you all over again, *il mio amore.*" His words send so much bittersweet pain through my heart, elation, yet a crushing, overwhelming ache. Not because his words have hurt me, but because they are exactly what I need to hear after so long. That in some small way they're a healing balm, a tiny start at making me feel whole again.

I wrap myself in him, pushing my head against his chest and listen to the sound of his heart, beating faster than usual, his breath more labored. My story has affected him physically, his body tense. I know he's mulling it all over, disgusted with what he's heard but not *at* me. I always believed he would look at me like some sort of slut or dirty whore if I told him, but he's not. He's looking at me like I'm a fragile piece of glass and he wants to mend it, he wants to protect me. I close my eyes and lean against him, surrounded by security.

"It's hard for me to talk about this stuff … When I do, it brings it all to the front of my mind and it plagues me for a long time after." I confess shamefully, unable to lift my voice above a breath.

"I don't want that … I'm so grateful you finally opened up to me. I know what it's taken, you've no idea how it makes me feel to know you trust me this much." His eyes are cool green again, he brings my chin to him to look at me deeply, clear and bright yet still so sad. "I finally understand why you shut me out anytime we got close, Emma … I get it … I'm sorry, *bambino*, I'm sorry that I was such an asshole and I kept pushing you." He looks forlorn, full of regret.

I don't want him to feel that way, we're here now, he came for me and he's changed everything. I needed his rejection to finally get me to this place where I can open up and let him in.

"You didn't know, Jake … You couldn't know … I was so used to pushing things down and being alone, closing doors, keeping people at arm's length to protect myself." I kiss him gently on the mouth. "It doesn't matter anymore. I'm here, you're here, we both want the same thing. Erase the past … Remember?" I hold his face with my fingertips, so we can look into each other's eyes, empowered suddenly.

"I remember." He looks down and frowns, so much

swirling in the depths of those eyes. "Some pasts may be harder to forget though. Some men will always be on my hit list, no matter how much time passes." There's an edginess to his tone and I brush my fingers across his lips softly.

"Forget them … For me. So, we can have a future, without the past interfering." He raises his head and once again locks green eyes on cool blue ones.

"Does that mean you will marry me someday?" He smiles, his eyes glinting, still haunted by my confession. I can tell he wants to talk more but he knows me, I've let it out and now I want it left alone. There's nothing more I can say, I don't want to be more specific, no more digging into it.

"Maybe, when you learn how to ask me properly … I'm not one of your leggy bimbos who's ready to drop their pants on command." I pout, pretending to be upset and deflecting talk of marriage. I'm not ready for that whole mess of emotions just yet, I've had no chance to consider a life with marriage in it.

The awkwardness is slowly dispersing, he smiles, pulling my chin down to kiss me seductively, his mouth effortlessly making mine surrender with tender fluttering kisses, then pulls away.

"I'm pretty sure I do get you to drop your underwear on command, *miele.*" He strokes my face with his thumb, tears drying and all but gone. He's steering the conversation away from my painful topic to let me move on, yet this new topic has me feeling antsy. "As for asking you properly … I'm Italian, *bambino* … When I ask you, there will be fireworks and a floor show … Trust me … You won't be able to refuse."

That Carrero confidence! He already knows I'll say yes, does he? I don't even know if marriage is something I even want just yet.

I wrap myself around him fiercely, wiping out everything

I've told him and just feel the safe security of his strong body, shielding me from every bad thing I have ever faced alone.

"We'll see." I bite my lip through a smile, squealing when that frowning face dives in with tickling hands and hauls me down with him.

Chapter 13

The departure from the boat this morning is tense, Marissa calls several times, ending in heated arguments over Jake's refusal to meet with lawyers until she agrees to Jake's terms and not hers. Every time causes Jake to hang up in agitation and throw his phone in various directions, violently, cursing and going off in a full Italian rant. I sit watching with my breath held until he calms down, unsure what to say to bring him back to a simmer instead, there isn't much to calm that hot temper and I know to let it run its course. His emotions are on edge with the topic of the baby and Marissa seems to know exactly how to push his buttons.

The flight home is silent, listening to music as he thrashes emails back and forth to his legal advisor about the meeting over paternity rights. He's tense and agitated and very much the Jake Carrero I used to work for; boyfriend Jake on hiatus as he frowns his way through a heated typing rampage, his poor laptop taking a beating. The Carrero glare, stuck firmly in place as I watch him hit the keyboard several times. That fiery Italian temper is always out of place in the cool calm demeanor of the most laid-back Carrero alive and I smile, despite the look on his face. I had even missed that part of him when he'd sent me away, his monumental arsey moods and dangerous glare never phased me at all. I watch him pull out his phone, give the screen the most hateful look I've ever seen then he rejects whoever is calling before returning to pounding keys.

"I think your laptop might need medical attention when you're done." I poke him in the rib lightly. Hoping to calm some of that brewing storm.

"I think Marissa will need it if I talk to her right now." He grinds out.

Ahhhhh, enough said.

* * *

We get to his apartment late evening; his staff dump our bags in his master bedroom and leave us in peace. We never spoke again about the things I'd told him of my past and I'm glad. I feel like all I had needed to tell him was now done, I don't have anything more to say about it, nothing else to get off my chest, putting an end to a chapter of my life in a way I wasn't even aware I needed. Sharing, telling someone who matters to me has done more than years of hiding it in the recesses of my mind. Having that person show me they don't blame me. He knows enough and now I hope we can forget about it. He seems to sense it too, always attentive and hasn't brought it up again, although I know he is still mulling over it, his gentleness since that conversation a testimony to the fact. He's treating me like fine china and even though I thought it impossible, is managing to be even more adoring of me.

He picks up his phone, his expression turns to death and he stalks out of the room, once again barking Marissa's name. I feel myself stiffen, she is already imposing on us and this is only the beginning. By my calculations, she must be two months maybe two and a half months pregnant, three at the most.

This is going to be a long six months if this is how she's going to play it, and then what? When the baby's here, how is it going to work?

There's a massive bang in the other room which makes me jump and freeze, listening intently as Jake curses and then appears in the room again, shaking his hand about as though he's punched something.

"I literally hate her." He snarls, pacing past me to the bar in the sitting room and reaching for the ice bucket, he throws some in a cloth and holds it to his fist. "Now I need someone to fix my goddamn wall." His glare breaks, and turns into a remorseful smile, looking at me with shame etched on his face. I shake my head and heave a sigh of relief at his change of mood.

"What could she possibly have said to piss you off this time?" I smile sweetly, my voice laced with sarcasm. She's only called him on average every hour, all day.

"Same bull … She doesn't want you around "her" baby … she wants me to promise not to bring you with me to LA. I don't know what her goddamn problem is suddenly. She stayed on a boat with you and never said a wrong word and now she thinks she has some leverage, she can call the shots. She'll soon realize that when it comes to you then she hasn't got a fucking chance!" He snaps again then sighs. Moving the ice bag on his hand to a new spot.

"I'm sorry, baby … I'm trying not to yell at you. This isn't you … It's her. She knows how to get under my skin." He leans on the bar and goes to lift a glass, thinks better of it and walks away. I had noticed over the last few days he hadn't drunk any alcohol at all, hadn't pushed me to drink either despite boss Carrero being someone who had wine with every meal and tried to get me drunk at every opportunity. It crosses my mind, but I let it go.

"She'll just keep hounding you until you agree, Jake … I think she's still in love with you," I say boldly, he pauses as he walks to the couch near me and looks me up and down in disbelief.

"I don't think so … It's been years and she's the one who screwed my best mate and caused me to break things off." He grabs my hand and pulls me with him, yanking me down on top of him when he sits, the soft leather cushioning me. He wraps me in his arms, pulling me with him as he slides onto his back and stretches out along the seat, me laying over him. His mouth against my temple and our arms wrapped around each other, face-t- face. I love this position, it always feels so restful and safe.

"I think it's why she hates me so much … I know you think I'm wrong, but I'm a girl … I understand girls … She's still in love with you, it was obvious even on the boat weeks ago." I point out with a yawn, tired from our trip.

"Well if she is then that's her problem, not ours … Good luck to her, because she's never going to get anywhere with it. Her problem with you better stay away from me, I'm the last person in the world you want to be around if they have a problem with you." His hand comes to the back of my hair, holding me against him tightly, he kisses me on top of the head.

"Want to have a movie night and some hot sex? I brought home that bondage gear we found on the boat, best way to kill stress." I hear the smile in his voice, he's already bored talking about Marissa and wants to forget about it for one night. My body is already responding to his suggestion. I lift my head up and grin at him, showing my full cooperation.

"As if I ever say *no* to you." I smile widely, eyes already heavy with desire and body churning with heat.

"Maybe we'll skip the movies and just go straight to bed." He grins back. "We can have dinner later."

Without warning he scoops me up into a bundle and jumps up from the couch, carrying me to the bedroom. He tosses me on his huge bed, kicking his door shut behind him and coming at me like a playful child, jumping on top of me and hauling me over on top of him.

Chapter 14

"Ready?" He looks at me as his car door is opened and holds out his hand. The Carrero building looms up in front of us and it feels like I haven't been here in weeks. So much has changed in such a short time. He slides out of the car, pulling me with him and straightens up as Jefferson shuts the door behind us. Normally, Jake would use the underground car park, but Jefferson has errands to run for him today, so we are being dropped at the front door. This is all very public, right outside the main entrance to Carrero House in the morning rush. I take a deep, anxious breath, pushing down the onslaught of emotions and nod.

I tense as we enter the building, the urge to pull my hand out of his as heads turn at our arrival. Faces beaming our way, quiet whispers, and stifled grins as people pretend not to be staring. We are obviously the talk of the building and very much confirming rumors while walking hand in hand through the foyer.

Ughhh, this is embarrassing.

I was surprised to find my work clothes hanging in Jake's wardrobe beside more of my outfits from my apartment this morning. Apparently, while we were away, Jefferson had Sarah pack me some essentials for our return at Jake's bidding.

Nice to know my commandeering man still exists in there somewhere.

I'm in my familiar gray suit jacket and pencil skirt and my favorite Louboutin black stiletto heels, I feel like old PA Emma except for the fact my boss is now casually walking with his fingers entwined in mine. Leading me to the elevator with a smug expression on his face of a guy who got a lot of sex before getting out of bed this morning. I shake my head at him, wishing he wouldn't make it so obvious but that glint in his eye serves as a warning that he will be far worse if I protest. I wouldn't put it past him to pick me up over his shoulder and drag me to the nearest elevator to make out.

He throws me a warning eyebrow lift when I try to slide my fingers out of his and I give up, he's never been a guy who it's wise to try to push. He has no qualms about making a scene and he doesn't care what people think about him.

We get to the sixty-fifth floor without too much drama, or people making it obvious they are outright mesmerized, I know most of the building has non-stopped gossiped about our dance floor kiss at the Marie Curie ball and as this is the first time most can see for themselves that the rumor is true, people are nosing our way.

Was that really just over a week ago?

I can't believe it's only been days. I feel like Jake's been with me for so much longer, that we spent a month on that yacht, so much has happened and things between us got so intense so quickly that I can't even begin to dissect that it's only been a week.

Luckily the elevator is full, so Jake's wandering hands can only skim my ass briefly, trying to be on best behavior.

"Want to come christen my desk?" he whispers as he

pulls me after him to my old familiar offices when we hit our floor.

"Jake!" I scold, my old PA mode kicking in. "When we're at work then I'm going to be the Emma you paid for." I let go of his hand haughtily and walk forward fast, toward my old desk, feet away. Jumping with a flinch as he smacks my ass loudly and I feel about ten heads snap around to look as I hold myself in check from reacting.

"I swear to god …" I begin to say slowly through gritted teeth, he only smiles with a flick of his eyebrows before walking past into his own office and leaving the door wide open. I stand outside it and throw my bag on the desk, my face flaming with embarrassment, pushing down the urge to throw something at him through his door.

I swear, I may actually throttle him.

I note that Margo's personal effects are gone already, she's cleared this in anticipation of my return. I feel sad at the evidence, I would really have loved to see her again, a chance to just talk to her about coming back.

"Miss. Anderson … I've something that requires your immediate attention." Jake's voice floats through at me and already I regret coming to work for him. I push down that inner irritation knowing that this is going to be some sexual reference, except unlike old me, I can't threaten to sue him to make him behave or brush off his advances anymore. I walk into his office, turn and walk back out when I see that him patting the new couch in his office suggestively, loosening his tie with a naughty look in his eye.

"Work! … Remember!" I yell back and stomp off to find a coffee, I'm going to need it today. We really need to set some ground rules about this working together or I'll end up choking him with his own tie.

"I forgot what PA Emma was like." He yells back, but

there's only amusement in his voice. "I've changed my mind … I might fire you after all." I ignore him and instead begin pulling out all the files Margo has left for me, briefs getting me up to speed on things I've missed and other things in mid-flow. I've missed a huge amount of work in the last month, this will be a nightmare to get my head around and the last thing I need is Jake trying to get me naked in his office.

I look up and spy Rosalie grinning at me from the outer office and smile back. She seems genuinely happy to see me, waving, she turns back to her desk and carries on working. It makes me feel a little bit warmer inside, a little less upset with my boyfriend, or boss's, overly public displays of affection.

An hour later Jake comes strolling out to my desk where I'm wading through all the documents Margo has left for me, two empty coffee mugs and a lot of scrunched up notes in the bin. He's lost his jacket and tie and is back in rolled up blue shirt with open collar, untucked at the waist, it's devastating to me, like it always is. I'm a sucker for this look on him and without looking directly at him I feel my temperature soar with my heart beat.

"I want to fuck you," he says quietly, leaning into my ear so only I can hear. My knee's press together under the table; I put my pen down and look up at his serious face with indulgence

"Jake. First, will you stop calling it that … Second … No! We're at work, to work … You get enough at home, and this morning," I whisper looking around nervously in case anyone can hear us.

Maybe I should shut my office door from now on, Rosalie is within ear shot most of the time.

"Fine … Lets screw, copulate, make love, have sex … Whatever you want to call it. You're literally ten feet away, wearing a tight ass skirt and stilettos and I'm supposed to not feel horny? *bambino,* please … I've a really convenient second room that locks, with a couch in there … Remember?" He looks at me in a way that sends my inner organs into a frenzy, my body clenching ecstatically, leaning in close enough to kiss without effort, his aftershave drawing me in.

I need to have more control than this.

I cast my mind back to the changing room type second door inside his office and the last time I saw that couch, months ago, before he ever kissed me, before I even knew how I felt about him and I'm more than tempted.

"You can't do this to me." I pout. "It's not fair."

"You think this is a one-sided deal?" he laughs. "Baby, I've had to stop myself coming through here about eighteen times in the last hour, just ripping that skirt off and taking you on the desk … It's not fair on me, you, looking like that and not being allowed to do anything about it." He leans down planting a chaste kiss on my cheek. "I'm going for a cold shower before I do end up making good on that threat." He walks off toward the outer office, toward Rosalie's external desk, his ass looking particularly hot in his tailored gray pants.

"Jake, wait," I say impulsively. He turns slowly and looks me up and down, his face blank but his eyes heavy, his pupils dilated still from his obvious horny state.

Oh god, how sexy he looks standing there. Screw it.

"Yes, Miss. Anderson?" His voice is low and husky and full of hidden intent, I feel my knees press together more firmly in response.

Jesus … what he does to me.

"I ummm, think I need you to look these over in your office," I say brightly, deliberately getting up to walk sexily into his room without a backward glance. I make sure I walk to his desk in full sight of the open door and bend over enough to slide the file down, just enough for my jacket to ride up, exposing my tight skirt, hugging my butt, lifting one foot slightly as though I'm reaching out, so my legs look shapelier in the confined material. I hear the door shut behind me almost immediately, his hands come up my thighs; I'm turned and thrown over his shoulder instantly, letting out a small squeal and giggle as he marches me toward that internal door.

* * *

I stretch out in my chair and arch my back, my desk is littered with papers, my laptop, files, and an overwhelming amount of random crap. It's been a hard few days, not made any easier by my oversexed boss-lover and his attempts at dragging me into his cupboard at every opportunity. He's succeeded more times than I want to admit, making that couch almost like a bed away from home.

He's finally settled down into some sort of work routine and left me alone today, I can see him through the open door, head down as he types, focus intent, that old Carrero frown in place, showing he means business. I watch him for a few seconds, feeling that swell of love inside of me. I can't stop it, every time I look at him, I have to pinch myself that this is real, that I'm really here. He senses my eyes on him and looks up, throwing me a knee weakening smile, his youthful boyish, "I'm way too hot to be legal", smile. I grin back and turn away, not wanting to give him too much encouragement. It doesn't take much to send that libido spinning out my way lately and I only just managed to get really absorbed in my work.

I hear his phone ring, he sounds agitated when he answers, and I know without confirmation that it's her again.

Ever since our return they have argued non-stop. He's refusing to sit down with the lawyers until they can come to some sort of middle ground on where I fit in on this whole thing.

I've told him so many times that I shouldn't be a factor in this, that I'll step out and keep my distance until the baby is born for the sake of peace. He's adamant he won't let her dictate his life and I know that stubborn streak too well, he will never back down. He's not capable of backing down when he's got the bit between his teeth, that stubborn side to him won't let him. I tune out and focus back on what I'm doing and try to ignore the way his tone and anger are rising slowly or the way my stomach aches at the thought of her.

* * *

A little after noon I get up and take him through the files I've gone through, some contracts he needs to check, a new start-up he's interested in investing in, and some minor publicity suggestions from Wilma. He's glaring at a document in front of him, obviously unhappy with something contained within, it makes me smile. Despite loving him as boyfriend, the Jake I had missed most was boss Carrero and his multitude of facial expressions when he was absorbed in something mundane. He had a face that could say a million things without opening his mouth, when he wasn't maintaining his poker face that is.

"Hey," I say softly, his chin lifts to look at me.

"Hey," he replies with a smile, getting up and coming around the desk to pull me against him. I glance back to see if anyone is watching through the open door and catch Rosalie turning away quickly. I try to push myself away, but he only tightens his grip.

"Stop caring about what people will think or say." He nuzzles my neck, making me melt against him a little too readily. I really have no willpower when it comes to his touch.

"It's easy for you to say that … You intimidate everyone … No one would say a thing about you, for fear of your wrath. They all think I'm some sort of gold digging whore who's bedding the boss to get my job back." I sigh. He brings his face to meet mine, frowning, he doesn't like what I've said.

"I'll fire anyone I catch saying that," he says seriously, his tone a tad harsh and sadly, I know he means every word. I push away from him and straighten my clothes, making it clear that I need to go.

"I've got to go to Queens and meet Sarah." I remind him. "I need more clothes and things from the apartment and I need to sit down and talk to her properly before she goes to work." He steps forward, closing the gap between us again and kisses me on the mouth, taking a moment to linger with his lips against mine. He has one hand on my face, holding me steady, slow grazing of lips and brush of tongue. It's hard not to react when he kisses me this way, the urge to grab him and kiss him harder makes my fingers twitch. He finally steps back.

"Jefferson is already waiting." He straightens my jacket and smooths down my blouse, lingering over my cleavage with a naughty smile that gains him an indulgent one back.

What am I to do with you?

"I've a meeting with my lawyer while you're gone, we'll eat when you're back, *miele.*" His fingertips come up to stroke my lower lip tenderly, his eyes focused on mine.

"She isn't going to be too pleased when I tell her you've asked me to move into your apartment full-time." I add. We had briefly talked about this last night, he'd been adamant and even though I want nothing more than to curl up in his bed every night, a part of me knows the thought terrifies me and Sarah will be upset at the speed this is all happening. It has all happened so suddenly, we are moving so fast. He shrugs, that infuriating mannerism of his when he couldn't care less about someone opposing what he really wants.

"She has her live-in boyfriend … You two rarely see each other because of your work schedules." He moves back around his desk, sliding back into his seat and picking up the file he'd thrown down. "It's going to happen, Emma … Whether it's now or in a month or two … You think I'm going to be happy with living apart for long?"

"You don't think this is moving too fast?" I tried to talk this through sensibly, but he'd closed me down every time, stubborn and set on what he wants. Typical Jake, it was always how he wanted things and I get no say unless it is to agree.

"Nope … We practically lived together when you were just my PA. Why is this suddenly something scary? … If you don't want to do it then just tell me." He sits back in agitation, childish pout face appearing, indicating I've hurt his feelings. He pushes away the file, in an almost temper tantrum.

Little boy Carrero.

"I do want this," I say quickly, trying to smooth the ruffled feathers of my man child. "It's just, it's serious, Jake … What if spending all this time working and living together makes you feel caged in … Restless … I just want to be sure that you've thought about it. I mean, you went from serious man-whore to a one-woman man overnight." I move to the chair beside his desk and sit down, moving closer so outside ears won't be able to hear us. "I'm just worried this is so full on so quickly that you'll start missing being free and single." I look away from him to the view outside, cursing myself for letting Miss. Insecurity show face again. I hear him sigh, he leans forward so our heads are close, his hand comes to find mine and pulls it between us. He starts playing with my fingers between his thumb and forefinger, dwarfing my hands.

"You've got to stop thinking that way, and you've got to stop measuring our relationship from the night I told you I loved you … I've loved you for a lot longer than that, I've wanted you for months. Our relationship started over a year ago, Emma, there's nothing rushed about where we are now, if anything, I've had the patience of a saint to wait this long to ask you." He smiles, his killer Casanova Carrero smile and I feel myself return it, he knows how to play me so easily.

"I don't want you to get fed up with me … Constantly being together can't be healthy." I add gently.

"It won't be like that, we're still enjoying being together in ways which we never allowed, this is the honeymoon period. When we get comfier we'll do things apart … You and Sarah, Leila … Sophie … I still will want to go out with Daniel. I have other friends too that you probably wouldn't be comfortable around. Friends I really wouldn't trust near you. I'll still have to take some solo business trips when things are hectic and you're needed here. There are no rules, we make them up as we go *miele.*" He strokes my fingers, voice low and sincere.

I know he's not saying it, but he also means trips to LA once a month, too.

"It makes no sense to me having you beside me at work, then you, going home to Queens at night … I want you home with me, to kick back and unwind. Here, we're starting to get back into our roles as boss and PA … I want my girlfriend when we're not working."

"Sarah's going to try and talk me out of it" I say, watching him play with my fingers one by one, enjoying the sensation. "She'll think we're rushing things." I look up at him and shake my head when he shrugs, his answer to everything. Infuriatingly so.

"I'm not going to force you, Emma … Go see her, collect what you need for this week anyway then let me know what you decide … I won't be mad, but I want you to know that it will happen." He moves forward, kissing me quickly before letting me get up to leave. I ruffle my fingers lightly through his hair for a moment, smiling at the way he looks up at me and our eyes instantly connect.

A face that could melt icebergs. And it's all mine. Stubborn to a fault.

I turn and walk off, grabbing my bag as I pass my desk. I can feel his eyes on me, but I don't look around. I like torturing him in subtle ways, it makes me feel good to know that I have a little power over him too, probably more than I realize, besides, he can be so commandeering sometimes that he deserves it.

I want to move in with him, but I'm also terrified. It's a huge step for me, to be dependent on someone else. His apartment, his things, he pays all the bills, his money, his furniture, his way!

I've always stood on my own two feet and what if it all goes to hell and we break up? I can't go crawling back to Sarah if I've nowhere else to go.

My head goes into overdrive thinking this all through as I make my way down to the underground car park to find Jefferson and one of Jake's four by fours, parked and waiting.

***

"Wow … Are you sure, Emma? … It's really fast!" Sarah remarks, sitting opposite me on the couch, her eyes wide in disbelief.

"I know it's just … He's right, though. We're working side by side, we spend so much time on business, flying places, sharing rooms … We dove straight into a committed relationship and missed out on dates and going slow. It's what he wants and as much as it scares me, I want it too. It just feels like this is how it should be." I answer a little stiltedly, I had rehearsed this on the drive over. She watches me for a long time, sipping her coffee and thinking.

"But? Come on, I can practically hear the hesitation." She raises an eyebrow at me. I sigh and sink back on the cushions.

"But a part of me is terrified, a part of me is running for the hills screaming right now. I don't even know why, I can't begin to analyze it." I slide my coffee mug on the table and slide off my stilettos, letting them drop to the floor as I tuck my legs in under me.

"No wonder. You spent your entire life being self-reliant, your own boss. Keeping people at arm's length so they didn't hurt you. He's asking you to just throw all in and put all your hopes and trust on your relationship after like a week … That's crazy." She waves a hand in the air as though to emphasize the point.

"Except we've been in love for so much longer. I can see why this isn't fast to him, he's that kind of impulsive person. He wants, so he takes, he's always had things his own way." I sigh and haul a cushion into my lap, picking at the fringe in agitation.

"I think that's just a male trait to be fair." Sarah slides her mug down and mirrors my pose with her legs underneath her. She's dressed in her chef whites ready for her shift this afternoon. "So, what are you going to tell him, what are you going to do?"

"I don't want to hurt him, he's always been right in the past when I've been scared to follow. Maybe this once I should just trust that he knows best." I rub my cheeks with my palms, frustrated at myself for feeling so torn about something that should be so simple.

"I don't want another room mate." She pouts. "What about, you move in with him, but we leave your room available for you? Like, you can leave stuff here that you wouldn't want to take and maybe have it ready for staying over sometimes?" she asks hopefully, her eyes almost pleading. I know her too well, she's offering me a way out of making a final decision, she's offering me a backup plan. She's being that girl who always helps me figure things out, that girl I love.

"I guess that could work … It's not like Jake will expect me to pay for anything, so I can still contribute here, like I've always done." I shrug, annoyed at myself for adopting his mannerism. "So technically I'll have moved out, but I'll still have the option of coming back? Maybe I could spend the odd night here to catch up." I smile, warmed by her enthusiastic nod.

I like this plan, it gives me an option C … Not living solely with him or her but choosing to stay with him unless I need an out.

Some stability, should he decide the full on committed relationship with someone so emotionally messed up isn't so great after all. The thought makes my stomach sink with a lurch.

"Okay, sorted! So, enough about that … I only have an hour before I have to get to work and I want all the juicy gossip … What being in love with *the* Jake Carrero is like! How good is he in bed, really? I want all the dirty, minute details." She giggles cheekily, and I sigh, I knew this was coming the second she got me alone.

***

I walk out of the elevator a couple of hours later, Jefferson is taking most of my bags straight to Jake's apartment and has dropped me back at Carrero House. I feel disappointed to see both Rosalie's desk and Jake's office are empty and check my watch. It's only mid-afternoon, I walk in and check my iPad on the desk, pulling up the schedule and see Rosalie has added in a meeting. Jake's meeting with the legal team overseeing the Hunter-Carrero ship merger, things must be moving along with the first hotel cruiser.

I sigh and make my way back out to Rosalie's desk to collect some letters and make myself busy. All the answer machines are on, the office is deathly quiet and even the other secretaries on this floor seemed to have disappeared. I miss him already and it makes me smile. I've only been gone a couple of hours and already I'm impatient to see him again, to feel his hands on me and kiss me the way he does. I keep telling myself that it's only been a week, that I shouldn't be this dependent on him so soon or even at all. I'm falling too far and too deep. Something inside of me tells me to let it go, to trust him for once and just go with it. See where this goes.

***

Absorbed in an email I'm typing I hear them finally return, it's late in the day and I ended up eating lunch alone when hunger made me feel faint.

"You missed an epic meeting." Jake's voice smooths over

me deliciously, he dumps files on my desk and comes around to haul me out of my seat by the arm. I squeal as he slides down into the chair he pulled me from and pulls me back on top of him in a heap across his knee like a child as he leans back casually and swings the chair so I have to hold on for dear life. He grins childishly and lifts his legs, planting his feet on the desk so I'm tipped closer to him, my face ending up nose to nose with him, he raises his eyebrows suggestively then plants a soft kiss on my mouth. "I missed you, sexy."

"Stop misbehaving." I laugh and try to push myself upright, I should give up trying to conceal the things he does from the floor staff out there, it's like trying to swim against the tide, he's always so inappropriately public.

"What did I miss?" I challenge playfully, giving up the fight and instead laying in his embrace just happy to be back in his arms and sliding my own around his neck to nuzzle closer.

"My father having a massive tantrum and glaring at everyone silently through the entirety of the meeting. Epic in every way." He grins, obviously amused. "He still hates the fact I put this merger in place, it didn't help that Daniel's father was there … if looks could kill. I felt sorry for the poor guy, though."

"Ouch." I respond remembering that Jake had told me Carrero had an affair with Daniel's mother years ago. The two men are still at war over it even now.

"Apart from that, everything is going to plan, they're moving to start production on the first two ships … It's a lengthy process, maybe two years or more before we launch our first five-star floating spa and hotel. Better book ourselves a suite now." I see his excitement and congratulate him with a kiss, as usual, he takes the opportunity to turn it into a full on passionate embrace, lasting minutes. Finally breaking away he tilts me back to him, so we're nose to nose again.

"So? Are you going to break my heart and tell me you only brought enough clothes for a couple of nights?" he asks seriously, his eyes coming to mine, there's something almost apprehensive about the look he's giving me. Always disarming me with that lost boy look in those deep green eyes.

"I packed up anything I want … Everything I need … To stay with you indefinitely." I smile softly, grinning as his face breaks into his famous happy as Larry smile. "I left my room with the stuff I would otherwise need to put in storage until I decide what to do with it and the understanding that I pay Sarah for it instead … In case you ever turf me out." I giggle as he pulls me back to his mouth for a celebratory peck on the lips.

"There's more chance of you leaving me, *bella.*" He swings us back in the chair like it's a rocker, and it creaks miserably under our combined weight. "Want to call it a day and go home with me to celebrate? … There's a huge hot tub with our name on it and I haven't seen you naked in seven hours, I'm getting withdrawals." He pulls his feet off the desk, moving to stand with me in his arms.

"Do you intend to carry me off regardless of the answer?" I laugh.

"Pretty much." He plants a chaste kiss on the corner of my mouth and puts me on my feet. "I need to go grab some files from my desk and my laptop … Get ready to go. Home it is. There's some advantages to being your boss." He orders with a wink before stalking off to his open doorway with a smile.

Chapter 15

We're sitting with feet entwined on the huge king size bed in Jake's bedroom, backs against the padded headboard and a mountain of cushions with some action movie playing on his oversized flat screen TV hanging from the ceiling. There are Chinese food tubs standing all over the bed around us, open and easy to reach for dipping into.

I'm wearing one of his T-shirts after our not so clean bubble bath and he's in a pair of dark gray sweat pants and a naked torso, showcasing his perfect chiseled body and tribal ink perfectly. I have a serious case of "my boyfriend's so hot" swoons as I watch his muscular arms and shoulders flex and tense as he shovels food into his mouth with the expertise of an avid Chinese food eater. He leans forward with chop sticks full of noodles and pops it in my mouth without waiting to ask if I even want any, his eyes glued to what he's watching. I'm being obedient and letting him stuff me full of food despite having the ability to feed myself. Amused by the way Jake has this constant need to tend to my every need like a mother hen.

Somehow, I like it like this, that he looks after me in small ways I would never have guessed him capable of. Force feeding me his food seems to be a recurring thing. He never seems to feel I've eaten enough and is always trying to ram food in my mouth.

There's a knock on the bedroom door, which is standing open and one of his security staff appear, dressed all in black. Another faceless person I've yet to find out the name of.

"Mr. Carrero ... Daniel Hunter is here to see you," he says apologetically, averting his eyes as he sees my long, naked legs on top of the sheets and his extremely scarce covering over my body. I'm glad I put some underwear on after our bath.

"Send him in," Jake replies with a mouthful, still not taking eyes off his movie, he leans to the end of the bed yanking up the throw which normally gets laid neatly there by the housekeeper and pulls it over my lower half. It makes me smile, he obviously didn't like the fact his security just checked me out. He covers me up while still chewing and watching his godawful film. Jake is a contradiction in so many ways, laid-back and confident yet also a little, green-eyed jealous child who doesn't like other men looking at me.

The green eyes suit him.

The man walks away, I make a mental note to learn the names and make friends with this almost invisible staff I occasionally see now that I live here, especially the house keeper, Nora, who seems to be the master of discretion. I feel ignorant and awkward when I see them in passing. It never bothered me when I was just his PA because they were his staff, and I was staff. But this was my home now and I didn't want to be rude.

"All right, bud." Daniel comes bounding in, stopping a moment when he sees me but continues almost flawlessly. "Was going to ask if you fancied a night on the tiles but I can see you're busy with the little woman." He looks me up and down oddly, I guess he's trying to figure out why I'm still on the scene, it's been over a month since the yacht trip he was on with us and he knows Jake's attention span for women peaks at four weeks, max. I guess he figured Jake would have got bored with my company long ago.

"I'm off the booze lately." Jake says; this surprises me, I had noticed his lack of alcohol on our trip, but he'd never mentioned it was intentional "She's not my little woman, she's my better half." He throws Daniel a look that's hard to translate, they have their own language these two. Goes hand in hand with the special bromance of Carrero and Hunter.

"Hey, better half." Daniel salutes me with a smile and I smile back, he's an odd one and our relationship is still in the teething stage.

"Hey." I smile back genuinely, for Jake's sake I really want to try to like Hunter, maybe form a mutual friendship now I'm no longer staff. I had never felt at ease with him as Jake's PA, maybe I would now that the dynamic had shifted.

Daniel comes to the bed, climbs on the end and gets comfy before picking up a box, Jake throws him some unopened chop sticks, as though granting permission to dig in and both men sit glued to the movie in silence for a few moments. It's some loud, all shooting, all exploding, macho male thing with a guy who looks a lot like someone who once felt me up in a nightclub in Vegas. Daniel starts eating, before pointing at something on screen with a mouth full.

"That twat still owes me $1500 for that bet in London," he mumbles.

"Jesus, Danny, tell me you didn't actually bed that weird chick with the wonky teeth." Jake drops his chop sticks into the tub of food he's eating and grimaces, looking at Daniel as though he's something disgusting. Something that puts Jake off his food. Daniel's sex life.

"A bet's a bet, Jakey boy. I just got really pissed and then she looked doable." He shrugs and continues eating.

"I thought you had some standards, maybe even really low ones. But that chick looked like a man in drag with a really shitty wig." Jake turns to me with a look that says, "you had to see her." He throws a chopstick at Daniel's head But Daniel ducks too late and it bounces off the top of his perfect blonde hair. Daniel may have a fetish for one-night stands and slutty girls, but he had the looks of a guy who should get any woman he wants. He's all blonde and blue eyed to Jake's dark hair and green eyes. As a duo, I'm sure the two of them must have pulled any women for miles.

"I thought Daniel's standard was porn star, isn't that like the lowest you can go. A girl who's paid to let everyone sleep with her?" I smile at Jake with a wicked gleam in my eye, Daniel frowns up at me.

"Hey! Some of those ladies are the highest paid in the profession, they're not prostitutes. I happen to like a girl who can get down and dirty and knows what she's doing." He throws the chopstick back at Jake who bats it away expertly.

"They're kinda like prostitute's, mate." Jake smirks.

"Shut up! Totally different. Besides, not so long ago you weren't so high and mighty with the standards. Just cos you're all loved up doesn't mean you haven't ground on a few—"

"I swear if you finish that sentence you'll regret it." Jake warns, an instant frost to the atmosphere between them. For a moment, there's a cold standoff of glares and eyeball communication. Seems Hunter is just as stubborn as Jake.

"I'd say keep your shirt on but it's already AWOL." Daniel breaks the tension with a smirk and Jake just throws another chopstick at his head. I wonder if this is how all men behave in the company of their so-called best friends.

"You're just jealous that my shirt's off for Emma and not you." He winks back. Lifting an arm and tensing a bicep with a sexy wiggle toward Daniel. I can't help but admire the bulge, I've never actually seen him tense a bicep on purpose and I almost faint with just how toned and muscular he is when he does it.

Is it okay to swoon over your own boyfriend? I think it is, right?

"Put it away, Carrero, I've told you a million times, I'm just not into you." Daniel seems to be fed up with his choice of food and looks through the extra boxes on the bed for something else.

"Says the guy who crashed my Chinese food party to come stare at a TV with me. Are you worried I won't love you anymore now I have Ems?" Jake discards his food and stretches out, leaning back into the sea of cushions behind us. Noticing I have long since discarded my food, he hauls me over to nestle in his arm and lay my head on his shoulder. I stretch out alongside him and snuggle in against his body.

"Totally heartbroken over here," Daniel says flatly without looking up, finds something he wants and settles back down to dig in and watch a particularly bloody scene on the screen.

Both men seem zoned in on the mass shooting and blood thirsty hero, hacking bad guys to bits with a large sword. I never understood action movies and all that bloodlust.

"Don't worry, Danny, I'll still keep you as my side chick, snuggle when Emma's not looking." He squeezes me, and I quell the urge to laugh at them.

"I'm too much woman to be your side chick, I'm an all or nothing kind of guy when it comes to you." Daniel doesn't even look back. There's a moment of pause, I see his body language change subtly as he changes tone completely. "Have you heard from Leila lately?" His voice sounds tense, I catch Jake frowning at the back of his head rather intensely for a moment.

"Why would you ask about Leila? I thought you two stayed well clear of each other?" Jake sits up, I know that look on his face. A dog with a bone, sniffing out some little secret. Whatever he's caught onto has peaked his Rottweiler mode.

"No reason. Just, you know, sometimes I wonder how she is." Daniel slides his food on the floor and lays out across the end of the bed lifting his feet up to get comfy.

"Okay, cut the shit. What happened with Leila?" Jake's domineering protective tone cuts in, he picks up the TV remote and pauses his movie, slides up, leaving me laying on the bed and leans forward, arms braced on his bent knees. Daniel gets up and looks sheepish.

"I kinda did a shitty thing. Don't go crazy … I know you're going to want to go crazy but swear. Swear on Emma's head—"

"Don't you fucking dare!" Jake jumps to his feet at the side of the bed and stalks toward him menacingly, all male testosterone flying now. "What did you do?"

"Look, maybe we should take this elsewhere, I mean, I know Emma and Leila are kinda close." Daniel's stalling, hands up defensively and Jake looks ready to start going ten rounds with him.

"All the more reason she should know, because if Leila needs a shoulder to cry on then I'm pretty sure she would choose Emma over me. Spit it out." Jake looks mad and Daniel hesitates, eyes darting to the floor and fidgeting with a chopstick in his hand. He sighs heavily.

"We had sex … And then I kinda bailed out and didn't call her again." Daniel at least looks sorry, his face losing all color. I tense as I see Jake go stiff, fighter mode engaging, and he stalks away angrily, pacing around and muttering a string of curse words as he clenches and unclenches fists.

I'm shocked that Leila would even look at Hunter, let alone sleep with him. I'm devastated that he would treat her that way and the urge to go call her hits me monumentally in the stomach, I just glare at him with severe hatred.

"What the fuck? I told you to stay away from her, you don't think you hurting her once was enough? Of all the women to fuck around on, she isn't one of them." Jake's yelling, voice tense and waving hands at Daniel. I sit biting my lip, nervous of the unfolding scene. Confused that Jake's implying this isn't the first time he's hurt her. I want to punch Daniel in his smarmy face.

"I know, okay, I was a complete shit. I didn't know how else to deal with it." Daniel is also pacing now in the opposite direction and they keep bypassing each other at the foot of the bed.

"You deal with it by not fucking sleeping with her. Did you learn nothing when you did it the first time around? You ripped her fucking heart out!" Jake's furious, Daniel even seems nervous of his rage and they're doing some sort of male walking around dance in a circle now with a lot of heightened tension. I almost choke on the thought that he and Leila had been together twice in that way. I couldn't imagine it at all.

"I know … I know. Okay! Leila's like goddamn kryptonite for me. I want her but then when I get her I want to run for the hills man. You know me. I didn't go out to intentionally hurt her, it just happened." Daniel slumps down on the bed and Jake looks exhausted. His anger drifting away quickly as his friend looks forlorn.

"How did it happen? You swore …" The two of them sit

down on the end of the bed, side by side and I watch intently. Silently drawing the back of Daniel's head daggers with my eyes.

Asshole!

"I know … We were drunk, partying … You know how it is, you know how she is. All fun and smiles and flirty and then she kissed me. That's all it took." Daniel gets up and runs a hand through his hair. "Leila is too good for me, I know that. I can't help myself though. I haven't talked to her since … Jake, maybe you could …"

"Hell no. Not this time. You do the decent thing and you talk to her. You man up and you tell that girl you're sorry, stop being the asshole you always make her think you are." Jake gets up too and they face each other.

"I don't know what to say to her." Daniel looks lost and they stand silently mulling it over, looking at each other, Daniel wary and Jake pissed.

"Can I just intervene? … Daniel, Leila would probably feel a lot better if you just sent her a text and said something like *I'm sorry I'm an asshole*. She doesn't hold grudges. She's not naive and if it was just a one-night hook up then show her some respect at least. Treat her like a human, not a cast off." I still want to punch him in the throat for hurting my beautiful little friend.

"That's the issue." Jake turns to me with a look that seems deflated. "Daniel's been in love with her since forever, he just can't admit it to himself. So, he acts like a prize moron instead." He throws an accusing glare back at Hunter.

I almost choke. I could never imagine the man-whore known as Hunter to give two craps about any woman let alone love one. I was with them on the boat, he had his porn star and she was with one of Jake's twin friends, neither seemed to care that the other had dates.

"I'm not in love with her, she just makes me crazy." He paces away and then back as though he's unsure how to behave.

"Scared. I think that's the word you're looking for." Jake crosses his arms across his chest and stands tapping a bare foot, watching Hunter mull around.

"Shut up. It's not love, I'm not scared. It's just … It's—"

"Complicated?" I butt in and sigh with a smile when I see the agreeing nod from him.

"Told ya." Jake smiles at me.

"Totally."

"What? What the hell does that mean? You two have some coupley inside language now, or what?" Daniel's almost pouting as Jake and I turn to look at him a little sympathetically.

"I think I used the word complicated maybe a dozen times to brush off how I really felt for Jake." I point out.

"I think it was more like thirty times for me." Jake shrugs.

"Fuck's sake. You two need to back off, okay. Leila is not the girl I'm in love with. Enjoy your Chinese, I'm going to hit the gym and then abuse your shower. I'm staying the night so keep the noise down." Daniel goes to storm off but Jake halts him.

"Stay here, *bella*, I need to have some words with my so-called best mate. I won't be long." He kisses me again, his hand smoothing my hair back before he jumps up, leaving all the food behind and stalks out, closing the door behind him. I sigh heavily, a weird trepidation in my gut.

I wait until everything goes quiet out in the sitting room before I get up and pull on some more modest clothing, pick up all the food and arrange it on the tray the security guard brought it all in on. I pad out of the room with it to the kitchen to get myself a drink and lay it on the counter. I notice neither of them are in the open plan space, they have obviously gone to Jake's games room, his room full of boy's gadgets, games consoles, and all things that I've zero interest in. It's far down the hall, opposite Jake's room.

I stand and ponder over what to do about Leila. Ponder over whether I should call her or wait to speak to Jake. She's my friend but all of this is so wildly outside my comfort zone, wildly outside my knowledge of sex and love and relationships. They all seem to have history and I know nothing until Jake comes back. If Daniel really is in love with her then Jake needs to talk sense into him, he needs to figure it out before Leila can hear from him. I ache for my friend, having been the one on the receiving end of heartache for the past few months and agonizing over how she must be feeling. I won't do anything until Jake tells me more, I need details, I need to know what's gone on between Daniel and Leila to get them here.

I feel the wave of exhaustion run over me, lately I haven't been getting enough rest thanks to Jake and his eternal energy and over potent libido, maybe I should just hit the sheets early tonight and sleep. No doubt Jake will come back and watch the rest of his movie, he could use the early night too.

Despite his appearance of boundless energy there's no way he isn't as tired as I am. It's been a long couple of weeks already.

Returning to the room I climb into bed properly, stripping back to his T-shirt and pick up a book from my bedside table, some light-hearted romance Leila gave me that had never peaked my interest back then. It's not too late but it's past seven, so going to bed isn't exactly unheard of. It's not long before my over exhausted mind drifts off mid-sentence.

* * *

"Baby, no!" Jake's disappointed voice breaks into my sleepy state. "I had plans for you." His voice is husky and thick but I'm too tired to open my eyes.

"I'm exhausted." I sigh, feeling his hands on my face, the heavy weight of his body on top of me, he smells good, a little too good.

"You're such a lightweight, *bambino* … I'm going to have to build your stamina up." He kisses me on the forehead and lifts his weight off me. "I'm going down to the gym with Daniel to expel some of this excess tension seeing as you're out of order. We'll talk tomorrow about Leila, okay?" he says softly, a finger stroking my cheek, I attempt to open one eye and see his gorgeous face inches above me, watching me with appreciation. "He's spending the night, we'll be an hour or two … Sleep, *bambino.*" He leans down, kissing me on the mouth again and leaves me to get the first decent night's sleep I've had since I was pulled into his arms on that dance floor.

* * *

I wake up alone in the huge bed, but Jake's side is messed up as though he's been here, I glance at the clock on his side, it's early, before 6.00 a.m. I vaguely remember him telling me that he needed to get back into his routine, early morning jogging and gym now that we're home. It seems that having me in his bed means he no longer drags me out to run like he used to, he's neglected it since we've been together. Not that he needed it with all the extra activity lately, I certainly didn't. I roll over to his side and inhale his pillows, the bed smells of him, his aftershave, and personal scent which is more comforting than any smell in the world. I wrap my arms around his cushions sighing heavily and fall back asleep.

I wake again with the alarm at seven and I can hear him in the shower off our room, it sounds like he's singing, and I stifle a giggle, he's surprisingly melodic. I close my eyes and listen intently.

Actually, he's more than melodic, Jake has a really sexy singing voice … I'm more than impressed.

I'm literally swooning with desire at this unexpected talent he has. He sounds like a singer from a band I was obsessed with in my teens, husky yet boyish, he could easily pull off soft rock with a voice like that. Desire over takes me, and I slide out of bed and pad into the open bathroom, I strip off and slide into the shower behind him. He seems to feel my approach, stops singing and turns, catches me and pulls me under the jets with him.

"She's awake!" He kisses me, wet faced and smelling of his familiar shower gel and shampoo.

"Barely. That sexy voice called me through here." I wrap my arms around his neck as he maneuvers me under the water and starts running his fingers through my hair, soaking it and letting it trail down my neck. He picks up the shampoo bottle.

"My irresistible singing in the shower, had your heart all of a flutter did it?" He dollops the shampoo in his hand and starts massaging it into my hair and scalp a little roughly.

"Maybe … Calm the hands, Carrero, you're not washing a dog." I lift my hands over his and slow down and ease his motion a little, helping him wash my hair. We stand for a moment while my hair is rinsed clean, his eyes flickering up and down the full length of me. I pause to reach for the shower gel which I'd put in here and he stops my hand.

"After ... You're going to need it." He gives me the naughty look I've come to know so well then knocks the breath out of me with his mouth against mine, in seconds he hoists me up to straddle him around the waist and pushes me back against the cold, tiled wall behind me. Deepening his kiss, his arms around me tightly, grinding against me with a fever that overtakes us both within seconds. My body never failing to react to this man.

"Do we still need a condom?" he asks gruffly, hands holding me up. I shake my head. I had begun oral contraception before heading out on the boat with him, the doctor had assured me we should be okay after two weeks to stop with condoms. Which would be today. He had remembered.

It feels amazing to no longer have anything between us, just skin on skin. He makes love to me up against the tiles, slow and deliberate, his mouth exploring me and bringing me to dizzying heights effortlessly, savoring the new sensation. Water pouring overhead and the noise muffling out my moans and cries.

* * *

Leaning against his body on my own feet as he washes me, I feel completely relaxed, my body still tingling, my breathing still labored. He bends down, kissing my shoulder and neck every few strokes of lathering my skin, his hands massaging me seductively. I could lay back and fall asleep this way, he has no idea how much I trust him, how soothing his touch is. I could literally curl naked around him and let him do whatever he wanted to me for an eternity without any fear or doubts.

"Baby?" he breathes softly behind me, his hands come

down over my shoulders and back, softly massaging soap into me with confident strokes. I can feel him tracing patterns with his fingers across my skin.

"Mmm hmm," I say, completely mesmerized by his hands.

"After you went to bed I got a call … I need to go to LA tonight. We're finally sitting down with the lawyers tomorrow … Marissa's agreed to some of the terms I laid out." His voice is wary, I feel myself stiffen. "I want you to come with me."

I close my eyes and shake my head, if he's going to see her then I don't want to go. I don't want to sit in a hotel twiddling my thumbs or pacing around waiting for him to come back. I could be here at work, or with Sarah. Not obsessing over the two of them sitting across a table, talking about a linked future, and their child. The thought makes me feel sick.

"I don't want to go to LA," I say quietly, I feel him move closer, pressing against my back, his hot body heat warming me.

"I don't want this to become something we fight about." He runs his finger down the back of my neck, sending shivers through every part of me. Planting a soft kiss between my shoulder blades before bringing his mouth back up to nape of my neck, pushing my head to one side and tracing his lips across my jaw. I know what he's trying to do, seduction as distraction.

Yeah, I'm well versed in all the Carrero tricks I'm afraid. I see through this.

"I don't want to go … To sit about waiting while you and she do whatever." I sigh heavily. I want to stay in my little ignorant bubble pretending Marissa and this baby don't exist for a little while longer. When the child is born, it'll be a part of our lives for an eternity, for now I just want the bliss of the two of us and no outside disruptions. Later, when it's here, I can accept and get used to the new dynamics it will bring to our lives, but for now, I don't have to like it.

"I told you, Emma … She doesn't get to keep you out, you'll be at the meeting too." His voice is determined. I spin on my heel so suddenly he almost loses his balance.

"No!" I snap "I don't want to go! … I don't want to be part of all that or to see her … And you … In the same place." Emotion fills me, and I try to turn away again, suddenly ashamed of my violent outburst. I don't want him to see just how insecure and jealous I am or can be. Embarrassed by my uncontrolled reaction.

"*Bambino*? … Emma? … Hey!" He grabs my face and hauls me back, pulling me against him, fresh tears rolling down my cheek. "Okay … okay." He soothes. "I'm sorry, I just figured keeping you involved was the best way … I don't want to upset you, *bella*." He kisses me softly on the mouth, trying to soothe away my distress. He nibbles my lower lip playfully trying to bring my mood back and quell my tears, it works a little and I feel myself begin to relax again. Sighing away the stupid emotions and wiping a hand across my already wet face. Completely pointless as every part of me is wet, Jake runs a thumb across my cheek with the same poor success.

Crying in the shower makes so much sense.

"I'll miss you while I'm gone." He smiles softly, bringing our heads together, the water from the shower still trickling over his hair and causing rivers to run down his cheek onto my breasts in an almost mesmerizing pattern.

"We haven't slept apart since you told me you loved me," I whisper shyly.

"It's been intentional." He watches my mouth, a finger coming up to trace my lips slowly. "Don't clam up on me, *neonata* … We should be talking about this." He sees my face change and backs off. My external bristle and cold mask connecting. Our eyes meet, and I see the indulgent frown.

"Okay, but we will talk about this at some point … The baby coming is inevitable. I know your instinct is to shut down and blank it but I'm not going to let you, not over this." That stubborn set to his jaw and raised eyebrow tell me that he means it.

I turn back around so I don't have to be interrogated by those eyes, tilting my head back so the water begins to rinse the left-over suds away from my hair, trying my best to make it clear that I'm done talking about this. I hear him take a slow steady breath, readying himself to say something else and cut in first.

"Just not today," I say quietly, relaxing when I feel his hands smooth over my hair to free it from the shampoo residue. He kisses my head and carries on washing my shoulders and back. The thing about Jake is that he knows me, maybe not every inner thought but he's learned enough about me to know when the wall has gone back up. Old Jake would have got pissy and tried to push, but all new and improved Jake knows when to let the battle simmer. I know it won't last, his impatient, overbearing, self will win over and he'll push me again and I hope to god by then I can get my head around this enough to talk.

"Stay home with me today … We won't go to work, if I have to leave you tonight then I want us to do something besides sitting in two different rooms stressing over paperwork all day." His hands move down my arms slowly, I can feel his body close, it sends tiny shivers through me but he's not actually touching me. His height towering over me, his wide frame making me feel small and dainty and suddenly so very vulnerable.

"You can't just take days off to stay in bed with your girlfriend." I turn and wrap myself in him, pushing away the sudden fragile emotional vibe I'm feeling. "Since I came back, workaholic Carrero seems to have run away." His hands come to knead my shoulders, I tilt my head to the side, closing my eyes, enjoying the way it feels.

"Well if we had stayed on the boat we wouldn't even be back by now, so I think I'm entitled to take days off, besides, I was focused on my job because I had nothing else worthy of my attention. I now have you." He tucks me back under his chin, so he can wrap his arms around me tightly and let his hands wander down my front teasingly.

"You had me before." I push back against him playfully, my butt molding into his groin.

"Hence why I made you work every waking hour and then some ... Had to find ways to be around your sexy little self almost constantly." His husky voice is right next to my ear, it sends tingles through me. "It's easy to be a workaholic when your PA is all you can focus on night and day and she's most definitely a slave driver." His mouth comes to my throat and up my jaw from behind, slowly, achingly good. Jake has moves, I'll give him that. He knows how to seduce.

"So, I must be slacking then, if now you're so lax about work that you're pulling constant sickies." I shove him off, giggling, batting his hands as they try to grope at me. He lifts me up off from my feet, wrapping his arms around me and squeezing me tightly, knocking the wind out of my sails, his mouth at my ear.

"Nope, you just got easy and let me do things I had only fantasized about." He drops me on my feet, turning me to him before bending down further and scooping me in a swift move so I'm up and straddling him within seconds. My arms coming around him and my legs gripping his waist. Back in the same position he had me in when he made love to me in here. He kisses me on the mouth, his elbow pushing the lever on the wall to cut the water off and carries me out of the cubicle, lifting towels from the heated rail with one hand. He slides me to my feet again, wrapping one around me the way you would wrap a child in an oversized towel and I pull it in, feeling the warmth envelope me as I watch him wrap one around his waist. He lifts another to dry his upper torso and then his hair, stopping to come and rub my hair a little brusquely.

"You're so romantic." I giggle, enjoying his lazy smile and the glint of his green eyes, he's amused, a good turn in our conversation. Away from her.

"Soooo?" He pulls me close by the towel at my neck, nose to nose. "Stay home or go to work?"

I hesitate, it feels so wrong to choose to not go in to work, it goes against all of PA Emma's ethics and principles, that version of me lives for her job. Girlfriend Emma, however, is already thinking about getting back in bed and being curled up in those tanned, tattooed arms with his wide chest only inches in front of me. I sigh with the effort of the decision.

"Times up!" He grins, bending down to scoop me up and marches me back through to the bedroom, throwing me unceremoniously down on the bed so that I bounce and lose the grip of my towel. I squeal as he dives on top of me, yanking the towels away and pinning my arms beside my head, his mouth coming in to devour my neck. I try to fight him off but he's relentless, pinning me down with arms and legs until I can't move, nibbling and biting and tickling me. I can't help laughing like a child.

I'm finally so exhausted from fighting and giggling that I stop trying, he leans over me looking utterly devastating. His hair ruffled and messy, his elated face more shadowy due to not shaving, muscles taut and bunching because of the way he's straining himself up. Carved perfection of ripples and lines that put most magazine models to shame and I can't believe it's all mine, I want to die from longing, my body reacting instantly. My lips part, my eyes get heavy as we gaze at one another, expressions turning hot and serious in an instant.

He leans down, planting a quick kiss on my lips then slides down the bed so his mouth trails down my abdomen. I giggle at the feather touch, tickling me, his hands come to my thighs, slide down slowly as he pulls my legs up at either side of him, pushing my knees outwards so I'm completely splayed out in front of him. I gasp in surprise, a little vulnerable at the position, catching a wolfish grin and naughty glint as I look down at him, he looks unbelievably young like this.

He bites his bottom lip, quirks his eyebrows, before yanking me down the bed a tad, making me yelp in surprise. He brings my pelvis underneath his face, my arms still stretched above my head.

He's in dominant mode again, his most comfortable persona when it comes to sex, I've never really had to initiate much sex related fun with him, he's always in control and ready to possess me. It makes him exciting and primal. It also takes away my insecurities about being too inexperienced with someone like him, not knowing how to behave or what to do to satisfy him, it's never been an issue as he's always just taken control of me effortlessly. Guided me, never made me feel like I had no clue to what I was doing. It's because I trust him.

He dips his head showing only dark hair and strong shoulders from my view point, my body arching as his mouth connects with my femininity.

***

Panting, I finally still, my legs flopping down with zero ability to hold them up any longer, my body sated and tired. He moves up and over me and gives me a slow, sexy kiss on my mouth, his tongue gently caressing mine with the taste of my completion on his tongue. Soft, erotic molding of mouths, gentle and toe-curling kissing. He pulls back with a satisfied look in his eye, the hint of a smile. Leaning over me like a predator surveying its dead prey proudly, I would let him dive in and devour me all over again just to feel this way every second. He bends as though to kiss me but pauses as there's a knock on the door. His face instantly changing to furrowed brow and irritation.

"What is it?" He barks back at the door. I stifle a giggle at his annoyance, it's a fate worse than death to interrupt Jake mid-sex. He smiles at me, shaking his head and jumps up to retrieve some sweat pants, throwing me a towel. I scurry up and wrap myself tightly before disappearing to the wardrobe, away from the view of the door.

He opens it once he pulls the pants on and stops to talk to whoever is on the outside, keeping it closed enough to conceal the bedroom, conceal me in stages of undress. I can only hear mumbles. I wait with my towel around me, unsure if I should dress, unsure if he'll come back to what we were doing.

My body feels like liquid, I'm sure if I look in the mirror I'll be glowing and flushed and showing signs of having been ravaged. He laughs, and it catches my attention. I love his laugh, it's so deep and carefree and male, yet there's a hint of boyishness to his normally husky tone when he laughs. I could close my eyes and listen to it forever.

He shuts the door and turns around to see where I've

gone, a look returning to lust when he sees me still draped in a towel. I'm surveying my clothes in the open cupboard in a bid to decide if I'm to get dressed or get back on the bed. He inhales deeply as though trying to calm his inner libido and a hint of disappointment on his face.

"We need to continue this later … I forgot Daniel was here." He grins, and I feel myself flush with embarrassment.

Oh, my god, how loud was I? Did he hear that?

I'm beyond mortified.

"He's coming to LA with me, *bella* … Seeing as you won't." He throws me a wary look but I only nod. Trying to ignore that remark. I don't like Daniel much right now, I don't like his influence over Jake, well the influence he had in the past, before us, and I don't like the fact he's just royally hurt my friend. We still have to talk about that.

I need to show Jake that I'm capable of trusting him, up until now it's been easy, we've been together every second, there hasn't been a need to test the limits of my trust. Going to LA with Daniel is going to be a test and it terrifies me. I don't want my inner doubts and anxiety to affect my relationship with him, my mind acting as my own worst enemy and obsessing over the man-whore he used to be, especially when he's going to see her.

"When will you get back?" I ask, trying to steer the conversation to neutral territory, to avoid any subject that may let jealous Emma rear her head and show her full ugliness.

"I'm leaving around four, it's about a six-hour flight, so if I leave LA same time tomorrow I should get home between eleven and midnight." He walks over to me pulling out a red dress from my wardrobe, one he'd chosen for me to wear the first time we ever went to his father's boat as friends. "Here … I like this on you." He hands it to me and kisses me on the cheek with a look that says "please". He knows better than to make demands on my choices, but I don't mind a gentle nudge if it makes him happy. It's a knee length summer dress with a floaty over skirt, a bit formal for lounging around the apartment. He chose this long before I was even more than just his PA, I look at him quizzically.

"We're all going out for breakfast," he answers. "Seems this apartment echoes a little too much, *amante,* and Daniel is threatening to come in and hose us down if we keep at it. What can I say? He's a little jealous that you get to have all of this." He gestures down his naked torso with a wink and I just roll my eyes in response. He bends down, fishing out the silver sandal wedges I had worn with this dress on the boat, I'm awed at his memory and smile as he hands them to me. The fact he remembered makes me feel all warm and gooey inside.

He really had been enamored back then to remember every detail of my outfit.

I reach in and pull out a soft gray cardigan for over the top of the dress, it's short and fitted and feels like cashmere, another Donna Moore purchase on Jake's expense account, his personal shopper for all things Emma-related, it seems. It'll take some of the formal out of the look and ward against the slight chill in the air.

He walks off to the other wardrobe door and yanks out his trademark black shirt and jeans, a leather jacket I hadn't seen before, with racing logo badges on one sleeve and a pair of black laced boots. I love him as sexy casual Carrero more than I like him in suits, it goes more with his bad boy look and youth, makes him less intimidating and more approachable. He walks off with his clothes into the bathroom leaving the door open and I hear the buzz of his shaver go on, he never fully shaves, just keeps his stubble trimmed for that sexy, designer look. I don't think I've ever seen him without a five o'clock shadow since the day I met him. Margo, my old mentor and now his PA once more, told me that he feels like he looks like a kid when he shaves it all off, that clean-shaven baby-faced look is just so not him anyway. It also doesn't last as his dark hair and Italian roots means it grows in fast through the day and never fully looks gone, even if he has a wet shave.

I dress quickly, brushing out my damp hair and blow drying it quickly, the one good thing about my shorter wavy hair is it requires no maintenance, it styles itself. I throw on the most basic of make-up and a spritz of perfume and am ready by the time he walks out of the bathroom, fully clothed and smelling divine. He looks me up and down appreciatively.

"Beautiful, as always, *mia cara.*" He takes my hand and brings it to his mouth, gently kissing my knuckles in a very gentlemanly fashion. "Have you got everything?" His eyes focus on mine, today they look hazy, softer green with hints of silver flecks, he looks relaxed and happy. I nod, lifting my handbag from the floor with my free hand and follow him out of the room into the sitting room.

Daniel is lounging on one of the long, low couches using his phone, dressed in practically identical attire to Jake. Either it's this season's hot look or we have a little bit of imitation going on and I can hazard a guess that it's on Daniel's part. He has both feet up on the leather even though he's wearing shoes.

Jake yanks at a leg and causes both feet to slide off, throwing him a look of disdain. I try to shield my smile, Jake has a lot of pride in his apartment, unlike most rich New York penthousers, he chose and designed everything in here. From paint colors to furniture and he keeps the place pretty neat, despite having a housekeeper that I rarely see. It annoys him that when Daniel comes over, he treats it like a hotel, leaving stuff around, putting his shoes on the white, Italian leather. Even as PA Emma, I used to deal with Jake's bitching fits whenever Daniel stayed with him. I think Daniel enjoys the reaction it causes, they have many a heated row, Jake never shy to voice his complaints.

"Ready?" He flicks Daniel's head as he passes him, and Hunter causally slides up, extending his middle finger toward him. The nature of their friendship has always amused me. Jake still has my hand, pulling me with him as he leads the way to the door; I catch Daniel looking me up and down and recoil at that slide of eyes down my legs and over my cleavage. My repulsion of the male sex still intact despite the ability to let Jake devour me.

I can't help it, even though I've let Jake do things to me, be with me in so many ways. I've learned that he's the exception. Men still make me cringe, I recoil at the touch of a strange man and feel my skin crawl when they look me over. I don't think I'll ever get over that.

We pass two black clad security men in the outer hall and smile our goodbyes and I catch a glimpse of Nora teetering into another room further down, she has a hoover in hand, off to tend to this apartment and go about her day. I sometimes forget how big this place actually is.

Jake bristles as Daniel gets extremely close to my rear nearing the door, so close he's almost spooning me from behind. His phone in hand, he's focused on the screen and walking faster than I am so isn't really paying attention to his proximity. I feel his body heat get close and instantly feel uncomfortable.

"Hey, never heard of personal space?" Jake pushes him in the shoulder playfully, knocking him backward and pulls me to his other side, a protective arm around my shoulders and a glance thrown at Daniel that looks less than amused.

"I'm sure if I wanted to butt hump your woman, I wouldn't let you watch." Daniel throws him a cheeky smile and ducks as Jake swings a hand at his head.

"You even try getting within a foot of her butt and you'll suffer like no man ever has." Jake lets go of me and grabs Daniel in a head lock, the two carrying on like teens in a playground. Batting at each other, Jake squeezes a little harder and Daniel turns puce.

"For goodness sakes, boys … Children!" I snap and see them separate to stand apart, sly jabs at each other and stupid pulled faces. Acting as though they just got busted by their mommy.

"Asshole," Jake mutters at him under his breath as he leans in, giving me a chaste kiss on the corner of my mouth.

"Dickhead." Daniel prods Jake in the back and swans past us to lead the way out of the apartment.

They exchange haughty glares, but I know it's only in jest.

I hope it's only in jest anyway.

I get the distinct impression that Jake would never leave me alone with his so-called best friend, there seems to be a distinct lack of trust and I hope it's for Daniel and not me. My mind casts back, trying to decipher if he'd ever given me a hint that he didn't trust him, and I falter. His childhood best friend and ex-girlfriend Marissa had betrayed him, I guess not trusting friends and lovers was ingrained now. I knew it wasn't Daniel. He'd told me he no longer had ties to the man in question, but I guess it was a deep insecurity inside of Jake, without knowing it, that he can never really trust best friends. I hope he realizes that not all women are like her. I've seen hints of jealous Jake but nothing concerning, nothing to make me think that he wouldn't trust me.

Chapter 16

The hotel restaurant is bustling despite the earliness of the day. Daniel was quick to invite a leggy blonde beauty to join us for breakfast and is currently trying to feed the poor bimbo strawberries, managing to drop most into her exposed cleavage and fish them out manually. It's cringe worthy. Jake watches him with a serious frown creasing his brow and he eye rolls every time he sees Daniel swoop in for another berry. We both know he's using the girl as padding, so Jake won't bring Leila, up again. That sweet bundle of blonde Daniel is hopelessly in love with. Jake had pretty much got nowhere with him on that front.

The girl giggles hopelessly, pretending to be embarrassed but the look on her face shows she isn't shy about it at all. Jake looks down and starts flicking through his phone with one hand, answering messages from his little brother, coffee held in the other while I eat my pancakes beside him. We've been here around a half hour and conversation has been strained. Jake stuck on wanting to talk and Daniel doing his very best to make it impossible.

I'm tired today, happy to sit in silence and eat while

Jake's beside me, absorbed in Arrick, on his cell and Daniel's acting like a complete sleaze in a five-star hotel's dining room.

I catch the girl throwing a flirty look Jake's way for the fiftieth time as Daniel's mouth heads back to her cleavage, I feel an inner rage washing over me. It was obvious that despite being Daniel's date and allowing him to eat food from her boobs she has the hots for Jake and a hope he might be interested.

My Jake … My man!

I look at her coolly, wondering if stabbing a fake breast with a fork would cause an explosion of silicon. I'm hardly able to conceal my jealousy as I glare at her across the table, she seems completely oblivious or just doesn't care. Jake's movement catches my eye, he puts his cup down, scratching his chin absent mindedly, stretching out his jaw in such a typically male way, his eyes still glued to his phone, unaware of the devastating effect any of his little macho mannerisms have on the female population. I catch her staring openly at him, her lips parting and her eyes growing heavy with desire. The anger inside me snapping finally, I throw down my fork and stand up fast.

"I'm going to the bathroom." I smile tightly, voice laced with venom. Jake's questioning look comes to meet me, seeing the direction of my glare, he looks across and catches the she devil's lusty focus on him. She has the nerve to bite her lip and smile, Daniel's face fully buried in her bust.

Ugghh.

Jake turns back to me quickly with a raised eyebrow, I smile as if to say "yup" and turn to leave but he catches me by the wrist, yanks me down toward his face and hits me with a jaw dropping kiss that's a bit too steamy for a morning breakfast table. It makes my knees go weak and I almost end up in his lap, my face flushing with heat and having to grab his upper arms to steady myself. Releasing me finally, I'm left panting, he smacks my ass firmly and loudly as I attempt to walk off, pulling a shocked giggle from me. Jake's devilish smile and wink, claiming his territory and sending the other girl a clear message.

Not interested, sister!

A glance back shows he's smirking to himself but fully focused back on his phone as the busty girl is looking more than a little annoyed. She looks utterly disgusted. My inner Emma swells with satisfaction, he's no idea how much what he just did made me love him even more. Only Jake could understand what I had needed in that moment, even if it was ridiculous.

It's why he's perfect for me. All my crazy fucked-up-ness and all.

On my return, I find Jake arguing with Daniel over some sport, something to do with the New York Yankees no doubt. The girl is staring at the plate in front of her, oozing boredom now Daniel has lost interest in her "assets" and Jake's given her zero attention. I slide down beside Jake, instantly smiling as his arm comes around my shoulders, pulling me over to him, he shifts in his chair so that he can stay this way, me nestled against him and continues talking to Daniel. I take a moment to look the bimbo up and down and catch her doing the same to me. She's wondering what I have that she doesn't. She's wondering how someone like me has managed to pull Jake Carrero into an actual relationship. I smile at her with malice and turn my face into his shoulder to snuggle in. A huge surge of satisfaction at her face and the sheer envy she isn't even trying to conceal.

"Emma could knock one out better than him." Jake's voice breaks into my inner dialogue and I look up at him in confusion, he's talking to Daniel about baseball still. "Guy hits worse than a girl." Jake motions for the waitress to refill the coffee mugs and sits back as she leans over to do so.

"You're clueless. Just stick with jumping out of perfectly good airplanes and leave the baseball to real men." Daniel swipes his mug and starts downing the refill. I move to the side as the waitress leans in to fill mine up with a gentle smile.

"You wouldn't know how to be a real man even if Emma wrote you a checklist." Jake leans out and flicks Daniel on the forehead, Daniel's delayed batting of his hand misses it entirely.

"Leave me out of this." I shove Jake's elbow playfully, catching his animated expression, he's entering childish Carrero mode and Daniel has no chance against that.

"Emma is way more man than you, Jake. Maybe get some pointers for yourself, I bet she talks sports better than you do too." He slides his mug back on the table and barely glances toward bimbo, she's making motions as if to get up. No one acknowledges her.

"I honestly don't know anything about sports and trust me, he's all man." I smile adoringly at Jake. "You, on the other hand …" I throw him a questioning look and smirk. I hear Jake laugh.

"Meaning?" Daniel's retorts in defensive mode.

"Real men don't sleep with girls they obviously have feelings for then leave them hanging." Jake interjects on my behalf, almost in tune with exactly what I had been about to say.

"Pot, kettle, black!" Daniel frowns at Jake and I see his stubbornness veil his face.

"Okay, I admit, I fucked-up when it came to Emma but look where we are now. Man up, Daniel. Leila isn't always going to be available, some guy will swoop in while you're busy chasing your own ass." Jake leans back in his chair, one arm draped across my back, so he can stroke my shoulder and the other on the table, sprawled down in his seat casually.

Daniel sits up and tenses.

"Look, can we drop this?" Daniel rolls his eyes toward the bimbo, like she matters, and both Jake and I smile in unison. Neither of us believe she cares, she's absorbed in her phone with a face that pretty much says she's oblivious to anything we're talking about. Disinterested.

"I'll drop it when I know you've at least called her and groveled. She deserves more; you know it as well as I do. You know her story." Jake looks fed up, sits back as his hand runs across my back. Daniel just looks evasive.

"I will … When I figure out what to say to her," Daniel mumbles and everyone is alerted to bimbo's leaving with the scrape of her chair and dramatic hair toss aimed at Daniel's face. Daniel sees it as an excuse to evade more interrogation and offers to walk her out. She doesn't acknowledge us as he guides her out, just a moody glare and she's off. I have to admit, I do feel a little bit guilty that we were just the most awful breakfast companions but then she did spend most of it eye-raping my boyfriend.

"Do you think he'll call her?" I ask when they're gone, the look on Jake's face says it all and feel myself bristle in anger.

"It is what it is," he says tightly, still looking across the restaurant. "Daniel's messed up in the head when it comes to women; thank his mother for that. Leila is caught up with a guy who's too afraid to feel anything for her and too in love with her to stay away." He puts down his mug without taking a drink and picks up his phone instead, his little habit making itself known. Jake fidgets with things when he's being evasive, when something is really bothering him.

"What exactly did his mother do to him?" I slide my arm through his, now that he's got both hands on his phone and rest my head against his shoulder. Looking up at him with wide-eyed, inquisitive adoration.

"Let's just say Daniel caught her in a lot of compromising positions from early in life with men who weren't his father. She had time for affairs but never any time for her only kid or her actual husband. The boy has serious mommy issues that I don't even think he understands and he completely idolizes his father."

"So that's why he surrounds himself with endless porn stars and one-night stands?" I blink in surprise, this little insight into a guy I thought was just a jerk and a sex addict. Maybe he has as many issues as me.

"Daniel doesn't trust women, he doesn't have much respect for them either. He looks at them all the same way he looks at his mother. The guy needs therapy but try telling him that." Jake throws me a look that means the conversation is over as we see Daniel swaggering back toward us, his hands jammed in his jeans pockets. Watching him walk over with renewed knowledge helps me see him in a different light. The face I always dismiss as smarmy and arrogant looks a little lost and vulnerable, the confident swagger more like a veil to hide an insecure person. Something I know about all too well.

"We done here?" Daniel looks us over and doesn't attempt to sit.

"We'll meet you back at the apartment before two," Jake says. "I want to take Emma shopping for some things we need." He looks at me with a blank expression as though checking if I've any objections, I just smile up at him. I've never been shopping with Jake. I used to either deal with it for him or had no part in it. He did it on his own time and despite most men avoiding any form of clothes shopping or anything shopping, Jake seems to enjoy it.

"We?" Daniel smirks and I dismiss the urge to make a face at him. Still a jackass under that sad look.

"She lives with me, Daniel. There are things *we* need. I know that's beyond any of your mental capabilities to comprehend. You know? What a relationship is." Jake smirks at him and throws down the napkin he was using on his hands, standing fast and pulling my chair out for me then offering a hand to help me up.

"I thought you were just shacked up temporarily for some hot sex and tension release, I didn't predict you joining the long line of shackled men in the world." He grins but Jake just shakes his head at him.

"Green isn't your color, princess. I know you're hot for me, Danny Boy, but don't belittle yourself in this way." Jake, now beside Hunter, pats his butt and gets a slap back in the chest.

"Whatever, asshole." Daniel grins and we turn to go. Heading out through the hotel foyer into the bright morning light.

"We leave for LA at two … Don't be late as I won't wait for you." Jake continues, Daniel shrugs then turns and takes off with a grin toward our car with Jefferson patiently waiting.

"He can drop me off first then. You pansies can enjoy your shopping without a third wheel." He throws back, but Jake just shrugs in return.

"Take him, we can walk … I need the air."

We watch Daniel slide into the car and turn away toward the busy streets. Jake's hand already entwined with mine. He stops me from walking forward with a small tug and I'm pulled back to face him.

"Can't go anywhere with you looking like that without doing this first." Jake leans down kissing me softly, his hand coming to the back of my neck before he deepens the intensity. Pretty soon he has me almost panting as his tongue smoothly caresses mine, his lips brush delicately and his whole mouth makes me melt against him. It's a sensual kiss, meant for the pleasure of the kiss yet he has me burning up with longing. Finally, he lets me go and I lean back on my heels, unaware I had been on tiptoe.

"Bit sexy for the pavement, wasn't it?" I giggle and feel him smooth the corner of my mouth with his thumb, fixing my nude lipstick smudges.

"Staking a claim on my beautiful girl. Too many men already checking you out." He grins and turns me with a twirl under his arm as though we're dancing before pulling me along the sidewalk toward the hustle and bustle of the busy, New York streets.

Chapter 17

I giggle as Jake finally releases me from his arms in the changing cubicle, shaking my head at him in disbelief. My face must match the color of the dress I'm trying to retrieve from the floor. His eyes dark and wicked, buttoning up his shirt with a huge grin on his face as I try my hardest to get dressed without being knocked into the narrow walls, it's so cramped in here.

I can't believe he managed to get me naked and have sex without knocking the feeble walls down.

"Was this your plan from the word go? Claiming to need me in the changing room to admire your shirt choices." I look up at him while trying to get my bra straps on untwisted, he drops his shirt and instead straightens the strap on my shoulder, reaching behind me to help untwist it. He answers with a wolfish grin.

Why am I even surprised by this? I should have known the second his hand ran under my skirt as we walked to the changing area.

He's close enough that I can practically lick his pecks without moving my head, the smell of him intoxicating, as always. It's insane how good he always smells, trying to keep quiet, knowing that the busy shop out front is probably aware what the young couple had been up to, it had taken almost forty minutes in the farthest dressing room from the front to try on two shirts.

We had tried to stifle the giggles and then the moans. Jake was incorrigible, only he could seduce all reason out of me and have me doing things in a boutique like this. He leans down and catches me in another passionate kiss, stilling me for a second, unable to ever refuse him.

"They won't care as long as I spend copious amounts of money before we leave." He smiles, returning to doing up his shirt. He turns his attention to his jeans, adjusting things before buttoning them up too. He looks effortlessly back to normal, not hard when you always look casual and slightly ruffled anyway.

On the other hand, I'm flushed, my hair probably wild and my dress has been crushed to death and looks wrinkled beyond repair as we have trampled on it a lot. I manage to step into the dress, holding it with an extended arm, the other hand against Jake's torso for stability and pull it up finally. Jake turns me to zip it up, presses his mouth against the back of my shoulder before helping me slide my cardigan back on, we had kept our shoes on as bending down in here was almost impossible. I look around for my lacy panties and don't see them anywhere. I frown, lifting first one foot then the other before noticing him watching me with the hint of a smile across his face.

"They're in my back pocket." He grins with a raised eyebrow, the look of wickedness returning.

"Why and how?" I laugh. I hadn't even seen him retrieve them.

"Because that's where I put them when I got them off you and that's where they're staying until we get home … Maybe even after I go to LA." He grins. I cross my arms and give him my best PA Emma look that means "I don't think so". He just turns, ruffling my hair, and opens the door before striding out. I follow him instantly annoyed

He was being serious? I can't walk around in a short dress without underwear …

I follow him, attempting a grab at his back pocket but his hand comes around catching my wrist and pulls me forward.

"There they stay." He commands with that glint of commander and chief, I furrow my brows and try my best angry glare, but it only amuses him more. "You're unbelievably sexy like this." He whispers pressing his mouth to mine, still smiling through his kiss.

"Why would you want to leave me panty-less while walking the streets of windy New York in a very floaty dress?" I say through gritted teeth, he stays close, his voice low, his hand coming to trace my lip seductively

"Because it's all I'll think about when we're walking out there, and it will make me want to fuck you ten times more."

"Like you need any encouragement." I smile, pushing a kiss on him then walk away. If he wants to play games then fine, he'll regret this one. Jake likes his little sexual games, he likes teasing me to death, likes to have little internal jokes.

Maybe I should start learning to do the same.

I walk into the shop, trying to push down my embarrassment as several women stop and glance at us departing from the changing area with knowing looks. He brought me in here because he wanted some new shirts, which he's left lying in that changing room. Half the shop sells women's clothes, so I stroll over casually, as though I'm browsing. I wait until I know he's followed me then I bend just enough to a lower rail so that my dress rides up dangerously close to my ass. I slowly straighten catching him watching, his hands move to his pockets as though he is about to surrender my underwear, then doesn't. He leans back against the pillar he's standing in front of, the look of amusement on his face spreading.

Hmmm, so he wants to enjoy the show, does he? He thinks he knows what I'm doing.

I know his desire to protect my modesty will kick in and he'll give me back my underwear. I walk around a tier of shelves with underwear laid out and bend lower this time to look at the bottom row of lace things, my dress rides up and slides slightly, exposing a lot of thigh. Even for me it feels dangerously close to revealing my secret parts, the air feeling odd against the exposed parts of me under the dress, but I give nothing away. I hear him inhale heavily despite being far away from me.

I spy a rail on the wall with some corset style basques and reach up to get one down, the motion of stretching lifts my dress high, not enough to expose me fully but enough thigh and long legs to get Jake to push off the wall and walk over behind me. I wait, sure I've won this little battle of the sexes and he regrets leaving my panty-less. But he just lifts down the one behind it and hands it to me instead, his body brushing against me from behind and a warm hand flicking across the thigh just under the curve of my naked ass.

"I prefer black." He smiles taking the harlot red and putting it back. I smile haughtily and turn away from him throwing it over my shoulder.

Fine, maybe he needs a new kind of message thrown his way.

I move over to a whole wall of sexy lingerie and stand as though I'm trying to decide, I pick up several pairs of boring panties in every color from the shelf below and throw him a defiant look. He suppresses a grin, still watching where I go and what I do.

I've no idea anymore … It's like trying to win over a master of his craft and I'm failing.

I decide I'll just buy all the panties, the most unattractive ugly, full butt-covering, practical ones I can find and then I'll go straight to the dressing room and put all five pairs on just to annoy him.

And, yes, I'll choose every color minus black.

I throw him a rebellious look and drop the corset on the pile of knickers as though it disgusts me. I see him narrow his eyes at me, he's thinking, then he turns to the nearest assistant and loudly says, "Can you help my girlfriend pick some new underwear out … Preferably black and fuckable as I ripped hers off and she's currently going commando." He grins and throws me a triumphant look as every face in the shop snaps around to stare first at him, then me. I feel my face turn puce and turn away completely mortified. I don't know whether to laugh, cry, or throw what I'm holding at him and storm out. I'm frozen to the spot.

"Ummm, sure … Yes." The girl stammers, and I'm not so sure if it's because of his statement or if it's him as she turns every shade of pink there is and hurries to my side. I throw him a glare as she comes over, fussing and taking the pants from me. She looks at the ones I've chosen with surprise and looks to him as though needing his permission. He shakes his head and she puts them all back down.

How the hell did this turn into a lingerie buying trip? One where he gets to dictate what I pick out? He's turning this to his advantage again.

"Actually, I don't need underwear," I say loudly, stubborn Emma kicking in. "I like the feeling of not wearing any." I remark and walk past her, then him, with my chin in the air. I stop at a rail of all in one cat suits and look at him pointedly. "Maybe I'll start dressing in such ways that my pants are inaccessible after this." I pout before walking out of the shop, his smirk following me before he even attempts to.

He's fast to catch up, trying to grab for my hand but I pull it away, keeping my face turned so he can't tell if I'm mad or not. I know I should be but somehow, I'm not, I feel strangely powerful.

I should torture him this way as I know it's one way I'll win … He may be the dark lord of sexual prowess, but I know how to shut him out, close down on him so he doesn't know what I'm thinking, and I know he hates that more than anything.

"You mad at me, *bambino?*" He soothes but I can hear the laughter in his voice.

So, he thinks he's funny?

"I'm perfectly fine," I say coldly, keeping my gaze averted as I walk fast, trying to stay in front of him.

"You're sexy when you're pissed." He breathes into my ear, my skin tingles in anticipation but I steel it back, keeping my cool. Old Emma effortlessly moving in.

"I'm not pissed … I'm not anything," I say matter of factly, all emotion devoid in my tone of voice. He catches my hand again; this time keeping a hold and hauls me back around to him. I don't look at him but down at our hands, keeping my face still, blank expression.

"Now are you mad because I stole these?" He holds up the black lace that he's retrieved from his back pocket and currently letting half the side walk see. "Or because I announced it to a shop full of uptight women that I fucked you and left you without them?" He grins at me, nothing in his face saying he's even minorly bothered that I may be in a bad mood right now. It only annoys me more. His normally clear green eyes look very dark, his pupils have enlarged crazily even in the brightness of the day. I push them aside as though it doesn't bother me that he's holding them for all to see, I act like I don't even want them and instead shrug.

"I'm not annoyed in the slightest … I happen to like this … Isn't the first time I've gone panty-less for a man." I smirk as his expression drops completely. That little flicker of doubt, and suddenly he's the one looking pissed. Luckily, he's no memory of the fact he was also the one who made me that way, the night he first took me home after the dance and shredded my underwear in the back of his limo and then the night he got me on his car bonnet then dumped me home. I turn to move away but he hauls me back a little aggressively, anger searing across his face.

"When? With who?" he yells at me, completely losing his cool. I suppress the smile I feel forming on my lips, lifting my chin defiantly.

He likes reactions, now I see why.

"Shouldn't start games if you can't handle them." I smirk, attempting to pull myself free again but his rage only heightens, pulling me hard into his chest so that I catch my breath. "Thought you weren't the jealous type?" I retort. I can feel the heat emitting from him, he's raging, aggression peaking inside but it only makes me feel a little bit empowered. Serves him right. He started this and when I tell him it was him it will end this little mood of his. So, for now I'm dishing it back at him and enjoying the rare upper hand.

"Over something like this, Emma, I'll literally rip heads off." He snaps at me, pure fury in those normally calm eyes and I lose my courage, his voice is venom. I flinch in fright as his hand grips my wrist harder. Feeling the inner fear take over, I reach up with my free hand and snatch back my underwear, hauling my hand free and shout at him impulsively.

"You've a goddamn nerve! With the amount of conquests, you've had? … It was *you*!" I snap and turn on my heel to storm away, tears instantly pricking my eyes. From our happy morning to this, I don't even know how we got here. I feel like bawling.

I should never play games with Jake, I learned a long time ago that it only ignites this side of him. Even before I was his, when I was just PA Emma I'd seen this side of him when I had tried to get a rise from him. Jake likes to be the one to initiate and control games on his terms, when it swings back at him he instantly goes into death mode.

So, stupid. People who love each other don't do things like this.

I feel his hand grab my upper arm and tug me back, turning me to face him and halting me once again in the street. People continue pushing past uninterested in the little domestic going on.

"*Neonata,* I'm sorry … Emma, baby, please don't." I feel the tear trickle down my cheek as he pulls me into him his arms, coming around me securely. He cradles my face against him, his hand on the back of my head. "*Perdonami, bambina, non è questo quello che volevo,*" he says huskily, falling into that habit of fluent Italian as he's overly emotional. It makes me stop and smile, I lift my chin up to him with a furrowed brow. It's rare that he does this, but on the occasions he does it's the most beautiful sound in the world. A sign he is overwhelmed.

"What?" I giggle through tears and his expression softens. He smiles and pushes our foreheads together, sighing in relief.

"Ignore me … Only you can make me forget the art of the English language." He grins, his mouth finding mine and kissing me softly yet passionately, all the hurt falling around our feet. He finally releases me from his kiss and searches my eyes with his.

"The first night after I told you I loved you and the night I stupidly dropped you at your apartment like an asshole too?" he questions, I nod. He remembers after all.

"I'm an idiot, Emma … Everything you ever told me, I should have known it would only be with me. I just saw red, *bella* …I know I've no right to be this way, especially with my past, but I can't help it. I know I wasn't the jealous type, but with you it's worse than bad. Do you think you can live with a boyfriend who gets so insanely jealous that even his best friend was riding close to a broken nose this morning?" He looks away as though he's embarrassed, but it only makes me elated, I push my mouth on his and kiss him thoroughly, panting when we finally break apart.

"I like it," I say shyly, no one had ever made me feel the way he does or reacted like he did over me. "I don't recall any time that I have given you reason to be jealous where Daniel was concerned though." I add thoughtfully looking at him quizzically. He raises an eyebrow with a dramatic sigh and shakes his head

"For his own safety he should just keep at least five feet between you at all times." He grins, grabs my hands in his, taking my lace panties back from me and putting then in his inside jacket pocket with a smile. I just shake my head at him.

"I'm still keeping these though … Until I get home again." He swoops down, silencing me with a kiss before I can protest, and I finally give up.

"So, in the meantime I'm to walk the streets without a stitch on under this skirt? What should I do if the wind exposes me and my overly jealous boyfriend catches another man ogling my assets?" I raise my eyebrows knowing this could very well happen. He frowns back at me only this time in thought and pulls his phone out, hitting the screen and putting it to his ear. He tells Jefferson where we are and to come immediately before hanging up.

"If I take you home and get you naked in my bed then we don't have to worry about it." He smiles and hauls me into the circle of his arms again, a hand moving down over my ass as though he's going to make sure the wind takes my dress nowhere. I laugh at him.

"No shopping? I thought we so desperately needed things like shirts and underwear." I tease.

"I don't need any more clothes right now ... You definitely don't need any more lace panties." He grins naughtily as we wait for our car to appear.

Chapter 18

Jake pushes the cream cannelloni into my mouth, almost choking me with the amount he's picked up from the plate. I struggle to push him away, stifling a giggle but he tries to ram it in further, close to choking me. I lift my hand and push him off, taking half out of my mouth and dropping it on the napkin in front of me, attempting to chew what's already there. He stuffs some into his own mouth, seemingly oblivious to what he's done to me.

"What is this deal you have with ramming food in my mouth?" I finally say, shoving his shoulder playfully. He leans around attempting another go at pushing more into my mouth, but I turn away. "Jake!" I scold, pushing his hand back, he shrugs redirecting it into his own mouth instead.

"Feeding you is part of taking care of you." He smiles but I only look at him with disbelief.

"There's feeding someone … You know like sexily in the movies? And then there's your version of trying to ram my mouth full in one fell swoop and almost choking me to death." I laugh.

"Seeing how much you can fit in there." He winks

suggestively, and I turn crimson as I get what he means.

Oh boy … we have never crossed the whole "me giving him oral pleasure" yet, I wouldn't even know how, and he's never tried to initiate it. He's never mentioned it despite doing it to me so many times. Is this a hint?

"Before your overactive brain starts going on a time out, thinking I want you to drop your face in my lap right now; I don't." He looks at me pointedly, always able to read me before I even finished thinking it. "You'll get there when you're ready and if you don't then it's not an issue." He picks up another piece of cannelloni and points it toward my mouth. I shake my head and watch him eat it instead. For some reason, eating our meals on or in his bed cross legged lately has started to become the norm.

We're in stages of undress again after coming home and making out on the couch. Actually, more grinding and squirming hotly on the couch and trying to stop his wandering hands incase Nora appeared. His lust led to the bedroom soon after as he was unable to function knowing I had no underwear on, and it was obvious with the speed in which he got me naked.

He's fed me what the housekeeper had left us for lunch. Steak dinner followed by cream cannelloni, which is apparently a Jake favorite. I'm full to bursting and his bed looks like a food explosion happened. I'm wearing his shirt over my nakedness and he's only wearing his jeans. All that delicious torso and muscular back and arms on show. My favorite view of him.

"I hate girls who play with food and eat nothing except lettuce." He finally adds, looking me up and down. "You're thin and seem to have a fast metabolism, I like seeing you fed." He smiles at me before another attempt at pushing food my way. "Something sexy about a girl who eats normally."

"I swear I'll be sick if you try that again … I'm not you with your endless stomach." I laugh, this time he aims at my nose smearing cream down my face then dives on top of me to lick it back off. I squeal and wriggle as his weight flattens me to the bed, his mouth sucking parts of my face the cream didn't even touch, he's trying to rub more on me that has smeared up his hand from my fighting him off. I squeal his name in objection, wriggling and battling those overly strong hands. Finally, he plants a kiss on my mouth, smiling as he does so, making me laugh in the process.

"Sometimes you're like a child." I push him up so he's no longer laying all over me and he sets his hands down either side of my head to take his weight. My favorite view of Jake.

"Yeah, well get used to it, men never grow up, baby." He picks up pieces of cannelloni and throws it toward the plate, the sticky mess on the sheets making him frown. I look around at the carnage from eating a full lunch here.

"Your bed is a total mess." I point out.

"It's our bed and I'm not sleeping here tonight so good luck with getting comfy in it." He grins, leaning down to kiss me again. I stop and sigh, reminded that he's leaving in a couple of hours, suddenly morose over that fact. It's only for one night but it's the why he's going and the fact we haven't been apart since we started this relationship that I'm feeling sad about it.

"Don't look at me like that." He breaks into my thoughts and leans in closer. "You make me want to cancel it and stay home with you, *bambino*." His eyes come to mine and I try a happier look, despite wanting him to do anything else but go.

"You need to sort this out or she'll just keep trying to call the shots."

And endlessly calling with her huffs and demands as though she owns him.

That makes me feel grumpier than hell and he grins before poking me in the frown.

"Definitely don't do that … Or I'll just run away with you and forget anything about responsibility." He frowns too, flopping down beside me on the bed then flinching in disgust, arching up off the bed swiftly.

"What the …? Ugghh." He leans up looking over his shoulder at the splodge of cream down his back and sends me into hysterical laughter.

"We should start using your dining table." I laugh as he slides off the bed and grabs a towel to clean it off, he surveys the mess we've made, seeing gravy spills from the steak when he'd tried to get a hand up my thigh mid-eating.

"You think that's funny?" He looks at me menacingly. I watch him, still laid flat on my back with amusement then squeal as he yanks the sheets completely off the bed, causing me to roll with them and land in a heap on the floor at his feet, rolled in white and gray bedding.

"Hey!" I choke, trying to get out and feel a hand grab my ankle and haul me across the floor out of it all. I'm picked up and thrown heavily on my back on the now sheet covered mattress and he comes to straddle me with a determined look on his face.

"Little girls who laugh at their boyfriends deserve to be disciplined." He pins my arms above my head with one hand then tortures me with tickles until I'm howling, pinned under him expertly. I squeal with laughter, writhing and wriggling with protest until I'm too exhausted to fight anymore and tears are pouring from my eyes. Finally, his relentless torture stills, and he moves to lay over me again, kissing me softly.

"You're a horrid boyfriend," I breathe, trying to wipe my face and catch my breath, exhausted by him. I can feel a smile forming on my lips as he moves close enough to rub noses, leaning over me, toying with almost kissing me but keeping it just out of reach.

"I guess." He smiles again, coming close as though he will, then moves back slightly with a look of wickedness, I get infuriated and lift my head to kiss him instead. He's quick and moves back smiling. "Too slow!" He's enjoying this … Playful, teasing Carrero has a new game. Torturing Emma!

"Fine!" I pout and turn my face away so he can't kiss me anymore, he grabs my chin pulling me back with a look of sheer annoyance on his face that his game has been turned on him and hits me with an extra seductive, passionate kiss. That glint of childish rage in his eye that he had been out maneuvered. He moves over me with more than a nudge of his intentions. My body instantly igniting, getting the slightest signal that he wants sex and she's already purring.

* * *

"Wake up, *neonata* … I need to go." Jake's voice rouses me from my sleep, I'm sprawled over the bed on nothing but a sheet with a fur throw over me, completely naked. He'd exhausted me to the point that I'd finally passed out, I had no idea how long I'd been asleep and now he was going. I open my eyes in protest, looking at him like a child who's about to cry.

"I know, baby … It's almost four, I'm late as it is because of this. I should have gone already … Daniel's already downstairs in the car." He kisses me, leaning over me on the bed, fully dressed in a dark suit and dark shirt left open at the collar and he smells like he always does. Aftershave and his own special scent. He kisses me longingly, his hand coming up to tangle in my hair, his body comes down to rest on mine gently, all of a sudden, I want to cling to him and not let him go.

He's going to see her, he's going to stay away from New York and talk about his future with Marissa's baby and I don't want it to be happening.

"Nora will come in and change the bed for you, *bambino*, she'll make you dinner around five … Make sure you eat, okay?" He lingers over me, a look in his eye of reluctance. "I'll be back before you know it … Don't go to work tomorrow, stay here and take some *you* time. I'll call you, okay?"

"Okay and okay." I smile, wrapping my arms around his neck one last time, pushing down all my inner upset before he slides up and waves. He grabs my foot at the end of the bed and strokes down my sole gently, causing me to flinch and giggle. He pauses, looking one more time as though he's reluctant to leave then turns and goes. I think maybe he's feeling it too, that trepidation at leaving me, at going to see her.

* * *

Jake finally calls me around midnight, when he's just getting to his hotel, he seems a million miles away. I miss him so much, even more so laying in this huge bed in his apartment all alone. The security staff have an outer hall that leads to a corridor of small rooms outside Jake's main apartment, so they rarely came inside unless needed. Nora left around seven to go home to her cats after I'd finally spent some time getting to know her while she cooked. Here I was in this huge, modern apartment, which lacked any home comforts, all on my lonesome.

"This hotel sucks," he says down the line, sounding so much huskier than his normal voice, he sounds tired and agitated.

"Are you slumming it in something less than five stars?" I ask giggling. Knowing that would never happen.

"It's a shitty Carrero hotel." He returns, his voice betraying he's smiling. Jake has always tried to avoid staying in his hotels for some unknown reason to me that I always found hilarious, all those trips all over and he had me booking us into anything but a Carrero hotel.

"Why on earth are you staying in one of those?" I ask, laughing at the irony.

"Seems my stand in PA is a bitch." He laughs, I know he has Margo still on staff, filling in for our disappearing acts. She asked that she be allowed to work on, even when I returned, finding the life of a retiree unfulfilling. So technically, he now has two PAs. Margo has been given an office elsewhere on the sixty-fifth floor all of her own, with regular office hours which seems to suit her much better.

"She must be mad at you to stick you like that." I giggle, turning onto my back in bed and twirling my hair above my head.

"Yeah, maybe replacing her with a younger PA I frequently bend over my desk put her nose out of joint."

I feel myself eyeroll and just ignore his comments about sex. It's always sex with him.

"I've never been in a Carrero hotel." I exclaim suddenly. It's true, in all the time I've worked there I had never been to one. Never even laid eyes on one. I would never have gone to one without Jake as its price tag was above anything I could ever have afforded, they were in the top tier of luxury accommodations.

"You're not missing much … Think old-world Hollywood glamour and ridiculously expensive … Nothing modern … Much like my father and his *Godfather* tastes." He sighs and then I get it right away. The hotels are his father's babies, the style and service something he established long before Jake was even a twinkle in his eye, and well, if it oozes Giovanni then I can see why Jake avoids it. He'd tried, in the last year, to have them updated but his father always came down hard on the styling of his chain.

"Can't be all bad … I mean I bet the staff are working extra hard to make you happy … Being the heir of their empire." I giggle at his defeated tone.

"*Bambino* … There is only so much ass kissing I can take, besides, they all dress like maître d's from Disneyland … My father really has no clue at all." He pauses, going silent for a moment and I feel that tug of longing hit me even harder. I want him here next to me already. I don't like this at all.

"I wish you'd come with me," he says softly, almost reading my mind. "I understand why, Emma, but I hate this. I want you here, laid next to me, not just a voice on a phone."

"I don't want to be a part of this, not yet." I admit honestly "I'm not okay with it yet. I need time." I sigh, waiting for the start of an argument; I've never said that before.

"That makes two of us, *bella.*" He sighs too, seeming so very, very far away from me. "Do you think you'll start coming with me sometime?" he asks.

"I don't know." It's doubtful that there's enough time before the actual birth for me to get over it but he didn't need to know that.

"I understand … It just sucks that I miss you this much already. This big old hotel room and huge bed isn't appealing without you in it."

"I miss you too." I feel that horrid tug inside me, regretting staying here but I know that going would have caused a different kind of pain. I didn't want to go and then feel angry at him the whole time we were in LA, I didn't want to address those feelings toward him for all of this.

"Daniel's giving me the evil eye, so I better go … Go to sleep, I'm going to get a late dinner. I hate airplane food … Then I'll be in bed dreaming of you soon enough and pretend like you're actually here."

"I love you," I whisper sadly, not wanting him to hang up. Aching for him to be in the bed beside me so I could trace that perfect face and snuggle in close.

"I love you way more," he says with a hint of a smile in his voice. "Sweet dreams, *bambino*, dream of a big hunky Italian with a shit ton of money stripping you naked."

"Most definitely!" I grin and feel my inner body heat for his touch.

"Goodnight, girlfriend."

"Goodnight, boyfriend." I laugh at him and his cuteness. With that he hangs up and leaves me feeling lonely, his apartment seeming so much emptier now. I move down under the sheets to his side of the bed, feeling disappointed at the lack of his smell on the fresh linens. I get up and go to the hamper looking for any of his clothes and find none. Nora is an efficient housekeeper. Too efficient it would seem. I climb back in bed feeling annoyed and emotional all at once, I force myself to lay down and close my eyes in the hopes that morning will come quickly, and it will be the day he's coming home to me.

What the hell is the matter with you, Emma? You had a whole life before him, a self-reliant, independent life.

* * *

I sit up bathed in sweat, crying out in the darkness. My heart beating fast and loud in my ears, fear gripping me as I come to, managing to focus on my whereabouts. I'm breathing fast and shallow, my hands gripping the sheets. I had been dreaming

What the hell?

I look around trying to gain calm from the surroundings, so different to where I'd been moments before. In Chicago, with my mother. We'd been fighting … No … Talking. I couldn't even remember exactly, the dream already starting to fade as my senses become fully alert. I remember the snarl of a face close up; I remember there was blood but it's hazy … My mother was sobbing and then she wasn't, a darkness in the shadow had enveloped us both and taken her from me … Lifeless, she'd fallen to the ground at my feet and I'd known she was dead.

With shaking hands, I reach out to the lamp on the bedside table and touch it, instantly springing to life with the merest trail of fingers. Jake and his love of gadgets. I look around me, grounding myself again and taking slow deliberate breaths, my phone on the docking port is nearby and I pick it up and dial my mother's landline, ignoring that it's only a little after 3.00 a.m. After a long wait she finally picks up.

"Hello." A grumpy, sleepy, slow, voice brings me more relief than I ever knew was possible.

"Mom?" I breathe softly, using the term I hadn't uttered since I was seven years old.

"Emma? Is that you?" Her voice instantly more alert and awake as it dawns on her it's me. "What is it? What's wrong?"

"I just … I dreamed you died." I break into a sob and there's nothing but silence between us. I know she must feel awkward, she doesn't know emotional Emma, I don't think she's seen her for a very long time. She's no idea how much

I've changed, what Jake has done to me or even that I'm with him at all. Last time we saw one another it ended so badly and she's probably wondering what's changed.

"I'm fine, darling … I'm just bobbing along, you know … Getting on with things." She sounds wary, she doesn't know what to say, which helps me reel back in the tears and regain my equilibrium, back to the Emma she's more able to deal with. My mother isn't one to be overly emotional and she sounds uncomfortable.

"I think I might come home for a few days … With Jake." I add, surprising even myself. Knowing her, she won't even ask why I would bring him.

"Oh, that would be lovely … For both of you to come, he's done so much for me and I would like to say thank you in person." She beams down the phone. It was obvious the last time she'd seen him she'd been enamored with the impressive Carrero heir. She doesn't even ask about us, about what relationship we have. Just accepts that I'll bring him, and she doesn't mention our last meeting. This is how she is, this is what she always does. My life is of no interest unless it has some point in hers.

"I better go and let you sleep." I finally add, my need to speak to her dissipating now, that inner nudge of disappointment she always makes me feel growing steadily inside of me.

I don't know why I always delude myself that she will be different. That for once I'll get some sort of emotion. The affectionate names are all just an act.

"Okay, sweetheart." She pauses as though she wants to say more but doesn't. "Just text me when you're going to come, and I'll get your old room ready," I say nothing, knowing we would stay in a hotel close by, too many harsh memories to stay there. We say our goodbyes and I hang up, feeling only marginally better. A different kind of emotion waving through me now.

I sigh and send Jake a text for him to get when he wakes up, part of me hoping he wakens with the vibration of his phone. I need to hear him.

"We're going to Chicago to see my mother ... I finally bit the bullet and called her. P.S I miss you xx"

I slide my phone onto the bedside table and lay down, he wouldn't be awake at this time. Jake had the ability to fall asleep anywhere and quickly, he would reply when he got up and maybe call me. I settle into the bed, trying to get comfy and toss and turn before I finally start to drift back off.

* * *

I wake early and feel slightly energized, knowing he's coming home today, and it thrills me in ways I never thought possible. I feel like he's been gone forever. I jump up and shower with renewed happiness, the memories of last night returning and thoughts of Chicago dampening it down again. I wasn't regretting calling her but somehow, in the light of a new day, I regretted agreeing to go back there. I knew Jake didn't quite see my mother in the same light anymore either, so maybe taking him with me wasn't a good idea after all.

Jake calls me a little after seven, he left it until after his gym workout and run time in case I was still asleep, and I'm so overjoyed to hear his voice again.

"Hey, *bambino.*" He sounds happy, I grin at the mere sound of him and melt at his usual affectionate term.

"Hey, sexy." I giggle, elated.

"Did you miss me? I missed you last night." His voice takes on a husky tone which sends shivers through me and the sudden urge to have him wrapped around me claws at my insides.

"Of course, not … Hardly noticed your absence." I jest and hear him laugh softly. He knows me better than that, can't get anything by him.

"I couldn't sleep last night, I think I tossed and turned until almost three before I finally got some shut eye," he says. "Think I was yearning for my live teddy bear." I hear the smile in his voice.

"That's odd, I woke up just after three with a horrendous nightmare." I admit "I dreamed my mother died and … Vanquis was here." It comes out a little too shakily as though I'm more torn about it than I am.

Maybe I am …

My hands are trembling at the memory.

"I wish I'd been beside you, *miele.*" He sounds somber. "I hate that you woke up alone after that."

"I don't have nightmares when you're here," I say to reassure him, my heart aching at the tone of his voice. The guilt he feels at not being here.

"I hate that leaving you means they come back then … You stopped having your night terrors when we started sleeping together?" He sounds genuinely surprised.

"I guess … I haven't had a dream like last night in a couple of weeks and that one night we shared a bed in Chicago I never had one either." I admit, feeling my face flush at the memory of that night and kissing him. I still hadn't told him that I had initiated it, maybe I would. He'd like that.

"It makes me happy to know that I keep them away, that in some way I'm protecting you from the past … Is that why you called her? Why you want to see her?" His tone changes subtly and it makes me feel a little wary.

"Yes … You don't think I should anymore?" I push gently.

"She's still your mother, maybe I don't favor her as much as I did, but only you can choose what relationship you have with her." I hear a noise from behind him, it's Daniel's voice and Jake tells him to get lost, playfully.

"Do you need to go?" I ask, feeling disappointment wash over me. He sighs lightly.

"Yes, but I'm not going to … Stay on the phone, baby." The noises coming down the call suggest he's getting up and moving around, maybe putting his shoes on. "Daniel is eager to get breakfast, but not here … The menu is as bad as the room." He jests, and I conjure up images of seafood platter banquets and over-elaborate poached egg dishes. Jake hates over fussy food displays, he likes food to look like food and a bit rustic. "I can still talk to you while I walk, though."

"Do you think you'll get everything sorted today?" I know I should ask, after all, it's the reason he's out there, but even uttering the words causes me a great amount of heartache. Life would be perfect if it weren't for this little hurdle.

"I hope so, I don't want to be going back and forth with lawyers for much longer … I'm not leaving until some sort of legal agreement is reached, money, visitation, boundaries." His voice goes quiet as he moves the phone away, I can almost imagine him sliding his jacket on. I close my eyes to see him in my mind's eye, aching to touch that face and those biceps.

"You think she's ready to agree?" I force myself to open my eyes again and not get lost in the memory of his touch.

"Yes … I told her that if she wanted me to have any sort of relationship with the baby she needed to back off because my love life was nothing to do with her." He comes back clearer and louder, the phone obviously back where it belongs. "I'm not going in there with her calling the shots on this … I made it clear that it goes my way or I'm on the first flight home." He sounds determined, typical commandeering Carrero on a role. Marissa has no idea what she's trying to come up against.

"I forgot you were the king of negotiation." I laugh, he's the king of manipulation and getting his own way more accurately.

"Right, *bella,* I'm heading into the elevator so I'm going to lose you … *Ti amo, piccola ragazza,*" he says it so seductively my insides tremble.

"I love you too … Goodbye, Jake." I smile down the phone when he utters his goodbyes and then, he's gone.

Chapter 19

My day is going to consist of sitting about here if I don't plan something productive. I end up sat in Jake's rarely used home office with my laptop and try to work through everything Margo has forwarded at my request. It seems taking that month away from this side of the business has made it so much harder for me to slot back into this life and I'm finding it less than satisfying.

The time we've spent at the office, I barely made a dent and found every file ridiculously hard to focus on. My mind always wandering to the six-foot two hunk in the next room. I used to love working for, and with, Jake but now, looking back, I think it was more than just the job; it was him and being around him, even if back then I couldn't admit it to myself, now that he is mine and all I can focus on, I'm finding returning to PA mode more than difficult.

Staying home today hadn't only been because Jake insisted, I just didn't want to go in and deal with the mundane right now. My head is all over the place and old in control and got her crap together Emma so far removed from who I have become, this is getting difficult. The change in dynamics between us has altered how I feel about my career, something which shocks me to the core. I have more than just a job now. I have a future to look forward to, I have hope. I have love from someone who makes me re-evaluate everything I planned for in my man free, single life I had painstakingly worked toward.

By lunch I am completely fed up, close to tears at my own inability to focus and decide I need a change of scenery. Looking through my clothes, I find something feminine and floaty, bought by Donna the personal shopper that I previously dismissed as 'not my thing' and throw it on. I'm aware of how differently I have begun dressing because of Jake. Romantic clothes that I would never have tolerated before. Soft, girly dresses, cute shoes, and accessories, my whole style losing the hard tailored and cold PA look and becoming far more young college girlfriend. A style I have never embraced but somehow, seeing that look on his face when I dress this way makes the world of difference. I don't have to be scared of attracting sleazy men anymore, I have my protector and he will rip men apart who try to touch me. I like the fact that Jake has that slash of jealousy to match mine, makes me feel less insecure and stupid. He is my security blanket now, I don't need my armor anymore.

* * *

I get Jefferson to take me to Queens to see Sarah before she heads out to work and spend some time with her in front of the TV, catching up. It seems like forever since I was here, even though it's been barely days. Marcus is at work, having finally found himself a regular nine-to-five position in an office block and things seem to have settled between the ever-sparring couple. I notice the apartment looks different, small, subtle, masculine changes such as a new stereo and upgraded TV. Part of me feels a little hurt that he's changing things with Sarah and I'm no longer part of the decisions or part of the atmosphere anymore. I guess it's a good sign, we're going in our own directions, letting life lead us.

I enjoy my time with her and while I sit watching Sarah make us food, I catch up with Sophie on the phone.

"I'm doing good … I really like my school, Leila takes me shopping almost every weekend. She's awesome and I love the fact that she says she's your bestie." She giggles, obvious affection for her new sister.

"Tell her I'll come next time you go. I could do with some new girly things." I smile and actually mean it, I catch Sarah throwing me a puzzled look and mouth, "Shopping", at her. She looks alarmed and makes me laugh at her reaction. I guess the old me would never have wanted to go on a girly shopping spree. The old me ordered all her clothes online and never cared about anything girly.

"That would be amazing, Leila never shuts up about you … And Jake," she says hesitantly then bravely asks, "Are you two really together now? Like, as in, properly a couple?"

"Yes, we are," I answer proudly and hear the satisfied giggle on the other end. I feel myself warm at her childish laugh, so good to hear that girl laugh in such a way. After everything, she sounded happy. Really happy and I feel the lump lodge in my throat.

"Good, because you already seemed like a really good couple. "He looks after you." She remarks as though giving her blessing. No hint of the scared and sad girl that she was in Chicago not so long ago.

"Yes, he does. He's perfect." I agree, that longing for him to come home washing over me again, I check my watch and catch another haughty look from Sarah. She's chided my constant time checking since I arrived. He won't be home until the middle of the night and it's only mid-afternoon. Not long now.

Emma, you're being one of those predictable, pathetic women who cannot function without their man!

The conversation soon turns to my mother and Sophie is overjoyed to hear I'm finally going to see her to smooth things over, the girl has real affection for my mother. Despite all my issues with her, my memories and my past, all Sophie has known was a woman who took her in when she needed someone and that led her to me. She begs me to take her next time, once she has a break from school and makes me promise. I can't tell her that I regret making plans to go, she would never understand.

Before long, Sarah needs to leave for work and I get Jefferson to drive her there before I head back to the city, it's still early but I'm restless so I swing by Carrero House to collect some files from Margo.

Maybe if I just throw myself into it without Jake around to distract me then I might finally feel capable of doing this job again.

I get up to the sixty-fifth floor, ignoring the looks from almost everyone I pass. For once, I can't decide if it's because I'm Jake's girlfriend now or because I'm dressed in a romantic floaty dress and look nothing like PA Emma. I stick my chin up defiantly and walk on regardless. Chin held high and a confidence glowing from me that seems to be flourishing with love.

***

I end up sitting in Jake's chair in his office with my feet, free from shoes, curled up under me, pouring over the documents Rosalie has brought for me. A lot of it is just reading and catch up, the merger details, some other small projects Jake has on the go, some new updates to the company policy. It all just blurs together and soon I'm distracted and bored.

Bored? I never bore of work.

I check my watch again, sighing that it's barely 4.00 p.m. At least he'll be getting on a plane around now, I frown as I realize he's not called me since this morning. I didn't want to call him in case it had interrupted the meeting. Not one text. I check my phone and realize it's died at some point between the apartment, Sarah's, and here. I go off in search of Jake's charging dock to plug it in on the other side of the room, it's too flat to switch on so I leave it alone for now.

Completely bored, I end up swiveling my chair around and watching the New York scenery with a heavy sigh, letting the papers slide down my lap. Leaning back in the seat and curling my feet under my legs I smile at the fact this is the first time I've sat in Jake's chair. Even as his PA I would never have dreamed of commandeering his office and snuggling in his chair, somehow it had seemed too intimate, yet here I was now. Using his chair in place of him, using his office to feel closer. This was as much his style as his apartment, all masculine colors and modern art and tiny, sentimental touches. If I close my eyes I can still smell his scent lingering in the room.

It's started to rain, nothing heavy just gentle rivulets of water running down the vast windows and it's almost mesmerizing, I feel tired. Last night it was hard enough to fall asleep but waking with my nightmare and then waking early has taken its toll on me. Lately I have been feeling the effects of living with someone who rarely sleeps. He's up early and waking me with him or keeping me awake late into the night with sex or talking. I need to start being firmer with him, this fatigue I feel almost daily right now is a little annoying and making me more emotional.

I hear a soft knock on the door and Rosalie comes in as I turn to face her, still tucked up in Jake's oversized chair.

"That's me heading off, Emma, I've a doctor's appointment, Margo said I could leave early." She smiles widely at me, hovering by the door.

"Okay, Rosalie, thank you … Just go, I'll probably head off soon." I reply before using the desk to push my chair back around to the skyline, the sky is darkening over, threatening a proper rain storm and I hope it doesn't affect Jake's flight coming back. The clouds are rolling and turning in the sky and it's almost mystical to watch. I slide down, getting comfy. I always loved watching a good storm from the safe inner-warmth of a building. I hear Rosalie depart with the soft click of the door and settle down.

I'll relax for a bit before calling for Jefferson to come get me, just enjoy the peace of Jake's office and this amazing view.

* * *

I jump awake to a warm touch on my face and almost launch myself at my attacker violently, my heart lurching in fear, stuck in a memory of an unwanted man.

"Woah, hey … It's me! It's Jake!" Jake grabs my arms in alarm holding back my fists and lifting them over my head as I scramble to throw him off. It's dark outside and I'm completely disorientated, panting, eyes darting around as I come to my senses.

I'm still in the office and it's lit with low lights only used when the floor gets put into sleep mode, I see his face close to mine, stopping my struggle and let out a long low breath in relief. I feel his grip loosen and he slides my arms back down slowly, eyes watching to make sure I'm fully awake.

What the hell is Jake doing here already? Where is everyone and why is it so dark in here?

"Where? How ...?" I'm still half asleep, relaxing my tight muscles as he pulls me forward slowly and cautiously, pulling my face up to kiss me softly, calming my panic.

"I didn't mean to give you a fright, baby." He lifts me up with a tight grip around my waist so I'm nose to nose with him and sinks a proper kiss on me, finding no resistance, he deepens it passionately, taking my breath away before putting me on my feet and leaning back to look at me with a much more relaxed expression. I think my little violent outburst has shocked him.

"What time is it?" I ask. He sighs and smiles at me shaking his head.

"It's almost 1.00 a.m., I got off my flight and Jefferson told me you never called him again ... I tried calling you a thousand times, *bambino.*" A look passes over his face fleetingly, relief with a tinge of apprehension. "I came looking, wondering if I'd missed something ... Like a fight we never had." He smiles with that panty-melting, megawatt grin, chasing away the look in his eye and pulls my arms around his neck. He smells amazing, he feels even better.

God, I missed you so badly.

I rest my head against his throat and apologize with small kisses to his exposed neck, between the open, top buttons at his throat, he tastes divine. I ached to be back like this and it feels like heaven.

"I fell asleep, I think ... Last thing I remember was the rain starting to fall when Rosalie left work." I sigh against him, closing my eyes to feel his heart beat below my cheek, he kisses the top of my head.

"What happened to staying home?" He bends and scoops my legs up over his arm, lifting me in a bride to be hold, snuggling me close and adjusting his hold until I'm molded against him, my arms comfortable around his neck. Our faces close enough to kiss.

"I got bored … I came here mid-afternoon to try to do my job … I failed badly." I laugh pointing toward my shoes on the floor. He nods, and Jefferson appears from the shadows picking up my shoes, bag, and jacket and turns to walk with them to the elevator. Jake follows him, carrying me.

"I can walk, you know?" I point out, enjoying being back in his arms, my nose against his neck, breathing him in. I've missed him so much and merely being here has my insides singing and fluttering like crazy.

"I know." He smiles down at me, walking effortlessly with my weight into the open elevator and just throws Jefferson another nod, indicating we're ready. He presses the ground floor button and faces forward keeping his eyes on the doors and not on us.

"Am I to be carried to the car then?" I poke fun at him and feel his mouth come to my forehead, lips grazing softly for a moment as he inhales me before planting a soft kiss.

"And then some," he answers, his arms tighten around me, lifting me up a little higher, he plants a kiss on my mouth then lowers me back to previous height. "I'm taking you home where I expected to find you waiting naked for me in bed." He grins; I flush and glance at Jefferson nervously. The man doesn't react or move, professionally ignorant of our conversation or at least pretending to be.

"I intended to be there," I whisper with a quiet smile just as a thought hits me. "Shit. I left my phone in your office, Jake." I yelp and attempt a wriggle to be let down, he just pulls me in and smiles.

"Jefferson has it … It's first thing he picked up when I

found you, he told me it was switched off and charging." He looks at me closely. "While I was waking my sleeping beauty up and instead finding karate kid." That smile has me shaking my head.

"I'm sorry … I had intended being curled up in bed for you coming home … I just got soooo …" I sigh "I can never focus on work anymore and your nocturnal habits are taking their toll on me." I admit in defeat

"That makes two of us, *bella*." He smiles at me softly and I see truth in his eye, he's been struggling as much as me. It makes me feel better though, he's a born CEO and if he's having a hard time getting on top of things then maybe I'm not doing as badly as I thought. "I'm way too focused on the nocturnal stuff to actually work right now." He winks at me and I flush, once again checking to see if Jefferson is listening. Jake has no cares about this sort of thing, I cannot think of a moment I have ever seen him embarrassed.

"I blame you." I sigh. "I can't seem to get back into PA mode, no matter how hard I try, she evades me."

"I broke you." He grins. "As much as I love PA Emma I think I prefer this version of you, *bambino* … PA Emma can retire if she likes."

"Not likely … But maybe a little break for now. Which version would I be now?" I giggle at him, my fingers tracing his open collar and stopping on the top button to play with it, his chin against my forehead as we talk.

"You sort of morphed into drunk Emma, kicking back Emma, PA Emma and this new sexy Emma, all in one … Girlfriend Emma I'm calling her." He kisses me on the cheek with a grin.

"I see … You don't think I should be concerned having these multiple personalities all collide into one?" I look up at him adoringly, again the surge of happiness at just how beautiful Jake is in the dim elevator light hits me.

"Nope … You seem perfect to me." He shrugs, this time dropping my feet onto the floor, so he can wrap his arms around my waist and pull me up to his height again, I slide my arms tighter around his neck as he swoops in for a killer kiss, this time getting a little more heated than I think he intended. Time apart bringing out instant fire and longing. I'm more than aware that Jefferson is so close and try to pull back, feeling that tighten of muscle behind me and he pulls me in, so my mouth comes straight back to what he's doing.

Seems I'm not getting out of it that easily.

Jake doesn't seem to care at all. A lifetime of being surrounded by staff and personnel makes him immune to their hovering presence, he stays nose to nose, holding me tightly until he finally releases me from the toe-curling kiss.

"What I'm going to do to you as soon as we get home." He threatens seductively, eyes heavy and dark, voice husky. Sending shivers through me and losing all thoughts of the nearby driver, he leans in, sinking another kiss on me, letting me down on my feet so his hands can slide down over my back and butt hungrily. He hooks me just under the curve of my ass and pulls me up against his groin, the urge to wrap my legs around him immediately pushed aside as I hear Jefferson clear his throat awkwardly. Jake thankfully releases me, turning me so I face the door and wraps his arms around my shoulders, his face against my cheek, tilting my head to the side. He nibbles my neck and ear softly, his breath warming my skin, sending a thousand hot tingles through me. My body aches to be alone with him.

When the elevator comes to the ground floor he pulls me around and picks me up again with a wink. He likes this game, he likes to manhandle me, carry me around like a Neanderthal. I think it gives him some macho man kick as he's been doing it since the first month I worked for him.

We pass the night security guards in the lower parking lot without a second glance. Jake's known to all who work for him, hard to miss that face when it graces so many magazines and poster boards. I smile up at him, watching his perfect profile, the smooth curve of his mouth and straight nose, his dark eyebrows over perfect mythical green eyes. He just makes me tingle when I look at him, so much physical perfection in one person, it's almost unreal. He doesn't have a bad side at all, no matter which direction you're looking at him and I know because lately I have seen him from every angle.

He slides me into the back of the limo, I note the screen is already up, separating us from Jefferson with a black out and I budge over, so he can get in beside me, his hand immediately coming to my legs and pulling me back against him when he shuts the door. His arm goes around me and cradles me against him. I get the distinct impression he's missed me and wants to be as close as possible, I feel the same way. I snake my arms around his upper body resting my head on his chest, his other hand comes up to play with my hair.

"*Mi sei mancato tanto.*" He breathes, kissing me on top of my head. I smile to myself and don't even ask what he's said this time, the way he'd muttered it had told me enough, he's missed me as much as I've missed him.

The car journey home is only twenty minutes long, we sit in silence, wrapped together, him stroking my hair and cheek while gazing out of the window lost in thought and me reveling in being back in his arms. Listening to the steady beat of his heart under my ear and my hand coming out to run across his abdomen under his shirt. It's fitted, showing the hint of his muscles laid flat beneath, he flinches as I tuck a finger underneath in the space between two buttons tickling his skin. His smile comes around to meet mine with a dark, wicked look in his eye

"Keep doing that and we won't make it home before I strip you naked, *bambino*." His voice gruff, he looks sexy and devilish and I feel my heart beat quicken, my inner body heating up and uncurling from slumber. She's been waiting for something more than kisses and caresses now that I'm fully awakened. I bite my lip in anticipation, his eyes move to my mouth, his own lips parting. In a mere second his whole face changes, from wicked gleam to complete seriousness, his pupils dilating fully. He pulls me up onto his lap to straddle him, his hands under my butt, and pulls me hard against him.

"If I even so much as kiss you right now I'll lose all control," he whispers huskily, his mouth hovering tentatively close, our breaths tickling one another's lips; it's highly sensual. I feel his body stiffen under mine, he doesn't break eye contact. "I don't want to fuck you in the car, *miele* ... I want a long, slow night in bed. It's all I've thought about since I left." His words send shivers through me, my body tingling in longing and I squirm in his lap. The heat radiating from within me.

"You could do both." I smile, aching for him to kiss me or touch me intimately. He rests his head back against the seat moving away from mine.

"You've no idea the self-control I'm exercising right now ... Please don't say things like that, I'm barely holding on." His hand comes to my face, stroking down across my cheek, then across my bottom lip slowly, his eyes following the progress intensely. I close my eyes, leaning into his touch, savoring every second. I hear him take a deep breath, he's trying to stay in control but the growing hardness under me tells me he's losing the battle. I don't get his sudden need to fight it, Jake has never turned down sex in cars, he's the master of sex in any place we feel like it. It's one of the kinky charms he has, no inhibitions about taking me any place he sees fit.

Feeling brave, I grind down on him gently, letting one hand come up to trail up his abdomen over his silky shirt. Feeling the hard curves of muscle underneath, his chest, across one shoulder then back along the top and up his neck before reaching his jaw. Tracing slowly along and up over his mouth, his body leaning into me at every touch, his eyes growing heavy with lust. I swoop forward and suck in his bottom lip, gently nibbling before I rub my mouth across his and push the tip of my tongue into the part that's opened for me. I feel him tense, he's on the brink of letting go, fascinated by my taking control. It's something I rarely do, it's usually him who initiates everything due to my inexperience and lack of confidence as a lover, or at least takes the lead as soon as I do. This time he seems more than happy to let me continue, fighting everything inside him to not throw me down on the seat and make love. It's highly erotic, the tension and teasing fueling me in a way I have never felt before … Like a game. And we both know how much Jake loves his games.

"Let's see how much willpower you really have," I whisper seductively. Leaning down to unbutton his shirt, down his smooth broad chest, my fingers trailing on his skin as I do so. He shuts his eyes, leaning his head back fully against the head rest, his arms relaxing around me. He's trying to disconnect so he doesn't react, and I giggle inwardly.

He likes games yet he's extremely competitive … He hates to lose, and I just issued a challenge.

I smirk before bending and trailing my lips across his exposed skin, my teeth finding his nipple and I bite gently. He flinches under me, his abdomen muscles stiffen and move as his pecks tense, his manhood twitching under the heat of my pelvis, straining in his pants. This feels beyond hot. I'm scorching with desire at this ability to torture him. I yank his shirt open wide, pulling it from his waistband and trailing kisses, licks, and nibbles everywhere I can reach. Bending low to taste the hard bumps of his crazily hard abdomen, he groans quietly but it's not doing enough.

I want to win this game and make him take me with force, lost in the desire of it, just to prove to myself that I have that much of an effect on him. I've seen Jake lose control and forcefully take me and I want it more than anything right now. I slide off his lap and move to kneel on the floor, pushing his legs apart to make space between them. Undoing his trousers, I glance up, seeing the flicker of a frown but he stays still, his eyes still closed. He is trying to be the model of control.

I feel the nerves rise but push them down, intent on my chosen path. I can do this, I understand the mechanics of it and even though he seems tense and unsure, I want to blow his mind. I free him from his pants and take him in my hands before lowering my mouth, taking a steadying breath and sliding him into my parted lips.

He feels hot and hard and large, the sensation new to me, desire overtaking me, I suck gently and start to enjoy both the taste and the feel of his hot skin in my mouth, the power it gives me. I'm surprised by the lack of gag reflex as I slide it as far back as I can manage, pushed on by the stifled moans coming from his throat. The heat inside my body swells and surges and awakens every sexual urge I have. He moans heavily and slides down the chair slightly, his hands coming to grasp my hair. I take this as encouragement and begin to move my mouth up and down, licking and teasing, sucking and swirling around as much of him as I can manage. Fascinated that doing this not only made him harder but made me even hotter for him, every suck causing a pulse deep inside my body and warmth flooding between my legs. He's longer than I'm capable of fitting completely in my mouth and fuller than is comfortable but somehow it only adds to my raging desire. His legs move, his knees come up slightly, indicating he's struggling to stay still and calm. He mutters my name barely above a whisper, yet I continue, sucking harder, empowered by every new squirm and moan coming from him. I must be doing something right. I feel his manhood tense inside my mouth deliciously, I wonder if this means he's close to coming and as much as I want to experience that, I don't want to give him any sort of relief when this game relies on him losing control. I pull away and stretch back, wipe my mouth with the back of my hand and begin mock yawning, raising my arms as though I've just woken up.

"Maybe I'll just take a little nap." I sigh, watching as his eyes snap open and focus on me intently.

Holy crap, I've never seen him look so primal.

"Fuck that shit." He sounds enraged, bends, grabbing me under my arms and yanking me up, throwing me on the seat onto my back. I let out a squeal. Within seconds he's on top of me, pulling up my dress and ripping my pants off, another lost pair of underwear at the hands of Carrero. There's no foreplay, no soft kisses or teasing he's just inside me within seconds, his hunger pushing all traces of sanity away and he's grinding into me with unleashed fever. I writhe and arch under him, burning with how this feels, my head meeting the door with aggression as he rams into me again, using his feet against the other side to lever his thrusts into me.

I like it, I like this hard, almost violent way he's screwing me, his need overtaking all rational thought and gentleness. This is a new side to him and I want more. Just desire so raging he needs to take me as fast as he can before he self-combusts, his hands come up, pinning my wrists to the seat beside my head, holding me down almost savagely, his face buried in my neck. My legs are up around his waist, the trousers causing friction because he's barely pulled them down, but it all adds to the exoticness of it all. For the first time in the many sessions of having sex with Jake this time really does feel like I'm just being fucked, and the contrast is mind-blowing. Hot, hard, and fast, I'm surprised by how quickly my body reacts, coming in grand fashion in seconds. He follows shortly then slumps on top of me, panting.

"Emma … Jesus!" He leans up with a weak smile. "That's not how I intended our reunion sex to be." His eyes have lost that darkness and now look soft and hazy and relaxed. I grin back at him.

Very proud of myself and the way I just played the king!

"I thought you were the master of second rounds." I tease issuing another challenge.

"Trust me, there will be a lot more when I get you out of here … And it won't be so fast or so goddamn fevered. You've no idea how much I've wanted this, *bambino.*" He grins, shaking his head at my ability to undo him. "Who knew my little icy Emma would be such a hot little seductress? I think you're starting to get too good at this and out maneuvering the master." He drops a kiss on my mouth and pulls me up, pulling my dress down for me and helps me slide up to sitting before sorting himself back into his pants. He bends, retrieving my torn lace and waves them triumphantly.

"I should stop collecting these or else I'm going to need a spare room to keep them all."

"You need to stop ripping my underwear off or soon I'll have to go commando from necessity." I joke, catching the lace in his hand and yank it free, I shove it into his inside pocket with a wink. I'm rewarded with a smile that makes me want to bite his lip again.

Who am I kidding? I want him again already.

"Baby, I'll buy you as much lingerie as you want, just show me what you like … I'm more than happy to keep ripping it off." He grins and then looks out of the heavily tinted window. "I think we should maybe get out of the car and head upstairs if you want a round two." He points out and it's only then I realize the car is motionless.

"When did we stop?" I ask in surprise, wondering if Jefferson was even still in the driver's seat. That would be beyond awkward with no engine to drown out what we just did.

"During that mind-blowing oral." He grins, pushing the door open. I see Jefferson standing a few feet away at the elevator holding my bag and shoes patiently and flush.

Oh, my god, does he know what we were doing?

It sends shame rushing through me.

At least that means he wasn't in the car when Jake was having sex with me, but did that mean he was outside instead, watching the car rock? And judging by the sheer aggressive nature of what Jake was doing I guess the car had to be rocking pretty badly. Oh, my god.

I feel myself die inside with embarrassment.

"That's something I haven't seen for a while." He points out, looking at me intently, no sign of shame on him at all, just a smirking confidence of a guy who just got laid.

"What?"

"That awkward Emma blush … Soon you'll be back to

twirling your hair and chewing your bottom lip … I miss those little Emma-isms." He leans forward planting a kiss on my mouth before sliding out of the car, I move along the seat, taking his outstretched hand and get out, making sure to hold my skirt down so I don't flash the poor driver with my panty-less self.

"You used to get mad at me for doing that!" I pout accusingly. "I didn't realize I had stopped doing any of them." I frown in confusion.

After years of trying to master those anxious habits, had they really just gone away?

"I hated that I made you stressed, *miele,* and you stopped the second I told you I loved you, *bambino.*" He grins and pulls me into his arms, lifting me again on the way to the lift. "Guess you don't have anything to be uptight over anymore and this time it was caused by something way more fun." He kisses me on top of my head and carries me home.

Chapter 20

Jake moves off me and flops down on his back, his skin damp with perspiration much like mine. There's a subtle smell of male sweat which only turns me on more, proof of his exertion in the last few hours erupting in multiple orgasms.

"Told you the second time would be slow." He grins at me but I'm too tired to move, I feel like I've just run a marathon. My breathing is labored and my body tingling and heavy. I could sleep for a week. The clock on the bedside tells me it's almost 5.00 a.m. and we've been awake since we got home just before two.

"We will never get up for work." I laugh. If I fall asleep now I won't get up for hours, he's exhausted me again, despite my long office nap.

"That's okay, because we're not going." He points out, his eyes coming to meet mine.

"Why?" This slacking off work is getting to be a bad habit with him lately, I'm not sure I have such a good effect on him anymore. He rolls toward me and leans up onto his arm, so he can look down at me, his hand comes to trace my jaw line.

I can't help but watch the haziness of those endlessly deep green eyes.

"Because I said so … And we need to talk about it." He adds with a slight furrow of the brow.

"Talk about the fact that you never go to work anymore?" I smile indulgently. He smiles, biting his lip thoughtfully. He always looks so young when he does that. I also know that means he's pondering a decision.

"Talk about the workplace dynamic … I think it needs changing. I did a lot of thinking on the flight home." He suddenly looks so serious, I feel a little jolt in my stomach, he has on boss Carrero face. I don't know if I'm going to like what he has to say.

"Go on." I urge nervously

"I think we should hire two new assistants to take your place and do more for me." His frown increases and he sit's up a little more. I sit up suddenly, the shock on my face apparent.

"You're firing me?" I yelp, confused and instantly upset. His hand comes up to my shoulder and pushes me down harshly back to the bed, he shifts over on top of me trapping me in his arms, his biceps straining as he keeps his weight over me. Over powering me.

"No! … Listen to me … Neither of us can seem to get our shit together since you came back … It's because neither of us can think about work when we're an office apart and just want to go fuck in the cupboard." He smiles at the memory. "We came back to soon, Emma … All of this is too new, and it was dumb to think we would just slot back into boss and PA mode. I don't think we ever can do that again, I don't think I even want to. We should have taken more time to get through the honeymoon phase before we came back."

"It was your idea." I pout, feeling distraught that he no longer wants me at work.

I should have known this would happen.

"It was … And it's why I've come up with a new way to try it … You're no longer going to be my PA … You're my number two in a new sense, like an assistant CEO I talk over the big stuff with. I always valued your opinion and trusted your decisions anyway. We oversee the major stuff but let two capable assistants do our jobs for us under Margo's watchful eye … I relinquish a little control and we get to just enjoy being together for as long as we need. No more stress on your shoulders, no more taking my bad moods out on you with work shit, baby."

I stay silent, watching his face while I run what he's saying through my head slowly. I can see his logic, but it isn't really taking the sting out of it.

"What does that mean exactly?" I ask a little too suspiciously.

"It means for the near future anyway, we only go in sporadically. Margo gets a promotion and has some suggestions for two assistants that will work under her, the three of them doing our jobs … We just sign things, make the big decisions and show face at meetings that I'm needed at. No more flying around the world for the menial crap we did … It's time I followed my father's example and spent less time working and more time enjoying being stupidly rich and young." He lowers himself to rest his head against mine.

"I want time to be with you, time for us to really get into this relationship. Working, focusing on work will just get in the way of that for now." He kisses me lightly. "I want to show you the world … Take you places you've never been … Stay in hotels in locations of our choosing. I want to take you to Italy to meet my family and lie on white sandy beaches with not a care in the world. We have six months, if we're lucky, before the baby arrives and I want to make sure you're so hopelessly in love with me by then that it won't change things between us." He looks so genuine and hopeless that I feel my heart melt.

"I'm already hopelessly in love with you," I admit quietly, his face lighting up at my admission.

"Trust me … By the time it arrives, I'll have turned your world upside down." He kisses me slowly and surely, lingering to tease my mouth with his, running his nose against mine. "So, are you in agreement that we try this out? Or do you love your job more than me?" He teases and watches me for an answer. I see that tiny fleck of self-doubt in his eye, that scrap of a waver in his overconfident self that I love so much.

"PA Emma is distraught," I say, "She's folding her arms and glaring at you like she wants your head to self-implode right now but seeing as she's on a long leave of absence, I guess it doesn't matter." I giggle, his smile matching mine.

This is temporary, as long as he knows I will go back to work. For now. This is temporary.

"That's my girl." He breathes before swooping on me all hands and mouth and working me into another fever, aching for much more than playfulness.

Chapter 21

"Come on, *miele* … We're going to be late." Jake is harassing me from outside the bathroom door. It's been a day of lazing in bed, food, and movies, but now he's rushing me to get dressed up to meet friends for his brother's birthday. The plan is to all meet up at a nightclub called Top of the Standard. Apparently one of the most exclusive clubs you can find in New York city. It didn't take much for Jake to swing entry for two dozen of Arrick's friends and closest family members.

"Well, seeing as you gave me zero warning, I'm doing the best I can." I pout, finally emerging in a black, strapless cocktail dress that is tight and short, gold high heels, and a gold clutch, I've made up my face with nude lips and a smoky dark eye shadow that Leila had shown me a few weeks back on the boat. My hair is its usual loose, tousled waves in a side parting.

"*Wow, si è assolutamente sorprendente, bambina.*" He exclaims, the look on his face telling me that it's most definitely a compliment. He swoops down to kiss me hard, taking my breath away. "Maybe being late will be worth it." He smirks, tracing a finger down from shoulder to cleavage diagonally and moving a little too close.

"Oh no you don't." I slap his hand away sassily. "I did not rush this kind of perfection to have you mess it all up with a quickie." I put my hands on my hips and see him sigh off the lust. He relents, his eyes still devouring me.

"Only because Arrick has text me twenty times already, that's the only reason I'm not bending you over the bed right now." He throws me a hot Casanova smile and I feel that annoyingly predictable internal flutter of heat.

Really? Weeks together and I still cannot control the urge to jump his bones.

He's in his trademark black shirt and leather jacket, only this time with black tailored trousers and black shoes. He looks every bit the billionaire playboy tonight, his hair spiked to the center and his designer stubble trimmed to perfection. He smells amazing.

"You look sexy." I grin as he pulls up the dark gray jacket from the bed and helps me ease into it, it's calf length and made of expensive wool and has the most flattering, fitted shape. A new acquisition from Donna at his urging that I needed a winter coat for formal events. New York was starting to get cooler already.

"You look far sexier than me, *neonata*." He leads me out of the apartment, nodding at the security staff in the outer hall.

* * *

The club is bumping when we finally find our party inside, taking over an entire corner of tables by the wide windows overlooking New York. We're up high with the lights sparkling below like a sea of fairy sparkles and plenty of high-rise buildings looking like neon shows in the dark. The club is bustling and glamourous with a center light reaching up from the floor and spreading out across the ceiling like an upturned chandelier, the whole place aglow with gold tones and shimmering magical aura. It's busy and bustling with people everywhere.

Jake's has his fingers entwined with mine as he introduces me to the hordes of new faces that swarmed toward him as we arrived. I recognize Arrick right away. He kisses me on the cheek and pats his brother on the back affectionately. I spy Leila and she waves frantically at me, too caught in her conversation with some tall blonde to come over and as I'm glued to Jake's hand, I can't go to her.

Daniel appears from the background, he looks toward Leila on the fly and heads in the opposite direction without even the briefest of acknowledgment of us. He's too busy eye stalking my friend, it seems. I turn back quickly seeing a slight creep of color run up her delicate cheeks and then she goes back to laughing loudly with her friend, it's obvious Hunter affects her more than she lets on. Her eyes never stray toward Daniel again which is a huge tell-tale sign. I long to go talk to her about it but I'm soon pulled into the arc of Jake's arms in front of his body as he introduces me to a vast number of unnaturally handsome people in expensive outfits.

There's a mix of both male and female friends, too many to count and Jake seems to be at ease with most of them. It makes me feel in awe. He's effortless with people, he knows everyone and yet I'm the polar opposite. People in social situations make me feel uncomfortable, I prefer the business deals and meetings where I can wear PA Emma face and demand respect. This happy social stuff is beyond my comfort zone. I'm a fish far out of water, but Jake seems to sense my apprehension and pulls me against him with an arm around the shoulders, keeping me in the middle of whomever he's talking to and involved; nudging me into the conversation at every opportunity. I just sip the cocktail he's bought me and listen for the most part, smile on cue and eventually start to relax under his attentive and protective care.

The music is good, the place is bumping and as I drink more, I feel myself loosen up. Jake relieves me from his hold, so he can lift his beer, a casual arm about my shoulders. I see Leila wind her way toward me and soon she drags me out of Jake's arms to dance with her near one of the windows. I find it easy to be a little freer in her company, she has that effect on me and her happy energy and bubbliness is infectious.

"Can I just say … Wow … I mean, wow!" Leila giggles and pulls me close to a quiet table by a window, she throws herself down and clicks her fingers toward Jake, motioning a drink. He sticks his fingers up at her then turns and walks toward the bar which only makes me laugh.

"What are you wowing at?" I laugh and slide down beside her, watching his sexy ass swagger across the club.

"Ummm, you and Jake! Like only the most loved up couple I have ever seen, like, ever. He rarely lets you out of his grasp, and for him, that's really something, Ems." She beams at me.

"Yeah, I guess we kinda like each other." I giggle and look over at him at the bar, he's propped his elbows on it as he waits for the bartender and is in full conversation with some guy on one side. I notice Daniel move up behind him and throw a casual arm around Jake's shoulder, motioning two fingers at the bartender over Jake's head. The contrast of the two men happens to be the most attractive sight in the bar. I guess I'm slowly starting to warm to Daniel enough to no longer see him as a sleazy creep. He hasn't a patch on Jake's looks, but he's a close contender.

"Pity he has such shit taste in best friends." Leila glares across at the two men and looks down at her lap, she's fiddling with her nails.

"You want to talk about it? He kinda showed up a few days ago and I got the brief outline." I throw her a supportive smile and see her eyes widen.

"He told you and Jake?" I don't know if it's surprise or hurt.

"He sort of asked after you and Jake almost beat it out of him, Jake was really pissed, too." I move to the seat next to her and take a hand in mine, pulling it to my lap and entwining fingers. "I'm here if you want to vent, he's not exactly my most favorite person in the world." I try for a laugh but her lack luster look, and down turned mouth halt me. I think she's going to cry.

I'm going to fucking kill him.

"No, there's nothing to say. I fell for it again, I slept with him and he never called me back. I'm so stupid when it comes to Daniel Hunter, I never learn." Her eyes fill with moisture and then she sniffs them back down, her inner strength forcing its way up. She lifts her chin defiantly and looks at me with extreme purpose. "I won't let him get to me, you know. He doesn't deserve the time it takes to talk or think about him, so let's just forget it."

"I think he does care for you, Leila, the way Jake and he were talking, it seems like overanalyzing and a huge case of cold feet." I try and soothe my friend, but I see the cold look move into her eye.

"Guess that's why he brought a date, right?"

I feel the color drain from my face and anger ignite. My eyes scan the room in fury and I see the tall porn star like waif hanging close by the bar where he's still hanging over Jake.

Asshole.

"What? He knew you would be here though?" I'm beyond perplexed, seems I had given him more due than he deserved.

"Exactly! Fuck him. Fuck men." She slides up as Jake approaches with two pink cocktails oozing with sparkly decorations. Leila reaches up and kisses him on the cheek as he slides one into her hand and then dips down and puts mine on the table. He slides in beside me and drapes an arm around the back of my chair as Leila stands, watching us and downing half the drink in one go. I think she's deliberately turning her back on the scene of Hunter and his date dancing nearby. It was pretty obvious they were hooking up tonight.

I could literally kick him in the face right now.

"I'll be back in a bit." She smiles and takes off toward the far side of the club with drink in hand and I feel Jake frowning at me.

"Is she okay?" I can tell by the look in his eye he really means, "How much has Daniel hurt her this time?"

"She will be, she's a tough cookie who knows she's worth far more." I stick up for her gallantly. It's all true. Leila is a feisty one and a fighter, it will take more than Daniel Hunter to break her. Jake looks after her departing figure for a moment, lost in thought then seems to shrug it off. Whatever thoughts had transpired, the alcohol obviously pushed aside. I can tell he's pretty mellow right now.

"Want to make out? I've been missing you over there." He smiles at me and I can't help the tug toward his mouth as soon as he even hints at kissing. It doesn't take long for us to end up wrapped in a clinch with mouths engaged in our second favorite physical pursuit. His tongue caressing mine softly and lips moving in perfect unison. His arms around me and one in the back of my hair keeping me held close. I could kiss him for an eternity.

"Will you two come up for air?" Daniel's voice breaks in and I feel a sharp shove transfer through Jake, obviously at Daniel's hands. "Seriously man, I've been standing over there for like twenty minutes waiting for you to stop."

"This jealousy thing, man, it's killing me. I just don't fancy you, Danny!" Jake smirks up at him, arms still draped around me and holding me close.

"Funny! … Look, I need to talk to you … Alone." Daniel looks serious and some sort of secret look passes between them.

"Okay, keep your wig on." Jake turns to me with a kiss and a smile. "I'll not be long, I can see Leila coming anyway." We both glance up and see her heading for us, her eyes deliberately zoned in on me and avoiding Hunter.

"Seriously, dude?" Daniel looks completely panicked and hurries Jake with him just as she approaches. Neither acknowledge each other and even though I see Jake throw him a glare, they both walk off.

"Asshole," Leila mumbles under her breath and moves back in beside me to grab my hand. "Was powdering my nose and having some girly bathroom bonding and now we're dancing, sexy Ems. Come on."

She hauls me up to a clearing where some of the other women from our party are already gyrating in time to music and pulls me to the inner circle. I get the distinct impression she doesn't want to talk about this at all.

A couple of the girls pull me over in sheer delight, asking me loudly over the thump thump of music, how I bagged *the* Jake Carrero as an actual boyfriend and they make me feel about twenty feet tall. I try to give the briefest and vaguest of replies, saying Jake just couldn't resist me and feel Leila start to unfurl back to that happy go lucky girl I'm used to. Seems

I'm the envy of most of the women in the group.

By the fifth cocktail, I'm decidedly drunk, completely accepted into the group of giggling women and stumbling on my own shoes frequently. I'm glad when familiar strong arms come around my waist from behind, his husky voice in my hair as he searches out my neck with his mouth.

"I feel neglected over there, *bella.*" He pulls me into his body, molding me with his. I see the envious and swooning looks from the women I've been dancing with and feel an inner warm glow spread through me. I like the fact that Jake is as irresistible to other women as he is to me, it makes me feel kind of smug and on top of the world.

"You should have come over to dance then." I smile, sinking into the feel of him, stumbling on my shoes again and feel him brace me.

"Think I should have, instead of sending over more alcohol, *bambino* … I think I see the return of drunk Emma, I've never got down and dirty with her," he says hoarsely into my ear, it sounds so good I turn and plant a kiss on his lips impulsively, instant touch searing into hot kiss. He cups my face and pulls me back to his mouth a little more firmly. The second kiss is more scorching than the first and my legs literally turn to mush as he holds me up. I hear the giggling and coos of the women behind me and ignore them although the warmth of knowing he's all mine seers through me in an instant and ups the inner heat and urge to rip his clothes off. When he lets me go I'm panting with the effects of that kiss.

"You might get lucky, then." I try my seductive look and see him smile in response, a perfect slow, smooth "Hollywood's best" smile.

"Maybe I'll be looking for a taxi about now." He smiles against my mouth as he moves in for a repeat. I don't get a chance to respond as Leila cuts in.

"Stop pawing at her and go back to your men folk." Leila smiles and we move apart slightly so we can both see her. "Your obvious amore for your woman is making me green with envy, Jacob!" She pulls his arms off me and attempts to push him away, back to where he came from. I frown with disappointment. He grabs Leila in a head lock and plants a kiss on top of her head as she battles to get his muscular arm off her face.

"Laylay, if you stopped eating the men who tried to date you then one would be around to romance you too." She shoves him off, throwing that famous pout at him.

"Stop calling me that ... We're not eight years old anymore, Jacob!" She huffs then breaks into a grin when he pokes her in between the eyebrows. I've always loved the almost sibling love between these too, I love Leila so much that she can be forgiven for teasing Jake, as often as she does.

"And my name is Jake!" He points out haughtily, he hates his Christian name so badly, it's adorable. I smile at the pair of them and shake my head.

"Children please." They glare at one another before Jake leans out, grabbing me by the hand and with a swift tug, has me back in his arms behind Leila. Raising his eyebrows in mock disdain before kissing me slowly and deliberately. I hear her unamused snort and inwardly giggle. I can almost visualize her hand on hip posture and dramatic eye rolling.

I hear Leila exclaim something, and Jake looks up and over my head, his body instantly tensing. The look in his eye goes from light-hearted and relaxed to sudden death glare. Dark and dangerous, his whole demeanor changing instantly.

"What is it?" I ask, straining to look around, but he's holding me against him so tightly I can't move more than a couple of inches. His jaw moves, eyes darkening heavily, teeth clenching—it can't be good. I feel a deep surge of anxiety, small ripples of apprehension in my stomach. I wonder what he sees that has fighter mode Carrero lifting its aggressive head from his fiery depths.

"Ummm, so, Emma …" Leila's voice drifts over, she sounds nervous. Jake makes no attempt to release me or even let me turn to see what she's doing. "This is Ben, my older brother."

"I know who he is." Jake's voice is venomous, the arms around me relentless, he won't let me turn and be polite. Just held as his prisoner and I can't even look at Leila. I look at him hopelessly, irritation rising at his behavior, only being able to see the upper side of his face and his strong steady glare on whoever Ben is. He's practically emanating hate in a way I've never seen from him.

"Nice to see you again, Jake." The male voice replies smoothly, he sounds flippant, unscathed by Jake's obvious hostility, in fact, he sounds pleased about it. "And you … Emma."

I feel the presence move away behind me and Jake finally lets me down enough to turn, I see Leila move toward the others with a tall, dark man standing at a similar height to Jake, but his back to us. His build and posture are remarkably Jake-like though, and that dark hair a perfect color match.

"Are you going to tell me what that was all about?" I ask pointedly. Jake scowls at the back of the person and fully lets me go, ignoring my question, he turns, grabbing my hand and pulls me to the bar and orders shots. Up until now he's been going easy on the alcohol, staying mostly sober compared to me, but I guess he's changed his mind. Not that I cared, I like Jake drunk or sober and never understood his recent sobriety.

He drinks three shots to my one for a couple of rounds until I protest, a lot. He's being evasive and as much as I try to bring up the mysterious Ben, he just blanks it completely. I'm already drunk and anymore I'll be unable to walk at all. Jake switches to vodka on the rocks and hands me a fruity cocktail which I leave on the bar for fear of passing out. He's avoiding conversation, so I let the subject lie, trying to get glimpses of Leila's brother when Jake's not looking at me to figure out who the heck he is.

Daniel appears and swings an arm around Jake's neck from behind, whispering something close to his ear that makes Jake frown. He turns his back on me in Daniel's hold and the two of them lower heads to one another and carry on the conversation in hushed tones. They look strangely cute yet totally male in that hunched way and even though he's being uncharacteristically weird, I try to ignore it.

"Dance!" Leila demands appearing with another girl in tow and grabbing my hand, her eyes dart at the huddled pair and for a moment, I see a flicker of pain. Then defiant Leila brews up in its place and the smile is pasted back on.

You go, girl!

"Sure thing." I beam, I turn, tugging the back of Jake's shirt to alert him to the fact I'm leaving. He turns as I'm motioning the dance floor and he smiles, kisses me quickly on the cheek and turns back to Daniel, who has the bar filling up with doubles and shots in front of them.

Oh boy, from sober to plastered in shortest time ever. Looks like that's what he intends to do.

* * *

"Wow." I scream as Leila spins me for the third time sending me wheeling across the narrow area we have chosen as a dance space; the place is jam packed and bumping into random strangers is inevitable. I catch Jake looking over from the group of men he's encompassed within and smile at him. He smiles back but there's a tension about him that wasn't there before. I'm pulled back by Leila minutes later, before being thrust out in a twirl and colliding with someone hard.

"Ouch" I yelp as hands come up to steady me, I pull myself from the person, apologizing profusely and stand on my own two feet. Hard to do when you're extremely drunk and I'm sure I'm slurring. I look up into the face of the tall dark wall of collision and I'm surprised by the resemblance to Jake, it's almost eerie, although, where Jake is casual sexy with designer stubble and green eyes this one has a clean-shaven face and blue eyes and more of a James Bond thing going for him. He smiles at me and extends a hand.

"A proper introduction … I'm Ben Huntsberger … Leila's brother." He smiles and I'm glad to see that he doesn't have Jake's heart-wrenching "I'm too hot" smile, he doesn't compare at all and his smile seems somehow all too white and all too engineered in that fake tan glow on his skin. Jake's tan is at least real, even without the sun, he has that Italian olive skin coloring anyway.

"Emma Anderson." I shake his hand and quickly pull away, not liking the feel of his skin on mine, somehow it feels wrong to be touched by him and sends a weird unease through me. Jake aside, I still cringe at men touching me.

"She's told me a lot about you." He grins at me and I get the distinct impression he's trying to flirt, I lower my brows, narrow my eyes suspiciously and move back, feeling a little uncomfortable. There's that same thing with him that I get with most men, most men except Jake. I never ever felt it with him, not even from the start. An off feeling of mistrust.

"Most of it's probably not true … She likes to embellish." I smile tightly, making sure I don't encourage him in any way, I know his type.

"I'm sure it's all true." His eyes wander up my legs and over my body before taking a second too long on my cleavage. "She tells me you're Jake's girlfriend?" I feel an inner wave of bile and unease. He's making my skin crawl. I don't get a chance to answer when I'm tugged back harshly into a hard chest and a very irate Jake, holding my upper arm almost painfully.

"Yes, she is … So, you can go letch someplace else, asshole." The aggression is oozing off Jake in overwhelming waves, making me feel extremely uneasy almost instantly. My alarm bells going off at being caught between them and the mounting alpha male vibe that Jake is throwing off in swarms.

"Well, didn't you turn out to be the jealous one after all?" Ben quips grinning, but it's the wrong thing to say and Jake's moved forward to him in a flash, face-t- face. Pushing me a little too abruptly aside so that I stumble into someone else. I catch myself and stumble behind him to keep my distance, eyes wide at this new version of him and unsure what to think or do.

"You think I'd be jealous of you? Emma wouldn't give you a second look." He snaps in Ben's face, the men nose to nose in a display of dominance, equally matched in height and muscle. The air sparking around them. I feel my inner body begin to tremble in fear, unsure how to react, I've never seen Jake come head to head with someone in this way. Never seen him behave like this. Only Ray Vanquis and that ended in bloodshed.

"I'm sure you thought that about Marissa too, yet she was only too willing to climb into my bed." Ben sneers and my brain instantly clicks the pieces into place and I gasp quietly.

This was Jake's best friend? The man who betrayed him so long ago. No wonder Jake feels this way about him.

I don't see it coming at all, it's so sudden and uncharacteristic of Jake that I barely see it happen. He hits Ben full on in the face with one perfect punch in his trained boxer stance, energy rippling around us and the room almost falling silent as the thud echoes in my ears. The other man crumples to the ground. Chaos immediately erupting around us as others jump to their feet and I hear Leila yelling.

I'm pushed back behind other girls by the force of those getting involved and can't see what's happening. For minutes I'm pushing and struggling to get out from the corner I've been trapped into, panic searing through me, surrounded by noise and shouting which is drowning out the music. I'm yanked forward by Leila finally, who drags me out between groups of people, and hurriedly leads me along the windows and out in front of the bar by a smaller side door before heading for the opening.

"Where's Jake?" I demand trying to wrench free. "Leila, stop! Where is he?" I yell in panic. I can't leave without him, I need to know where he is, what's happening, and if he's okay.

"We're following him!" Leila barks. "Security threw him outside with Ben, I need you to calm him down before he fucking kills him." She looks distraught.

"Wait, what?" I grab her hand, pulling her to a sharp stop. "I thought Jake hit him and that was the end … Everyone got in the way and I couldn't see anymore." The fear that has taken hold in my stomach is most definitely in panic mode.

"Ben got back up, when Jake went to walk away he lurched at him and tried to hit Jake back." Leila starts to cry, and I wrap my arms around her. "I got pushed aside and I couldn't see anymore … Next thing I knew both Ben and Jake were gone and apparently heading out of the building to finish what they started." She starts sobbing. "I love them both … I don't know what to do."

"It's okay." I soothe, trying to act more sober and braver than I feel, the shock of what's happened has improved my senses. The deep pit of worry inside me takes over, pushing good old familiar PA Emma head in place. I pull Laila along, following others who are leaving the building, hoping I'm going the right way. I spot one of the men who had been with us upstairs ahead of us and follow him at speed, dragging a silent and tearful Leila along by the hand with determination. My heart thudding through my chest.

We get outside after the longest time ever, people in the way hindering us. Arrick appears, looking less frantic and just shakes his head in our general direction, like this is something normal and every day. I feel ill with nerves, but my outward demeanor is that of cool and controlled PA Emma, she was always best in a crisis.

There seems to be a crowd in the street. Pulling Leila by the hand, I spot more familiar faces and finally see Ben being held back by two men. His face is bloody, his perfect hair messy, and his shirt pulled and torn. He's yelling and struggling to get loose, but they have an arm each and are doing their best to keep him back.

I follow the direction of his hateful gaze and see Jake standing about twenty-feet from him. He has another few men in front of him, talking to him. He looks completely unscathed, less agitated than Ben and requiring a lot less force to keep him still, not a hint of anything wrong with his attire at all. I let go of Leila and run for him, pushing in between him and the man shielding him back with a hand

and throw myself around him. The tears coming from nowhere. He seems to jolt back to reality at my touch, and instantly relaxes, tension I hadn't seen in his face seeping from his rigid body. His hands come to my face and pull my chin up to bring our eyes to one another.

"Hey … Don't cry." He soothes, the furrow on his brow deepening and showing remorse instead of anger.

"*Bambino*, hey … Stop now." His arms come around me completely, his face and mouth come into my neck, surrounding me wholly. He squeezes the life out of me, lifting me from my feet in a bear hug that almost winds me.

I feel the rage inside of me rise surely and so suddenly now that I know he's okay, the fact that Jake physically pushed me out of his way in a nightclub to fight with some idiot over *her*. It sparks to the surface without warning, I shove him off hard and square up to him as best I can, being so much shorter.

"Don't ever do that to me again," I yell at him, tears replaced with anger, his face a picture of disbelief. He goes to grab me, but I hit him away angrily, the fire inside me fully igniting.

How could he behave like that in a nightclub, he pushed me aside and physically attacked someone? No. He attacked the person who had stolen Marissa from him, the girl he doesn't care for anymore—apparently!

That, more than anything, was at the root of my fury. My insecurity peaked and sensitized and irrational Emma on a full-blown tirade in her drunk state.

"I'm going home!" I snap, giving him no chance to answer. I turn away, looking around for Leila, for anyone to get me away from him and the utter rage I feel at him right now.

"Emma?" Jake comes at me again, apprehension all over his face. I'm beyond livid, I need him not to touch me. I spin away and march back in the direction of Arrick, who's standing nearby, looking toward Leila with Ben. She's got her arms around his waist and is talking to him, crying her eyes out, pleading with him, all the while he's glaring over her head at Jake with unveiled venom.

He looks at me storming past, pushing Leila aside, he marches forward grabbing me by the wrist and tries at a revengeful kiss on my mouth. He wants Jake to go for him again and he's using me as a weapon. I slap him hard across the face as I see it coming, instant defensive Emma, so honed and acting impulsively. Incensed with anger.

I'm thrust forward into Arrick Carrero with a hard shove from behind, it makes me fly forward straight into his arms as though he's expecting it. Falling like a rag doll and being enveloped in his hold.

Shocked and winded and trying not to fight, I turn in the younger man's arms—he's strong for someone so lean—and I see Jake and Ben rolling around on the ground, going at it on the hard, concrete street. Jake is most definitely getting the upper hand and the look of sheer hatred emanating from his face sends chills down my body. I try to lurch forward but Arrick keeps a tight hold, picking me up off my feet and marching me away from the craziness. I squeal and struggle in protest but it's futile, he has Jake's strength and iron will and in no way am I a match.

I'm deposited into a waiting car, Arrick slides in holding my arm tightly and looks toward the scene from the window.

"Take us to Jake's apartment," Arrick commands the driver, I wriggle, trying to get my hand free and protest.

"Hell, no! … Your brother is back there fighting … I'm not leaving him." I yell aggressively and try another twist at my arm to get free. His grip only tightens, and it begins to hurt a little.

"Jake's a big boy … I know him well enough to know this is the only way to get him home and away from Ben Huntsberger in a hurry … Jake used to spend a lot of his younger life beating the crap out of people, Emma, I'm seriously not worried. Ben should be though … My brother is an accomplished fighter and Ben just touched the one thing in the world that flipped Jake's psycho switch." He seems almost proud and is smirking as the car pulls off.

For the first time ever, I see a slight resemblance to Jake in his face, it's in the smirk, the slight curve of his mouth and it quietens me momentarily.

"Why would dragging me away make him come? He's back there fighting over his ex-girlfriend." I snap, tears biting at my eyes.

Arrick looks at me with a confused frown then shrugs and murmurs, "Women," almost sarcastically. When the car is up to speed on the road, he finally lets go of me and pulls out his phone, sticking it to his ear.

"Hey, Daniel … Tell my brother I'm taking his girlfriend back to his place … Tell him she's absolutely livid with him and thinking of packing her bags." He throws me a triumphant look, as though he's just put the best master plan in motion, then sits back comfortably. A master of dominance and manipulation, just like his brother.

"Look, Emma, just relax and let me take you home. I know him better than most. Trust me to get him home … Deal?" He holds out a long, slender hand and throws me his most charming smile as though asking me to shake on it. I see Jake's smile in a face that is nothing like it. I soften a little, despite my head being full of anger, insecurity, and chaos and stuck back somewhere on the street of New York where my boyfriend was reenacting a scene from *Fight Club*.

"Thanks. I guess. Deal … I'm sorry Jake ruined your

birthday." I shake his hand then look away, my mind still racing back to what's happening with him.

"Ben's an asshole. Any chance he gets, he likes to start this shit with Jake, it's been ten years or more and he still won't give it up." Arrick shrugs in that annoying Carrero manner.

Jesus can he have anymore of Jake's mannerisms?

"Wait, what? If Ben's the one who hurt Jake, then why is Ben the one causing an issue?" I look at him pointedly, confusion muddling my already muddled brain.

"Ben's been in love with Marissa since forever … Even after Jake broke up with her, she just kept trailing after him and pushed Ben aside … Ben has never got over the fact she still picked Jake over him." He checks his phone as it lights up and texts someone back absentmindedly.

"So, this has happened before? Anytime they meet?" The thought makes me feel sick to my stomach.

"Well yeah, in a way. Never as physical as tonight though … Jake's normally a lot more in control … He normally just blows him off with sarcasm and a lot of posturing. Tonight, is the first time he's hit Ben in years." He's back to looking at me across the back seat. A small smile of assurance on his face.

I guess Arrick does have more of Jake in that face now I can see him up close, he doesn't have that devastating, male-dominant thing going on with flawless masculinity, but he has something. More boyish and cute than rugged. Like a little brother should, especially one who is still so young.

"Jake had drunk a lot tonight. Maybe that's why?" I turn away to watch the passing scenery, a horrid heaviness inside of me waiting to burst open.

"I think Ben saw something he's never had before … A weapon to rile my brother, that's why he tried to kiss you."

He smiles at me and I shake my head, that inner anguish firing back up and tears threatening.

"No, the first hit was after he mentioned Marissa … You're wrong." I shrug, the emotion inside of me raw. I start biting my thumb nail anxiously, fingers instantly finding a strand of my hair to tug at.

"Jake wouldn't hit him if he wasn't already riled, Emma … He started growling the second he saw Ben talking to you, I was beside him … As soon as he saw him near you, he put his drink down in readiness for battle." He smiles gently and disarms me with Jake's most annoying trait ever. He pulls my fingers out of my hair and puts my hand on my lap with a gentle tap before letting it go. It causes a surprised shock to run through me.

"Look, stop worrying … Jake's a trained kick boxer, he spent half his life fighting for fun, he'll be fine. Ben is no opponent."

I can do nothing but blink at him. So much like his brother but not, the hair thing totally threw me. And the fact that not once that he's touched me have I felt any repulsion or fear. I only felt what I feel when Leila or Sarah touched me. Quiet trust for someone who's almost family. This is so new to me I don't even know how to process it.

"Jake will follow as soon as he gets my message." He grins at me. "He's got it bad with you. You'll see."

I relax back into my chair and close my eyes, trying not to picture Jake sprawling in the street with Ben Huntsberger. Trying not to picture that smug face as he'd moved in to kiss me. Maybe Arrick was right, he'd honed in on me to get a reaction from Jake, not once but twice, and Jake had behaved in a way that was so uncharacteristic of my old boss and friend. Maybe boyfriend Jake was just overprotective and jealous, or maybe it really was about her.

I'm so confused.

When we enter the underground car park to Jake's apartment building, he asks if I want him to escort me up to the door, but I refuse. I thank him for getting me home and point out that I lost my coat somewhere in the nightclub, he assures me he will have the staff locate it in the morning and I say my goodbyes.

I like Arrick, there's something so very Jake-like about him yet in a less macho package, he's sweet, in a little brother kind of a way, and I feel safe around him. Not once has he eyed me up or checked out my cleavage and every sentence from his mouth is delivered with eye contact throughout.

Jake loves his brother, they're always texting and calling each other and now I can see why. Arrick is the calm and sensible of the two, the grounding force in Jake's life. The quieter brother who idolizes him and makes him want to be a better role model.

I pass Mathews, one of Jake's security guards, in the hall, he's doing the night watch this weekend, we exchange brief smiles before I head to the bedroom and throw my shoes off, aiming them at Jake's wardrobe in a temper now that I'm alone. I feel completely up and down about tonight.

I'm angry with Jake for ruining the night but I also get it, Ben is an asshole of the worst kind and he deserved that punch in the face. But if what Jake really hit him for was past hurt over Marissa, then I just cannot look at him tonight. It hurts too much.

I stomp around angrily.

On the other hand, I'm upset because of the way he manhandled me, there was no love or care about his shoving me into Arrick.

Even pulling me away from Ben the first time had been aggressive, and it's left me feeling shaken up. I can't handle aggressive behavior toward me, especially not from him. It opens deep insecurities and fears that I can't even begin to untangle.

If I had let Jake just hold me, kiss me, and then begged him to come home then the second half of the fight would never have occurred. Ben wouldn't have used me as bait. We would have come home, and he would be here right now with me, instead of god knew where, doing what.

I strip, pulling on a loose T-shirt over my panties and pad to the bathroom to use make-up wipes to clean my face. Tear stained and smudged to hell, I look awful.

I don't even want to try calling Jake, in fact, I can't. I realize with dismay, I didn't even pick up my bag when I left that damn club. My phone and lipstick were all that was in it, I groan at the realization that I had left it on a table beside Jake when I'd been dancing.

I wander around the room pacing and checking the time, looking at the door and then walking to the window to try and peer down at the street below but it's too far down to see anything. I'm sick with nerves.

Where is he?

I walk to the kitchen and pour myself some orange juice, taking two aspirin now that my drunkenness has dissipated fully with the events of the night, adrenaline killing it all. There's still no sign of him when I walk back to the bedroom and sit on the bed, I don't want to lay down until he's back and I know he's not harmed in any way.

I'm angry that I can't call him, that he's not home, and my mind is running at a million miles an hour with the worst scenarios. I curl up in a ball on the bed and sit waiting, tense, and twisting my hair to death, my feet scrunching into the sheets and biting my lip all at once. Emma in fidget overload.

Guess I didn't lose my tells, at all.

Chapter 22

I sit for what feels like an eternity, waiting with bated breath and extreme anxiety coursing through me. Finally, I hear the door open and voices come into the apartment, there seems to be more than one and I can't tell if any are Jake. I wait and listen. I hear a male laugh that sounds like Daniel, possibly Arrick too and then I hear Jake, low and husky and my heart constricts with relief.

The bedroom door opens, and he sticks his head around sheepishly, his brows furrowed as he locks eyes with me. Like a child about to meet the headmaster. There's no evidence of any fighting on him at all, no messy face or mussed hair, no torn clothing. I look away from him, emotion rising in my throat, relief and upset. I want to cry suddenly.

I hear him walk toward me, I can smell the outside air from his clothes and the faint smells of nightclub and a lot of alcohol as he gets closer.

"You still mad at me, *bambino*?" he asks, he has my coat and bag in hand and throws them to the chair in the corner, sliding across the bed and gently pulling my legs out from under me so he can lay me flat. I ignore him, looking away still as my body starts to slide down with his maneuvering. "Don't do that, *miele.*" He tugs my hand out of my hair, it's followed by a tug on my chin to make me stop chewing my lip. He's being gentle and cautious, wariness in his voice. He pulls me so I'm flat out on the bed then slides over me, resting a knee between my legs, his weight on his arms so he's above me and looking down.

I stay steady with my head turned to one side, fighting the urge to cry, fighting the urge to curl up into that body. I want to search his face and body for signs of injury, but the overwhelming emotion has me stone cold still, like old Emma would be. Emotions bubbling inside in chaos leaving a blank expression and icy demeanor.

"I see through this, you know." He breathes, leaning in to touch his lips against my cheek, his nose traces gently across my skin igniting that familiar fluttering and crazy tingles. I close my eyes, so he doesn't see any hint of response.

"The silent treatment, huh?" He kisses my neck gently, trailing down to the neck of my shirt, one of his hands comes up under the shirt, skin on skin, across my abdomen and up to my breast, slowly and surely. I hold my breath, biting my inner lip to quell any noise that may come out involuntarily, I can't just give into him and let him think his behavior was acceptable.

"I can make you respond, Emma … I know you better than you think." He whispers, still a drunken slur to his voice and the overwhelming fumes of alcohol seeping from him. He starts gently sucking my ear lobe, his hand still moving over my breast, his fingers stop over my hardening nipple and I feel him smile against my ear, "Doesn't take much." He smiles against me, lifting my shirt up and putting his mouth there instead. I flinch as desire courses through me, my body dying to turn and wrap around him.

I hold myself steady, trying to find that inner anger and hold onto it, angry at myself for being so weak when it comes to him and angry at him for thinking all it takes is a slow seduction and I'm won over. His hand moves and trails down toward my underwear, skimming the waist line suggestively before sliding inside, his fingertips moving to my core slowly and finding it more than willing.

"See." He stops his assault on my nipples and concentrates on the apex of my thighs instead. I bite my lip hard to kill the moan that threatens to erupt, his teasing is working but I'm not ready to back down yet.

I can do this, I can fight Carrero's charm.

He leans down low to my navel and licks my abdomen suggestively, I feel my pulse quicken, desire coursing and hoping his mouth moves further south, hating my own weakness to his advances but he stops, jumps up from the bed and walks off, turning at the door.

"I'm not going to rape my girlfriend, Emma … Come find me when you get over it." With a smirk he pulls the door shut and walks off to the low hum of male voices in the sitting area. I feel my rage ignite fully, grabbing the nearest thing to me I throw it hard at the door, the hard-back book Jake's been reading hits it with a loud thump before sliding to the floor amid a flutter of pages.

I jump out of bed and storm to the bathroom, holding back the tears and slam the door shut, locking it tight before sitting down on the fluffy bath mat and crying my eyes out.

I've no idea what the hell is wrong with me, this overwhelming need to be angry at him, to punish him and now this broken heart because he refused to play my game.

I'm a crazy bundle of emotions that don't relate to one another, probably still more drunk than I realize with an overwhelming need to hit something hard. The bathroom door handle moves a little then stops, then again as he tests that I really have locked it before it stills, and I hear his footsteps walk away. I wait and watch, unsure if I want to even see him, but then feel that rage erupt again because he didn't even try and coax me out to talk to him.

Jake always pursues me, always wins me around, it's one of his most infuriating qualities. He never just lets things lie, always pushing to get me to open up. So why not tonight? Why is he being an asshole and acting like I don't matter?

I get up wiping my face dry with fury and unlatch the door, storming into the bedroom; surprised to see him standing, waiting for me with folded arms. His eyes meet mine with a hint of triumph which only annoys me further.

Damn him for always anticipating my next move.

"So, she's in a temper tonight. Drunk, horny, and angry. Interesting combo for my beautiful little hell cat." He tilts his head watching me. "Poor book didn't much like meeting the door though." He shrugs in amusement. I glare at him frostily, tilting my chin up and go to march to the bed to make a show of how pissed I am. He catches my arm, tugging me to him abruptly.

Catching me with both hands around my upper arms he leans down to kiss me, his mouth finding me weak, betraying me. My senses snap back into focus and I bite him on the lower lip. He moves back in surprise, his hand coming to his mouth for second, a frown enveloping his face and then he tightens his hold on my arms tugging me toward him and kisses me again. This time it's harder, I respond greedily and then bite him again as rage surges in front of lust. This time it's done with more intent, feeling a rush of something inside of me when he clutches me tightly and tosses me back on the bed.

For a moment I think he's going to storm out, but he

doesn't, he follows me slowly, climbing on top of me, catching my hands and pinning them by my head and staring at me in a very calculated way. I struggle and start fighting him off, unable to tear away from his gaze, his pupils widening with lust and something terrifying. A look he's never given me and I'm not sure if he wants to kiss me or hit me. I struggle weakly, but he has me expertly pinned down.

His lip looks red where I bit him and the urge to soothe it comes from nowhere. I reach up mid-fight and suck it, that gains a groan from him which only pushes me further. Confusion ripping through my mind at my inability to pick a mood and stick with it. Feeling anger at myself for being weak I bite him again, he pulls back harshly, forcing my arms higher above my head, aggressively, so that I can no longer move my upper body. I bring my knee up impulsively but his leg pins me down swiftly, anticipating it.

"So, she wants to fuck, but she also wants to fight, huh?" he growls, looking at me wolfishly, a smirk moving across his face. "If you want angry sex, baby, all you need to do is ask … I'm all yours." He moves down, nibbling my neck, aware I can't fight him off, all I can do is glare at him.

Do I want him to have sex with me while feeling this way? Yes … The desire building within me is threatening to explode if he doesn't take me like he can't control it. This is what I need, an extreme reaction from him … To take me as though he's no control anymore, even if I'm fighting him. To heal the wounds his fighting over Marissa has left me with.

It's what I want. It shocks me, that after everything in my life, every man who ever tried to force himself on me, I want him to do this to me. He's right though; the thrill of what he's suggesting has me writhing and arching my body below him in wanton desire, almost begging him to take me with force. I've so much anger and aggression within me tonight and it needs release. This endless need to have Jake forcefully take me must have deeper, emotional roots but I don't care. Whatever messed up part of me switches this on is beyond my comprehension and I don't want to begin analyzing it.

He sits up, letting go of me suddenly so he can lift his weight over me at a distance, giving me space. He releases my legs, too. His eyes meeting mine.

"One little word, Emma, and I quit, okay? Just say stop and I'll leave you alone." He looks at me differently, apprehension in his eyes for a moment. His voice unsure. I steel my gaze, lift my hands and shove him hard so he falls onto his back beside me, swiftly moving to straddle him. I yank up his shirt exposing flawless perfection and rake my nails down his chest with every ounce of venom I can muster, watching him flinch and bite his lip at the pain. Releasing my anger in a very satisfying way.

This is what I need.

A grin breaks across his face, he grabs me by the hips and throws me back down on the bed jumping over me once more into dominant position.

"Game on, baby," he mutters, coming in for a crushing kiss and starting something he excels at. Games are Jake's forte, his weakness when it comes to sex and he can flip it like a switch.

I fight, I bite, and I even attempt to slap him, but he's fast with quick reflexes and grabs and pins every one of my movements down on the mattress. It ignites something between us so hot we're almost engulfed in the flames, releasing teen Emma and her pent-up fury. I yank his shirt over his head, he follows suit, yanking mine off and ripping my underwear free. I have to sink my teeth into my bottom lip to quell the urge to moan out.

He flips me over on the bed, grabbing both my wrists and

splaying me out star shaped under him, my face buried in the pillows as his weight moves up behind me. His pants grinding against my ass heavily, he bites and kisses my exposed shoulders roughly, holding me down. Using his foot to kick my legs apart and nestle in between them. I can feel every part of him against my ass and the effect only causes a rush of warmth and excitement to surge through me. I fight and squirm, but I'm so powerfully held that I can do nothing but lay, flattened.

"I'm going to fuck you any way I want, baby." His hoarse growl is nothing like any Jake I've ever known, and it sends a thrill through me. I can barely breathe, held this way, my legs forced open by his body, his weight crushing me and his grip merciless on my wrists. All I feel is extreme hunger and desire coursing through me, an ache so overpowering I've never felt it before.

I really want this, some crazy internal need to be forced.

Chicago Emma is being allowed free for the first time without consequence, a part of me I never wanted him to see and he's almost goading her out to meet him. I try to buck him off, but he pushes me down, a hand coming to my neck and holding me from behind, fingers firm and constricting. He grinds into me some more, increases the force with every one of my muffled cries into the pillows. My rage is pulsing from me, but it only serves to increase how turned on I am.

Jake has never been this way with me, even when consumed by lust there's always an element of gentleness, a feeling that I'm always safe with him. Tonight, it's gone, he's primal and aggressive and it pushes me beyond control. He's drunk and wired from fighting, pushed on by my mood and I want this more than anything I have ever needed. I need this release.

He lets go of my hand and neck, his body moving back

off me a little, I can feel him maneuvering his trousers off, wriggling about behind me, face still close to the back of my head. I reach back with my one free hand and tug his hair, it's all I can reach, struggling to tangle my fingers in its shortness, but managing enough. I tug at it again, feeling satisfaction as he comes down biting me on the shoulder, not enough to draw blood but enough to sting. I buck and lift my legs to try to kick, but it's futile.

Moving back, he leans off me, yanking his hair away and smacks me hard on my bare ass. Enough of a slap to cause a sting and then a wave of heated warmth. I yelp in surprise, my first instinct is to feel outraged, maybe even upset by him hitting me so ruthlessly. I bite down the reaction, pushing my butt back hard so I collide with his now naked groin in mid-air with a satisfied grunt from him. His hand grips my hips hard, fingers biting my skin, pulling me back to him with a thrust. I can feel all of him, he's fully aroused and the tension only seems to be getting thicker around us.

Bent over like this, resting on my elbows, my face still in the pillows, I feel vulnerable. I've got myself into a position where he can do anything to me and I can't do a single thing in defense. He seems to realize it too, both hands coming to my waist and pulling me back further, so my knees are bent below me. He enters me roughly, no foreplay and soft touches, only the wetness of my earlier arousal and what we've been doing. He isn't gentle, he thrusts in hard and I yelp out again in surprise at the movement. My head jerking forward further into the cushions.

Yessss!

I start moaning out as he begins thrusting hard into me, I want to fight but I also want to grind into him, making his thrusts harder. They feel better than good and the tiny stars going off inside of me already are a sign of just how turned on I am. I'm practically unraveling without any effort from him. He grabs my hair from the back, yanking my head back with a tug so my chin lifts from the pillows, his other hand between my shoulders, holding me down to the bed so I can't raise up from my chest. He's got me under complete control and even though the waves of pleasure are already coursing through me, that inner instinct to fight back surges out and I start to resist him.

Using my hands to reach back and try to grab at his arm and hand on my back, to claw him, to hitch onto anything to give me a fighting chance. I'm struggling and twisting, his thrusts becoming harder and more relentless, he grunts and groans in a way he never has, and I moan out too. His heavy weight is crushing me, his hold biting into my skin and his grip tightening cruelly but I want it harder. Unable to control the first waves of orgasm approaching, he feels my body start to tighten and bends forward over me to put more pressure on me, changing the angle and pushing into me further. I cry out, giving up the fight, my hands instead grabbing the sheets below me.

I can't let go and lose control, let him win so easily. I need more.

I bite down hard on my lip, pushing back with all my might, using my hands as leverage on the mattress and somehow, we both end up falling backward, his arms coming around my waist, taking me with him. We're too close to the edge of the bed and fall with a thud to the floor, me coming to land on his front rather dramatically, he's still inside of me.

I feel that wave of satisfaction, a smile widening on my face now that I'm back in control and on top. I begin moving in rhythm, too horny to not want it. I feel his body go from tense to relaxed, his hands unwrapping from around me and moving to my hips instead, slow steady and intense grinding as a soft sigh leaves his lips.

I don't think so, Carrero … I'm not ready to switch to sensual love making just yet.

I arch myself, lifting my arms over my head and sliding around his neck at full stretch. He seems to feel it coming and as I try to tighten into an angry head lock, he thrusts his pelvis hard, my body, losing focus for a moment, enough for him to yank both my arms apart. Holding them either side of his head, his grip tight and biting. He ups the rhythm, thrusting into me so hard I'm moved up and down on his body. His feet are on the ground lifting us up, so he can get momentum, my legs splayed with feet dangling over the floor and unable to steady myself.

I feel that anger ignite, no matter what I do, he gains control. Using his sheer muscle against me. He anticipates my every movement. His mouth comes to my ear biting and nipping my lobe.

"Yield, baby, because like it or not, I'm going to make you come when I want you to. Not the other way around." The gravelly tone sends shivers through my core and kills all my resolve. His voice can push me into submission effortlessly. His movements inside of me harder and faster, that wave that threatens to envelope me building again and I'm so near it's starting to consume me.

I want it too badly, giving in too easily. I'm screaming out for that release, aware that I'm moaning and panting out loud, but I don't care who hears us. I only want him to make me come loud and hard, so I can feel that peak and fall come over me finally. The building yearn threatening to consume me with his aggressive thrusting. He senses the change in me and pushes me off him so hard I roll onto the floor with a squeal and then a thud. Unceremoniously dumped but I feel a smile break my face.

"I don't think so. I said when I choose, not you." He lifts me up from the floor around the waist, igniting my flight or fight mode and I begin clawing and kicking furiously. He laughs at me when he dumps me back on the bed. The anger searing now, teen Emma so undeniably on show and spitting teeth. All hands and claws, slapping and launching at him. No hiding my crazy from him anymore, she is on full show and he isn't fazed by her at all.

I was so close to orgasm that his stopping has sent me over the edge. I throw myself at him, trying for a slap, his hand catching my wrist, I try with the other, but he catches that too. Throwing me on my back hard on the bed and following fast, he kisses me harshly, his mouth demanding, his touch forcing me to open and let him in. His tongue pushing against mine almost commandingly. He's forced my arms at the side of my head, his body bringing mine to heel once more. He's never kissed me this way, it's almost punishing, a fierceness I never knew him capable of. I'm distracted by what he's doing and then shocked into a gasp as he thrusts himself into me again. No love, only sheer need to screw me. I cry out with our mouths still locked together, at the harshness of it, yet somehow it only reignites the closeness of my orgasm.

Why are you liking this so much? Emma, what the hell? This is worse than anything any of those men tried to do to you, this is beyond perverse. You have serious mental issues.

He pushes against me harder than before, pinning my arms higher above my head, aggressive dominance pouring from every cell, a hint at his strength and ability to hurt me should he want. He holds me down, biting my lip hard as he moves fast and finally makes me reach that pinnacle of orgasm with speed. I have no way of fighting back, no control anymore, he has me completely at his whim. A dominant, aggressive man taking what he wants from me and not caring about how he gets it.

It's not the same, it's Jake. Jake would never do this to me if I didn't want it. I trust him, even this way, even acting like he wants to hurt me. I know that I'm safe, that he is still holding back his strength. I need this, some strange broken part of me aches for this, despite everything.

I come loudly, screaming out and spasming out of control around him, my vision going black with the sheer intensity of it. Stars igniting all around and I lose sense of time and space as everything goes blank for a moment. My body finally stilling as I feel him come inside me. His body tenses over me before falling heavily, breathing and panting in unison with me. All my last ounces of anger and rage are dispersed with that explosion and I suddenly feel fragile, vulnerable, and emotional as my body stills from release.

He rolls off me onto his back to catch his breath and we lay silent for a moment. Neither moving or saying anything, only the deafening silence between us in the now pitch darkness of the room. The sudden urge to cry hits me, I don't want this version of Jake anymore. I want my gentle Jake who kisses me softly and strokes my face. I had my fun, expelled all that anger and energy inside of me with that crashing release, now I want my security back.

I want my Jake!

I don't like this version. I shiver, the internal war of emotions getting to me, afraid that he may just go to sleep or go back to whoever he has in the next room, still angry and oozing aggression. There's a moment of pause, I stop breathing as I try to listen and see if I get any inclination of who he is right now and then he moves. He rolls back to me, his hand comes to my face and gently strokes my cheek softly, slowly. I can feel his breath over my skin.

"Are you okay, *bella*?" His voice is soft and soothing and normal, I feel the relief wash over me and move into him, curling myself around him possessively, burying my face in his neck.

"I'm sorry," I mutter quietly, fighting the tears. His arms come around me fully, wrapping me against him. My gentle Jake was always there. I've nothing to worry about, he never left me.

"No, baby, I'm sorry … Sorry that I made you upset tonight. I'm sorry I left you in that club and I'm sorry I shoved you out of the way … I'm sorry I made you feel the way you did when I came home, you know I can be a prize asshole. Especially when I drink." His voice is husky, his hand finds my face to lift my chin as he kisses me slow and soft. A perfect Jake "I love you" kiss that melts every part of me.

"I was so mad at you," I whisper unsurely, closing my eyes against the feel of his skin. I feel confusion running through me at what I had just made him do.

"I noticed." He grins against my mouth, it makes me smile despite myself. "I liked this … Angry Emma sex … But I don't think I want to do it very often, *bambino* … I feel guilty now, guilty that I hurt you." His hand traces my shoulder and upper arm slowly, coming down to stroke across my ass where he struck me.

"Are you okay?" He sounds genuinely concerned and remorseful, his face hovering over mine.

"You didn't hurt me, not really." I breathe. "I liked it … But now I want normal Jake." I sigh, my body fully relaxing as his face moves against mine, bringing his nose across my cheek, small playful kisses.

"I'm always here, *bambino* … Even mid angry fuck, I would have stopped and just made love to you had you said the word." He brushes his lips against mine, still cupping my face. "You can always trust me, Emma … Even when I'm acting like a violent, crazed, jealous, idiot." He smiles against my mouth again and moves his body to mold against mine a little better. I feel him pull the bed sheets up over us now that we're calm, and our body heat is cooling.

"Jealous?" I repeat, confused and wary.

Had he been jealous when Ben brought up Marissa … Or had it been me? This is what had started my rage after all.

"As soon as I saw him touch you, I wanted to hit him, he gave me enough reason by bringing up the past … It wasn't about her though … I told you, Emma, with you I get crazy jealous. I can't even think straight, and this is new for me, I don't know how to handle it … It just makes me so overwhelmingly angry and I want to hurt people and lash out." The tension in his voice surprises me. "I've never been this way, hence not knowing how to deal with it … Marissa used to try to get me jealous a lot, she would flirt with Ben for a reaction. I guess half the reason things went so far with them was because she wanted me to react and I just never did." He sighs, tracing my eyebrow with his thumb. "I never loved her the way I love you … This … Us … It's all-consuming. It terrifies me, Emma. The lack of control I have when it hits, I'm scared of my own reaction. I would give up everything to just be with you. I would do anything to keep you, you have to realize that?"

"But why?" I finally answer, so quietly, so unsurely, tears rolling down my cheek at the words coming from him. I've never understood what was so special about me. He was everything any woman could want. Rich, successful, beautiful, fun, and confident. Amazing in bed. He made me feel like the most desirable women in the world. He took care of me in every way. And I had just made him abuse me in an almost rape-like way for my own perverted release of anger.

What did he see in me? A broken abused nobody, a skinny girl from a horrible past who was just his assistant. A cold ice-maiden who had kept him at arm's length for so long that he'd finally sent me away. How could he have fallen so badly with someone so unworthy?

"Because you're you ... Everything about you ... Even when you're trying so hard to be cold and distant. I can see through it for the most part. I remember thinking you would be a challenge ... An ice queen I could melt with my irresistible charm." His mouth comes down to find mine and gently grazes my lips, soft and sweet.

"So, the lure was because I didn't want to sleep with you?" I push him playfully but only half of me is joking, I've always wanted to know why he pursued me, why he feels for me what he does. So many thoughts racing through my head, overanalyzing everything.

"At first, it confused me, I've never had a woman so obviously uninterested in me. I'm not going to lie. I didn't like it, but it wasn't just that, it was something which caught me off guard in the first week you worked for me." I feel his fingers begin tracing the curve of my bottom lip and trail along my jaw.

"What?" I rest my forehead against his, pulled in by the gentle words and gentle touch.

"You took your hair down ... It sounds so nothing when I say it aloud, but I saw you at your desk, sitting engrossed in work. I watched you for a moment, transfixed by the difference it made. You looked soft and innocent, almost vulnerable, like losing that polished, school mistress hair had made you forget the mask for a second and I knew straight away that I was in danger of having my head fucked over by a girl who didn't seem to want to know me." He kisses me again, more meaningfully this time.

"How could you know that when you barely knew anything about me?" I giggle at him and his earnestly. Feeling my racing thoughts calming away as we lay here.

"Because I had come to realize that you didn't trust men. You didn't trust me. There was something about you, a fear about letting me, or any guy, close, I could sense it even though I didn't understand it … And seeing you just for that moment without the mask, a glimpse of a girl you were trying to protect … I wanted to pull her out of you and protect her for you." He frowns against me, sighing deeply. "I made it my mission to make you trust me, *miele*, to let me touch you without you flinching, without that look of fear that you had first time I ever laid a hand on you. I wanted it more than anything … The harder I tried to make you relax with me and saw the crazy number of layers that there was to you, the harder I fell for you."

"Why would you try? The truth must have been disappointing." I close my eyes at the memory of first admitting to him I was damaged. The way he had looked so torn and ravaged by it.

"Why would you think that? Finding out why you were so guarded only made me crazy protective of you in ways that made me lose my mind. I had never been that way with any woman. Emma. When are you going to realize that I fell in love with all of you, every bad thing that happened only contributed to who you are … I've never known anyone like you. You're beautiful, brave, strong, smart, sexy, sometimes even funny. I love all of that, but what I love the most is this." He kisses my nose softly. "The scared, vulnerable, insecure you, who lets me in, who lets me protect her. The part of you who lets her sexual inhibitions go and feels safe enough to let me do anything with. You make me feel twenty feet tall. I want to squeeze the shit out of you. I love this part of you so much more, because it's only for me, because you trust me. Because you love me." His voice is hoarse and low and filled with emotion. In one sentence he had removed my shame about the way I'd just let him screw me.

"You're effortlessly easy to love." I admit quietly, blown away by everything he'd said. My own voice torn with emotion and my eyes glistening with unshed tears.

"I think there are a lot of people who would disagree, *miele*." He laughs, kissing me more slowly this time, more purposefully, pushing my mouth open to explore mine with the tip of his tongue. I feel that same rush of desire inside of me. Longing to have him devour me.

"I'll never tire of kissing you … Of touching you. Of finding new ways to have sex with you." His nose touches against mine again in the darkness, his body heat all around me and his breath gently playing on my mouth. "You may tire of my jealous outbursts though, but then I did enjoy being punished, so maybe that's not so bad."

"You? Punished by me?" I giggle at the ludicrously of it. "That never happened, I think I had the upper hand for all of ten seconds, Carrero … Your dominant self isn't one to just let it go and relinquish any sort of control." I giggle, amazed at this ability to talk about what we had done as if it was normal.

Maybe it was, maybe couples had angry sex all the time and I was putting too much emphasis on it being related to my past.

"Well next time just fish out that bondage gear and tie me up, then I get no say." He smiles, I feel it even though I can't see him anymore.

"Don't tempt me." I laugh, feeling an inner glow, his mouth coming to mine again gently, my body curling up into his with longing already. Relaxed and happy, pain and fury forgotten and now aching to have my normal Jake's love.

"As fun as it was baby … Can I just make love to you the normal way now, as much as I like our kinky fun, I love just making love to you slowly and gently. I really want to just get lost in the feel of you and forget tonight ever happened. Sex with you is healing, it brings me so much more than I ever knew possible." He breathes, moving over me suggestively, his hands coming to brace his weight at either side of my head as he eases his body between my legs. I ache at how in tune we are and that it makes us both feel the same way.

"Can I ever refuse?" I smile as I feel his mouth coming to me, I'm lost to him with every touch. His kiss taking over and pulling me back to a gentler, more satisfying long, slow love making session lasting until dawn and pushing away any shame at what I had made him do.

Chapter 23

"You said you wanted to go see her, so we're going." He hands me my case to pack, but I put it back down on the bed moodily.

"I've changed my mind." I pout, trying to avoid his gaze on me, sitting on the edge and pulling at my hair. I feel emotional again and I've no idea why. This was decided by me and yet now he's making good on my decision, I've changed my mind.

"Look, Emma … I know things with her are messy, but I don't want you waking up one day and regretting this. Go, talk … Just do it." He picks up my case and flips it open, pulling my fingers out of my hair as he passes, wandering to the wardrobe he starts pulling out some of my casual clothes and throwing them toward it.

What is this obsession he has with packing for me?

"Why do you care if I see her or not?" I snap, irritated by his pushiness. We've had a week of lazing around and lots of bed time play. Suddenly, he wants to vacate the apartment and take me to Chicago.

"Because I love you … And I want what's best for you. I

happen to think this is going to help. You need to talk to her." He walks over with a pile of clothes and dumps them onto my lap, I've no choice but to take them. He leans down tugging on my chin to pull my lip free of my teeth and replaces it with a chaste kiss and a ruffle of my hair as though I'm a child.

"You're a bossy ass." I pout, glaring at him as he grins. He stops, looks down at me in a very manly manner, his shoulders relaxed and his hands slipping to his back pockets.

"Baby … You haven't seen the full extent of my bossy assholeness … I don't think you should tempt fate." Our eyes meet and lock … Simmering, stubborn, fire on fire.

"Fine." I finally break, not in the mood for a head to head when I'm feeling so fragile. "But I'm not staying in that house." I look away from him.

"I've already booked us into a hotel nearby, *miele*. Close enough to walk if that's what you want to do. Look we don't need to stay for the whole weekend, just go and see her once." He bends to kiss me, his green eyes distracting me, and I surrender, letting his mouth capture me and push me back onto the bed slowly. He slides up over me, his heavy torso pinning me to the bed. "Just don't argue with me over this, can we just get ready and go and argue on the plane?" He kisses me again, slowly and teasingly before getting back up, satisfied that he's quieted me for now.

"You need to stop using your sexpertize to get your own way!" I pout up at him from the bed, my body still tingling from his touch.

"With you it's the only weapon I have … You're infuriatingly stubborn and strong-minded, baby. I've never known a woman like you." He grins down at me before padding off, barefooted, across the plush carpet of our room to drag his case out of the wardrobe and start filling it with clothes.

"Well, you better hope I don't get as good as you." I smile wickedly "Else you will have zero chance of bending my will." I lift my chin with a defiant smile, watching as he straightens from the lower half of his wardrobe and turns.

"Baby, your sexpertize is already beyond my capabilities … You've no idea how crazy you make me." He winks and leans down to scoop shoes from the bottom shelves, his sexy ass tight and alluring as he bends over in tight blue jeans. I feel my inner body react and press my knees together.

Okay, my horny levels the last few days had certainly peaked, even for us I have been insatiable. What's up with that?

I watch him for a moment, biting my lower lip and squirming on the bed. The downside to a super-hot boyfriend I guess was the inability to think about anything other than sex. Even when you were mid-conversation and mid-argument about a trip home.

"Jake?" I purr seductively, my eyes almost attached to his ass now. He stands up and glances over, his face breaking into a wide smile, his eyes instantly changing to dark.

"I guess the plane could wait an extra half hour." He strides over to me. "The upside to owning it I guess." Sliding onto the bed he catches my mouth with him in a sweeping effortless motion, his hand immediately coming up under my dress to find me already willing.

* * *

Chicago is cold when we get out of the car, I look around the familiar street and close my eyes, taking a steadying breath. Jake's hand comes up over my shoulder giving me the extra strength I need.

"You okay, *bambino*? he asks bringing his face to my ear and kissing me lightly.

"Yes." I smile up at him, inner peace washing over me at his touch and I lead the way to my mother's apartment. The street is dull and gray, matching my mood as we pick our way up the internal stairway of her building. It stinks of urine and the corners of the concrete stairs are littered with condom wrappers, dried leaves, papers, and broken needles. I pick my steps carefully, angry that this place seems to fall into more disrepair the longer it stands.

Jake's hand comes up to my ass behind me, holding me from behind to guide me, I smile at his choice of grabbing place already knowing, without looking back, that he's grinning. It lightens my mood and as we finally round the corner into the hall leading to my mother's door, I take a deep heavy breath. His hand comes up my back resting on my shoulder.

"It's going to be just fine … I'm right here," he whispers before leaning past me and knocking on my mother's door confidently. We barely have to wait as she yanks the door open, the waft of baked cakes and perfume hits us in the face with an almost alarming force.

She's certainly gone all out!

I see she's obviously tried a little too hard for this visit. Her long gypsy dress, in rainbow colors, is on over silver sandals and, for once, her hair is down, gleaming in all its tawnyness and brushed into long, loose, shining waves. I can see why men flock to my mother, she's still beautiful, with her delicate face and calm, blue eyes. She smiles, leading us in with a flow of idle chatter.

"Seeing her minus bruises, I can see the resemblance," Jake whispers in my ear. I frown up at him, I've never seen the resemblance with my mother apart from the color of my hair. Maybe the same pouted lips and eye color but my mother is beautiful, whereas, I'm just average.

"My mother got the looks, but I inherited all the brains," I whisper back as my mother swans off to fill the kettle while still gushing and chattering animatedly about our arrival.

"*Bambino* … You got the beauty too … More than your mother did." He leans down quickly, kissing me on the mouth and moving off to accept the serving dishes she's holding out to us. I can't help but smile at his back, a warm feeling washing over me because I know he isn't one to make empty observations. Jake really does think I'm beautiful.

"Take them to the table." She grins, nodding to the lounge as he carries the cooked chicken and salad bowls over to the dinette set in the small room. It's already set up with other dishes and plates. Coming out of the tiny kitchen she walks up to me and lightly kisses me on the cheek.

I stiffen automatically, we didn't do this kind of touchy feely stuff, ever! Feeling awkward I reach out and pat her on the shoulder before making a swift exit toward Jake and sliding into the nearest chair, draping my jacket on it behind me.

"My beautiful daughter is home." She gushes toward me before choosing the seat facing me and sitting down, Jake sits beside me after sliding out of his leather jacket and slides it onto the back of his chair. He seems to occupy this space a little too much, it's always been a small table in a small room and he seems massive in it. We bang elbows as we both reach for a plate in the center of the table and laugh.

"Ouch," I say rubbing my arm, he pulls it up automatically and kisses me where we connected, before handing me a plate.

"Sorry, *bambino.*" He smiles at me and I catch my mother watching us closely with a strangely serious look on her face. She looks away when our eyes connect and continues dishing out food for us.

Strange.

"I'm really glad you're here … Both of you." She smiles without looking up. I hand Jake the bowl of salad after dishing my own and watch her, I feel like there is so much to say yet I don't have the words at all.

Where would I start? Twenty-six years of pent-up emotions and accusations, yet here we are, acting like me coming home for a weekend with my boyfriend is normal. Not that she's even asked if that is what he is now. Maybe that's what that look was all about, maybe it's obvious.

Jake digs into his food, his normally chatty self, quiet, he's leaving me to take the next step and for once I would rather ultra-sociable Carrero would just step in. He's a master at idle chit-chat and dominating a conversation, normally.

"I'm not sure how long we'll be staying," I say to break the silence.

Maybe it's best to say it now and not let her think the whole weekend would be "catching up".

I take a forkful of my chicken and dressing and watch the frown develop on her face. I try to ignore it.

"Well, even being here for a quick visit is enough for me … I do miss you, Emma." She finally looks at me and smiles warmly. I smile back but I know it doesn't reach my eyes, we're doing what we always do. Playing nice and polite and pretending there's no issue in front of other people.

Being back here, in this apartment, this town, and already I can feel myself closing. Old Emma mannerisms pushing in. The wall coming up between us. That controlled mask of indifference that Jake has spent months peeling away. I don't want to go back to her, to who she was. To that empty cold and feelingless shell of myself, the person who let no one in and never experienced real emotion. That girl was gone.

I was stupid to think I could come here and do the whole heart to heart thing with her. Being faced with her acting as though life was so fricking normal just reminded me that she would never see my side of it. She would never take any blame in how I turned out and why would she? Here I was with my millionaire boyfriend doting over me, dressed in expensive clothes and living the high life in New York. To her, she'd been a success as a mother.

I'm jolted out of my head by Jake's warm hand on my back and I glance at him, he's studying my expression and frowning lightly. I realize I've been silently staring at my empty fork, probably with a blank expression as I mulled things over. My mother is chatting about nothing of importance, unaware that neither of us are listening. Jake strokes my back gently, relaxing his hand when I continue eating and returns to his own food, a silent little message between us that he knows I'm not okay being here. He smiles softly at me and a small look in his eye tells me he loves me. I inhale slowly and pull it all back down to the calmness he gives me. That peaceful place I spend most of my time now.

"So, Mom, how's things at the homeless shelter nowadays?" I interject to try to connect with her, try to make things less awkward for Jake.

Calling her mom? Since when?

"Good, really good. I managed to get some funding help and with the volunteers and the grant from the city I have the place ticking over really well. We managed to convince some of the food stores in Chicago to donate the food with sell by dates instead of sending them to the trash." She grins, obviously proud of herself. She turns her smile on Jake impressively. "And the donation from the Carrero Corporation went toward fixing up the building and redecorating the shared sleeping rooms, thank you so much for that, Jake." He smiles back but I just blink.

What? When the hell did Jake donate anything to my mother's charity?

I look at him, questioning with my eyes and he just shrugs. I feel irritated by this little new piece of information, something else he swooped in and solved with a cheque book, something else he didn't tell me about.

I look down at my plate and push my food around, I've no idea why I feel so tetchy lately. My emotions up and down for the last few days. Of course, I've no right to be mad about this, it's nothing. Jake's company donates to causes every year as part of a tax relief move, of course he would donate to her. She's my mother and he loves me. He probably hadn't even written the cheque, just forwarded her details to finance to be added to our list of preferred causes. I know because it used to be my job to do it. I sigh heavily and try to force more food into my mouth although I have zero appetite. Being here is just making me irrational.

"I'm glad it helped." He smiles, and I can feel his eyes on me, but I ignore him. Finally, fed up with the way I'm feeling, I get up.

"I'll make the coffee," I say and walk off toward the kitchen without looking at either of them, I keep my back turned as I lay out cups and get them ready. I can hear my mother carrying on the conversation about the home, but Jake sounds only half interested, his replies polite yet he's not really conversing. I glance back and catch him looking at me every few seconds. He's trying to read me, trying to gauge what's going on in my head. I look away and close my eyes.

This fucked-up part of me that he doesn't see as much in New York, she rules down here in Chicago. Her moods all over the place, her temper short, and the suffocating air of this wretched place makes her agitated.

I carry the cups over and lay them down in front of them, returning for my own before I finally sit back down. I push my uneaten food away, curbing away the urge to start tapping my nails on the table. There's a growing energy of restlessness inside of me, that familiar pang to run very far away from here.

"So, Sophie seems happy, doesn't she?" my mother points this question at Jake and I feel myself bristle at the mention of her name. My protectiveness of her standing to attention, my mother needed to stay out of her life.

"She does yeah, she really is blossoming with the Huntsbergers." I hear the affection in his voice, just like me, he's been keeping tabs on her and calls her once a week to check in.

"Such a lovely girl, such a sad past … She deserved better." My mother says innocently. I choke on my coffee, a snort of disbelief setting it off and begin coughing badly as Jake pats my back and tries to console me with circular rubs. Finally, I clear my lungs and, gasping for air, I look up at her in complete disbelief.

"You think Sophie deserved better?" I ask, my voice holding the slight hint of disdain.

"Of course, I do." She blinks back at me with wide innocent eyes as though she has no idea. "Such a horrid life for a young girl … Being sexually abused by her father is just awful." She shakes her head and swallows down with a face of disgust as though she can't comprehend it at all.

"So, because it was her father, it's wrong … What if he'd just been her mom's boyfriend?" I ask, sarcasm oozing. An inner argumentative teen Emma aching to be let loose. Since our angry sex a week ago she had been showing herself in small ways, subtle tells that Jake didn't seem to mind at all. My inner voice jumps to attention, telling me to let it go but my peaked anger ignores it. I feel Jake shift in the chair next to me awkwardly, his hand stilling on his coffee mug as he waits for a response, he's letting me act out because he thinks I need this. I can't look at him.

"Darling, what a silly question … Any man touching Sophie that way is wrong." She smiles toward Jake as if trying to excuse my weirdness but my rage kicks in stupendously. This was just typical of her in every way.

"It's just not wrong when it's me … Right?" I snap. Gritting my teeth and lifting my glare toward her with full fiery fury. She blinks, lays her mug down very carefully and looks at me steadily. This was how she used to deal with me as a teen, this cool and calm control she had over me.

"I don't know what has come over you, Emma, but I really don't think this is a conversation we should be having in front of Jake." She grits her teeth, her blue eyes icing over. If I ever wondered where I got the ability to bring up that icy wall and shut Jake down with a look, I see it reflected at me.

"Scared Jake will find out something less than favorable, Mother?" I laugh at her, sounding a tad manic and notice he's still not moved his cup. "He already knows … I told him everything." I smirk, shoving myself away from the table and walk off toward the counter to put space between us. I can feel that inner anger growing, and I don't want to lash out in front of Jake. He's never seen psychotic Emma in complete crazed mode beyond that night of sex. I don't think I ever want him to see that part of me. He would leave.

"There is nothing to tell, Emma … The exaggerated versions of a child's memory, nothing more." She dismisses me so easily that it physically wounds me, a pain slashing across my chest.

"What the fuck?" I spin, yelling at her. "Is that how you justify it to yourself? That I just imagined it?" My fury can't conceal itself. "Or was it that I asked for it, Mother? Like I seduced Ray?" I swipe the counter in my rage, sending crockery flying and smashing to the floor. Jake's on his feet and comes to me in two strides, pulling me to him as tears fill my eyes and he tries to reign me in a little. I push him away and turn on her again. Putting myself in front of him so I can face her.

"Why do you always do this?" I yell but she continues to sit with her eyes faced forward on the wall across from her, her expression blank as though her child is just having a tantrum. "You always make me feel this way! You always act this way whenever I try to broach this subject." It's all ripping loose from inside of me, teen Emma not caring if Jake sees her in all her ugly fury.

Jake tries to haul me to him, to embrace me but I fight him off. I need to get this out. I need more of a reaction than this same bullshit, every time I find the courage to face her.

"This is why I left … Why I ran … This is why I don't come back." I cry in desperation, Jake stands behind me his hands on my upper arms, trying to support me, he stays silent but just feeling him close helps me find courage. "You can never admit what you let happen to me, can you? You can never acknowledge that I'm a fucking mess because of you … You've no idea the shit that goes on inside of my head every second of everyday, because of you!" I yell at her, the pain in my voice raw as the tears pour down my skin pathetically. I've never felt so close to hysteria in my life. She stays sitting and doesn't move one single inch. Her focus intent on the wall. Jake's grip has become reassuringly tight, his strength keeping me up. I'm the unraveling mess of a child who can never understand why her mother just didn't love her enough.

"Look at me!" I demand, but she doesn't. She just picks up her mug and takes a long, slow drink. I feel myself breaking, the crumbling of resolve as tears begin to pour. "What did I do to ever deserve any of that? … Any of this? I was your only child, Mom … I was your baby. Why didn't you protect me?" My voice is oozing absolute heartbreak. Jake's arms come around me and this time I don't fight him. He pulls me under his chin, turning me into his chest and holds me close, his heart beating a little more rapidly than normal. I break. So much heart-wrenching pain and tears pouring out of me. Jake saw who I really was and yet he's not letting me go, he's holding me closer than before.

"Jocelyn, for the love of god … If you don't acknowledge her and what she's saying to you, I think I'll be the one to fucking lose my shit in here." His deep gravelly voice holds so much anger, yet it's steady and strong. It snaps me out of my misery and I turn to look at her. This makes her snap her attention to us, so good at always blocking me out yet add a dominant male with an edge to his tone and she's all ears.

You're pathetic.

"You believe the things she says about me?" she whimpers like a child, switching on doe eyes and blinking at him expertly. I had seen this face a million times. Her victim act and she was damned good at it.

"Emma has never lied to me and I know she never will … I met Ray Vanquis … I beat the shit out of him and I would do it to every guy you ever let touch her." The malice in his voice wipes away her expression instantly. Gulping back unsurely, she slowly stands.

"I think you should both leave … I've nothing else to say." Her face may look unaffected but her voice wobbles, her hands tremble as she crosses them across her waist in such a PA Emma way.

"Emma deserves so much more of a mother than you," he growls, his temper letting loose. I feel the vibration of rage rippling through his body. "Your daughter is scarred to hell because of the shit you let her endure, everything she became was a coping mechanism to blank it all out. You've no idea how far she's come, what she's gone through. Yet you stand here like she means nothing. That her pain means nothing. You make me fucking sick … As a mother … As a human being." Jake wraps me in his arms more forcefully, trying to blot out the pain for me. "I made her come … This was a mistake. I see that now and it won't be one I'll be making again." He snaps and finally pulls me with him toward the table. Lifting our coats but keeping one arm around me, he finally turns to her. My champion, with every word he's pulling me back from desperation. "There is so much that she had to say to you, but I see now why she never could … I finally see why Emma spent her life so closed in and keeping people at arm's length, even me. You taught her that she wasn't worth anything, she wasn't worthy of love, only being abused. You taught her that letting people get close at all only left her open to be hurt. That men would only hurt her and no one but her was going to protect her. When I marry her, I don't want you there, you would just jade it." He snarls and turns, pulling me with him toward the door without a backward glance.

I had never heard or seen Jake this way, especially not with a woman, the fairer sex. His body bristling with anger, he guides me out of the apartment and into the hall. My tears still falling silently. I've lost all ability to do anything except be pulled around by him like a child. I watch him as he pulls my coat around me, his eyes flashing and sizzling, he bites his lip to curb his temper, his jaw tense and stiff with so much aggression brimming in his muscles. He sighs dramatically before leading me out into the Chicago air and back to the car he's hired.

"We're going home," he says as he pulls the door open for me, deposits me inside and clips my seat belt as though I am a child. He leans down planting a soft kiss on my tear damp lips, wiping my face with the back of his fingers before closing me in, walking around, pulling on his jacket, and slides into his seat and slams the door. Starting the car, he slams his hand on the wheel, making me jump, jaw tensed, fingers bunching into fists, he finally relaxes and turns to me.

"I'm sorry, baby … I didn't know it would turn out this way … I finally get it. Completely … The parts I could never understand. You learned all that closed in bullshit from her, you know. The icy demeanor and inability to just talk. I know you probably don't want to hear it, you probably don't even see it." He sighs and leans toward me, his hand capturing my face and pulling me to him.

"I'll never make you come here again … I'll never question anything about your relationship with her. As far as I'm concerned, she's the fucking problem, the reason you couldn't trust anyone. The reason you can't ever talk about the past." He kisses me a little more firmly, it's as though he is trying to push his own anger out as well as mine. I relax into his touch, lost in the way he opens my lips and feels his way inside of me, leaving me breathless when we part.

"It isn't just what those men did, Emma … She's a huge part of the problem. What she did was far worse and probably had the biggest effect on you, but you don't even realize it." He pushes his forehead to mine and finally lets me go.

"Just get me away from here, Jake," I whisper finally, unable to say anything else about what just happened or to even acknowledge anything he was saying. That part of me that's so emotionally damaged taking icy control.

"Don't worry about it baby … We're as good as on a plane home, we just need to pick up our bags from the hotel and we can get the hell out of this place." He thrusts the car into gear and maneuvers out of the parking spot, getting us back to the hotel in mere minutes.

He stops before getting out to call his pilot and tells them to ready his plane for a trip back to New York.

In our room, he pulls me with him to the bed and hauls me down on top of him, wrapping himself around me like a second skin and just breathes in my hair without saying a word. I nuzzle close, listening to the steady beat of his heart, my tears dried, my demeanor calm but the ache inside me engulfing my body in pain. His body emanating sheer anger. He stays that way with me for long minutes before finally rolling us onto our side and bringing his face to mine.

"I love you more than anything in the world, Emma … I love you so much that there isn't anything I wouldn't do to protect you. I need you in ways that I never knew were possible, in ways I didn't think I could ever need anyone. You're my world." He pushes his face to mine, raw with emotion. "She isn't someone you should ever measure your worth up against. You should only think about me; how much I love you and need you and measure your worth against that. There is no one else in the world who compares to you, *neonata.* You got a shitty deal when it came to parents and yet you turned out like this, you're perfect. You're amazing." He kisses me hard, pouring as much feeling as he can into this single thing, pushing the meaning into me. Trying to convince me of my own worth as a person.

"Jake," I whisper breathlessly when he finally releases me. "You've no idea how much I need you." Tears roll down my cheeks and he pulls me back into his arms, crushing me against him in an effort to take it all away for me.

Chapter 24

He helps me pack my things back into my bag silently. We had lain in silence, just entwined, until the pilot called to inform us the jet would be ready for take-off by the time we got to the airfield. He watches me steadily but leaves me alone with my thoughts, he knows I won't talk about this anymore. The wall is up on the matter and I'm already filing it into the back of my head with all the other crap I never want to face. I won't bring it up again, much like I never bring Marissa up. He knows me well enough to leave it alone, now that he seems to finally understand how I tick inside.

I feel like a complete failure. I'm numb from over thinking, pushing it all back into the recess of my mind, back into that little black box with the rest of my heartache and terrors.

Back with the child who used to cry herself to sleep in fear of her bedroom door creaking open in the darkness.

* * *

As we settle into the plane, Jake looks me over thoughtfully and slides my hand into his. I've been quiet ever since we packed and left alone to my internal dialogue.

"Instead of going home I want to take you someplace … After this, I think you need it." He leans down, brushing his lips across mine, followed by his fingertips.

"I just want to go back to New York, Jake." I sigh and close my eyes, willing this to be over and for us to be high above Chicago already. I need the miles between me and this wretched memory.

"It's in New York … My parents' house in the Hamptons. I want to take you home for the rest of the weekend, *miele*. To the place I grew up." He straps his seat belt on.

"I don't know." I look away out of the window, feeling utterly deflated and exhausted. I just want to close my eyes and go to sleep now. I want to wake up back home and act like none of this ever happened.

"Trust me, change of scenery will do you good … My mother wants to meet you as my girl, finally, not just as my PA. She's been driving me mad with calls about bringing you home. The trip will make you feel a hundred times better, *bambino*." He flashes his charming smile at me and I feel myself melt. Bending me to his will again with a smoldering look and a flash of pearly whites. I shake my head at him, a hint of a smile playing on my lips and see the relief wash over his face.

"I already had the pilot plot the flight plan to the Hamptons." He admits sheepishly, I bat at him with my hand, but he only catches it and kisses my fingertips.

"You're the most overbearing man I've ever known." I smile quietly at him.

"Who else would have the steel to break down the Emma

walls?" He grins. "Or the determination?" Pulling my hand to his lap and wrapping both of his around it, he sits back, sliding down to get comfy. That perfect, handsome profile looking mighty pleased with himself.

"I'm glad you did," I whisper at him affectionately, feeling my heart heal a little as he gives me his best "You're welcome" smile and a look that sends me into a frenzy of longing.

* * *

"*Ahh, il mio bel ragazzo è a casa e lui mi porta la sua bella ragazza troppo.*" Sylvana Carrero gushes at our arrival and sweeps Jake into a motherly hug. This isn't the first time I've met the tall, lithe, beauty of a woman, but it's the first time I've met her in a non-professional capacity and at her own gorgeous home.

"*Si guarda bella come sempre, Madre.*" Jake responds before kissing her on the cheek and moving out of the way for her to wrap herself around me enthusiastically. I feel a little overwhelmed but hug her anyway. Jake had been getting me used to being manhandled so much of late that this kind of affection was welcome when it was from women.

"Emma, my darling girl, you look so very different … *Belissimo.*" Sylvana has a strong Italian taint to her accent and is the reason Jake litters his English with Italian affections. Standing tall with dark hair and Jake's green eyes she looks like a woman in her early thirties and not the mother of my twenty-eight-year-old Adonis, more like a sister.

"Thank you, Mrs. Carrero, it's a new dress." I look down at the short, floaty, floral print dress I had changed into at the airfield, a present from Jake via Donna.

"Please, call me Sylvana, or even Mamma, and I mean everything … You look so soft and rosy cheeked and glowy, your hair is lovely this length too, really makes you appear very cute and young." She grins, kissing both of my cheeks dramatically and I feel myself blush at the attention.

"She is young and cute, Mamma." Jake cuts in and pulls me around to nestle in his arm, pulling my cheeks together so I pucker my mouth at him. "Crazily cute, so much so I sometimes just want to squeeze the life out of her." His mother beams at us with unconcealed joy. I attempt to bat his hand off my face and am instead rewarded with a kiss on the nose before he lets me go.

"So, in love, *chi l'avrebbe mai detto?*" She pinches his cheek before heading to the kitchen with us in tow across the grand marble hall, past a huge sweeping staircase. The house just screams money.

She chatters on to Jake about the others she has coming to stay this weekend, it seems Arrick and his newest love interest are to come. Jake's cousin and his wife and a couple more of the extended family that I've never met. I listen, fascinated by the rapport between them and the crazy similarities in how they look and move.

"Mamma, I brought Emma for a quiet weekend, not a family gathering … I do want her to still be here by the time I'm ready to go." He jokes and receives a pout from that beautiful mother of his. Mock sadness on her unlined, timeless face.

"Jacob, you know how much the family has been dying to meet the girl who finally reigned in the *stallone Italiano* and tamed him." She laughs, patting him on the cheek in a very motherly way.

"Promise me there are no parties, Mamma?" He groans as she winks playfully at him. "I swear you're killing my relationship before I even get a ring on her finger." He scolds as I giggle at them and she spins suddenly.

"So, there will be a ring on the finger will there?" She hones in like a blood hound, her eyes flashing merrily as she searches our faces. A little too energetically and I feel my stomach lurch with that familiar doubt.

"Eventually." He smiles, pulling me in to kiss me quickly. "When I ask her." He looks at me warily and I feel myself bite my lip and hold my breath. We had barely covered this subject and it was way too soon to even contemplate.

"And when will that be?" she pushes and I can already see her calculating which part of the grounds would make a good wedding alter. My heart rate quickens in panic.

"When we feel like it." He smirks and pulls me forward, past her to the fridge. "What's for eating, *Madre*, we're starved." He lets go of me and pulls open the huge built-in double cooler and looks through the covered plates. Master of misdirection, batting away anymore wedding talk and I sigh with relief. I haven't even begun to analyze that yet.

"I've been cooking all morning, go sit and I'll bring you some *pomodoro cremosa e gnocchi di spinaci*, it's *delizioso*." She smiles, I knew Jake's mother loved to cook, he'd told me many times it was her way to relax on a weekend, and I follow him eagerly to the next room to sit down at the large oval table. Despite my lack of appetite in Chicago, I'm ravenous now.

* * *

The food is amazing, creamy tomato and spinach, light fluffy gnocchi, as delectable as his mother's company. The three of us sit and fill our stomachs with the beautifully made dish and lots of crispy bread. She's easy to relax around, with

Jake's same chilled personality and easy joking manner. The same social ability to chat and carry on conversation. The two of them are so alike it's almost alarming. I feel better being here, Jake's right. His mother is like a soothing balm with her endless cheeky jibes and loving nature. She exudes the same laid-back confidence that Jake oozes and it's obvious they are very close.

Soon the conversation turns to Sophie and his mother's work with abused children and I start to feel uncomfortable. Jake had admitted to me that in our separation period he'd spoken to his mother about me, about us, and some of what he'd known about my past to gain a little insight to why I was the way I was. She didn't seem the type to pry but when the conversation pushes along this line, I feel ready to close down and blank them both out. Jake seems to sense my change and instead looks to me, grabs my hand and pulls it to him quickly.

"Mamma, I'm going to take Emma around the grounds and show her this place, maybe take her on a tour of the house, too." His eyes meet mine, holding so much gentleness, it makes me smile.

"Feel free, I'm going to clean myself up for the others arriving this afternoon *miele.* Go wander and let your mamma put her face on." She smiles at us both warmly before sliding up and with a kiss on each of our cheeks, leaves us to it. Not that she needed make-up, she was as stunning as her flawless son. Good genes.

"Want to come see my old bedroom?" Jake winks and I shake my head.

"How did I know that within seconds of being left alone you would be thinking about getting me near a bed?" I giggle at him.

"*Bambino,* I'm always thinking about getting you in a bed,

no matter what I'm doing." He grins wickedly. "Unless you want to go see my mother's greenhouse, it's hot and full of roses and pretty private." I feel the tingles run through me almost on command, that actually sounds fun. I bite my lip in response and feel the thrill as his eyes move to focus on my mouth, his eyes darkening instantly.

You are so easy, Emma!

* * *

The greenhouse is massive, more like a glass palace, full to bursting with flowers and bushes everywhere we turn, the scents strong and heady and blocking out most of the lower windows. It's so hot it's like a tropical jungle. Jake pulls me against him from behind, so my ass nestles his crotch, showing me how turned on he already is, and I giggle.

"You haven't even touched me yet." I laugh as his hand skirts up my dress, cupping my breast.

"I don't need too, just looking is enough." He catches my chin from behind with his free hand, tugging it back to reveal my neck to him so he can move in and devour me. I instantly lose all willpower, my body sagging back into him, his teeth toying with my jaw line and throat seductively. His hand on my breast, moves down my dress pulling it up and disappears under to find my lace panties.

"Baby, you're already so wet." He groans into my ear in unison with me as his fingers find their way inside of me. It's not hard to be turned on all the time when your lover is Jake Carrero.

"Jake, if you do that here my legs will give out." I breath heavily, aware that my legs are already trembling with what he's doing. He walks us forward into a tiny open room that seems to house nothing but a chaise lounge, a small table covered in gardening books, and empty pots and vases stacked on a set of metal shelves against one frosted glass paneled wall.

Jake lets go of me and shrugs out of his coat, pulling my cardigan off and dumping both on the chair in front of us. I feel his fingers skim behind me and turn to see him unbuttoning his shirt fully. I clench internally, that heavy ache of longing, throbbing already in anticipation as I watch him expose the smooth expanse of chiseled perfection only interrupted by the black ink of tribal tattoos curling across one of his pecks. I move to turn and help but he catches me, turning me back away, unzipping the back of my dress and sliding it down so I'm standing in the expensive lingerie he had delivered for me only hours before our flight to Chicago. His hands come up my sides softly, tracing up under arms, sending goosebumps everywhere, my skin tingling with the contact.

"I want to screw you over that chair, *bambino.*" His husky voice bites into my ear as his stubble tingles over my cheek. Obediently, I lean forward to place my hands on the higher edge of the seat so I'm bending, his hand coming up from my thigh and over my ass before he pulls my thong down over it, sliding it down to my ankles where I step free from it.

***

"Shit!" He murmurs, bringing a hand to my mouth as I cry out in first waves of orgasm mid-thrust, covering it fully, leaning down close to me so he can pull my covered face into his neck. I feel him soften the thrust making the waves calm rather than build and writhe in frustration to make him go harder.

"Shhhhhh, baby. Someone's coming in." He whispers,

keeping his hand over my mouth, he keeps pushing into me slower, trying to keep me quiet but it's too late, the continued movement has me unraveling below him unable to be quiet. His arms tighten around me as I convulse, and my body gives out, flopping forward onto the chaise longue. He leans down, kissing me on my back for a second, before finally releasing my mouth, lifting his head off my back as he strains to listen. He keeps me still, holding me against the couch which is now under my abdomen and serving as a resting place for my slumped body, my arms curled beside me on the arm.

Voices come dangerously close and I feel him tense, they move away again, and he relaxes. Pulling away and sliding me upright in one easy movement, he turns me and sinks a passionate kiss on me. His tongue exploring my mouth before breaking away.

"That was close, too close to finish here." He grins and pulls his jeans up, concealing himself. "That was my father and my uncle Dimitrio." He kisses me on the cheek before leaning down and getting my underwear for me, handing them to me he scoops up the dress and holds it out so I can step inside of it. He zips me up with another kiss on the back of my shoulder and runs his hands through my loose hair.

"I'm going to screw you in every part of this house before we leave." He threatens huskily and my body tingles in anticipation, his hands skimming my butt through the thin fabric of my dress, making me aware that I'm still holding my panties between us. He takes them and shoves them inside his jacket with a wink.

"We're not done yet, I'm way too horny to let it go." He kisses me on the back of my head, catching my hand as he lifts our coat and cardigan and pulls me with him toward the side door of the green house toward a building across a large lawn. Pulling me closer he throws his arm casually around my shoulder and brings his mouth to my ear.

"Would you rather be fucked on a Ferrari or a Lamborghini?" His voice is heavy and gruff, I know he's not kidding as we make our way into a low building which turns out to be a dark garage. He presses codes into a panel on the wall and opens a door which he locks behind us. Inside is a row of shiny expensive cars in various bright colors. His eyes scan them all and he drags me to a low yellow car with a sloping hood that just screams wealth.

"Jake?" I giggle as he turns me, he's really going to attempt to push me on the hood.

"What? You don't want to bang on top of my dad's car? I really do … Can't think of a better way to piss him off without him even knowing, payback for interrupting us. Besides, baby, I told you we would finish making out on the bonnet of a car someday." He grins wickedly, and I know refusal is pointless, he lifts me up under the thighs and props me on top of the shiny bonnet, sliding my dress up before he is back inside me in seconds, only fully dressed this time.

* * *

The sex on the car is hard and fast but also fun, the awkwardness of the angle and the slide of the slope has us giggling as much as groaning and finally turning me over to lean on it serves better in getting us both to come. He pulls me up into an embrace afterwards and holds me tenderly. This is the Jake I love the most, this fun and impulsive and thoroughly naughty version of him. The one who makes me pant and self-combust and can still make me laugh while doing it.

"My little freak." He grins and kisses me soundly,

smacking my ass as he pushes me in front of him to lead the way back into the outside world, panties fully intact and on under my dress.

"You're a bad influence on me." I smirk, stretching out lazily as we walk, his hand coming to entangle with mine.

"That's so not true … If anyone had any influence on the other, then it's you, baby." He smiles at me and pulls me close again as we walk, lifting my hand to my shoulder so he can have his arm around me and keep his fingers entwined with mine.

"I didn't turn you into a kinky sex addict." I giggle. "You were already one and you just made me join you." I look up at him pointedly, grinning at his smirk, he knew he couldn't deny it.

"You just turned me into a one-woman man, by keeping up with me, and making me far hornier than I could ever imagine." His hand moves from mine and he slides his arm down my back to pinch my butt. I jump as we walk and give him a jab in the ribs. His hand sliding back up to my shoulders.

"You don't like being a one-woman man?" I throw on a mocked painful expression, my eyes wide. His mouth comes to capture mine surely.

"You know I love being an Emma only man." He catches my lip with his mouth, gently sucking. I'm shocked at how quickly my body starts aching already, this insatiable need in me. I groan loudly and catch him looking at me in disbelief

"Now who's the sex addict?" he smiles. "I've created a monster."

I shrug and look away, feeling the blush on my cheeks, his hand comes up to grab my chin and pull me back to him.

"As long as I made you feel better and forget about this morning." His tone is soft, I look away again and shrug.

Making it clear I don't want to talk about it. He sighs and then kisses my temple, affirming that he understands and still drags me toward the house.

* * *

"You two look very relaxed." Sylvana points out, standing by her kitchen island making a salad as we enter, and I feel my body flush seven shades of morbid embarrassment. Jake mock frowns at me and leans in to whisper for my ears only.

"There's no hiding what you've been up to is there?" His mouth lingering seductively by my ear and I give him an elbow jab to move him away. Luckily, Sylvana seems oblivious or at least has the good grace to pretend she is.

"We had a little stroll in the greenhouse and the garages." He answers his mother smoothly, no hint of shame in his voice or manner. I keep my face down so my hair hides my hues of pink skin.

"Oh, my roses are looking beautiful today, I only watered them this morning, that's if you noticed the flowers, of course." She beams at us and I catch a knowing look in her eye which only makes me want the floor to open up and take me.

Jake lets go of me and dives into the fridge for two bottles of water and hands me one, I didn't think I needed it but I'm soon dragging it into my throat like someone who has been stuck in the Sahara for a week. Trying to push down my shame and calm that internal flurry of panic and awkwardness.

Jake's quizzing his mother on anything he's missed within the family for the last couple of weeks as this is the first time he's been home since being with me. I get lost inside my own head, thinking of nothing in particular just a sense of fatigue and a slight surreal feeling in the back of my mind. I blame him and his undying energy and libido. I'm in much need of a holiday from him to just lay down and sleep.

I feel a little warm too. I feel both of their eyes on me and look up warily.

"Emma isn't really okay with all this yet, Mamma." Jake warns and pulls me toward him and slides me into a stool by him. I feel confused but say nothing. I must have completely zoned out for a bit.

"Well, it isn't going to go away, and it isn't exactly the way I expected my first grandchild to come into the family." She sounds upset and I feel my stomach tighten at the topic.

Great time to zone back in, well done.

"It's not how I imagined becoming a father either," he mutters, looking to me for signs of anger or even emotion but I keep it all locked safely inside and just focus on my bottle of water and the growing heat up my spine. I catch him looking at me with a frown, second guessing my blank expression. Sometimes his knowing me this well is a curse. I tighten my resolve to give nothing away and ignore him.

"So, what did you finally agree on?" she pushes, oblivious to anything I may be feeling as she doesn't know my PA Emma face at all, or my ability to lock down and act fine. Jake looks at me warily, seeing nothing, he carries on.

"I attend classes to prepare for the birth, I go to the birth and after it's here I get fortnightly visitation two days a week until the baby is older. Then we'll re-meet to arrange weekly times and days." I can still feel his eyes on me, waiting for a reaction, instead I focus on peeling off the label on the bottle, my lip finding its way between my teeth absentmindedly. I catch his frown in the corner of my eye and take my lip out of my teeth.

"Well, it's best to get these things sorted out and legal … Marissa has always been one to change her mind like the weather." Sylvana retorts and I see for the first time a dislike in her for the girl. "Has your father discussed the DNA test with you?" she adds in hastily and averts her eyes to her task. I feel Jake bristle instantly; his body close enough to send out signals in every which way. The air buzzing with him.

"Do you mean has he ordered me to enforce one after the baby comes?" I catch the icy tone and look up at him in surprise.

"He's only making sure the name of our family is protected, Jacob … That you really are the father." She leans out and pats his hand gently. "Women can be very manipulative with a means to an end, *miele*."

"Marissa doesn't need money, she doesn't need my name either. Her family does just fine on its own." He huffs, moving back to reach for an apple in the fruit bowl and starts tossing it between his hands in agitation. Jake is entering the "I'm done with this" mode. Fidgeting is his tell.

"You never told me about a DNA test?" I finally butt in quietly; Jake's eyes snap up to me in surprise at hearing my voice.

"You never want to talk about it, *bambino* … I didn't think there was point in telling you, seeing as it's a moot point." He looks annoyed with Sylvana yet wary that I've started talking about something I normally avoid like the plague.

"Why?" Sylvana demands. "Because Marissa and you had sex? Jacob, women who want something will sometimes do all in their power to get it … Marissa has always wanted you back, this isn't about money or title."

"She's definitely pregnant and she knows that she has no chance with me … Ever." He snaps and turns, pacing to the patio doors, looking outside, his body emanating aggression. The pain coursing through my heart right now is enough to make me stay seated, unable to go to him.

"I don't doubt she is … And despite you saying you believe her, I think it would be best for everyone if we just made it official after the birth." She was trying to smooth over his bad mood. I look at his straight, stiff posture and know best when to leave him be. He was in angry mode and she needed to stop talking and leave him be.

Back off, Mamma Carrero, your son is on the verge of rage mode.

"Maybe we should drop it for now." I smile quietly at her. "I really don't feel so good." I add without thinking and realize it's true, since sitting here and gulping down water I have started to feel really light headed. It's come over me almost instantaneously. Jake turns and comes to me quickly.

"What's wrong, are you okay?" His hand comes to my face and it's the last thing I see before darkness over takes me.

* * *

"She's coming around." I hear Sylvana's voice over the top of me and something cold and damp across my head, Jake's face comes into focus, leaning over me, etched with concern. His normally playful expression now dark and foreboding and his green eyes almost black. Sylvana appears further back, removing the dampness on my head and replacing it with another, colder, one.

"Hey," Jake breathes, as I flutter my lashes open. "You scared me, *bambino.*" His voice is husky and shaky, his hands gripping both of mine tightly and I can feel the tension radiating from him.

"What happened?" I ask weakly, closing my eyes again as exhaustion washes over me. I feel woozy still.

"You fainted, *miele.*" Sylvana cuts in softly, a warm gentle hand stroking my cheek. "Luckily, Jake was quick enough to catch you before you did yourself a terrible injury, you were only out a couple of minutes. I think we need to get a house visit from our family doctor." She smiles at me as I focus on her face again. I feel nothing but fatigue and disorientation, as though I've been asleep for days.

I realize I'm lying flat on my back and there's a large ornate ceiling above me and central light fixture with elaborate center rose, I'm in some sort of grand sitting room.

"Emma, look at me." Jake's voice urges, and I obey, focusing on his worried face, his mouth set in a thin line, he's frowning deeply. His shoulders hunched forward as he scrutinizes me. "The doctor is a good idea, *bella*."

"No. No doctors," I say, finding some inner strength and trying to sit up but he pushes me back down.

"You don't get a say." He commands, that furrowing brow coming close to commandeering Carrero face.

"Yes, I do … Look, it's been a long day, we had an early start and two flights today followed by an … erm … long walk." I add blushing wildly and avoid looking at his mother, I catch the smirk on his face at my meaning. "I'm just exhausted and a little overwhelmed." His hand strokes across my face, sending tiny shivers through me. "I don't want a doctor, I think I just need a nap, I'm so tired." I point out.

It's been an emotional day and I'm seriously flaking right now.

"I don't think that's wise—" Sylvana starts but Jake cuts in.

"I'll take her upstairs and let her sleep, if she's still shaky later then I'll be the first to get her a doctor, Mamma, I swear … Okay?" I feel myself relax as Jake sides with me. I know he wants nothing more than for me to obey her, but he also knows if I want to be stubborn I'll point blank refuse to let a doctor touch me. She regards his expression for a moment and then me.

"Okay, take her to your old room, *miele* … I had all the beds made up fresh when you told me you were coming." She leans and kisses him on the cheek before moving back.

"Come on, you." Jake's leans in, scooping me in his arms and hoists me up revealing that I had been laid on an expensive looking white couch and carries me out toward that sweeping marble staircase in the grand hall.

* * *

I wake in the darkness, my body held tightly in Jake's arms and maneuver to free myself a little. I'm surprised to find that both of us are undressed and under the bed clothes. When I had fallen asleep I had been fully dressed, lying on top, laid on his chest as he watched a movie. It's dark around us and reaching for the phone in the semi-dark room I'm shocked to find it has gone 4.00 a.m.

How long have I been asleep? I must have been exhausted.

I look down at his completely still face, breathing heavily in slumber, his strong arms encircling me protectively. It takes away the urge to get up and instead I nuzzle back down into him, nose to nose and watch him sleep before slumber over takes me again.

Chapter 25

Jake stills over me, bracing himself on his arms, biceps straining impressively. His naked skin has a soft sheen of moisture and is glistening at me from inches above my own nakedness.

"What's wrong, *bambino*?" His intense gaze dissecting my face, his breathing rapid. I wriggle impatiently, unimpressed with his sudden halt.

"Nothing …What are you doing?" I stay nestled in the pillows watching him in confusion. My heart rate still elevated and my breathing shallow.

"Baby, we have been having sex for the best part of a half hour and I haven't made you come once … That's unheard of for you … I'm starting to feel a little more than inadequate." He pulls off me, indicating he's not going to continue.

"Jake, don't stop … It still feels better than good." I pout, trying to pull him down against me but he only resists.

"Not until you tell me what's wrong." He persists, his face serious.

"Nothing's wrong." It's not exactly a lie, I had been more

than enjoying what he was doing but my head had been all over the place making it impossible to succumb to the growing waves of orgasm every time they started.

"Are you still dizzy? From yesterday?" The concern etched on his face tugs at my heart, guilt rising inside of me.

"No. I told you when we woke up, I'm fine today." I bite my lip anxiously, I know he's not going to let this go. As sex crazed as Jake seems to be, he always seems honed into how I'm responding and feeling. He's an attentive lover.

"Is this about Marissa?" He leans down so he's closer to me, his eyes locking fully on mine for any hint of hesitation.

"No … Maybe." I break. It's true. All I've been thinking about is her and the baby since his mother brought her up. The DNA test foremost in my head. A mass of confused thoughts eating away at my brain.

"In general? Or more specifically?" Intuitive as always and straight to the point. I turn to look at the bedside clock, uneasy at his intent gaze on my face. It's after ten in the morning, most of the house will probably be up now and I wonder if maybe we should go downstairs instead of this interrogation. His hand catches my chin and pulls me back to face him.

"I can stay here all day, baby, and drag this out of you one letter at a time." He threatens, and I know he means it, no one has more stubbornness in them than him.

"I think you should have the DNA test done." I blurt out then cringe, biting back on my lip in remorse. His face tightens but he doesn't fully react. I watch as his pale hue of green changes to a darker shade with more brown flecks than normal and he narrows his eyes with a frown. It always mesmerized me the way they could change depending on his mood. A typical green eye characteristic.

"You don't think the baby is mine?" He questions flatly,

face devoid of any expression, except a subtle furrow. I can feel the ripple of tension, though, and my stomach lurches with the energy.

"I don't know … What your mother said, Jake, the fact you say you don't even remember sleeping with her and I know you … No matter how drunk, you've never forgotten to use a condom."

Didn't I used to order your goddamn supply for you?

"You don't think my lack of memory indicates just how drunk I was? That not using a condom in that state is likely?" His voice has an edge to it but he's still not giving much away.

"If you were that drunk then how did you even … You know." I look away awkwardly, hating this conversation, a deep pit in my stomach building up. My nerves tightening and nausea threatening to take hold. Something prickling all the way up my skin and making me nervy.

"Get it up?" He replies sardonically and all I can do is nod mutely with a flush of shame and warming cheeks.

"It's never been an issue; even drunk enough to forget what I've been up to." He points out. I feel that inner hope I had been starting to cling to die immediately. He rolls off me onto his back and stares blankly up at the ceiling. "You really want me to do this?" He sounds almost exasperated. Maybe angry.

"Don't do it if you don't want to," I reply numbly, this shift in his position and mood throwing me. Ten minutes ago, he'd been inside of me, breathing heavily in my ear as I had groaned and writhed under his body, mounting again to another wave of pleasure. Maybe I wouldn't have come but I was certainly enjoying it way more than this.

"You can't just hit me with what's wrong then say something like that." He snaps. "Of course, I'll take the fucking test." He gets up quickly and stalks off toward the en-suite. "I would do anything you asked of me … Doesn't mean I have to be fucking happy about it." He slams the bathroom door as soon as he's inside and I feel myself well up instantly. A tremor of emotion running through me painfully. I didn't want to fight. I roll on my side and wrap my arms around myself, an effort to push away the threatening tears. I didn't know what the issue with the test was.

Didn't he want to be sure? Why was he so against it? Why did he get so angry about it? I would want to know if it was me. It's not like he had reason to trust her, she had proven that years ago.

He finally emerges wearing sweat pants and a T-shirt, I can smell toothpaste and he looks like he's trimmed his stubble, his hair styled. I guess he's no intention of coming back to bed.

He walks past the bed, hauling his running shoes from the bag on the floor that held his gym clothes and sits down on the edge of the bed to put them on. I say nothing, just watch him silently, hating the atmosphere between us. He finally gets up, stretching out his arms over his head and flexes his large shoulders, rotating them before throwing me a look.

"I'm going for a run … Stay here or go for breakfast … Don't wait on me, I don't know how long I'm going to be." There's nothing in his tone, no anger yet no love and he doesn't stoop to kiss me before lifting the zip of his hoodie up and walking out. No backward glance or even a smile, he just stalks out, emanating all kinds of anger and then he's gone. All the tension bubbling inside of me to epic proportions.

I immediately burst into tears and bury my face in the pillows of the bed to drown it out. Pulling them around me to blot out the world, I pull my knees up to my stomach and let the full force of the pain run through me.

He's no idea how he can make me feel, how little effort it really took to hurt me. Especially about this, he had no clue to the depth of insecurity it had inflicted me with.

"Don't cry, baby, please." His sudden tone in my ear makes me jump as his arms come around me tightly from behind. "I'm sorry, Emma … Please, *bambino.*" His tone is soft and gentle, his fingers uncurling my grip in the cushions, so he can pull me into his body, encircling me with his face in my hair by my cheek.

"Shhhhhh, come on. Turn around." He breathes, finally coaxing me to face him and pulling me against his chest. "I'm sorry. *Neonata*. Stop. You're making me feel even shittier than I do already." His fingers come down across my face, wiping away the dampness, his nose coming down to mine so he can look at me. I'm nestled in his arms under him. I take a breath, stilling the onslaught, sniffing back any more threatening to come. Confused as to why he's back.

"I've stopped." I sigh emotionally, sniffing again and suddenly embarrassed. "Why did you come back?" I look up at him with wide eyes.

"I didn't get far … This overwhelming guilt that after finally getting you to actually tell me how you're feeling, I just acted like a prize asshole and you would probably never open up again. You can't help that you feel that way, *bambino*. Being pissed at you for it was a sure-fire way to make sure you never trusted me to talk to again. I couldn't let that happen." He looks at me remorsefully, his brows lowered in regret. "It's a touchy subject … Do you forgive me?" He leans down as I nod and kisses me gently on the mouth, soft and reassuring, his hand comes to curl in my hair. He breathes heavily and looks away across the room over the top of me as though trying to find a focus.

"I'm not mad about taking the tests, Emma … I agree.

It's just Marissa can be a prize bitch normally and hitting her with this will set her off again. She's going to flip out and cause me all sorts of agro, *miele*. I can't blame her though, it's doubting her honesty and probably going to look like I'm looking for a way out." He sighs again. "From day one she's been accusing me of not being invested … This is just going to look like she's right."

"You're putting up with so much crap from her and running to LA for all of this," I retort. "How can she say that you're not invested?"

"You really want to know?" He looks at me warily. "You never ask about any of this." He watches me carefully. I bite on my lip, and twirl my hair nervously, everything in me wanting to push this topic away and clamp shut, but the way he's looking at me stills me. He lifts his hand to mine, cupping it slowly and pulls my fingers from my hair with a frown. He keeps my hand in his yet uses his thumb to stroke my cheek.

"I want to talk to you about this, but not if it's going to upset you." He finally admits but I stay still, looking intently at him.

"I need to stop pretending it's not happening." I finally let out quietly and watch the indecision flit across his face. He knows I probably won't lead the conversation, so he volunteers it instead.

"I asked her to have a termination." He grimaces as though he's not proud of the memory. "The night in the hotel, the first time we ever had sex … I didn't know what was happening with us, all I could think about was you. She wanted me to marry her, for the sake of her pride and I told her no. I thought a baby would mean I would never have a chance with you, so I told her I didn't want it." He looks anywhere but at me and despite looking ashamed there's an inner glow inside of me, a tiny spark calming over my insecure heart.

Does that make me a complete bitch?

"I was a complete jerk. She showed up at the wrong time, things between us messy and all I wanted was to march to your room and talk about everything that had happened; not be pacing around my room with an angry Marissa preaching to me about responsibilities."

I love you so much!

"You think I don't agree? I would have done the same if I had been you." I reach my fingertips up and try to smooth away the furrow of his dark brows. "This baby has been a massive cloud over us from day one."

He sighs and turns his attention back to me, his knuckles running down my cheek.

"I keep trying to feel some sort of peace with this, trying to get things legal was an attempt at being okay with it but I just can't. No matter how many times I tell myself I'm going to be a father, I just can't seem to accept it." He exhales heavily. "The DNA testing just points out to me more than ever how much I'm desperate to find a way out, Emma … I'm ashamed that I can even think that way. It's why I don't want it … Because I don't want to focus hope on some miracle that it's not mine."

Hearing him verbalize all of this makes me cry, only not with insecurity or anguish but with relief, a part of me needing to hear all of this finally. He rests his forehead to mine, his fingers tracing my mouth.

"This isn't how I planned any of this. It was supposed to be just you and me and a whole future ahead of us to get married, have kids … Marissa and this baby turn everything upside down. It kills me to know how much it hurts you and that hurts me too."

"I wish it never happened." I admit shyly, my cheeks heating at the admission, afraid to show him how selfish I am.

You're an awful person, Emma!

"I wish it never happened either, I'm not just saying that because I got her pregnant … I wish I had realized the moment I fell in love with you that sex with anyone else was never going to fix me. I was stupid and only gave you more reason to push me away." He's gazing deeply into my eyes intensely; every shade of green has come into play with every emotion and right now I'm mesmerized. I look away, swallowing down the surge of hurt, the memory of him leaving me on that boat to expel his sexual tension with other women in a bid to get over me.

"It never helped me. I just felt shitty." He whispers against my cheek. "It just made me even more messed up in the head, feeling more and more distraught."

"You don't need to tell me this." I start, feeling the panic rise that's he's going to admit to everything I didn't want to hear. I didn't need to know about the women who kept him occupied while we were apart.

"I need to tell you this, Emma … You need to hear it, if anything so that I stop feeling guilty about it every time I look at you. I regret it so much."

"I don't want to know about other women when you left the boat." I start, wriggling to get free but he holds me still.

"There was only one … Once. I swear. Then I sent her away and took some alone time because I realized sex wasn't going to straighten my head out, it wasn't going to fill this emptiness inside of me that you left."

It rips through my chest but in no way near the destructive way I had expected. I had been waiting to hear about a multitude of women and non-stop sex, yet his admission took it all away.

"But you came back to New York with a date." I point out. My brain scrambling at the memories in disbelief.

"I'm capable of sharing my bed with someone and not having sex you know, I brought her with me to make sure I didn't try anything with you." He shrugs. "I didn't care if it pissed her off, I just didn't trust myself to be close to you."

"Before the boat?" I blurt out, my mind a chaos and trying to think back to the women he had around me back then. So sure he'd been keeping up with his dates throughout.

"Probably less than half you thought I was sleeping with, slowly, over the months I couldn't find anything in them that turned me on. I pretty much lost all interest in every woman that I laid eyes on after the first time I kissed you." He smiles at me. "Up until that point, I didn't really understand how I felt, I knew I cared about you a lot. I knew that you drove me crazy with your tight skirts, hints of cleavage, and high heels but I figured it was lust … Challenge of the unattainable. I was confused."

"But we barely kissed, and I pushed you away?" I frown, my memories falling into one another haphazardly.

"I know. But in that brief second, I knew I was crazy about you, the feel of you." He stops and runs a gentle fingertip across my lower lip longingly. "I've never felt that way kissing anyone, the deep lurch in my stomach and goddamn butterflies" He grins. "All that mushy girl crap you hear them talking about … It actually happened for me."

I grin back at him.

Who knew Carrero could turn into a teen girl?

"Pity all I could think was how terrified I was, it drowned out everything else for me." I admit apologetically but he only smiles and throws a quick kiss on my mouth.

"I felt it baby … That fear, that instant terror and it only made me want to be the guy to rescue you even more. I knew I had to gain your trust slowly. I made up my mind that I was going to be the guy to bring you out of yourself, no matter what it took."

"Not enough to abstain from sex though?" I pout.

"Hey, no fair. I was still figuring it out. I tried to just carry on as normal, but I didn't get the same kick out of casual sex anymore and I didn't sleep with most of them." His brow furrows and his gaze lands on mine again, that remorse overtaking his beautiful face.

"So, your break in women? You were really celibate by then? That must have been hard when surrounded by over sexed bimbos," I say, unable to conceal my jealousy.

"Why? You don't think I could cope without constant sex? I kept up the pretense for a while, baby, in case you caught on something had changed and then I just let the dates fizzle out until I didn't bother with them anymore. Which, can I add, was a relief, because man, you women sure get prissy as shit when a guy refuses sex. I knew what I wanted, Emma. No one else held any interest for me. It was harder to be around *you* and not want sex with *you* every minute of the day."

"Jake Carrero gave up sex for me. Hell must have frozen over." I'm grinning, this admission has completely blown me away. I squeal and giggle as he goes for my stomach with tickling fingers.

"I told you … This relationship didn't start after that dance, *neonata*, for me, this has been a very long time coming. I'm amazed I still had the lasting capability the first time we had sex. It had been a hell of a while and the way you got to me I was shocked I lasted more than thirty seconds." He was on top of me now, brushing back my hair and nuzzling his nose against mine.

"I guess it explains why you're making up for it nowadays." I giggle, he laughs too, flooring me with the beauty of that perfect white grin.

"Trust me. The lack of sex is not the only reason. You, my love, drive me insane with lust." He kisses me more thoroughly, pinning me down to the bed and moving against me suggestively. "See." He points out as the hardness in his pants pressed through the sheets against my pelvis.

"I didn't stop things." I remind him. "You did."

He frowns and takes a deep breath, his eyes on mine as he stills. That serious, all-business look coming across his face.

"I'll have my lawyers draft in the request for DNA for as soon as the baby is born, this may change things with our current arrangements knowing how Marissa can be. I'm not going to get my hopes up, Emma … I may not remember it happening but I'm pretty sure she would never stoop that low." He brushes his nose against mine before stealing a soft kiss. I smile in response despite the inner trepidation and sudden flutter of anxiety.

There's nothing more to say on the subject and knowing that he will get the test helps put it out of my head. This whole conversation has helped put it all out of my head. Lifting my chin up, I kiss him more passionately, catching his bottom lip and sucking it sexily. I feel the stirring in his sweat pants harden and grin triumphantly.

"Want to get naked and finish what you started, Casanova?" I lay back watching with satisfaction as the heavy dark lust clouds his eye color.

"*Bambino*, I'm on a mission to make you come at least once before we head down for food." He grins, pulling away to peel his clothes off.

Chapter 26

Entering the dining room so late in the morning feels like a huge giveaway as to what we've been doing but I'm glad to see it's absolutely deserted. Jake's walking behind me with his hands on my shoulders and is much more relaxed, he's practically horizontal now, his mood is so mellow. I guess finally making me orgasm multiple times had him in a much better mood, all my inner thoughts and emotions no longer a hurdle when he'd started making love to me again. In fact, his confessions had only made me extra responsive to his touch and barely able to last minutes before the first waves had overtaken me.

He kisses me on the back of the head before letting go and taking my hand to lead me to a sunny breakfast room laid with bowls and cereal. Almost as soon as we sit a maid comes in bringing us hot plates of pancakes, eggs, sausages, and bacon and a fresh bowl of sliced fruit. He doesn't even acknowledge the girl, but I smile warmly at her with thanks.

"That's really rude you know?" I chastise him lightly, sitting opposite him and watching him lift his mug as he scans the newspaper and picks up his phone.

"What is?" He looks up from the phone in his hand with a quizzical expression.

"Not thanking people for bringing you food."

"It's her job, she does it several times a day … If I thanked her for every time she served us something she would think I fancied her." He grins at me cheekily but is met only with my unamused frown. I shouldn't be testy about a lifetime of being blind to the people who served him. He hadn't known any other life except the one with money and servants.

"She's still a person, Jake … An employee. No different to what I was to you." I point out, feeling a surge of irritation, that weird overreactive feeling again. I don't know if it's all that's going on lately that has me so touchy. My emotions and moods had been touchy to say the least.

"You know as well as I do no one could ever compare to what you were to me … Are to me." His intense look floors me, yet this time when the girl brings the pitcher of fresh orange juice, he thanks her with a winning smile, which makes me smile too. Satisfied I have that effect on him. The girl blushes and twirls off, almost skipping away.

"I bet I find her naked in my bed later." He points out sardonically but I glower at him and shake my head.

"Being a gentleman doesn't automatically encourage sexual advances." I scold but then bite my tongue when our server returns with the day's newest papers and lingers a little too long next to Jake with a very improper twinkle in her eye. I sigh and look away, resisting the urge to throw my plate at her head.

"Did you forget who you're in love with, baby?" he says in front of her, staring at me fully with a raised know-it-all eyebrow and ignoring her completely. His reputation even in this house preceding him. She moves away and then a thought occurs to me and I lean forward in irritation.

"You never? ... You know? ... With her? Or the staff?" I hear the jealousy in my voice and instantly hate myself.

God, will I always be this insecure?

Jake lifts a fork and digs into the fruit bowl, a smirk on his face. Dragging out the silence a moment before answering.

Asshole, he's enjoying this!

"No, *bambino*. Never touched any of my staff ... Never touched any employees until you." He throws me a wink then settles down to start stuffing his face heartily. That appetite as always is huge. If Jake didn't work out religiously then I was sure that huge muscular frame would carry a lot more weight.

"Beneath you, I assume?" I say haughtily, annoyed with the fact he's enjoying this. He laughs and despite myself I smile.

"No, my sweet little hell cat; not beneath me at all. I don't care what a girl does as a job or what she earns, I don't however like messy law suits over the misuse of my position or shocking headlines ... Anymore." He throws me a boss Carrero look and I feel myself relax a little with a smirk. I dig into my food, stopping to pour syrup on it first. Ravenous isn't close to how hungry I feel right now.

"I guess you better dig out my employment contract and make some amendments under the sexual harassment section." I smile, lifting an eyebrow in amusement.

"*Miele,* I literally burned that thing the second I knew I was going to chase you to the ends of the earth. Technically you haven't been an employee for a very long time." He winks, and I feel my face drop. I wasn't sure if he was being serious or not, his face giving nothing away at all.

"You're kidding, right?" I look at him warily. Surely Jake really wouldn't have done something so underhanded as to remove me as an employee of Carrero Corporation. He wasn't that kind of manipulative.

"Am I?" He smirks, between mouthfuls and carries on digging in, turning over the paper to the business section and dipping his head.

"Of course, you're kidding." I add shaking my head at my own stupidity. "I still got paid every month, I'm pretty sure legal wouldn't dish out cash to anyone not on the payroll."

"Oh, but for a second there, you doubted me." He grins without looking up. I pick up a grape and toss it at him, hitting him in his shoulder.

"With you, I can never tell!" I point out innocently.

"You think a contract would stop me from laying my hands on you?" He looks up, his eyes almost glittering and I feel myself blush. I shake my head knowing only too well it would have never stopped the tornado that was Jake Carrero. He smiles at me and tosses the grape, which had rolled to his lap, on to the table, leaning over to dump some fruit on my plate and steals a bit of my syrup-soaked pancake.

* * *

After breakfast, we wander the gardens in the sunshine, enjoying the quiet before the rush of people getting up. It seems most of the Carrero family ate in bed on weekends and stayed out of sight until afternoon. All of them worked and had demanding careers so they used this time when they were all together to be lazy and relax. This big house and its grounds was all but deserted, only the meandering staff running around doing whatever they were paid to do.

Jefferson arrives a little after twelve with a black folder for Jake and several brown envelopes, taking his leave immediately to go be wherever he went when Jake did not require him. I guessed it was to go back to New York.

Pulling me with him to the kitchen through the wide patio doors Jake sets about opening the mail and smiling at me as he fumbles through papers.

"Here." He holds out a gold card to me without looking up, automatically I take it and notice my name on the front. It's a credit card.

"What's this for?" I look at him in confusion.

"For abusing, *miele.*" He pulls out some papers and flips them over, practically ignoring me.

"Why do I need this?" I put it down on the counter and slide it back to him, but he only stops my hand mid-push and slides it back toward me with a frown.

"Because you're my girlfriend and I pay for the standard of living I'm trying to get you used too." His tone is edgy, we glare at one another for a moment and I feel myself bristle internally.

This was not part of the deal, Carrero!

"I'm fine with how things are, I don't need you giving me this on top of everything you already pay for and buy me." I retort, but this time I catch his full undivided angry glare.

"Well you're going to be pissed with this then." He flops down the paperwork in front of me, almost in a challenging way. I take it, eyeing him warily and notice it's a contract. My contract. My new position in his corporation with a wage rise of almost ten times what I had been paid previously. I almost choke on it.

As a PA I had always earned top dollar, but this sum tops some of the company executives' salaries. I snap up to him in complete confusion.

"I don't need this." I gasp but he only shrugs. So many conflicting emotions hitting me at once.

"Regardless to whether you do or don't, I told you we had reshuffled our job roles. This is just an informality required by legal." He leans down kissing me on the temple before moving off with the rest of his papers to the table and sitting down. Picking up both the credit card and the contract, I walk over and toss them down in front of him, folding my arms stubbornly.

You will not buy me or control me this way!

"I do not require any more money or a new title. This says I'm your VP … Your second in command?"

"Well, you're already that. Time you got paid for it, and some recognition." He's already flicking through papers and trying to dismiss me.

I don't think so!

"Jake, first, you don't even let me go to work anymore so I shouldn't be getting paid anything at all!" I snap haughtily. "And second, everyone in the building will think you did this because you're screwing me." I balk, emotion rising inside of me at an alarming speed.

"Don't turn this into a fight." He sighs with a wave of his hand, commandeering Carrero returning in full.

"Don't make our relationship about money," I snap again, tears brimming to the surface with this damn crazy sensitivity I have lately.

What the hell is with that?

"You're the only one doing that," he snaps back, equally riled and slides his chair back in agitation. "Emma, get used to being rich, because I'll marry you and like it or not, I've no plans to go bankrupt in my lifetime. My money will be your money too and trust me, there is a lot more than either of us can spend in a lifetime." He gets up, pushing past me and stalking to the fridge, retrieving a water bottle and taking a drink before he turns back to me a little more calmly. I'm still glaring at him with my arms crossed across my chest defiantly.

"Look, I get it … I'm not stupid. I know you. It's hard for you to ever just accept anything from anyone that you don't think you've earned your crazy independence in case everything goes to shit. This … Us … It's not going to end, Emma, and you do deserve everything I have to give. I just happen to have shit loads of money and I want you to not need to ask me to splurge on yourself. This way, you can have your own money and do what you want with it, the credit card is for when you get used to abusing my finances and let me pay for things instead." He sighs watching me, my face still bathed in irritation. Walking back to me he lets his hand wander up my arm to my jawline. I nudge my face away. I don't know how to feel about this right now. That inner war waging. Independent and fearless Emma showing her face.

"Baby, please … I know you're not with me because of this … You don't have anything to prove, it's okay to enjoy having a filthy rich boyfriend. There's no shame in it." He kisses me gently and relaxes as I start to respond to it, always incapable with maintaining a mood when he touches me. His mouth opens mine and is soon engulfing me in a hot, searing kiss.

"I don't want this," I finally say, calmer and push the contract back at him. "I don't need it." It was true. Jake already paid for everything, leaving most of my wages every month untouched. Only the regular bills toward the apartment with Sarah came out. Jake was generous to a fault with having Donna bring me clothes and lingerie often, he fed me almost ritually, and I never wanted for anything. I never had to spend anything. I didn't need a bank account filling up with money I wouldn't even use, money I wasn't even earning anymore. I wasn't one to go shopping often or splurge on things for fun.

Since Jake had decided that work was out of the question, I didn't do anything to deserve any money at all. I was only accepting my monthly wage on the understanding we would eventually go back, and I would eventually do something to be paid for, so that I could pay Sarah for my room.

"If you don't sign it I'll stop sleeping with you until you do." He smiles wickedly but I see that stubborn look in his eye. He means it.

"You would cave before I did," I retort, turning my back to him in defiance, folding my arms across my chest again. Not too enamored with threats right now. His hand comes down my summer dress, across the curve of my ass gently and ignites a million sensations so effortlessly.

"Baby, you held me at arm's length for almost a year … I'm sure I can handle it." I hear the amusement in his voice, he really believes he has me over a barrel and it only spurs the determination in me. A battle of wills.

"Fine … You want to play games over this then we're on. No sex until I sign? Get used to a very platonic relationship, *baby*." I grin smartly using his own term of endearment, wiggling my ass into his crotch before sauntering off and leaving him standing alone with his contract and credit card on the table. An inner goddess lifting her sassy head and deciding to beat him down with his own methods. He follows close behind, catching me by the arm and pulling me back, a smug look on his face.

"Game on, sweetheart … No rules. First one to cave loses. Either you sign the contract, or I can't take it anymore and fuck you. I've no doubt that you'll sign it before we head home, *bambino*." His voice thick and laden with intent, I can see the glint of excitement in his eye at the chance for a new game. That cocky confidence that he will win only ignites something inside of me.

Well really?

"No rules? At all?" I flutter my lashes innocently before letting my hand run up his sweat pant leg, pushing into his waist band and seeking out his manhood, rubbing him under his boxers until I feel a response. He catches my wrist and yanks it away, nose to nose.

"You forget whose better at the art of seduction, Emma … You're the one who likes instant gratification and can never wait … I, on the other hand, like to drag things out, remember?" His mouth lingers close enough to mine, I think he's going to kiss me, our breaths getting heavier as lust builds in both of us. The excitement of this little game sparking something naughty and pushing all anger out of the window.

He moves forward so he breathes against my lips, his hand comes up my inner thigh slowly and deliciously under my short dress, creeping closer to my now wet underwear until he sees my lips part and my eyes get heavy with longing. His mouth teasingly near, the urge to reach up and suck one of his perfect smooth, soft lips. He smiles and pushes off me, turning and walking away. I'm left reeling, my body tingling and my inner core throbbing with heat. That backward smug look of his as he saunters away only ignites the self-doubt.

Why did I start this? I knew better than anyone that he has more sexpertize than most.

I tremble at the thought of what he's capable of, but I push aside the shrill of excitement I feel. The lure of being chased and turned on by Jake in an effort to have me begging him for sex. The thought of him pulling out all stops to make me yield, is strangely appealing.

We'll see. I know one thing for sure. When he said, no rules, he didn't take into consideration that by turning me on he would have to fight himself not to lose control … I, on the other hand, could seduce to my heart's content and that made the odds tip in my favor. I could make Jake insane with longing, push him to take me forcefully.

I feel the shiver of excitement course through me; I could pull out all the stops to seduce him, but he had to keep it at a level that left him able to stop. I knew how to push his buttons, it was almost a certainty that I would win if it came down to that. I couldn't deny that inner excitement at seeing my aggressive lover again. That part of me that needed primal sex and his lack of control.

I walk out into the hall to go in search of him and find him embroiled in a friendly group of people in casual clothes as they all appeared from various directions, talking animatedly. He pulls me close to introduce me to his brother again and his current girlfriend, his cousins with women in tow, and a few other family and friends his mother has invited.

Arrick and Jake head off into a quiet corner together laughing and joking, I know he's trying to put distance between us in the name of his game and I'm left in a throng of loud, energetic people all vying to get each other's attention, in the maternal hold of Sylvana's arm. The overall atmosphere is loud and bustling, but you can feel the genuine warmth and energy. These people actually like one another.

Before long, Sylvana moves us all out to the pool side loungers where everyone seems to spread out and form little huddles. Arrick's young girlfriend seems painfully shy and sticks close to me, feeling somehow as left out as I do with both our men seemingly ignoring us. Jake has barely looked my way and is doing a magnificent job of making me feel invisible.

Just great!

I like Arrick's girlfriend, I guess, she's sweet and shy and despite being maybe five years younger than me it's striking how similar we look. Both with tawny hair, highlighted to blonde in waves, both small and busty with soft gray blue eyes. I guess the Carrero brothers have a type. The only obvious difference I can see is she seems incredibly shy and mousy whereas I'm more of a silent, outwardly confident type by manufacture. She shadows me to the loungers and seems relieved to get a seat right beside me on the double bed.

Jake and Arrick strip off across the other side of the pool, so different in build. Arrick is athletic and young with a lot of lean muscle to his frame whereas Jake is all hard ridges, muscle, and manliness. There is a lot more of him next to his smaller sibling. He throws me a look and a smile that screams "game on" and then dives expertly into the water, closely followed by his equally stunning younger brother.

"Wow, Jake has a lot of tattoos." Cara exclaims, watching the men in wonder. I look over at her and feel that familiar hint of jealousy starting to rise from my stomach. Her eyes are wide with appreciation and her mouth parted, I can see she's starting to pant.

For god's sake.

"Yeah, I guess … He got them all in his later teens I think." We had never really talked about the tribal ink across his upper torso and scattered down his arms. I knew he also had one on his upper back spreading across his shoulder blades, all black and no color.

"It's kind of hot, I wonder if Arrick would get some?" she says dreamily watching the two swimming easily across the pool before splashing water at each other. I can hear Jake's laugh echo my way and it makes my insides clench.

Is it now? Want to put your eyes back in your head sweetie?

"I'm sure his parents wouldn't be impressed," I respond flatly. "I know they both hate Jake's." Which wasn't entirely dishonest. I knew they had both given him a lot of grief about them at first, but no one seemed to notice the additions in later years. Jake had mentioned wanting a new tattoo briefly.

"What's to hate? I mean on that body they only accentuate things." She grins, then immediately drops it when she catches my look, inner green-eyed me scowling unnecessarily. I know it's normal to check out Jake, everyone does it, but I don't need someone sitting beside me verbalizing it. Especially not someone so young and beautiful with an obvious resemblance to me. A younger less fucked-up model.

That's called severe insecurity, Emma!

"Sorry, I didn't mean to upset you." She adds hastily. "How long have you been dating?" She asks quietly, obviously trying to make amends for the eye ogling, her eyes still on the water and the now swimming men.

"A while," I answer, contemplating poking her in the eyeballs. In truth not long at all but as Jake always tells me this relationship started long before it did and I'm happy to let her believe it.

Marking your territory?

"Wow, so like as in real dating, not just sex?" She looks impressed. Her eyes once again flicking to him as he pulls out of the water at the far side. A vision of slick muscle and gorgeousness.

Maybe you need a poke in the brain, followed by a sharp poke in the throat!

"If you're asking if we're serious then yes, I live with him. He loves me." I point out flatly and turn to the magazines on the low table, picking the first on the pile. Trying to act indifferent to her and succeeding. Something I was always good at.

"How did you manage that? I heard Jake was a hopeless womanizer, more chance of getting blood from a stone." She looks me up and down and I can tell she's comparing us as she pushes her bust out and rearranges her legs on the lounger.

I swear, honey, you're going to meet the water in a second and I'm sure swimming will be hard with my foot on your head.

"I didn't do anything, Jake is the one who pursued me … Relentlessly." I smile to myself, even though our relationship is far more complex, it sounds good to summarize it that way. I glance over at him and see his smile turned our way, that same inner heat hitting me with the contact and distracting my crazy jealousy for a second. I still my response and just raise an eyebrow at him instead.

He's the one keeping his distance, he doesn't get a smile for it.

"I guess you either had a chastity belt to stave that off or were an absolute tiger in bed to keep him interested." She smiles, her eyes focused on Jake as he pulls himself out of the pool, his shorts now clinging to his butt and thighs and showing off every muscle perfectly, not to mention how much he was packing below the waist. Her head follows his saunter across the side, eyes widening at his obvious bulge and the way his muscles flex and tense as he moves and lifts a towel from a nearby lounger.

I hate you.

The girl has irritated me enough, I ignore her and turn to my side, away from her, to get a grip of the irrational thoughts and violent intentions. Opening the magazine to make it clear I'm done.

I feel her shift on the lounger and her foot touches me as

she maneuvers herself into a new position. Glancing back in anger I see she's posing like a wanton tramp, thrusting her bust forward and exposing her leg through her open wrap as Jake approaches.

I guess I was wrong about this one, not so sweet and nice after all. Definitely ripe for a brutal beating.

I jump up and walk away from the lounger. Jake doesn't stop, he just walks on to where I've moved off and sits beside her instead, making me stop dead in my tracks.

What the F …? Jake always soothes my jealousy!

She positively beams at him despite him shedding water all over her. Giving him a haughty glare, I go back and sit on the lounger next to them, I'm not leaving with him acting like an asshole. I sit a foot apart and pick up my magazine again, ignoring his grin and jutting my chin out in anger. I can feel that wicked gaze flicking my way and see the way he's sprawled out casually beside her, all tanned, carved torso and long legs.

Asshole.

"So, Cara … Arrick tells me you're a freshman in college?" His smooth Casanova Carrero voice eases over her and I literally want to throat punch him. He's in flirt mode, I can just tell by his entire manner. I suppress the urge to openly glare at him, pushing the magazine open to another page aggressively.

"Umm, yes, Jake." She rolls his name on her tongue as seductively as she can. I look up seeing Arrick shaking his head in amusement and it only angers me more.

Isn't this his girlfriend? This girl, practically spreading her legs for my boyfriend to bang her?

Feeling my rage ignite I get up and storm off toward the house, I need to get out of this sundress and into something that Jake will take notice of. I reel as I notice he doesn't follow me. Hurt and anger battling one another, I catch that smug look in his eye as I glance back. All part of his little game, he thinks he can make my jealousy work against me, so I'll cave and beg him to come make love to me.

I think not.

I lift my chin defiantly.

* * *

In the room, I pull out all of my clothes and feel rage when I can't locate a bikini at all. I hadn't packed for a weekend in the Hamptons and have nothing that will turn his head at neck breaking speed. Looking through, the only thing I can find is my running clothes and I chuck them down in dismay. I get up and stomp out of the room, feeling more than a little annoyed and run into the girlfriend one of the cousins. Alessandra. She's a swimwear model with a body to die for and a heavy Italian accent.

"Ahh, hello, Emma? Right?" She smiles warmly, a towel draped over her arm and a sun lotion bottle in her hand. She's heading back down and looking devastatingly sexy in her own black molded two piece.

"Yes … Hi … You wouldn't have a spare bikini, would you? I didn't pack for this." I laugh shyly and see the sparkle in her eye.

"Of course, I always pack many. Come with me, I have something so perfect for you." She smiles and turns, leading me back to her room with a sexy cat walk thrust. I can't help but be awed by this sexual being swaying in front of me. She has the body of a woman who works out religiously and eats only organic bagged fresh air.

* * *

"You don't think it looks skimpy and kind of slutty?" I look at myself in the mirror in the smallest red two piece I've ever seen and feel completely self-conscious. I'm not against a bikini, Jake's seen me in them plenty of times, but this is borderline indecent. Somehow, while still covering all the necessary areas it has managed to lift up and push my cleavage into something most impressive, my stomach and hips look longer and leaner when edged with the low-cut briefs which seem to sculpt my lower half too. She has put me in high heeled red sandals to complete the look and my legs look endless.

"Trust me, it suits you very much." She gushes, coming behind me and tucking my hair back from my face before applying a little bronzer to my cheeks and between my breasts. "You have gorgeous body … You work out? I think you should keep it, suits you much more." Her heavily accented English is almost sensual, and I'm swayed by her purring praise.

"Sort of … And thank you." I blush; lately all my work outs have been at Jake's hands but before that I did used to run and keep fit so I'm toned and bikini ready. I just feel majorly underdressed.

"You look perfect, keep Jake on his toes, huh, with all those man eyes on that derrière." She tweaks my breast unabashedly before turning and walking out with a confident air, my face flaming from her lack of inhibition and I follow reluctantly.

I had stupidly confessed to her that Jake and I were having a little bet. She'd grinned with the wise words, "All is fair in love and war," before digging out this red number for me to wear. She had that same wicked glint in her eye I had seen on Jake many a time and was hard to not think of this one as his cousin rather than her boyfriend.

Getting back to the pool with a towel over my arm, I lift my chin defiantly, I can work this and make it look like I would wear something this revealing every day. I see Jake engrossed in conversation with two men, Cara has been moved to a chair with Arrick nearby and all eyes turn as we approach. One of the men nudges him in the shoulder and nods toward me, Jake's face literally drops when he sees me, and he clamps his mouth shut with a frown. I walk past him with a smile and follow Alessandra to the loungers across from the pool. Smiling only briefly at him in passing, as if he were no more than an acquaintance.

Eat that, Jake.

Getting comfortable slowly and surely, aware his attention is on me from afar, the girl asks me to rub lotion on her back with a wicked smile. I can feel his eyes boring into me without looking, every one of my senses on high alert and goose bumps littering my skin.

"You want men to be hot for you, baby girl?" She whispers seductively. "Then take my lead, rub me good, yeah." She hands me sun tan oil and rolls onto her stomach untying her bikini at the back and encouraging me gently. Feeling brave, I stand up and slide beside her onto the lounger so I'm leaning over her and slowly and deliberately start to take small amounts of oil and cover her naked skin. Far enough to not be heard by the men, she gives me direction, enjoying this little chance to tease our menfolk. I know one of the boys sitting with Jake is his cousin, her current beau and judging by the glances from them our little ploy has not gone unnoticed. They can barely keep the conversation flowing or control the looking over.

"Men are easy, Emma," she says huskily, watching me from her tilted head on the cushion. "They think everything is sex, sex, sex ... As a woman, you can make them think it is." She giggles huskily, a strangely seductive sound and encourages me to massage the oil lower.

"I think Jake's on the verge of taking a cold shower." I giggle as I see him shift position more than once in his seat. He's laid a magazine on his lap and seems to be struggling with his facial expressions. I can't decide if he wants to punch someone or come over and strip me.

"Want to really make him squirm?" She sits up, pulling her bikini back and quickly tying it before turning onto her back and sitting up. "Your turn, *bambino* … See men they like to see their women being touched. Gino's fantasy is to see me fuck a girl … I'm not into girls but teasing him is fun." She gets up, pushing me down on the lounger onto my back and immediately comes to straddle me, her small pelvis resting over mine in a completely awkward manner. I feel myself take a quick breath and hold it. Sexual display makes me feel unbelievably uncomfortable even when it's from a woman. Well, unless it's Jake, he seems to have cured me of any inhibitions when it comes to him.

She drizzles oil on her hands and begins working it onto my skin across the exposed part of my stomach and up onto my exposed cleavage, grinning at me because she's facing away from them enough not to be seen. From their angle, they can see her hands working me over, her face concealed by her hair.

"What they doing now?" She smiles innocently.

"Breaking necks to see what you're doing." I giggle and see Jake almost topple off his lounger at the angle he's leaned over. He rights himself, moving to stand and pulls shades over his eyes in an effort to coolly cover it. I can tell by the way he starts adjusting his shorts that he's having a hard time.

Literally.

"Turn over, *bambino.*" She whispers and moves up, so I can flip. I gasp as she smacks me lightly on the ass before tending to my back in the same way I had to hers. I feel the bikini loosen as she unties it. I close my eyes, trying to relax and enjoy the feeling of her gentle hands and then freeze as her body comes down on top of mine, her feet pushing my legs apart to nestle against my butt and starts nuzzling my neck softly. Her breath on my skin. I stiffen at the contact and immediately pull out from under her, pulling my bikini with me to stay concealed. It's beyond uncomfortable and I'm barely keeping the panic under control.

"Aww, *bambino* … too much? You will be thanking me in a second." I don't get a chance to respond as Jake is over me in an instant, pulling my hand and barely giving me a chance to tie my bikini. His focus is dark and piercing, his manner agitated, and he seems to be oozing sexual tension. I feel my heart rate skip up a gear.

He's so easy!

"Wow, wait!" I yelp, aware I'm losing my scrap of fabric, he stops, turning to see me clutching it across my breasts and turns me to tie it.

"I need you to come with me, we need to be alone … Right now!" He rasps in my ear huskily and yanks me with him away from the poolside gathering, eyes lifting in curiosity as he practically hauls me at speed. I'm not sure if he's angry or craving sex but either way his body is radiating enough hot energy to power a planet. I feel a ripple of apprehension and try to gauge if this is sex mad Jake or green-eyed jealous Jake.

Surely not jealous over a woman?

We barely get out of sight behind a building close to the house when he yanks me around, pushes me against the wall and crushes a kiss on me so hard it catches my breath. His mouth devours mine in a frenzy of passion and need and I surrender weakly. His hands yank my bikini down under my breasts to ravage me, lifting me up so I'm around his waist and pushing me so hard into the wall behind I'm practically compressed. His obvious desire is bursting from his damp swim shorts, his hands claiming me carelessly as though he's lost all sense of gentleness.

This is who I wanted.

He grinds into me, kissing every ounce of rejection and defense away before moving to my breast and sucking my nipples to attention. I feel a sense of triumph, celebration at how easy this win was. Mentally thanking Alessandra and trying my hardest not to moan out loud. The growing heat inside of me is throbbing manically for release as his hands bite into my skin under my butt, his fingers of one hand slide further under the edge of my bikini pants and slides into me. Finding me more than ready he groans into my mouth.

He drops me to my feet, pulling his hands away and turns me against the buildings smooth cream walls roughly, forcing me to brace my hands against it. He has one hand on my breast, his mouth against my neck, his other hand finds its path back inside of me under my pants and starts pushing in and out from the back. I'm moaning and grinding into his palm, eyes screwed shut so I can get lost in the sensations. I can't control the build of waves that he always effortlessly begins in me, he's hard against me yet doesn't escalate to sex, just fingers and mouth on my skin bringing me closer.

"Is that good, baby?" He growls into my ear, breathless and hot. His voice doing as much to me as his hands and I tremble under his power.

"Uh, mmmmm huh." I moan, equally breathless as he slowly tortures me with his fingers, his other hand skillfully teasing my nipple. I'm so wet I can feel it throbbing and sliding effortlessly. My hands braced on the building which is scratching slightly under my smooth palms, unable to do anything except surrender to him with legs wide apart. His hard body molded to mine while those wicked hands pleasure me deeply.

"You want to come like this?" He pushes against me again, showing me how turned on he is. His strong naked torso against my own naked skin, that in itself causing a wave of sensation. I'm so lost to him it's pathetic.

"Mmmm, hmmmmm." Is the only answer I can give, unable to talk as I move back against him, the building pleasure soaring through me, making my body tingle and nipples ache. He continues to probe and slide into me, feeling me start to tighten around him, his mouth tracing my neck and shoulders slowly and seductively. I moan and writhe as I start to climb, the orgasm merely seconds away and my legs trembling with the threat of giving out completely. I breathe harder, my moaning pitching as it comes closer and closer to the almost brink, the internal building and tingles coursing through me, legs turning to jelly and insides tingling in anticipation, my whole body heating and vibrating.

"Pity we made that little deal then huh?" His voice changes like night from day and his hand pulls out of me fast, letting me go to sag against the building in outrage. All sensations cutting off like being dunked in ice water in a flash. It takes a moment to recover from the ecstasy of what he was doing, and I turn on him and am faced with a smugness and complete control on his face. He looks like the cat who got the cream. I stare in open-mouthed disbelief.

"Denying a woman an orgasm when she's as close to it as you, baby, is almost torture." He grins, leaning out to yank up my bikini to cover my breasts and turns to walk away while adjusting himself in his shorts. "I recommend a change of outfit, Emma, you're not really concealing how much you want to be fucked right now." With a wink he adjusts this manhood once more and walks off toward the house without a backward glance.

I erupt into a violent spew of curse words and anger, if I had something to throw at him then I would have. Unable to control the internal wave of anger and sexual frustration and just letting rip with no cares as to who can hear me.

He's right in a way he didn't even mean. Stopping when I was so close to the brink makes me crazy mad and I storm after him yanking his arm, so he faces me.

"What the fuck?" I yell at him, concealed by palm trees from the pool so no one can see us. I don't even care if they can hear us right now, I'm that pissed off.

"You agreed to this game, Emma … Think you can play out some little lesbian fantasy scene with Alessandra and I'll what? Come begging to have sex? I told you, baby … We're not matched in this, I've been around a lot more than you have. I was just reminding you of that little fact."

He leans down, kissing me chastely on the corner of my mouth and moves off again. Smugness personified over that face of his. I literally have no words at all. No retorts or violent outbursts, just complete speechlessness and the urge to hit him over the head.

I march into the house and throw him a glare as he nestles himself down at the breakfast bar, ignoring the overly pleased grin across his face. I walk past to the stair and run for our room in complete rage. So many emotions racing through my head I think I may self-combust in a grand fashion.

* * *

Even the icy blast from the shower doesn't help alleviate the burning ache inside of me, he's never left me mid-orgasm before and its agony. Every part of me crying for release and I even consider finishing the job myself. I don't though.

Maybe that's what he wants … I can't forget how manipulative he can be when he sets his mind on something and I won't give him the satisfaction.

I shower quickly and then storm into the room to start getting dressed for him.

He wants seduction? Then he'll get seduction.

I packed enough lingerie for this trip to see me through a week, he likes to rip enough of it off me and I've a new lacy, see-through set that I had meant for bed that he hasn't seen yet. A tight see-through underdress and black lace I had ordered online as a surprise to rile my sexy man up in all his aggressive fury.

We shall see, Carrero!

Chapter 27

I finally look at myself in the mirror; smoky eyed make-up and full red lips. Killer contouring on my perfectly made up face. My see-through under dress over black lace lingerie which has pushed and perked everything up. High cut lines and seductive contouring making my body look awesome. I topped it all off with lace edge top black stockings, suspenders, and a look on my face of pure lust.

I slide my feet into the black stilettos I take everywhere, like a security blanket; and spritz perfume on across my bulging cleavage. This underwear does me wonders so I spill seductively, straining cleavage above the low cut of the dress and I bronze between them to enhance them some more.

Can always use a little extra help.

The panties are a thong that shows clearly under the shimmering dress, everything made for seduction and I'm mighty pleased with myself.

Look at you go, girl.

I pick up my phone with a smile. I've been up here for about an hour and a half now, there isn't much time before dinner tonight. Most of the company get changed into formal attire to eat, according to Sylvana. So, if I ask him to come zip me up then he will just assume I'm dressing for dinner. I text him and wait, standing in the center of the room, my blonde hair extra wild and falling over one eye.

I need your assistance in zipping up my dress for dinner, and your opinion as to whether I'm underdressed. xxx

My dress for dinner is laid across the bed and if I fail at my *before dinner seduction* then it will easily pull over what I'm wearing, leaving him a clear image throughout the meal. The dress for dinner is one of his favorites, classy, black, and tight. I'm betting on succeeding and skipping dinner altogether though.

He walks in after a few minutes, adjusting a cufflink and pauses, faced with me standing sexily, legs apart and hands on hips, jutting out my bust toward him with a look of "fuck me" on my face. He looks me up and down, slowly and physically changes, immediate apprehension as I see the confidence waver in his eye. I've at least thrown him, so I give myself brownie points for that. He moves past me, his eyes unable to tear free, saying nothing but goes and picks my dress off the bed and holds it out to me at a distance. His face is such a picture of confusion it makes me smile.

"Maybe I need help putting it on." I bite my lip seductively and see his mouth part in response, he sighs heavily. Those green eyes are dark and heavy, he can't conceal his longing from me.

Casanova Carrero where have you gone?

He looks almost nervous, like a tongue-tied teen. I'm waiting on him starting to fumble with the dress, he looks ready to. He's never met overly sexual and forward Emma. I'm kind of liking her.

Was it really only five minutes ago that all sex abhorred me, and I kept everyone at a firm distance? Look at me now.

"Sure." He swallows hard and opens up the dress to find the shoulders, he holds it up, looking how to drape it on me. He's already changed into a dark shirt and pants, looking devastating as always with freshly styled hair and I wonder when he came in here to get a change of clothes. Possibly when I was showering.

He walks forward, lowering the dress so he can hold it open for me to step into, his eyes skimming me achingly as he pulls it up my body and over the tight mesh dress, keeping his hands away from touching me.

He doesn't trust himself to touch me. Strike two.

It's only being this close that I can hear his breathing is a lot shallower than normal, his eyes fully dilated and almost ripping my clothes off with desire. I give myself a little internal applause. Leaning forward smoothly as he gets to face height, I open my lips mere millimeters from him, seeing him stop. He doesn't move just waits, anticipating my kiss. Eyes heavily focused on my mouth, every muscle in his face pausing and waiting and that overwhelming lust radiating from his expression. I tilt my head, breathe on his soft mouth gently and linger achingly close, inhaling him and heating up with his closeness. It makes me ache so badly and my fingers are almost itching to touch him. I swear he holds his breath for a moment, his head moving forward a touch as his desire to kiss me grows. I pull away with a smile.

"Don't want to ruin my lipstick." I feign innocence, basking in the furrow of his brow as he pulls the dress the rest of the way up with attitude. His eyes narrow and he spins me, zipping me up a little forcefully and smacking me hard on my ass.

"Ouch." I yelp and move away from him quickly. The storm starts brewing in the delicious face and I can see his body stiffening, muscles tensing.

"Dinner is going to be interesting." He growls huskily, and I can tell I have more than thrown him, he's possibly about to self-implode. "Sure, you don't just want to sign the contract, and admit defeat, *bambino*?" He moves close to me this time, his mouth even closer than I had dared. I shake my head as I watch his eyes locking with mine, his hand trails up my leg lazily, skimming the tight dress until he grazes my breast and ignites the usual sizzling response in me. His hand, feather light, makes its way to my jaw until I'm almost breathless with its journey. He pulls me forward for the softest kiss of my life, his lips barely brushing mine, moving into me further, teasing and grazing. His hand grazes along my jaw softly as his other comes to cup the other side. Soft and sensual kissing that's so in contrast to every signal he's sending off right now.

Moving deeper into my mouth, he teases my lips open with the sheer strength of seduction, he kisses me gently, easing in slowly to a more passionate motion. His tongue slipping across my bottom lip and tentatively touching mine. As kisses went, he'd never hit me with the expertise of this make out session. This was a different kind of assault, a new tactic with sheer softness. Within minutes he has me fully wrapped around him, dragging his arms to me to try and push the kiss further, completely panting at how much he'd turned me on in a matter of seconds. Still locked together, tongues still caressing, and lips molded together, I was so close to surrender. If he had a pen I would have signed the contract while still being kissed this way. Jake knew exactly how to weaken me, he didn't even need words or his body, he could always do it with a kiss.

Realizing that was exactly his plan, I pull away sharply, heaving in air and trying to steady myself against him. He sucks in his bottom lip seductively, eyeing me with satisfaction, tasting me and smiles upon releasing it.

"Your lipstick tasted good … Pity it now looks pretty fucked-up." He lets go of me the way you would drop a piece of trash and smirks before walking off toward the door. That look of strike two on his face and I internally rage. Turning to the mirror I see the mess of my mouth and grit my teeth. This was because I'd refused to kiss him on grounds of the lipstick and now it was so smeared and smudged I had no alternative but to wipe it off and start again, or just go without. He had made a mess of all of my make-up around my mouth. I see him grab for tissues as he leaves, wiping off the berry shade evidence of his assault, with a whistle and a slight bounce to his walk. I just played right into his hands for the second time.

Asshole! He's just too damned good at this!

I feel that inner strength kick in, he had me so close to giving in and he didn't even know it. Well, that was my one weak moment and from now on, I was going to strengthen my resolve. If he was playing dirty, then I had every intention to play dirty too. Fight fire with fire.

* * *

Emerging twenty minutes later, the stains replaced with a sheer gloss instead, I make my way to the huge, opulent dining room and slide in beside him at the table amid the arrival of some of the others. He's using his phone and completely ignores me. I bristle, knowing this isn't a normal Jake move but I'm not going to let it get to me, I'm going to act like I don't care at all and just sit down. I stop myself from looking at him, even though it's almost impulsive to eye up how gorgeous he always looks.

As soon as everyone is seated, he puts his phone away,

leans back on his chair and places an arm across the back of mine while throwing me a triumphant look. I note that his father watches us from a distance at the head of the huge dark wood table and feel myself still. I had managed to avoid him until now, but dinner would be interesting. I got the distinct impression Giovanni was not all that enamored with his son hooking up with an employee from his own office. Especially a nobody with no fortune and a troubled past.

"You can still back out now, *bambino,* and we can just enjoy dinner and a lot of fun after." Jake says quietly, commanding my attention, his eyes steady on my face. He drops his gaze to my mouth and smirks some more at the lack of red lipstick. It only ignites that inner stubbornness.

"Why would I? You're obviously struggling, Jake, I'm sure if it's too hard you can just admit defeat." I smile salaciously and turn my attention to my champagne glass, running my finger around the rim teasingly. He watches me with interest for a moment then gets up with a smile.

"I told Cara I would sit beside her tonight." He smirks cruelly at me then saunters off to the seat beside the girl, receiving an award-winning smile from her. I feel myself inwardly curl up and tremble. Nausea and anxiety equally consuming my stomach and a tight gut-wrenching throb. Jealousy punching its way into my gut.

What was he doing? Surely Jake would not do this to me for the sake of a stupid challenge?

Arrick appears in the doorway and immediately sits next to me, greeting me with a warm hello and no sense of surprise at all. I try to smile but it doesn't come naturally.

"Don't worry about Cara." He leans into me conspiringly. "She wouldn't know what to do with someone like Jake and he only has eyes for you, *mia cara.*" He nudges me with his shoulder and this time I smile genuinely, at his niceness and at the family trait of mixing English and Italian. Something they all seem to do.

"You're not worried if your girlfriend tries to run off with your brother?" I pout keeping my eyes away from Jake who's engrossed in his deep conversation with a devoted fan. Cara is almost salivating over him.

Slut!

"Nah, Jake would never do that to me or you, besides Cara isn't my girlfriend, she's just a passing interest." He studies my shocked face. "I'm more like my brother than you realize and, yes, he told me you two have some sort of bet going … Abstaining from sex until one of you breaks." He winks and picks up his glass. "I suggest you play him at his own game, Jake hates to lose but he does love the thrill of the challenge."

"What do you mean?" I look over, seeing Jake effortlessly sprawled in his seat commanding not only Cara's attention but the quiet brunette that came with his other cousin too, both fluttering lashes and smiling at him coquettishly. He's in full flirt mode, demanding adoration effortlessly.

For god's sakes!

"You've a table of virile young men to charm, and a face pretty enough to do it." He pats my hand and sits back as his starter is laid before him. I lean back as my plate of asparagus spears, boiled egg, and hollandaise sauce piled delicately on top is placed before me by one of the uniformed maids. I smile warmly at her and get one in return, catching Jake from the corner of my eye and seeing him thanking the girl who gave him his food. Stupidly, I feel myself smile internally and push it back down.

"I'm not, Jake. Commanding the attention of men isn't my style." I turn back to my dinner mate. Arrick is unaware that despite how I am with Jake, most men still make me feel uncomfortable. Arrick seems to be an exception and sitting with him now, I couldn't feel more at ease. I guess it's because he is enough like Jake to feel relaxed around, something about him, much like his brother, made you feel safe.

"You know Jake better than most, Emma … You know how to push his buttons and throw him off his game. Use what you know. It's obvious that you have an influence over him that no one can even come close to." He smiles and tucks into his food while I sit and look at the plate, pondering his words. Arrick was a wise one, he had that quick Carrero mind and that flawless confidence. He was one to watch in coming years as he came into his own. Jake may have a competitor within the family business with this one.

It was true though, I knew Jake well enough to know a few things about him. One, that he can get insanely jealous and it's never a good route to take. I had already proven that more than once. Two, he's better than most people at games and seems to get a kick out of winning and can read people and situations with deathly speed. Three, when it comes to me he always takes care of me obsessively, that even when he's mad he still can't help but be protective. I glance at him for a second, catching his eye as he eats and look away. A small plan formulating in my head.

This had gone beyond a battle of sex, this had become a game of the upper hand, and if I had to play a low card like he'd done with his sexpertize already, then I would. My strong point wasn't sex, it was Jake's inability to see me hurt or cry. His never-ending need to fix things for me. It was Jake's love for me that was his ultimate weakness. I feel that internal smugness at figuring this out, I couldn't beat him at sex with my inexperience, but I could bend him with emotions. My emotions. Tucking into my food slowly I remain impassive and stare at my plate as I mull it over.

I know how to play this. PA Emma's cool emotionless outer shell always drove him crazy.

I stay quiet through dinner, never looking at him, even though I can hear him flirting and trying his hardest to affect me, but I don't react. I don't want him to see that it's bothering me a lot because it brings him amusement to see my fiery green-eyed reaction, but I want him to feel it, feeling my emotions hits him differently. It brings out that need to fix it. So, my plan to appear somber and un-chatty is put into place. Jake will agonize over what I'm thinking, I know him well enough to know that my obvious closed mood will worry him.

It comes easily the longer it carries on and I start to feel tearful at his over-interest in the women around him, it's not hard to picture him as Casanova Carrero when I can hear it. Jealousy growing inside of me. With upset comes the ability to remain cool and devoid of any outward emotion at all. At first, he tries to up his game when I seem quiet but as the dinner wades on, I can feel his change in mood. The listless way he fidgets with his glass and cutlery, the small glances at me. I see him tapping his fingers on the table and listen to the almost uninterested tone in his voice as his dinner mates lose all interest to him. He's pre-occupied. So in tune with me that my mood is seriously affecting him. I wonder if he's thinking of calling it quits and have to quell the surge of smugness from affecting my expression.

I occasionally converse with Arrick on my right and avoid all looks to my left, luckily the seat next to me is filled with a rather drunk elderly man who sits the entire night playing with his phone, a hand of black jack on some online gambling site. He's some uncle or relative that never seems to converse with anyone but is making a great barrier from

Giovanni. I have a feeling he may be Dimitrio, Jake's uncle, there is a slight resemblance to Giovanni. His body is blocking me from his view and letting me get through dinner without his interest swaying my way. Jake has spoken to him only in Italian and there seems to be a constant coolness between them. There are enough family between my seat and his, further up the table, that there is no need to converse with him at all. The whole table has been noisy through the meal, people throwing conversation at all angles and I only had to sit and listen so far.

I feel Jake look at me several times, but I resist all urges to even catch his eye. I can't tell if it's getting to him or not in the way I want it to, unable to read anything from the corner of my eye. As dessert is handed out, I become completely silent, gazing at his mother as she tells a story or listening quietly to those around me and never really engaging. I hope no one else is as attuned to me as him or else they all might think I'm the most ignorant dinner guest of all time. I hope they just assume I am reserved and listening.

I have to play this out if I've any chance of beating him.

Lifting my wine glass to wash down the cream cannelloni, I feel the smallest breeze behind me as someone passes and look up expecting to see the maid. The elderly gentlemen walks by, and leaves the room with a puce colored face and bored expression. Heat envelopes me as an arm comes around my shoulder unexpectedly and a firm hot mouth kisses me on the exposed skin.

"Hey, *bambino* … You okay?" I feel that inner triumph as Jake surrounds me with his heat and smell. Sitting in the recently evacuated seat next to me. I glance down, noting he's brought his glass of wine with him and push down the urge to beam in his presence, instead keeping my tone controlled and flat.

"I'm fine." Just enough of a sigh to portray that I'm not.

I should get an Oscar for this.

"You want to go for a walk or go upstairs?" He sounds concerned, a hesitation in his voice that maybe he's pushed things too far. My little boy Carrero in full flow, so unsure and sweet.

Don't melt at it, stay strong.

"No. I'm good, thanks." I keep my face turned from him and push the rest of my dessert around the plate absentmindedly. I know it looks to him as though I'm upset.

"You know I would never do anything, baby? I love you, I'd never hurt you like that." The tone in his voice betrays more than apprehension, he's trying to reassure me. He's back peddling this evening and I feel that inner smugness rising up. I keep my face blank and my exterior controlled.

"I know." I smile tightly and pull away from him to get up, announcing I need to go to the ladies' room and excuse myself quickly. Jake follows close behind me, catching me in the hall.

"Emma, wait." He catches my arm, pulling me to him and encircles me with his arms. "Baby, I'm sorry, I shouldn't have behaved like this and made you feel this way. Look, can we just forget all of this, *bambino?* You know me. I would never do anything to make you leave me. Come upstairs and we can just go to bed early. Veg out and watch one of those trashy movies you love so much." His narrowed brow and genuine concern makes me melt and even feel a tad guilty.

This is the guy I love to death, right here. This one with the beautiful green eyes and loving heart.

"You would do that for me?" I lower my lashes and look away as though I'm surprised he cares and he falls for it hook, line, and sinker.

"Baby, it was just a game, a stupid game. I don't need the

contract signed. I just need you." He kisses me and wipes away all my resolve. His arms sliding around me firmly and pressing every inch of me against him. My inner body almost self-combusting.

"Take me upstairs, Jake." I breathe into his mouth as his hands work down my body, he doesn't need to be told twice and grabs my hand, leading the way.

* * *

Minutes later he peels me out of my dress and under dress in the bedroom and pulls me down on top of him on the bed so I'm straddling him in my lingerie and stockings. He leans up against the headboard, my shoes discarded on the floor with his and I kiss him full on while unbuttoning his shirt. I can feel the heat rising inside of me, his knees bent behind me, so it keeps me against him. His hands skate over the soft skin at my ass as he pulls me closer into his groin with a moan. The heat of our mouths together ignites, and he flips over so he's on top of me, my legs coming around his waist and his hands running down the silkiness of my stockings hungrily, finding their way into the lace of my thong. His mouth covers my neck and the swell of my breasts trying to burst out of my bra. I'm panting and heaving as he devours me, grinding into me with his hardness and making me even more wanton than I had been down at the pool earlier. The unquenched orgasm still lingering inside of me ready to be reignited and almost begging for him. We moan in unison as we grind together, and his hands come up, lifting both of mine above my head in the way he seems to love holding me down. His fingers slide up my arms as his lips tease my cleavage mercilessly, fingers trailing all the way up to my wrists.

I hear a clink and a strange noise as cold metal encircles

my wrist causing a startled yelp. My head snaps up at the direction of the noise and Jake pulls away, sitting back on his haunches with a satisfied grin as I realize he's handcuffed me to the bed by one hand. I tug at it looking to him in confusion.

"I know when you're upset, Emma, and I know when you're trying to play me. Sweet dreams, baby … Only way I'm sleeping next to you tonight is if your powerless to touch me." He climbs off the bed and strolls to the bathroom, fully untucking his shirt and throwing it into a hamper by the door.

"What the hell, Jake?" I writhe and tug at the cold metal, trying to free my hand and glaring at him angrily as it clanks and digs into my skin. Inner rage igniting, torn between disbelief and sheer mortification that he would do this to me.

"Do you need a pen?" He asks mercilessly, turning away as I hurl abuse at him, rolling and trying to get free.

"No point in struggling, shorty, those ain't coming off unless you rip that headboard off too, and before you ask, I borrowed them from Alessandra. Seems she's no loyalty to which side wins." He walks into the bathroom and I hear him turn on the tap, brushing his teeth and leaving me leashed to this goddamn infernal bed.

I manage to maneuver myself to my knees and sit up, pulling with all my might but it's no good. The biting pain in my wrist makes me give in long before the bed does, and I slump. Sitting down dejectedly I feel the rage rising inside of me. He's always one step ahead. Always knows how to shut me down at every turn, even using Alessandra to borrow these cuffs as payback for my borrowing the bikini and her behavior. It's so typically him! Cold and calculated and bloody merciless. He has no qualms when it comes to winning, all that somber shit at dinner had been an act. Playing me for playing him.

For fuck's sake!

He finally walks out of the bathroom wearing sweat pants and smirks when he sees me.

"You can't sleep like that." He slides onto the bed and pulls over a book from the bedside table, settling down to read it and flicking the TV onto a chick flick for me, pushing cushions behind him and getting comfy.

"You're really going to leave me like this?" I blanche in disbelief, raising my hands in question and feeling the bite of the cuff again. The clunk of metal.

"If you lay down and go to sleep I'll maybe take it off when I'm sure you're out cold." He doesn't even look my way. Turns a page in his book and crosses his ankles. I feel like screaming at him or at least slapping that book out of his goddamn hand. I am beyond livid.

"Fine!" I snap, hauling back the comforter and maneuvering inside of it awkwardly, I slide off my stockings one at a time and throw both at his face angrily. He doesn't react, just lets them fall down his shoulder and leaves them propped there with a satisfied smile on his face. "Well, goodnight then." I snort and lay down so that my arm is held up above my head on the cushion, it's not wholly uncomfortable, it's just awkward. I huff and sigh and try to get comfy, but I can't. The anger simmering inside of me is too much.

"Goodnight sexy." He chuckles. Actually chuckles.

Fuck you!

"You're a jerk," I snap and turn away from him so I'm leaning on my arm as a pillow. Close to tears with sheer frustration.

"Sadly, I am." He jokes but doesn't move.

"All this over a stupid contract," I mumble to no one in particular, rage seeping from every pore.

"Nope, all this over you issuing a challenge, *miele*. I stopped being interested in the contract the second I stopped looking at it." I hear the arrogance in his voice and bristle.

"Well, I take it back." I smart and kick my feet back in an attempt to get him, being under the sheets and him on top means I achieve nothing except awkward wriggling. He doesn't even acknowledge it.

"Told you, sign it and we're done with this … That's the same as taking it back." He sounds highly amused and I just want to stab him with my stiletto.

"Go to hell, I'll never sign it, just to show you what an asshole you are." I pout, my voice high and childish.

"We'll see." He smacks my ass through the sheet and flicks off the bedroom lights, I hear his book being laid down as he moves in the bed to get comfy. I feel his breath on my back, meaning he's laid on his side, facing my back and I stiffen. The sound of some annoying love-based movie playing on the screen facing the bed.

"I guess you better get used to never having sex again." I retort angrily. "I think handcuffing your girlfriend to a bed just to break her will is unbelievably bad form." I hear him laugh quietly at my rage and it only fuels it further.

"Asshole!" I jerk my body further into a ball to tell him not to touch me.

"Emma, I happen to think you're even sexier when you're this seething mad, definitely more amusing, baby. I know for a fact that if our relationship has a sex ban placed on it you'd be the first one to cave. Women need that physical connection to feel secure more than men do … If it's a game of waiting, then I've more than enough patience." He reaches out, running a finger down my spine and makes my body shiver in response. "Besides, if I really wanted it I could make you break so easily, I've gone easy on you so far, baby … I'm enjoying this way too much." That voice laced with complete amusement makes me grit my teeth.

"Screw you." I bite back angered more as he finds even that funny. The overwhelming rage building to a height where tears are starting to threaten.

I should never play games with him, he always makes me feel so … Soooo … Alone.

"Soon enough, sweetheart … Now go to sleep." He leans forward and kisses the back of my head before turning away and nestling away from me in the dark.

Chapter 28

I lay awake in the night with his body coiled around me possessively, his face buried in the back of my hair breathing soundly. My arm free of the restraint and only the sheets of the bed keeping me captive as he's still not got under the comforter with me. I must have dosed off at some point and he'd taken it off, but I could only remember turning and tossing until he switched off that damn movie.

His arms are wrapped around my upper body and fingers entwined with mine, I sigh and relax into his hold, needing this to balm over the events of the day before. I'm too weak for this game, already that ache of insecurity threatening to engulf me at the lack of his body joined with mine. He was right. I didn't just need the sex though, I needed the small things. The gestures and touches, the attentiveness and kindness too. All the things he deprived me of when he wanted to win a stupid game. This helps though, that even in sleep he needs to cling to me and revives my will a tiny little bit, giving me a little inner strength.

That stupid stubborn part of me, that inner teen Emma, who can't relinquish control, won't give into this challenge and let him win. Jake's too good at these games, he always wins, it's his mission in life to always come out on top. It's why he's a ferocious CEO and more than a match for his father, he just can't help it, it's in his nature to dominate at everything. Even though he's a laid-back and easy-going kind of man, there's an inner alpha male dominance that shines through and shows face whenever pressed. I shiver as the thought comes over me that maybe in this, I've bitten off more than I can chew.

If neither of us breaks, then what? Jake won't back down, it's not in his capabilities to do it. Will I?

I'm suddenly saddened by the fact that this game has turned into something more, a battle of the wills and feelings are starting to get bruised. My feelings are starting to get hurt. The knowledge that he doesn't need any emotional security to get through it, because emotionally he's stable while I'm flailing. Always that internal fear in me that this is only temporary for him. That he will see what I really am and get bored or just hurt me, the way everyone else did. That was his upper hand, not the sex alone. He was emotionally capable of playing this game because to him it was just that, harmless and thrilling. He had that inner confidence and self-assurance, he was stable in my feelings for him and felt secure in our relationship.

He mumbles in his sleep and it makes me smile despite the turmoil of emotions brewing inside of me. His low sexy voice, husky as always, seems even more so, and I hear my name among the garble of words he whispers into my hair. He shifts lazily, his arm letting go of my fingers and coming across my upper chest, pulling me closer to him. His face and mouth coming down to bury into my neck and warm me with his return to steady breathing.

I let my fingers trail his muscular arm, the light feathering of hair across that perfect olive skin, surprisingly light considering his dark hair and Italian coloring, but then he was overall not a particularly hairy man and the amount of time he spent in the sun would probably bleach away most of the darkness.

I trace my fingers over the symbols tattooed along his arm almost reaching his wrist. A long straight row of black ink, possibly Arabic, maybe Buddhist and wonder at what they mean in the early dusk light. I had never asked him about his tattoos or the meaning of each, he'd such a weakness for symbols and tribal patterns.

I close my eyes to try to return to sleep but find it near impossible, that sudden urge to cry envelopes me again and for no reason at all it springs on me from nowhere. Maybe it's the calm gentle way I'm being held and being able to steal genuine moments of affection with no games, maybe it's how lonely he made me feel yesterday by his distance and commitment to winning. Before I know it, I'm breaking my heart, face wet with tears and trying to be silent; trying not to move despite my racking sobs. My heart breaking without any good reason to. I curl up into the fetal position on my side to try to silence it, try to hide it.

"Baby?" His voice comes at me through my pain, his arms tightening slightly. "Emma, baby, what is it?" His body moves so he's leaning over me, trying to see my face but I only bury the evidence of my sadness into my palms and try to hide from him.

"N … N … Nothing." I stammer out amid silent tears, gut-wrenching and pain so sharp inside of me I can barely breathe.

"Emma, this isn't nothing … Hey …" He pulls me toward him so I'm on my back in the crook of his arms and tries to tug my hands away.

"Is this about yesterday? Emma, you know none of it's serious. Baby, talk to me." He sounds different, huskiness from sleep and gentle concern mixed to make him sound devastating, it makes me cry more. I can't answer and finally he tugs my hands down, bringing his nose to mine.

"Baby … You know I love you more than life. Don't do this. I hate seeing you cry." He runs a hand across my face gently and wipes some of the tears away. Realizing just how tear stained I am, he slides out of bed, flicking on the lamp and grabbing a box of tissues before hauling me against him again. I take a few, unable to meet his eyes and wipe my face, only to feel fresh tears roll from my eyes.

"I'm calling an end to this. Seriously this time." He sighs and pulls me against him hard. "Nothing is worth this." He kisses me then, not forceful or passionate but needily, his mouth taking mine and pushing all the emotion he can muster into kissing me intensely. I kiss him back hungrily, needing him more than air right now. It's as though he's trying to push away my heartbreak and I'm clinging onto him.

Pulling back, he stays nose to nose, his fingers tracing my face and finally I sniff back the newest tears. Gulping down an onslaught of more.

"Talk to me." He pleads, his eyes never leaving mine. "It kills me to see you this way, *bambino*."

"I miss you." Is the only thing I can force out and it's true, in only a day Jake feels a million miles away from me, my security shaky in the name of a game, and the carpet ripped out from under me in ways I don't even understand. He groans regretfully.

"Baby, I've never left you." He kisses me harder this time, sliding over me to cover my body with his, impatiently he yanks the sheets from between us, so he can mold himself to me. I'm still in the black lingerie and he's in sweatpants. His hands come to my wrists pulling them to the sides of my head and he pushes himself up, still connected to my mouth but shifting so his body and mine so we become wrapped up sexily, my legs automatically wrapping around his hips. His mouth is hungry for me and kisses me so thoroughly I'm left panting. "No more games, Emma. I can't do this to you anymore." The steel in his voice makes me feel reassured and I surrender to him in every way possible.

Jake makes love to me slowly and tenderly until my body is beyond exhausted. His hands cover every inch of my skin as though they had been starved for an eternity, from lack of my touch. His passion brims under the surface, threatening to break free, staying harnessed so that he can look into my eyes while taking me. I had experienced gentleness from him many a time, but this was beyond anything I knew him capable of. His mouth soft and fluttering on my face and lips, his hands light and gentle. For the first time, I knew exactly how it felt to be made love to and Jake was wiping away every ounce of pain and insecurity with every second.

Despite its low-key motion, and the lack of fiery passion, he makes me climax spectacularly, twice, before finding his own release and covering me with kisses. Laid in the crook of his arms I feel sated, both mentally, physically, and emotionally.

"Feel better, *neonata*?" He kisses my ear, his arm across my neck and hand buried in my hair, cupping my scalp on the opposite side, holding my face to his.

"Much." I blush and turn into him, nuzzling closer at his affection.

"I can't stand seeing you cry." He moves to my temple, kissing me firmly, our bodies still entwined. "Makes me feel like someone rammed a poker straight into my chest." His confession sends a bittersweet knot of pain through my heart.

"Maybe I should feel victorious." I sigh. "Jake Carrero threw in the towel while he was ahead." I glance up at him with a shy smile, he smiles back.

"I knew the second I saw you crying, baby, that I was never ahead, winning should never come at that cost." He presses his forehead to me and frowns. "I guess you found my Achilles heel. Lesson well learned."

"I learned that I'll never be a match for you." I pout in jest, but he only shakes his head and moves a hair from my cheek. A small, intimate motion that makes me wants him so much more. His eyes grazing my face as he lifts strands of my wild hair away.

"You've no idea how crazy you were making me. I was losing badly, I couldn't stand to touch you for long or I would have folded, so I tried to keep my distance instead." His mouth lifts at one corner, a self-defeated smile of sorts.

"Maybe I just should have held out after all." I reflect with a cheeky smile on my face, he bites his lip, his eyes moving to my mouth and grins.

"You almost had me so many times, that sexy set up when I walked in here … Jesus, Emma. I almost came in my pants, you've no idea the restraint that took. Why do you think I got away from you at dinner?" He grins at me and brings his eyes back to mine, light green and clear.

"To make me jealous!" I pout again, throwing him a haughty glare.

"*Neonata*, I knew if I sat next to you picturing what was under that dress I was going to end up banging you on the table in front of my family. I couldn't keep my eyes off you through the entire meal, I don't think I ate anything." He brushes his mouth against mine with the gentlest of kisses.

"You're a jerk … You had me believing I had zero effect

on you." I smile as his fingers move down my naked cleavage and start circling my nipple, bringing it to immediate attention. His focus most definitely honed in on what he's doing.

"I've been a walking hard-on since you issued the challenge." He leans down and kisses the swell of my breast before turning back to me with a wicked glint.

"I know I said no more games, baby, but I've other plans for those handcuffs and I'm pretty sure it's a game you would like." He leans in fast, kissing me hard and I know before he even slides his hand under the sheet to my warm hot core that he will find no resistance.

Chapter 29

Lounging in between Jake's legs on the huge sofa in the family room feels amazing after the events of the day before, my head against his chest as he concentrates on a document in his hand and strokes my hair and neck with the other. I'm attempting to read a book, but the sheer blissfulness of our morning has me daydreaming idly instead. Every so often he plants a kiss on top of my head before turning his papers and silently focusing back on work, he's reading through contracts for something I've no idea about.

When did this happen? When did I become so disconnected from the business side that I don't even know what Jake's reading through anymore?

I realize it doesn't bother me at all, I like laying here detached from work while he still keeps tabs on things going on in his empire. I'm in danger of becoming a kept girlfriend at this rate and I'm not sure how I feel about it right now.

The maid comes in a little after ten and leaves us a fresh tray of coffee and bagels, we had been up early for breakfast, revived, even with a lack of sleep. Both in the happiest of moods and playful, tickling, and play fighting as we had walked through the house.

Jake sighs heavily.

"This is the agreement with Marissa." He strokes my face again as he feels me tense up. "I called the legal team and requested a new meeting to discuss the DNA test and some other minor details in the draft Marissa's lawyer sent me."

I curl around to my side, so I can look up at him, he smiles when we lock eyes.

That beautiful face.

"You look relaxed today." Leaning down he kisses my nose bringing out a smile in me, despite his mention of her.

"I feel it." I sigh and tug the corner of his document held slightly to the side. "What details?" I remind him of his topic. He sighs heavily.

"I'm refusing to fly to LA every month for classes. She's no commitments like I do, it makes more sense if she relocates to New York until after the birth. That way I can fit her into my schedule and not vice versa." I look at the paper rather than at him, aware how much it still aches to talk about this and swallow it down. I knew he had to go to LA again soon for the first of the maternity meets, but with things still in limbo he'd refused to do anything until this was settled. My hatred for her never ceased to eat at me.

"Why is she making this more awkward?" I ask finally, once I had my emotions fully under control.

"Marissa likes to think she's in control, she likes to play stupid games." I watch his mouth and inwardly blanche. I wonder if Marissa's games had been the start of Jake's need to always have the upper hand. He has no idea how ironic his statement is.

"She wants you to jump through hoops and agree to anything she decides?" I push my other thoughts away.

Trying so hard to commit to talking about this; he obviously wants to.

"I guess … She doesn't know me very well then does she, *bambino*?" He winks at me and despite myself, I smile. It's true, she's no idea what she is coming up against in him. He wasn't a fifteen-year-old boy anymore and if she hadn't really known him as he grew up then she was about to get a rude awakening.

Jake will wipe the floor with you, sweetie!

"No, she doesn't." I admit with a degree of somberness which makes him frown at me, he leans down giving me an almost upside-down kiss on the mouth, sticking his tongue in unexpectedly and then licking my lip playfully. I squeal in disgust and wriggle to get free, trapped in his muscular arm. He nibbles my cheek before releasing me and hauling me up against him from where I had slid down. Grinning at me. Despite the shitty topic of conversation, he's been playful all morning and that little maneuver had been one of many similar since dawn.

"I'm done with negotiating with her, most of her demands are plain stupid … She's acting like a woman in a relationship." He closes the papers and throws them onto a nearby table with a dramatic inhale. "It's not even close to what I'll agree to."

"I thought you sorted things out when you flew out there?" I nestle my head in his neck again, feeling a little less likely to run and hide with the topic being opened again, feeling like I needed to try to face this. Knowing how he really felt about all of it had helped me, taken some of the sting out of it. Or maybe I was just starting to get used to the idea that this was happening after all.

"We did, to an extent … The basics were agreed on. Marissa keeps adding demands anytime we get close to signing and now she wants me to spend a weekend a month in her condo with her, going to maternity and parenting classes. Plus, an additional day, every two weeks, going to some bonding shit so that we will work together for the sake of the baby. I don't know what she's been smoking but she can forget it." He wraps both arms around me tightly and squeezes me.

"Sounds like she just wants excuses to have you with her." I pout jealously, anger overtaking me and filling my stomach with a heavy knot of hatred.

"Well, she can try." He lifts me up, sliding his legs under me so I'm sitting on him instead, my head just slightly higher than his. I open my legs to sit more comfortably on top of him, still being spooned by his body.

"Are you going to come with me this time?" I hear the serious tone and despite really trying to agree, I shake my head. I still can't do this. He sighs but says nothing.

"I'm sorry," I whisper, leaning my head back against his cheek. Feeling that overwhelming guilt but I just can't, it's still too soon, too raw for me.

"I understand, *bambino* ... If it were a role reversal I wouldn't be able to handle it either." He hugs me tight before getting up and sliding me onto the couch.

"I need to go make some calls, I'll be in our room if you want me." He leans down and kisses me on the mouth before turning and lifting a coffee and a bagel. "Go roam the gardens or take a swim, no one shows face until noon around here on weekends." He walks off and throws me back a smile with a glint of wicked in it. "Or maybe come see me in a little while and I'll occupy you." With a wink he's gone, and I'm left to lay back on the cream plush settee and stretch out like a satisfied cat.

***

I end up taking a walk in the gardens and looking at the view of the distant shoreline visible from the Carrero home. It's peaceful and sunny despite the late season, the view is so beautiful and calming. I'm surprised to hear footsteps lightly coming up behind me and turn in curiosity, a smile breaking across my face as I see Sophie running toward me at full pelt with a massive grin on her face. Turning with complete joy I grin right back and am soon met with the crushing hug of an overexcited teenager.

"Oh, my god, it's so good to see you again." She gushes, looking every bit the pampered and tanned socialite, a far cry from the skinny tomboy in oversized clothes of weeks ago. I feel my heart swell at the sight of her.

"You look so healthy and happy." I hold back the emotions that threaten up inside of me, hugging her back with equal force. Tears brimming in my eyes; she looks so good it's painful. Happiness bursting out of me in every direction. That tawny hair is highlighted and silky in a plumper face, deliciously tanned, and sporting hints of make-up.

"I can't ever thank you and Jake enough for the way my life has turned out, Emma. I can't believe you're actually here. I almost died of happiness when I got Jake's text." She releases me, looking me over with appreciation, she can see the change in me just like everyone else.

"I'm happy to hear you're doing so well here, Sophie. I must say, you look completely different." I lift her hand and make her twirl under my arm, all skinny jeans and flattering sparkly T-shirt with a cheeky logo, her body fuller from a better living and losing the skinny gauntness of Chicago.

"Likewise." She giggles and hugs me again for added

measure, her energy infectious and soon we're walking along, hand in hand, catching up with anything we forgot to add in our emails to each other. Sophie is infectious, her happiness brimming over into every word and mannerism and I can see Leila's influence in the quirky Converse with animal print laces and the sparkling diamantes on her jeans. Leila always liked a little bit of showiness.

We make our way back to the main house, lost in easy conversation.

"There she is!" Jake's deep tone catches us both and she beams at him, she doesn't, however, close the gap between them, the way she had with me and it's the first time I see she has that same distance with males that afflicts me. It causes me a moment of pain. A flicker of heartache for her.

Jake strides forward, giving her a light hug quickly before releasing her and scooping forward to plant a kiss on me. He unashamedly makes me blush with the sheer passion in its brief touch.

"Well look at you two nowadays." Sophie giggles with open eyed wonder. "Nice to see that you finally stopped fighting it and just got around to giving her a good kiss." She laughs as I throw a jab at her shoulder and she ducks away.

"What are you? All of fourteen?" I giggle, affected by her youthful fun so easily.

"Can I just point out, I never fought it." Jake's smiles, the face of a boy trying to earn points. "I always tried like a bear." He slides an arm around my shoulders, coming beside me, his other hand in his pocket. Sophie looks at him thoughtfully and smiles with maturity.

"Thing is, with girls like us … Sometimes it takes a lot to trust people. We need the ones who try like a bear to get in." She throws me a bashful look and we pass a smile of solidarity.

Jake says nothing but kisses me on the temple; no explanation required.

He definitely was someone who tried like a bear.

"So, who's ready for lunch, because I'm starving?" He cuts in with good humor after a few seconds and is delighted to get two very strong "*Me's*".

* * *

Sophie is easily integrated into the Carrero family lunch, it's obvious that she's a frequent visitor with the Huntsberger family home being a mere walk away from here. Sylvana clucks over her like a mother hen and family and friends pull her into easy conversation on topics they seem to already know about. Arrick slides her in beside him through lunch and it's easy to see the rapport they have already built. A very brotherly Arrick watching over her the way Jake did for me.

We're all sat around a garden table that's big enough to seat about twenty people or more and eating a light chicken salad lunch with lots of side dishes. Jake's beside me with a casual arm around the back of my chair, already full from his huge mountain of food the minute he sat down, while the rest of us picked and made polite conversation. He's lazing in his chair and laughing at whatever Arrick is saying to the left of him.

The bustling noise of this family is a joy to be a part of, having grown up with just my mother. It's a little overwhelming but so very enjoyable, a complete contrast to the life I had known in my own family. The conversations are littered with fluent Italian as well as English and it seems not one of them knows how to speak without crossing over each other and butting in at every direction. They are a fun and verbal family and I see where Jake learned the art of being social and finding his confidence. They also endlessly touch one another, prod, poke and push or throw sarcastic gestures around. I absolutely love them all.

His fingers come up trailing my back and I throw him a sweet smile.

"You must be hungry." He grins, watching me clear my plate for the second time, lately I've been ravenous at meals.

"I told you I was starving," I say defensively, wondering if he's having doubts about me staying thin. I put my fork down feeling that bite of anxiety.

"Don't stop on my account. I like seeing you well fed, *bambino*." He kisses me lightly on the cheek and runs a finger across my cheek with a smile.

"Voi due siete così appassionati di belle, mi fa così caldo dentro." Alessandra gushes toward us, but I can only look in confusion as Jake smiles at her.

"E facile amare, Emma, non-ho potuto chiedere per una ragazza più perfetta." Jake responds with a look toward her then at me, a look of complete infatuation but I just stare at him, completely lost.

"What now?" I burst into laughter, and he shakes his head, leaning in close to talk quietly.

"Alessandra is envious of how we are together … She appreciates people in love." He kisses me on the corner of the mouth. I feel that rise of inner-warmth spread through me and blush.

"And you said?" I tease playfully.

"That it's easy to love you … Because you're perfect." He grins and this time it's me that throws a kiss on him with a smile of complete devotion.

Smooth! My man is so smooth he's slick!

"You've no idea how perfect you can be sometimes." I gush. "Sometimes, it's easy to love me." I correct him and get a look of agreement in response. "Hey." I protest with mock outrage, but he just pulls me into a headlock and devours me with nibbling kisses across the face and cheek which has me squealing for help. No one at the table helps but I catch Sylvana watching us with extreme glee across her face.

"*Mio figlio, così innamorato.*" She gestures at Jake and I can only assume she's happy that he finally settled down with one woman as most of the table turn and smile at us. It makes me feel warm inside. Jake slides his hand down my arm and gives me a cute squeeze against him. Beaming with pride.

What's with this family talking Italian though when It's obviously about us?

* * *

The day seems to go by effortlessly, we shared time with his family, laughing, joking, and relaxing, and time alone, wandering the beach, late in the day, with naked feet in the sand. All too soon it's Jake who's telling me we have to catch a flight home in the morning.

"I could stay here forever." I grin lazily from his embrace as we lounge in a double swing bed in the huge manicured gardens. "It's so peaceful and so unlike the city. I love it here so much."

"Maybe we should just buy a house here and make Mamma happy." He smiles and kisses me on the side of the head, wrapped behind me. Our breaths intermingling from close proximity. I shift around so he's spooning me from behind and pull his hands into my stomach.

"What and leave your much too adored bachelor pad

behind? I'm not that cruel to you, Jake." I giggle and toy with his fingers.

"Maybe I realize having a bachelor pad isn't for me anymore." The seriousness in his tone makes me turn around in surprise, catching a look that is anything but humorous.

"You're serious?" I blanche, a sudden winding fear hitting me in the gut.

He's talking long-term houses, future, plans. Forever …

"Why not? I don't need to be in the city to stay in contact with Margo … You like it here, so why don't we get a house here?" He shrugs it off and goes back to nuzzling into me.

"No …Stop it." I snap pushing myself out of his embrace and climbing off the bed, agitation prickling my skin. His face drops and he follows, coming to stand in front of me.

"What? Why the reaction? It's okay to talk about marriage but not a house, Emma?" The confusion all over his face makes me falter, waving my hands around and trying to get my thoughts in order. I have no idea why I'm reacting this way, fear gripping my heart.

"It's serious, Jake … These houses cost millions … You're moving too fast, so soon. We have barely had time to just be together and you're talking about uprooting and moving away from the city. You're talking about buying a house that most families can never dream of affording and just setting up home in the blink of an eye." My voice is high and breathy.

How can I make him understand how terrifying this is? It's easy to slot into his life and his apartment because it doesn't really change it in anyway and if we were to break up then he wouldn't lose anything … Just me.

But buying a mansion, moving to beside his family like a little married couple. He will never let me go back to working in the Carrero Corporation now, it's too much. To be a kept woman with no chance of being able to just slide back into city life should he ever get tired of me. To get cozy and make bonds with these people who I have loved being around.

What if it all blew up in my face and I had to give up more than just him? His family. Sophie close by.

It's all so overwhelming I can't think straight. My fear and anxiety threatening to choke me at the huge change he wanted to make in my life. He had no idea how hard this was. Not so long ago, I had been alone, reliant on only me. I had my own money, my own plans, and my own life and I didn't want to let anyone else in. Now here I was, willing to gamble everything on uncertainty and faith and let someone else take control. I need control.

"If this is about money, Emma, then it's not a problem. I've my own money … I can more than afford a house here. I won't even need the apartment in New York, but we can keep it if you want a place to stay when we do go back there, if it makes you more comfortable?" His face is dark and closed in, his voice edgy and husky. I can see the rising of commandeering boss Carrero, that no nonsense temper moving in.

"It's not the money," I snap. "It's how fast this is moving, Jake. How you think that it's just so easy to up and move in the blink of an eye. To change everything in life on a whim, because you get an idea and impulsively want to act on it."

No discussion. It's just what he wants, and I have to accept it. I know this means my career will be over.

That overwhelming emotion hits me again and I step back to sit and steady my legs on the edge of the swing. Nausea rising up and blinding fear threatening to engulf me. He had no clue how much this was scaring me, he was changing all the rules, changing all the players, and knocking things on their head.

"Emma, I thought we were on the same page?" He snaps at me and stalks away to stand stiffly, his back turned. I can feel his rage, even from here, that fiery temper of his bubbling under the surface like molten lava and that pig-headed logic moving in.

"We are, Jake, but so much is new, so much we're still getting used to … So much we haven't even agreed on … It's terrifying and so final." I blurt out, eyes watering with unshed tears. My hands trembling.

"No, Emma, it's not … If you love me then it's no different to staying with me in New York. It's just a house." He turns, flashing me with a cold green glare that does little to hide the tornado brewing inside of him.

"Don't say it that way. I do love you!" I snap back, the urge to storm off in rage surging over me.

That's right, Emma, you always run when you're scared. You're pathetic!

"Then what's wrong with looking for a home we can actually make together?" He pleads, his voice laced with anger, but I can only shake my head.

"I'm not ready." I almost cry with the panic gripping me inside like a vice of coldness. I can't explain it, I only know that this is too much too soon. There are a million thoughts racing through my head, what ifs, outcomes of things going wrong. Moving here, away from the city, away from the closeness of Sarah as security. It's not even a drive away, it takes hours to get there if I ever needed to try to leave. Everything choking in my throat as it piles up and I fear a panic attack starting.

"So, if I hadn't suggested a house but had proposed instead … Would the answer have been no?" his eyes flare in rage and hurt. Spitting it at me accusingly, Carrero ego well and truly bruised and seeing only what he wants to see.

"That's not fair … It's not the same thing." I flail.

"It's exactly the same fucking thing … Answer me … If I had asked you to marry me right now, then what would it have been? Yes, or *fucking no*?" He moves to me menacingly and grabs my arm in a biting embrace. I can't answer, my throat closing in panic and unable to formulate a response that will satisfy him. It's too soon and I'm terrified, I wouldn't say *no*, I love him, and I want a life with him, but I can't say yes to that when he's asking me in this way and being this way. I stay silent and just grasp for words to come, the panic all over my face under his intimidating glare.

"That speaks fucking volumes." He grinds and storms off toward the house angrily, wearing his bruised feelings openly. I reach for him with a sob in my throat but can't find the strength to move my legs. Unable to call out to him. He throws me a hateful glare that catches in my lungs and almost slaps me into sense. I feel my inner panic spike into rage instead.

So, goddamn typical of him. It's his way or no way and he won't entertain any defiance or wait to find out why I even feel this way. He doesn't care how I'm freaking out about this, just doesn't like the refusal so storms off. Too used to getting his own way in everything. Screw you, Carrero

I bubble inside, storming around with my internal rage.

I don't want this, I don't want the pressure of him buying me a home. Playing happy families with all of these people who actually matter, so soon … Not yet, not when everything is still so new, and I still feel so insecure all the time. And work?

I know for a fact he won't want me to fly to the city and take up my old position, he barely wants to go back himself lately and moving here would make it more final. The truth is that I thought it would change, that I would have some sort of epiphany that I was finally with the man I would be with forever and it would all just go away. That I would be happy to be kept by him. But all the doubts, fears, and insecurities remained, and I wondered if I was destined to be plagued with them forever, that Jake would bore of it and leave me.

My insecurity wouldn't allow me to ever think beyond right now, think about when Marissa's baby came, or Jake and I in any long-term sense. I could only think about the here and now, so sure that I would be tempting fate if I dared to hope for more than I had been given. I wasn't someone who was used to happy ever afters, of people sticking around. Not even my own father had seen a reason to stick around. Somewhere, inside of me I had convinced myself that Jake would never stay, that one day he too would walk away.

Jake's obsession with always thinking ahead and trying to plan our forever was terrifying. He was putting so much emphasis and hope on an imagined future with me without hesitation. It felt like a huge weight of responsibility. I had never been someone who thought of other people taking the lead in my life. All my careful plans and goals had been self-orientated, leading to self-dependence and security, without relying on other people. Other people could hurt you, let you down and walk away. Everyone was capable of it, everyone capable of changing toward you and Jake was no different. All along, a part of me had held her breath waiting for that fateful moment when he would realize I wasn't everything he wanted in life and he would cut me loose.

That's why I couldn't let him do this, couldn't let him push me deeper into the comfort and security of being his forever, starting to build a home and a life so different to anything I had ever known because I knew, one day, he would tire of the broken little girl full of fears and anxiety. When I was no longer so much fun or mystery. And then the devastation of so much loss would end me. The loss of a life with him would kill me.

I take deep steadying breaths, trying to calm the manic panic inside my head and getting my shit together. I need to stop rambling and focus. I need to pull it all in and calm the hell down.

Stop letting teen Emma control your thoughts.

I finally follow Jake's route to the house and bypass all who are milling around in the family room, going straight to our bedroom. I see Jake packing and my stomach drops. His body radiating aggression, his face dark. I stop for a moment to look at him by the door, I know he sees me, he pauses mid-stroke throwing his clothes in the case but then continues without turning my way.

Well and truly pissed then.

"I guess we're leaving today?" I try with a gentle tone. But Jake blanks me. He walks to the wardrobes in the wall and yanks more of his clothes out in a manner that screams *fuck off.*

"Jake?" I try patiently, hating this thick atmosphere and the way he's practically massacring his expensive shirts as he rolls them into balls and almost punches them into his case.

"Yes. We are … I'm not in the mood to hang about any longer." He snaps and then continues tossing and throwing his clothes in haphazardly.

"You don't think you're taking this way out of context?" I push, feeling my own anger rising but trying not to lose it

"Hmmm. I don't know, Emma, am I? The woman I want a life with tells me she doesn't actually fucking want it with me." His anger rises at the closure of his sentence, his husky voice turning more to a growl. Deathly venom lacing his tone. That stubborn, impulsive, logic clouding his normally quick brain.

"I never said that … I said *not yet*, there's an enormous difference." I can feel my resolve crumbling and some sort of weary feebleness creeping over me. I was used to Jake's crazy violent temper when I was his PA, but I had never seen it as his lover. Right now, I didn't know how to react or calm him.

"Why not yet? I know how I feel already. If you don't feel the same way after everything, then I doubt you ever will." He slams his case shut and yanks it toward him to zip it up. The strength in the way he savages it is almost enough to snap it off.

He's being impossible, how can you even argue with such stupid logic. Just because self-assured, always knows what he wants in life Carrero has decided this is his chosen path, it doesn't mean I'm there yet. He has to understand that my past, my life has taught me to be cautious. To be wary of letting others take too much of my control away. It's an ingrained reflex to survive and I need time.

"You're being ridiculous, Jake." I bite my tongue, wanting to say so much but knowing by his simmering temper that it will lead to an all-out fight in his mother's house. That rage inside of him is bubbling dangerously close to an all-out explosion. I couldn't deal with the humiliation of a blow-out while they're all here.

"Look … I think we need to drop it. I have to go say goodbye, you need to pack. I called the airfield; the jet will be ready by the time we get there." He's gritting his teeth as he talks to me, inner fury seeping out and for once, I'm glad that he's leaving the room. I feel shaky and vulnerable and so close to tears it's unreal. Jake's temper never used to phase me when I was just his PA but now he has this ability to make me feel young and stupid and insecure. He has the ability to wound me deeply. A pain starts gnawing through my chest.

Why can't I just say yes? … *Yes, I want a home with you, Jake. It's what I want more than anything. I know why … I can't because I've an inability to back down or verbalize my fears, the same as he does, and this isn't going to change until one of us changes our argument. I'm not the one being unreasonable. He is!*

Chapter 30

Jake continues to refuse to acknowledge me, even when we get on the flight; his earphones in and his music blaring. He submerges himself in work across the aisle from me on his laptop, laying a bag on the seat beside him, making it clear he wants space. I grit my teeth and jut out my chin in anger. Getting up and shaking my head at him in fury.

Screw you, Jake, act like an asshole and I'll happily treat you like one.

I move down the plane, picking a seat facing away and haul out my book. Not that I can focus. I'm seething that he's behaving this way.

Why is it always about what he wants, and I must go along or be frozen out? Sometimes he's impossible.

***

"You're not coming?" I balk at him as I slide into the car that Jefferson is holding open for me, my heart falling to my feet like a heavy sand bag. Pain constricting in my throat.

"No, I've to go take care of a few things." Jake avoids

looking at me, his expression hard as he gazes off across the airfield toward an approaching familiar car. He lets Jefferson take our cases and load them in the boot as I stare with open astonishment through the wide car door.

"Jake, we need to talk about things?" I plead, feeling my angry resolve that had lasted through our entire flight dissipate, replaced with hurt. Anxiety and panic rising inside of me.

How ironic that now I'm the one who wants to talk. When did that flip?

"I've nothing else to say," he says coldly, he turns and heads off toward his car, now parked on the runway about twenty feet away, I note Daniel sliding dutifully out of the driver's door with a confused look on his face. He obviously had orders to drive Jake's pride and joy here and is wondering what the hell is eating his ass. Daniel looks him over, noting the tense scowl, the rigid posture and the way he completely blanks my existence without a backward glance. Daniel looks at me hesitantly and I see, for a moment, an almost worried expression. My stomach lurches.

"You're being an asshole," I spit at his retreating back, but he only lifts a hand in a gesture that dismisses me. A wave at an irritation that he doesn't want to deal with, I feel the pain rise up my chest and threaten to suffocate me.

He stalks to the driver's side and thumbs Daniel out of the way arrogantly, he reluctantly moves out and around the car to get in the passenger side. Taking one last look at my direction and a quick flick to Jake's profile, his face says it all. Daniel thinks we're over.

Oh, my god.

My breath catches in my throat with the overwhelming despair inside of me as I try to figure out if we really are.

Jake slides into the P1 and pulls down the door

aggressively, firing it up, and revving the engine so it roars across at me. The sound is both intimidating and terrifying. I'm pretty sure that if he had something to smash right now he would be focusing all his energy on beating the crap out of it, he's practically aching for a fight.

The car reverses at death defying speed with a squeal, a huge drift of black smoke billowing from the tires as he spins the car around in a show of idiocy. Hand brake spinning it, so it's facing the other way in a blink. He slams his foot down, wheel spinning viciously for a few seconds and takes off like a bat out of hell, the air ringing with the powerful engine and squealing of brakes. The stench of burned rubber and god knows what else tainting the air around me. All I hear is the roaring hum as it clings to the tarmac and speeds out of sight, it makes me want to scream in frustration.

What the actual fuck, Jake?

We had arguments before and none where he'd ever just walked off and left things in the air like this, he's obviously in arrogant prick mode. Not since the boat, so very long ago, has he behaved this way. Surely, he wouldn't end things over this, even he wasn't that dumb.

I get that I've hurt him, maybe more than I realize, but there is no need for him to behave this way toward me. Things are different between us now.

I slam my door, not waiting for Jefferson, and throw myself into the seat in a tearful rage. If he's trying to punish me then it's working but I'm not going to let him know that. He can be a prick, he wants to act like this then he should never have chosen me as a girlfriend. Of all the women in the world, I'm not one who will chase after him like some pathetic girl with a broken heart and try to make this right. This is on him; his stupid asshole behavior and he needs to get a grip.

"Take me to Queens," I command as Jefferson slides in. "I'll be staying there tonight." I sound more in control than I really feel, my inner body twisting and aching in pain.

"Yes, Ma'am." The cool gentle tone responds, I see a flicker of a frown in his mirror and know that he's pissed at Jake too. It soothes me a little.

Before long, we're heading out of the city and forward in search of Sarah and solitude. Jake needed to realize that despite his domineering ways, I was still my own person. Maybe I had let him take the lead a little too often of late and he was getting used to dictating my life. He could take his mood and sulk as long as he needed and then when he finally saw just how much of a jackass he was being, he could come find me. I wasn't playing this game again, if one thing his leaving the boat had taught me was, that Jake was an impulsive ass when his feelings were bruised, and he acted like an adolescent. He carried on like a child and lashed out at those he loved.

Hadn't he done that to me once before?

I would leave him to simmer. God knew how long this would take him to get over, that one time on the boat had seen him in a mood for almost two weeks but he had come back, and he had made things right. I had to trust that he would do that now.

* * *

Sarah isn't home when I let myself into the apartment carrying my case. I had let Jefferson go, assuring him I could manage and despite his fatherly protests, he had finally gone. I still had a key to the apartment and wanted nothing more than the coziness of that couch and throws and space to mull over Jake's asshole attitude.

I text Sarah informing her of my arrival, so she won't be surprised when she gets home but my heart sinks at her response. Marcus had taken her to Florida for a few days to meet his family and she'd only left this morning. She told me to help myself to the freezer contents and to call her later. My heart aches but I don't tell her why I'm here.

Meeting the family equaled seriousness. It signaled forever!

Maybe Sarah and Marcus were really making a go of it this time, the thought bothered me, but not as much as it did before. I feel lost that my stability isn't here to lift my chin and help me get through my first meaningful relationship fight with Jake. Not that there was much of a fight. Just him acting out like the spoiled brat he could sometimes be and trying to domineer his own way as per usual. Sometimes I liked Jake's wealth and the confidence it gave him but at times like this, when his tantrumming spoiled into asshole moods and attitude that money had ingrained on him reared its ugly head, I hated it.

I submerge myself in catching up with Margo and work via email. Step one of showing Jake this was not how a relationship worked. I was going to reacquaint myself with the current tasks he'd been overseeing, touch base with Rosalie, and make it known I wanted to be involved again. I had become too used to being kept by Jake in eternal vacation mode and stubborn PA Emma was stamping her foot in defiance at his behavior today. He seemed more than happy to slide me into his personal life more and more, taking me worlds away from PA mode and partly it was what was wrong with me lately. The weird moods and emotions, the tiredness and listless feeling deep inside. I had lost my value as his partner in work and was left only as his girlfriend with no real security the way I needed it.

I wanted to be more than just his bed partner and cuddle

buddy, I needed that challenge back of being his partner in work; decision making and overseeing things. I was so out of touch with all of that and disappointed in myself.

The thought of making a home in the Hamptons with nothing to do but twiddle my thumbs left me terrified. I didn't know how to be nothing—a doting girlfriend and kept woman. I didn't know how to slot into a domestic life and leisurely existence and I didn't want it. I wanted to be worth something, to be something worthwhile for me, something to aspire to.

Margo soon dumps the email catch up in replacement for a real phone call and has me up to speed, lost in idle chit-chat and asking how life as Jake's love is treating me. It feels so good to talk to her, to talk through everything, and even to confess to the fight at his parents. This opening up to people had slowly been getting more natural with me, shockingly so, and I was finding it helping me right now.

She assures me that Jake will come around and realize that pushing me has never worked in the past and always sent me running away from him. To have a little faith in his ability to retrace his bad decisions and make things right. I smile when we hang up, feeling more assured and less heartbroken. She's right. Jake may be an impulsive ass sometimes but eventually his logical brain brings it back around and he sees the error in his judgment. I'm just not sure how long this is going to take him.

You made him feel like he wasn't what you wanted in life, Emma, good move. That ego alone has taken a massive dint today, never mind his heart.

I sigh in exasperation and try to focus on anything that's not him.

By late evening I've returned to despair at his lack of contact and check my phone endlessly. That pit of anxiety and tension coursing through me and the absolute agony of not knowing what he's thinking anymore. Finally, I can't stand it anymore and call him, beyond hurt that my absence has been ignored.

So much for caring about my feelings!

"Jake?" After endless ringing, he finally picks up and all I hear is noise and music all around him, it's obvious he's at a nightclub and my heart thuds hard through my chest, winding me painfully. Jake has never just up and gone out without me like this, not since he told me he loved me. He's out getting drunk and ignoring my existence.

What the fuck?

"Hello?" his slurred husky voice comes through the noise, he's extremely drunk, but I hear him talking to other people in the background, some female voices too. Giggling and chattering and a lot of hilarity. I feel my tears well up and anger fly higher.

"Hello?" He can't seem to hear me over the music. My jealousy rages, my heart and temper sparring with one another and it engulfs me.

"Jake, where are you?" I feel tears slip out unexpectedly and warmly roll down my cheek, despite my rage. My heart's breaking. I hate the way he can twist a knife in me this way. All he's done is go out, but somehow it feels like a momentous thing considering how we left things.

What's he doing and who with?

I suddenly feel so alone and so insecure it's almost strangling me, cursing my inner stupid self and her eternal inability to believe Jake will never hurt me that way.

"Look, honey, I can't hear you … I'm staying out, maybe see you tomorrow or something. We'll see." He sounds distant, cold, just like the Jake who left me on that boat to go have sex with other people. He doesn't wait but just hangs up and leaves me staring numbly at a blank screen, my heart ripping free.

He obviously hadn't been home, never realized I didn't get there or if he had, then it didn't matter to him and now his attitude … calling me honey … The word he used on his casual sex buddies. The anger soars through me and I yank the phone back up calling back again. This time when he answers the noise isn't so loud as though he's moved to another room or maybe the bathroom.

"Where the fuck are you?" I stand up, rage coursing through me. My body trembling with so much emotion ripping through me at one time.

Who the hell was he to treat me that way, like I didn't matter? He'd spent months making me believe that I mattered more than anything in the world and on the back of one stupid disagreement, he was treating me like one of his passing whores. Some of whom he's probably with. I mean who in New York hadn't he had sex with? Our relationship was more than this.

I'm so angry I can feel the pulse beating in my head.

"Calm the fuck down and go to bed. I'm out. I told you. I need space to figure things out." Was his reply and it only made me seethe even more. I hear a girl say his name and giggle, the phone muffles as he replies to her and I can't make out what either are saying. I see red, jealousy spiking to psychotic levels, and my lungs exploding to battle the pain I was feeling.

Screw him. Screw Carrero and his stubborn, arrogant, prick-faced attitude! Screw him and his whores and playboy fucking lifestyle.

"Don't worry I'm going to bed but it's not yours, asshole." I almost crack my screen with the force I hang up. I storm through to the kitchen to get a drink of water for my suddenly sand dry throat, my hands are shaking but I'm literally vibrating with anger. This is so stupid, so goddamn over the top dramatic, even for him. My phone rings again, Jake's name flashing like a red flag on my screen and the urge to hang up bites at me. I pick it up and hesitate but then answer. Rage consuming me.

"Whose bed exactly are you climbing into?" his venomous jealousy fueled response winds me.

What the f—? Does Jake really believe me capable of climbing into someone else's bed? I'm not him!

I glare at the screen; my inner logical self has jumped out a window but instead, this need to wound him raises her ugly head.

How could he accuse me of something like that?

"I'm fucking waiting on an answer!" He shouts down the phone at me with so much hatred I feel myself recoil.

Stalking back to my room I haul the huge teddy bear out of the closet and pull him upright, he wears a tag around his throat with his name, I flip it over and read it before slamming my mouth back to the phone.

"Joey's … An old friend from Queens." I know how stupid his reaction to the bear had been the first time he 'met' him, whether it was in jest or not, it had highlighted Jake had a severe jealous side and would probably miss the name of the bear. I hope it made him suffer in the way he was making me suffer right now. I hang up just as he explodes. Silencing the onslaught of Carrero abuse and craziness. I stand trying to calm the panic surging through me, my body shaking violently and my nerves trembling. I feel weak and hysterical, my heart pounding through my chest. I know everything is falling apart around me.

I jump as my phone rings and his number flashes across my screen, I red button him in defiance. He wanted to be a prick and now he suddenly wants to talk. I red button him a second time when it rings again.

Answer the fucking phone! The text beeps on almost as soon as I lay it face down on the bed. I feel that inner fear sweeping over me.

Jake's angry, angry. Maybe I pushed things too far?

My anger almost drops out of me with insane speed to be replaced with immediate remorse. I should know better than to rile the jealousy card with Jake, it makes him irrational and aggressive, even with me. He sees red and can't seem to control it. He admitted to me he'd never had any feelings like that in his past, all so new to him and overpowering and I've just handed him a lit grenade when he's drunk and already pissed. I know him. I know his need to lash out and hurt things, hurt people when consumed like this. As a teen he beat his way through a drunken fueled haze many a time and made the headlines. Last thing he needed now was another front-page mess because his girlfriend tipped him over the edge.

What had I done to him? I'm so stupid! So, fucking stupid! I'm supposed to make him a better man, want to be a better man.

I pick up the phone, swaying with indecisiveness and try to call him, my hands shaking violently. I feel sick with nerves. I get his voicemail and feel my stomach drop. I try again and again, five times in twenty minutes but I get his voicemail every time and it suddenly dawns on me he's switched his cell off.

He's beyond raging with me, he's gone off the charts angry. I text him quickly, hoping to god he switches it on and sees it before he does something beyond stupid or calls me back.

Jake, I'm sorry, I was angry, please don't go mad … Joey is the bear you won for me, remember? I'm in my old apartment xxx I love you.

I send it with the overwhelming feeling of fear tightening my stomach. Choking on tears and regret.

Maybe I should go back to the apartment tonight and be there for him coming home; fix this. Fix my stupidity. I should know better than to ever play that card with him, it's the guaranteed way to make him lash out and do something stupid like get in a bar brawl or come home and smash another wall.

That much testosterone fueled by booze and jealousy was a lethal combination and I had just lit the fuse. If he'd done the same to me I would have flipped the psycho switch and no telling what I would have done. I feel so stupid.

I sit shaking for what seems like an eternity before I finally get enough courage to gather my things and call for a cab, it's going to be one expensive ride home and the most agonizing journey, but I need to be there when Jake finally comes home. I need to show him that the only bed I was climbing into was his. I pick up my phone and send one last text.

Please come home, Jake … I'm getting a cab back to Manhattan. I'm sorry xxx I need to see you. I miss you.

I take a deep, steadying breath and swallow down the urge to cry. Body shaking violently, and all resolve gone. Pulling myself together, I call for a cab and get ready while awaiting its arrival.

* * *

The journey feels endless and the driver makes no attempt at conversation, luckily Jake always insists I carry cash for emergencies and his generosity means it's more than I had realized was even in my purse. It warmed me a little knowing he'd put it there should I ever be caught somewhere in desperate need of assistance; that I had money to use. It just makes me feel even more wretched for hurting him this way, for letting him think I would do that. I feel like an idiot and try his phone for the hundredth time, it's still off. Tears pour down my cheek and my heart aches. I had so much to make up for.

Mathews lets me into the apartment with a warm smile and a look of concern, yet he knows his place and doesn't ask. I know as soon as I walk in that Jake has never been here. I can just tell from the emptiness and the fact his case is sat by the kitchen counter, that only his things were dropped off and he'd never set foot back in here.

I drag both of our cases to the bedroom and get ready for bed, pulling on one of his T-shirts for comfort. It's late, Jake probably won't be home for hours if he refuses to turn his phone back on and well, he assumes I'm doing god knows what with someone else. I wouldn't be surprised if he never came home at all. I want to find him, but I don't know how and all I can do until he reads my messages is wait.

I pick up my phone for one last attempt and stifle a sob as it hits voicemail immediately. I have no idea where he is or what he's doing. I want him home with me so badly. I would agree to anything right now. Eloping, mansions on the moon, and a lifetime of only saying yes to his every whim.

I finally curl into his side of the bed, crying my heart out until I drift into a hazy tortured sleep, dreaming of Jake consumed by rage and ripping apart men trying to lay hands on me.

***

I'm torn awake by noise in the apartment, I jump in fright realizing the darkness around me is more of a soft gray and it's now almost sunrise.

It has to be Jake.

I jump out of bed and run through to the sitting room,

my pulse beating crazily in my throat, slamming to a halt as our eyes meet across the calm spacious room. My heart elated at his final appearance and almost jumping out of my chest. He looks devastating to me and I just want to run into his arms.

"Where have you been?" I cry, stilling the urge to run at him when he moves through to where I'm standing. He looks at me with emptiness; he looks tired, disheveled, his eyes dark and ravaged. His appearance makes me nervous, it could not be more un-Jake if he tried and he doesn't seem anywhere near as drunk as he had been.

I'm desperate to talk, to try to convince him that nothing happened last night. I've been frantic with his absence. He sighs and takes in my appearance with the most gut-wrenching look of despair I've ever seen. He swallows hard. Something in his manner starts sending off a million warning bells and the atmosphere he's creating sends a cold surge down my spine.

Has he really ended things with me?

"Emma, sit down … We need to talk." His voice is hoarse, he can't seem to look me in the eye and his manner is making me feel queasy. He loosely catches my wrist and pulls me with him toward the couch to one side. I don't fight, my body on high alert and screaming that something is majorly off. Terrified of hearing the words that will rip my soul from my body. Nerves still the words on my lips. Something feels wrong, despite our fight, despite the events of late something has changed in him. Panic rising inside of me. He sits me on the couch, sliding down next to me, close. Close enough to reach around me and hold me tight but he doesn't, he sits touching legs, maneuvering me into the corner so I'm caged in by him. He's unable to look at me. I can feel the tension from his body, my nerves choking me.

This isn't Jake, not my controlled and overly confident Carrero, this version of him is making me feel sick with nerves.

"What is it?" I breathe, my hands beginning to tremble, aching to reach for him but his entire body language keeps me at bay. I can feel his distance pounding out at me.

Does he think I betrayed him? Does he really want us to be over?

"Emma … I want you to know how much I love you … I mean really love you … There's no one else in this world for me. I need you …" He gets up and paces around for a moment, making me feel sick with worry but relieved that this isn't a break up speech. He comes back to his previous position and swallows hard. "Last night, when I thought you'd done something, after the talk about not wanting to marry me and pretty much breaking up … It fucked me up in the head." His eyes are focused on my hands and I can see they are filled with unshed tears, he can't look at me. "None of this changes how I ever felt about you … I need you to know that I still love you every bit as much as I did, I still want the same things with you, and I acted like a complete fucking idiot at the airport … I believe you when you text me that nothing happened. I wish I'd had the sense to realize it last night, but I was so drunk and jealous, and I wasn't rational … *bambino* I was so goddamn distraught." He lifts my hands to his mouth rubbing my knuckles against his face, his stubble scratching at me achingly and kissing them lightly. I hold my breath. Closing his eyes for a moment, savoring my touch, my smell as though they were to be his last. I feel the inner trembles begin to shake my whole body, my breath held.

"I did something really stupid, *miele* … …" His words instantly send a heavy dread inside of me, pulsing out through every limb, an ache in my chest so strong I think my heart is going to give out. I can't do anything except stay like stone and wait, wait for whatever it is he needs to tell me with the growing trepidation that this could change everything.

"What?" It's so strained I don't recognize my own voice, the question impulsive at the agony of what's coming out of his mouth. I'm frozen in fear, knowing only this man had the power to destroy me.

"I was drunk, Emma … Seriously raging … Upset … Not thinking straight." He tightens his hold on me as though the words are painful, and he's scared I'll run. I feel terrified, my mind racing at a hundred miles an hour.

What has he done? Why is he being this way?

"Tell me." I beg, desperate to end this torture, tears already finding a path down my cheeks as if some part of me already knows what's happened and is mourning in advance.

"I kissed someone." My hands pull from his in reaction, my body darting back as though he's hit me with an electric volt. My heart sears with pain and a blinding ache through my head. I gasp and try to catch my breath but only a sob comes out.

He looks up, panic in his eyes yet stays still, he's prepared himself for my reaction. This is why he sat so close, so I'm hemmed in, even if I try to pull away. I can't run without pushing him away and he knows I don't have the physical strength, he thought about this first.

God knows how long he's played this over in his head in the last few hours.

"What?" I cry in shock when I can find the words. "What do you mean?" I can't comprehend this, I don't want it to be true, for those painful words to be coming from my Jake's mouth.

My Jake the one I trust, my security … My heart. My betrayer.

"Someone who was at the club. She wasn't there with us,

someone we know. Just a coincidence she was even in town at all. I kissed her. I guess I wanted to lash out, so sure we were done." His eyes come to mine, keeping his hands steady on his lap, he knows not to touch me. He can see I'm perched ready to react, only held still by my shock. Unable to make any part of my brain function beyond the shock of what he's said. The world spinning around me.

I feel my body go before my mind does, the racking sounds of sobbing and the dissolving of my posture. The wrenching pain of someone ripping your very soul out. His face crumbles and reaches for me but I slap him away, hard, shoving his chest in anger.

I don't know what to do … What to think, what to say; the pain is so unbearable, unlike anything I've ever experienced in my life.

"Why? … How could you, Jake? … Who?" I can't breathe but my voice is screeching out. I can't think straight; my heart is being ripped out through my stomach and I'm lashing out in teen Emma mode. He tries to restrain me, but I battle him off until he stops. Unable to let him touch me. I think I may fall down and pass out. I think I may die.

Oh, my god this may actually kill me.

"I'm sorry. Baby. I'm so sorry … I didn't think about what I was doing, I just wanted to lash out … I was drunk and stupid, I'm an idiot when I drink … I knew immediately I'd fucked-up so badly … When I turned on my phone and saw your messages, Emma … I died." His cheeks are wet with moisture, his voice low and shameful, his face reflecting the agony of what he's telling me. I don't doubt that he regrets it but he's killing me inside. This pain unbearable, I can't bear to even think about what he's done to us, it destroys everything. It takes all that we are and sets it alight, reducing it to nothing but ashes.

"Who?" I say again more venomously, it's the only detail

I can focus on right now. I don't know why it matters but something inside of me says it matters a lot … I need to know.

What if it's Leila? I trust Leila, I love her as a sister and she's meant to be in France; it would fit. The pain of both betraying me that way would end me. A final, fatal blow.

He hesitates and looks away, standing to tower over me and I see his hands shaking as violently as mine. He's putting distance between us because he knows his next confession is going to be just as bad. I can tell, I can feel it.

He shoves his hands in his pockets and stares at the floor between us. His distance makes me afraid, he thinks I'm going to freak out, lash out again. He's getting ready to move out of the firing line.

Oh, my god, this can't be good. He's going to tell me it's Leila, he's going to turn the knife and make it hurt more if that was even possible. He's going to kill me with his words and I'll die right here on the couch.

"Who?" I press again more firmly, my heart ceases to beat, my breath held, still sitting with my hands clasped so tightly my nails draw blood from my own palms and body rigid awaiting the blow.

He takes a long slow deep breath, locks eyes with me and I see nothing but fear and regret and tears. The look of a man who has just lost everything and doesn't know what else to do. I know that no matter what he tells me the damage is already done and this is just adding salt to the wound.

How can I ever trust him again?

He swallows, as though preparing himself for the worst moment of his life and breathes the name slowly.

"Marissa."

.

About the Author

L.T. Marshall is a Scottish born and bred romance writer with more than the average person's life experience. She has been a torrent of wild things—including singer in a girl band, animal rights activist and charity owner, worked in radio and offered jobs in TV.

A passionate, restless soul, who has always found peace in writing—the only way to calm that fiery spirit. She uses her wit and dark humor to her advantage in her works and has been an avid reader for most of her life.

Her influences vary, but from early life and a teen stint in journalism, she applies logic to most of her plot lines, is a self-confessed research fiend, and likes a lot of psychology behind her characters actions.

She currently resides in Central Scotland with her two children and fiancé of 13 years, making waves in the book world with her signature "WTF moments" she likes to apply in each story, hints of humor and devastating emotional rollercoaster rides.

A note from the Author

I hope you enjoyed my book, it would mean a great deal to me if you took the time to leave me a review on Amazon or Goodreads—or even both. My reviews are something I regularly, and actively read, and appreciate you taking the time to leave me one. x

L.T. Marshall

Find the Author online

You can find L.T. Marshall across all social media and she regularly interacts with fans on Facebook.

Website: ltmarshall.blog
Facebook: facebook.com/LTMarshallauthor
Twitter: twitter.com/LMarshallAuthor
Instagram: instagram.com/l.t.marshall

32018388R00274

Printed in Great Britain
by Amazon